MILLION
DOLLAR
COWBOY

Lori Wilde

MILLION DOLLAR COWBOY

A CUPID, TEXAS NOVEL

AVONBOOKS

An Imprint of HarperCollinsPublishers

Excerpt from *Cowboy, It's Cold Outside* copyright © 2017 by Laurie Vanzura.

MILLION DOLLAR COWBOY. Copyright © 2017 by Laurie Vanzura. All rights reserved. Printed in the United States of America. No part of this book may be used or reproduced in any manner whatsoever without written permission except in the case of brief quotations embodied in critical articles and reviews. For information, address HarperCollins Publishers, 195 Broadway, New York, NY 10007.

First Avon Books mass market printing: April 2017
First Avon Books hardcover printing: March 2017

ISBN 978-0-06-266020-6

Avon, Avon & logo, and Avon Books & logo are registered trademarks of HarperCollins Publishers in the United States of America and other countries.

HarperCollins is a registered trademark of HarperCollins Publishers in the United States of America and other countries.

16 17 18 19 20 LSC 10 9 8 7 6 5 4 3 2 1

To my editor Lucia Macro, who sparked the idea for the Lockharts of Texas. Thank you so much for your support and guidance!

Acknowledgments

I MUST acknowledge the amazing team at HarperCollins. From the editors to sales and marketing, to the art department and the fabulous publicity team. They are the best in the business. I wouldn't have the career that I do without them.

MILLION DOLLAR COWBOY

Ridge Lockhart was three years old when his mother abandoned him on the doorstep of the second-richest man in Jeff Davis County.

His father.

It was his first clear memory. The forever event stamped on the retina of his life.

Midnight. Or so it seemed to a kid. Late. Way past his bedtime. Deep dark in far west Texas, except for the glittering stars overhead.

Desert sounds. Coyotes howl. Hoots of a night owl. Whispers of wind blowing across sand.

Mommy left the car parked at the gate, crawled over the cattle guard, carried him and a small duffel bag stuffed with his things thrown over her shoulder. Stumbling the half mile hike to the big house in pink cowgirl boots. She was humming a lullaby and crying. Crying so hard he patted her face to comfort her.

"Don't cry, Mommy. Don't cry."

"Shh," she cautioned.

The odor of a burnt-out campfire, barbecue and beans, filled his nose. His stomach growled because he was hungry, and there was nothing to eat but the stale graham cracker clutched in his fist.

She reached the front porch, and set him down.

He wore Mutant Ninja Turtle house shoes and Batman pajamas. She let the duffel bag fall off her shoulder, dropping it onto the cement beside him. *Thump.*

A strand of blond hair fell across her face. She did not push it back and he could not see her eyes, but he could see her breasts pushed up high against the low neck of her tight blouse. She smelled like vanilla and sadness.

He tried to press his head against her chest but she yanked back. "No."

His hands shook and his tummy turned upside down. What had he done wrong?

She pulled a square white envelope from her purse with one word written on the front and fastened it to the front of his pajamas with a safety pin, right through Batman's head.

He tugged at the envelope.

"Leave it," she said, moving his hand away.

He stared at her, the funny feeling in his tummy wriggling into his throat. "Why?"

"Because I said so." She took a deep shaky breath. "Okay now," she muttered. "Ridgy, you can count to ten, can't you?'

He bobbed his head. He could. She'd taught him. He held up his fingers one by one. "One . . . two . . . free . . ."

"Good boy. Good boy." She patted his head. Her lipstick was smeared and there were tears in her eyes. "Listen to me."

He cocked his head sensing something big was happening. Biting his bottom lip, he nodded again.

"Be my big brave boy and count to ten. When you get to ten, you ring this bell right here. See it? Press right here."

Ridge reached up to press the button glowing orange in the porch shadows, but she snatched his hand back.

"No. Not now."

Tears burned his eyes. He'd made her mad. He hated to make her mad. "Sowwy."

"It's okay. But you must wait until I hide. Wait until you count to ten and *then* press the bell. Do you understand?"

"Uh-huh." The funny feeling in his throat and tummy slipped down to his knees. *Mommy's gonna leave me.* He was scared. Scared all over.

"It's a game." She laughed but she didn't sound happy.

"Like hide-and-seek?" His tummy felt better and his knees stopped shaking. He loved when she played hide-and-seek with him.

"You smart boy." She kissed his forehead. "So smart. You stay here and count while Mommy goes and hides."

He studied her. He wanted to play, but this felt wrong. Why were they playing hide-and-seek in the dark? In a strange place? Why did he have to push the orange button? He didn't like it.

"Give me a head start before you start counting. Understand?"

"No, no." This wasn't right and he knew it. He wrapped his arms around one of her legs.

"Ridge," she said in her mad voice. "Let me go."

He clung tighter.

She pried his fingers open, peeled him off her leg, gripped him by the shoulders, sank her thumbs into his skin, shook him gently. "Close your eyes now."

His entire body trembled, and he felt like he was gonna throw up. "Mommy?"

"Close your eyes."

Slowly, he closed his eyes, heard the scoot of her cowgirl boots against the sidewalk. Scoot, scoot, scooty-scoot. Going fast, then faster.

His tummy hurt really badly. He didn't want to play hide-and-seek anymore. But he'd promised her he would count, and then ring the bell. So he counted. Got mixed up at seven. Started again.

When he reached ten he opened his eyes. Mommy was gone. Everything was dark except for the glowing orange button by the front door.

"Mommy?" he called.

Only the coyotes yipping and howling answered him. Goose bumps spread shivers over his arm. Where was Mommy hiding?

Remembering what she'd told him, he pushed the orange button. Heard a loud *ding-dong* from inside the house.

Ridge jumped back. A light came on above him. A light so bright it hurt. He put his hand up to shield his eyes.

The door opened, and a pretty brown-faced woman who looked

kind of like his babysitter, Carmen, peeked out. Her long dark hair was in braids and she wore a yellow housecoat and had round little glasses perched on the end of her nose. She blinked.

"Who are you?" she asked in a soft voice.

He was so scared. He wanted to run into the dark and find his mommy, but he raised his chin. "Ridge."

"Who is it, Anya?" another woman's voice called.

Anya shook her head, and before she could say anything, the other woman appeared, holding a baby in her arms. This lady was blond like his mother, but not as pretty and not as young. She peered over Anya's shoulder, and she too blinked at Ridge as if he was a strange zoo animal.

"What's this?" the woman asked.

"A boy," Anya answered.

"I can see that." The woman sounded like a buzzing mosquito, mean and mad. The baby in her arms swiveled his head to stare at Ridge. "But who is he and why is he here?"

Anya shrugged. "The answer could be in that envelope."

"I don't like the looks of this," the woman mumbled.

"What do we do?" Anya asked.

"Bring him in," the blond woman snapped. "We can't very well leave a toddler standing on the front porch."

"Mr. Duke's name is on the envelope."

"I can see that too." The blond woman's voice got tighter, higher, stringier. "Here." She shoved the baby at Anya. "Take care of Ranger while I get to the bottom of this."

Anya nodded, took the baby, and skittered away.

Leaving Ridge facing the mean lady.

She crooked a finger. "Come here."

He shook his head.

Snorting, she reached out, snaked her hand around his wrist.

"Mommy!" he screamed, and jerked away. "Mommy, help!"

She grabbed for him, missed, but snagged the envelope and used it to yank him toward her.

He fell backward.

The safety pin holding the envelope ripped, tearing a hole where Batman's head had once been.

Ridge lay quivering on the porch, tears burning his nose.

The woman tore open the envelope, read the note. "Oh no she did-*n't*!" The woman howled louder than any coyote.

Ridge rolled into a tight little ball, tried to make himself really small. Willing himself to disappear the way he did when his mommy took him to the club and he fell asleep on the pool table.

"You're coming with me." The lady snatched him off the porch, dragged him inside the house. He dug his feet into the floor, trying to stop her, but couldn't.

She towed him after her into a living room with animal heads on the wall staring down at him with glassy eyes and sharp horns.

A dark-haired man sat in a recliner in front of a really big TV. Ridge had seen him before at the club, and sometimes at his mother's house. He wore a black T-shirt over arms as big and hard as rocks. And he had a thick bushy mustache that hid his upper lip. There was a can of beer on the table beside him and a big fat brown cigar smoldering in an ashtray. The smell burned Ridge's nose.

The blonde woman had the envelope balled into her fist and she raised it at the man. Called him a bad name.

"This!" The woman snatched Ridge up by his arm, yanking him off his feet, dangling him in front of the man's face. Shook him hard. "This is your mess!"

Pain shot from his shoulder, spread out in two directions, up his arm and down his side. Ridge's heart thumped so hard he could hardly breathe. He wanted to cry, but he promised Mommy he wouldn't cry.

The man said nothing, did nothing, just glared at Ridge with angry eyes as if this was his fault.

"Clean it up!" The woman let go of Ridge's arm, and he tumbled to the rug, falling facedown at his man's feet. "Clean this up or I'm leaving you!"

The man stood up calmly. "Sabrina, calm down."

"The boy is your son, and his mother is leaving him with us."

"That's bullshit."

"Are you denying he's your son?"

"No," the man said. "But that was before I married you and settled down. She's not going to get away with dumping him on us. I'll take care of it."

"You son of a bitch," Sabrina screamed at him. "People warned me about you, but I wouldn't listen. Stupid. So stupid."

The man glared hard. "That's enough, woman. Hush."

"I'm not raising this kid. I won't." She walked back and forth across the room. "I've got my own son to raise. Your *legitimate* son."

Ridge cowered against the couch, rubbing his shoulder. It still hurt from where the woman had jerked him up. He was scared and hungry and had lost the graham cracker.

Then in the middle of the yelling and crying, Ridge heard sirens outside the house—sirens, strobes of flashing red and blue lights, a hard knock at the door. Men in boots and Stetsons and silver stars pinned to their chests marching into the living room.

Stern faces. Low voices. Serious tones.

Single-car accident. Excessive speed. Missed the turn. Hit the cement wall at the cemetery entrance outside Brooklane Baptist Church.

And Ridge never saw his mother again.

Chapter 2

Twenty-nine years later

FOR the first time in a decade Ridge Lockhart was coming home.

He circled his Evektor Harmony over Silver Feather Ranch—the hundred-thousand-acre spread sprawling across Jeff Davis and Presidio counties—that had been in his family for six generations.

A cheery sun peeped over the horizon, greeting him jovially. *Hey buddy! Good morning. Welcome back to the fifth circle of hell.*

His jaw clenched and his stomach churned and the old dark anger he thought he'd stamped out years ago by working hard and making his mark on the world came roaring back, leonine as March winds.

He was in town for one reason and one reason only. Do the best man thing for his childhood buddy, Archer Alzate, and then get the mothertrucker out of Cupid, Texas.

ASAP.

Ridge took his time coming in, buzzing the plane lower than he should have. Taking stock. Sizing things up. No matter how you sliced it, this was where he'd been hatched and reared. He could not escape his past.

Miles of desert stretched below his plane, land so dry a man got parched just looking at it. Land filled with cactus and chaparral flats. Land teeming with rattlesnakes, horned toads, and stinging insects. Land that claimed lives and crops, hopes and dreams in equal measure.

This land was a far cry from the cool, green country where he lived in Calgary. But damn his hide if he hadn't missed it.

The Chihuahuan Desert. The Trans-Pecos. Cupid. Silver Feather Ranch.

Home.

And that was his personal curse. To hate the very place that called to his soul, the place where he did not belong, but secretly yearned for.

Throat tight, tongue powdery, he reached for the gonzo-sized energy drink resting in the cup holder and guzzled it.

Ah. Much better. Thirst quenched. Caffeine buzzed. Cobwebs chased.

Ready or not, here I come.

His chest knotted up like extra string on a wind-whipped kite. He dipped the plane lower, coming in, coming down.

Their paternal grandfather, Cyril, had left all four Lockhart grandsons two-acre parcels of land on each four quadrants of the ranch, with the stipulation that none of them could sell their places without approval from the entire family. Which was the only reason Ridge had held on to his house.

To the north, he spied Ranger's place. His brother had built an ecofriendly, solar home out of reclaimed wood and recycled everything.

Out of the four Lockhart brothers, he and Ranger were closest in age. Ranger was thirty-one to Ridge's thirty-two, but they were as different in temperament as wind and earth. Maybe it was because they had different mothers. Maybe it was because Ranger was a brainy astrobiologist and Ridge was an act-first-ask-questions-later entrepreneur. Or maybe it was because Ranger was a legitimate Lockhart, whereas Ridge was the bastard.

His two other younger brothers, Remington and Rhett, had the same mother. Lucy Hurd had been his father's second wife and the closest thing to a real mother Ridge had ever had. He'd been devastated by kindhearted Lucy's death from ovarian cancer when he was in junior high.

Army Captain Remington was twenty-eight and currently deployed in the Middle East. He had stuck a travel trailer on his parcel of land on the west side of the ranch for a place to stay when he was home on leave, but hadn't bothered to commit to construction. And the youngest, Rhett, was a PBR bull-riding rodeo star. He had built a rustic log cabin on the south end of the ranch in Presidio County.

Ridge flew over their places, taking it all in, but resisted the urge to buzz the east side of the ranch where his house stood. The house he'd built, but had never lived in. The house he hadn't seen in ten years.

Up ahead, in the dead center of the ranch, lay the landing strip put in for crop dusting planes. Around the landing strip were stables, bunkhouses, three barns, numerous sheds, the foreman's farmhouse where Archer lived, and at the top of a small hill, the extravagant mansion where Ridge had once stood on the front porch and rung that orange bell.

The mansion where his father lived with his third wife, Vivi.

Yep. Gossip of the decade. Vivi Courtland. Ridge's onetime girlfriend was now his old man's spouse.

His stomach churned and deep-rooted resentment covered him, thick as the hard pack soil. Back. All the useless feelings he thought he'd conquered were back, as layered and nuanced as ever.

Anger. Shame. Fear. Guilt. Disgust.

"Damn it," he muttered, settled a straw Stetson on his head, and climbed from the cockpit, an unwanted lump in his throat and the morning sun in his eyes.

He forced himself to breathe. In. Out. Smooth and steady. Nothing disturbed him. He was the boss. In control. In charge. Tough.

Ridge pocketed the plane's key remote control, turned to the cargo hold to get his gear, and . . .

. . . that's when he spied her.

Lumbering up in a battered, blue, Toyota Tundra extended-cab pickup truck and parking catawampus beside the tallest barn on the ranch.

He cocked his head. Who was she?

The woman hopped from the tall truck with the fluid grace of a playful water sprite more at home underneath a cascading water-fall than smack in the middle of the Chihuahuan Desert.

She wore faded blue skinny jeans that fit like spray paint, cupping rounded hips and a firm lush fanny. A neon-pink, V-neck T-shirt showed off a hint of sweet cleavage. Her flat-heeled cowboy boots were scuffed and dusty. From this distance, it appeared as if she didn't have on a lick of makeup, and her thick dark hair was pulled into twin braids. A gust of hot, lazy June air blew across the sand, and her nimble fingers reached up to tuck a tendril of loosened hair behind one ear.

Ridge had a startling vision of easing the elastic bands from her hair, undoing the braids, and watching that tumble of hair fall over his hand soft and smooth as liquid silk.

What the hell? Why the instant lust? Normally, he went for tall willowy blondes like Vivi. Not petite, shapely brunettes.

Why?

That was easy enough to answer. A) The brunette was smoking hot. B) There was something familiar about her, something warm and cozy and inviting. C) He hadn't had sex in so long he'd almost forgotten what it felt like.

Hope cut into him, gutted him open, leaving him raw and hungry. Hey, who knew? There was a wedding this weekend—alcohol, food, music, slow dancing. Maybe they'd hook up.

Easy Lockhart, getting ahead of yourself.

He didn't even know her name, or if she was involved with some-one, or if she'd even been invited to the wedding.

No, but that didn't stop steamy sexual fantasies from unspool-ing inside his head. Nor could he shake an odd feeling that he'd gone fishing for shad and managed to hook a mermaid instead.

The woman opened the extended cab's passenger side door and bent over, butt wiggling as she ducked her head inside to retrieve something from the backseat. That round wriggly rump robbed the air from his lungs, highjacked his brain as effectively as a gun-toting bandit.

As the owner and CEO of Lock Ridge Drilling, he made snap

decisions on a daily basis and he'd honed the skill of sizing up people at a glance.

From the click-quick snapshot trapped in that breathless time of his mind, Ridge knew she was the spunky girl-next-door type. Able to climb trees, make chicken soup for a sick neighbor, organize a charity drive, spike a witty barb at smart-ass-know-it-alls, passionately root for her favorite sports team complete with face paint and logo jerseys, park her butt in the church pew every Sunday morning, and cheerfully answer three a.m. phone calls from friends in need.

She was, in fact, everything Ridge was not—perky, happy-go-lucky, laid-back, a rule-following, people-pleasing team player.

Not his type. Not in the least.

Which probably explained the pounding lust. He had a knack for picking women who were all wrong for him.

At this distance, with the width of the landing strip between them, he hadn't gotten a clear view of her face, but his initial impression was that she was more pretty than beautiful, while her body language exuded a come-sit-by-me friendliness that drew him. She was curvy enough to let him know that she enjoyed a good splurge meal now and again, but she was also healthy and fit. Her skin was tan and supple, her eyes soft and bright, her teeth straight and white. She took good care of herself.

But it was the way she carried herself that totally wrecked him. Confidence mixed with humility. She had an authentic stride full of wholehearted openness. The last person he'd known who'd possessed that special combo was Archer Alzate's kid sister, Kaia.

He hadn't seen Kaia face-to-face since she was sixteen and she had attended his and Archer's graduation from the University of Texas. But two years ago, Archer called him to tell him that while working on her doctorate in veterinarian medicine at Texas A&M, Kaia had been in a terrible car accident and fractured her pelvis. Ridge had flown straight to College Station to see her only to discover she was in a medically induced coma.

The waiting room had been packed with her family and friends, and no one noticed him standing in the doorway. After so much time away he'd felt awkward and misplaced, an outsider. Not wanting to turn Kaia's accident into a stage for his return, he'd slipped quietly away without speaking to the family.

But later he texted Archer to meet him in the parking lot to get an update on Kaia's condition. Archer gave him the rundown, including the fact Kaia had such a high medical deductible he didn't know how she was ever going to afford to finish her degree.

Once Ridge knew she was stable and going to pull through, he went to the business office, anonymously paid the fifteen-thousand-dollar deductible toward her medical bills, and swore Archer to secrecy.

Later, when she was out of the coma, he sent flowers and a card and he'd gotten back a kind thank-you note, and their correspondence had ended there. Archer kept his word and Kaia never knew Ridge had come to see her or that he was the one who paid her deductible.

Ridge slipped off his sunglasses for a clearer look at the provocative woman. From the back seat of the Tundra, she extracted an oversized present wrapped in gold foil. The package was so big and the backseat so small. How she'd managed to cram it in?

She tossed her head, a triumphant smile on her face, and turned in his direction. Their gazes met across an empty desert.

For a split second, his heart stopped.

Her obsidian eyes arrested him, a mysterious color that suggested hot summer nights and low, deep-throated whispers. Ripples of recognition jolted his nervous system, both shocking and exhilarating. He knew her.

Kaia Alzate.

Freakadilly circus, he'd been lusting after little Kaia Alzate. Hot for the girl he'd once dubbed the Braterminator.

Ridge coolly slipped his sunglasses back down over his eyes. She'd pestered the hell out of him and Archer when they were kids. Tagging along everywhere they went, tattling if they stepped out of line, and generally being a run-of-the-mill pain-in-the-ass.

He might have hidden his eyes from her, but he couldn't hide the goose bumps spreading over his skin, pushing an insistent heat into his bloodstream as he watched her from behind the safety of the polarized lenses of his aviator Ray-Bans.

Her snapping black eyes sparkled with glee, as an enthusiastic grin split her mouth wide. She had recognized him too, and she looked more than happy to see him.

His gut dove the way it did whenever he'd practiced a stall in pilot training, spinning, whirling, and hurtling headlong toward the earth.

Thank God her hands were full because he had the distinct impression that if she'd been empty-handed, she would have come flying across the tarmac to hug the stuffing out of him.

He didn't mean to do it, told himself he wasn't going to do it, but damn if he couldn't help sliding his gaze over her body. After all, she had no idea what his eyes were doing behind the sunglasses.

Thank you, Ray-Bans.

She moved toward him, arms strapped around the oversized present. Stopped. Cast a glance over her shoulder at the main house. Swung her gaze back to him. She wanted to come over, but didn't seem to know what to do with the package.

He kept his face unreadable, but gave her a respectful nod. *I see you, but no need to rush or gush or make a fuss.*

Deliberately, he turned away, telling himself it was to chalk the plane's tires, and it had nothing to do with the fact his chest was tight and his head fuzzy. And a smile he could not stop was pushing across his face.

He was happy to see her too. So happy it freaked him out.

Once the chalks were in place, and he reined in his galloping pulse, Ridge raised his head, ready to dish up a slick greeting.

But she was gone.

Yay. Great. Perfect. He'd avoided her exuberant hug. Good work.

Why then, did he feel so bummed?

Holy tidal wave!

It was Ridge Lockhart, and he was more devastatingly gorgeous than ever.

Of course, Kaia had known he was coming home for Archer's wedding. She expected to see him. Thought she was braced for it.

Fat chance!

What she hadn't expected was that he'd be so damned sexy.

Her initial impulse had been to run to him and fling herself into his arms and tell him how thrilled she was that he'd come home. But she wasn't eight years old anymore, and he was no longer that lanky boy who'd yanked her braids and called her irritating names.

Her heart jackhammered, and she clutched the oversized wedding present tighter and hurried up the stone walkway to the mansion where the wedding party was assembling before the rehearsal. Instead of the traditional rehearsal dinner, Casey Hollis, the bride-to-be, had decided on a rehearsal brunch. As soon as everyone arrived, they would all head out to the cowboy chapel to rehearse.

Ridge included.

Kaia's pulse gave another sharp hop.

The gift was a crate for the German shepherd puppy that Archer and Casey were adopting from the shelter when they returned from their honeymoon. But ugh. She hadn't fully thought it through. Per usual, excitement had swept her away.

Then again, she'd used the gift as a shield against Ridge's steely gaze. It provided a great excuse not to talk to him until she was prepped.

Seriously? She was not a silly teen with a monster crush on her big brother's best friend. Why did she need to prep to speak to the man?

Why?

Because just seeing him standing there in the sunlight sent her blood swirling the way it always had.

Darn it. Shouldn't she be over puppy love by now?

There ought to be a law. No one man had a right to look so handsomely heartbreaking.

The past decade had been kind to him. More than kind. He'd

grown from the lean, skinny kid into full-blown manhood. Big-framed. Rugged. Untamed as ever.

He moved with the predatory grace of a mountain lion on the hunt. Intent, alert eyes and muscles, but with loose limbs and fluid joints. He looked like he should be on a high mountaintop staking in a pennant flag, claiming his territory.

Dressed in jeans, Stetson, suit jacket, tie, aviator sunglasses, and lizard-skin boots, he was part businessman, part pilot, part cowboy, and one hundred percent alpha male. Muscular fingers and scarred knuckles hinted at his roughneck past.

He was both rawboned and polished. Cheeks and jawline sharp, primal. Nose perfectly straight. Eyebrows orderly. It was a dizzying combination of refined poise and rough-edged virility.

Everything about him caused her insides to quiver and her heart to flush. She couldn't have been more surprised if she'd unearthed pirate treasure in the desert.

Oh no. Oh damn. She was in trouble. Felt the truth of it overtake her. Nothing had changed. She still pined for him. How could she not even know it until now?

Stop it. Just stop it.

She was letting her imagination run away with her. All she had to do was steer clear of him until he went back to where he'd come from, and that would be that.

Turmoil over. Crisis avoided.

Except that she had to be around him for the wedding. He was her older brother's best friend and the best man and she was a bridesmaid. There was no way she could avoid him completely.

Chillaxe. No need to flip out. He would only be in town for three days. She could keep her hormones in check. All she had to do was make sure she was never alone with him. Considering all the people who'd been invited to the wedding, that should be a piece of cake.

Armed with a plan, Kaia chuffed out a relieved breath, kicked on the front door with the tip of her boot in lieu of knocking, and called out, "Open up. It's me, Kaia. I come bearing gifts."

Chapter 3

Some days hovered over the desert like God's fist, big and omnipresent, pressing heat into the barren earth until the ground burned with low, undulating energy. Steady as a locust buzz, squirming circuitously across the Trans-Pecos.

Ridge looped his thumb in his waistband, raised his face to the wide expanse of hot blue sky. He could smell the sun.

Relentless.

A pizza oven that blazed mad mirages until the soil smelled of it too, leaving the plants withered and crisped, lizards darting for shade in the cracks, tears drying long before they hit cheeks. The desert had the power to strip a man of everything, even his right to grieve.

An involuntary shudder ran through him and instead of immediately heading into the mansion, Ridge wandered the grounds, stalling.

This wasn't like him, avoiding problems, but here he was, loping along, checking out what had changed, and what hadn't. Looking for Archer, and putting off facing the people inside of the house for as long as possible.

Christ, he'd had ten years. What was it gonna take? Truth? He could have a century and never belong here.

He walked around, impressed by the improvements. He spied a fleet of ATVs in the barn, gassed up and ready to go. Archer had told him the ranch used ATVs now for herding instead of horses, cheaper and more efficient, but it felt wrong somehow. The end of an era.

The ranch hands in the barn greeted him as Mr. Lockhart, so

they knew who he was, but he didn't know any of them. They'd always had a big turnover in staff. While the old man paid well, he was notoriously hard to work for. Ridge had no idea how Archer had lasted so long as the Silver Feather's foreman. When he asked his friend about it, Archer would say, "You just gotta know how to sweet-talk him."

Yeah, about that, Ridge refused to kiss the old man's ass. Why should he? He had nothing to apologize for, and no desire to pump up the old man's ego.

Although to be fair, Duke Augustus Lockhart was a smart sonofagun with a masterful ability for making money.

Duke had taken the modest Lockhart fortune he'd inherited, invested heavily in real estate during the boom, and managed to get out just before economic sands shifted and things collapsed on Wall Street. With that move, he'd become the richest man in Jeff Davis County, finally surpassing the privileged Fants.

The Fants had come from Baltimore old money and had a family history that harkened back to British royalty, and at one time had rubbed elbows with the likes of Wallis Simpson and Prince Edward.

The Lockharts had none of that pizzazz. Their pedigree was hard work, dogged tenacity, and Texas-sized chutzpah. Levi Lockhart, Ridge's three times great-grandfather had come to the Trans-Pecos in 1852 looking to strike it rich at silver mining.

From all accounts Levi had been a persistent cuss, part outlaw and part idealist, with a grand imagination and even grander schemes. Although many pronounced him a damn fool for daring to encroach on territory claimed by the fearsome Mescalero Apaches.

Levi not only managed to survive with his scalp intact, he also gained the lands that became the Silver Feather and a personal truce with the natives when he found a young Apache brave wounded in the desert.

Rather than leaving the teen to die, Levi nursed him back to health. The young brave turned out to be the tribal chief's son. In gratitude for saving the boy, the chieftan presented Levi with a silver hawk feather and a solemn vow that the Apaches would forever leave Levi and his family in peace.

That framed silver feather hung in his father's mansion.

While Levi did settle the homestead in the town that later become Cupid—so dubbed because of a stalagmite found in the local caverns that resembled the Roman god of love—he never did find the silver he came looking for. That discovery went to Levi's oldest son, Malachi, who took up his father's quest, staked a claim, and in 1884 founded Lockhart Silver Mining Company.

Stalwart ancestors, peace treaties with the Apaches, ranching, and silver mining cemented the Lockharts' legacy deep in the history of the Trans-Pecos. Ridge had a huge birthright to live up to and he did not take his responsibility lightly. He was the oldest son, of the oldest son, of the oldest son all the way back to Levi.

Never mind that he was illegitimate. Each subsequent generation of high achievers kept raising the bar.

The urge to prove himself to Duke drove Ridge. He was as good or better than any other Lockhart, and he would do whatever it took to show them all up.

Drive gnawed at him like hunger pangs. Spurred his galloping ambition. Dreams mattered. Success mattered. Money mattered.

The urge to excel colored everything he did. And that went for the best man duties he'd signed on for. If Ridge promised something, he delivered.

Always.

Where was Archer and why hadn't he come out to greet him?

Probably wrapped around his fiancée's little finger. The way the man talked about Casey made Ridge's teeth ache. He didn't mean that in a disparaging way. He liked Casey. Archer had brought her to Calgary to meet him at Christmas, and they'd gone skiing at Banff. She and Archer had cuddled and canoodled and got along like two peas in a pod.

It was just that . . . well . . . Ridge didn't much believe in all that sappy romance stuff. It colored people's reasoning and judgment. He knew that falling in lust could make for some pretty bad decisions.

He passed through the stables, rounded the corner of a stall and boom!

There was Duke, saddling up a mature stallion named Majestic, a horse that was once so untamable that only a rare few dared ride him. Was he still as wild? Or was he age-mellowed?

Involuntarily, Ridge's gut clenched and for a whisper of a breath, he was that three-year-old kid again, snatched up by his arm and dangled in Duke's face. *This is your mess. Clean it up.*

Majestic whinnied at the sight of Ridge. His gut loosened, and his heart swelled, and his pulse broke like floodgates.

Duke had bought the stallion for Ridge as a college graduation present, and he had loved that horse. But he'd left Majestic behind when he'd fled the ranch after catching Duke in *his* bed at *his* house with *his* girlfriend.

Ridge ground his teeth. Ancient history. Let it go.

His father raised his head, met Ridge's eyes. Grunted. "Son."

"Duke."

The old man had aged in a decade. Wrinkles lined his sun-weathered face and his hair was thinner, his moustache grayer. His father made an I-suppose-I-deserve-not-being-called-dad sound. Not an actual admission of guilt or regret, but it was something.

What had he expected? That his father would hug him and beg his forgiveness? The prospect of hell icing into a frozen Arctic skating rink was far more likely.

Duke Lockhart did not apologize. *Ever.* In all honesty, neither did Ridge.

Ten years had passed since they'd seen each other. They were standing four feet apart, the smell of hay and horse manure in the air. Staring at each other as if they were strangers.

Weren't they? Truly, had he ever really known the man?

"You made it," Duke said mildly.

"Archer's my best friend."

"Whom you rarely see."

"We talk." Which was more than Ridge and his father did. "And text."

"Well there's that." Sarcasm pulled his voice down into a yeasty dark brew of contempt. Ah, there it was. Duke's real feelings.

Showdown at the Silver Feather Corral, and Ridge wouldn't have been half surprised to see pearl-handled pistols sticking from Duke's waistband.

Neither of them blinked.

A column of silence marched between them, tension stretching long and flammable. Picking up on the tension, Majestic tossed his head.

"You look good," Duke said finally, his tone softening, but his eyes stayed flinty, unrelenting.

"Wish I could say the same for you."

"You always were a little bastard," Duke said, but there was affection in the word and the tension thawed. Not much, but a little.

"Where you going?" Ridge nodded at the saddle in his father's hand. Duke's forearms bunched and corded from the weight of it. He was still strong as an ox.

"Chapel. To turn on air conditioning before the rest of them get up there and start squawking about the heat. Casey's folks are city sissies."

"Vivi doesn't much like the heat either, if memory serves."

At the mention of Vivi's name, his father's pupils dilated and the pitch of his tone lifted. "She is a rare flower, our Vivi."

Our Vivi. Jab. Stab. Take that Oedipus. Daddy's still in charge.

Ridge raised his palms. Not a gesture of surrender, more like not-my-circus-not-my-monkeys-don't-drag-me-into-it. "Hey man, she's all yours. You claimed her. You're stuck with her."

Duke settled the saddle on Majestic's back and the stallion gave a kick just to let them know he stayed spicy.

"Why are you taking Majestic?" Ridge nudged his Stetson back on his head.

"He doesn't get ridden enough."

"You're taking that horse around a bunch of people he doesn't know?" Ridge pressed his mouth flat in a you're-a-dumbass expression. "Playing with fire."

"You haven't seen the horse in ten years and you're making judgments? Telling me about my own horse."

"I know Majestic. He was my horse."

"Until you ran off and left him. He's aged." Duke jutted out his chin.

"Has he?" Ridge hitched his thumbs through his belt loops. They were no longer talking about the stallion.

"If you came home once in a while you'd know things." Duke's bushy eyebrows pulled into a glower.

"Some things aren't worth bothering about."

"Meaning me?"

"Take it any way you like, old man."

Duke shifted his weight, rocking onto the balls of his feet, sinking his hands on his hips, spreading out, making himself look bigger, fiercer.

Ridge knew the ploy. Expand your body; expand your territory. Taking control. Taking over. Man-spreading.

But Duke was already in control here. It was his home. His place. No need to expand. Unless . . .

Was his father feeling insecure?

Ridge smiled big as Dallas. Had his arrival thrown Duke? Hmm. He liked that idea. Liked it a lot.

Their gazes locked, and Ridge did not have a key. They stared at each other until all he could see was Duke's chocolate eyes and he supposed that all Duke could see of him where his navy blues.

Yeah, okay, he'd admit it. He'd gotten his stubborn streak from the old coot.

Another five seconds of staring each other down and they would have gone to fisticuffs. He could feel it in the air, his own body, in the way Duke sank his feet solidly into the ground. Bracing.

They'd been here before. Just like this. More than once. He

didn't want to fight an AARP member, but he wasn't afraid to defend himself if Duke made the first move. The old man had a right hook like a bulldozer, the kind that could knock a son out with one clean snap.

It would be like old times. Ridge felt his fists bunch, and his body loosened with readiness. If that's where this was going, so be it.

Majestic snorted and tossed his head, ready for action. That broke the stare down. Duke was the first to drop his gaze, and he mumbled, "We're going to use it."

Huh? Ridge blinked, confused. "Use what?"

"At the mine. The Lock Ridge drilling method."

Knock him down with a feather duster.

"Everyone in silver mining will be using it," Ridge said without a trace of ego. It was a fact. If you mined silver and you weren't using the Lock Ridge technique, you were squatting behind a giant financial eight ball with spurs on. Only a dumbass would ignore that, and Duke was anything but dumb.

"Saw that write-up on you in the *Wall Street Journal*." Duke cinched the saddle on Majestic.

Ridge raised an eyebrow, waiting for a tart rejoinder.

"You didn't mention a word about me," Duke said.

"I did not. Why should I? I made it on my own. Besides, Bridgette Alzate taught me that if you can't say something nice, don't say anything at all."

Duke snorted again.

Anger heat pushed its way up Ridge's neck. *Do not rise to the bait. He's an alligator waiting to attack. Anything you say can and will be used against you.* "Got something to say?"

"Gave you my DNA. You're welcome."

"If I could give it back, I would."

Duke laughed a fat, wet sound like mud sucking around bogged work boots. "I imagine you'd like to shove it down my throat."

"The thought has occurred to me."

"Congratulations." Duke bobbed his head up and down once,

as if he were reluctant and rusty at praise. "You took my DNA and ran with it. You achieved what you set out to do."

Ridge cocked his head, closed one eye against the glare of the sun coming through the open stable door, and gauged his father. Tried to puzzle out his angle.

"How's Vivi?" he asked, poking the bear.

Duke tightened his lip. "All in a fluff over this weddin'."

"Archer told me you built a wedding chapel on the east forty."

"Vivi's idea. Renting the chapel out for weddings brings in more money than hunting leases. Who knew?"

"You've stopped the leases?"

Duke rolled his eyes. "Vivi's liberal claptrap. Don't kill Bambi, wah, wah."

"And you went along with it?"

"Some things ain't worth getting in a snit over."

Ridge couldn't help grinning. Duke was bending over backward to please his trophy wife. "Hey, keeping her happy must be working for you. You've managed to hang on to her the longest of all your wives."

"It ain't all gumdrops and roses, but this one's gotta stick. I'm too old to start over."

"What? No tick-tock of her biological clock? She's thirty-two. There's gotta be a countdown. Ready to become a daddy again?"

"Hush it." Duke's eyebrows bunched together above his hawkish nose. "Last thing I need is another squall bag."

"You should try for a girl," Ridge teased, enjoying watching his father squirm. "I always did want a little sister."

"You're enjoying this."

"Immensely."

"Gloatin' bastard."

"Yep."

"I need to get up to the chapel."

"Turning on that air conditioning and all."

Another long stretch of silence, but this one was less tense than before. Something had shifted.

Duke grunted. "Good to have you home."

This was as close to saying *I'm sorry for stealing your girl* as Duke was ever going to get. Good enough.

Hey, shocker of shockers, coming home didn't feel as bad as he'd feared. But he didn't trust this feeling or his father.

Not by a long shot.

Chapter 4

"You're late," Mom hollered above the beehive hum of female voices gathered in the mansion's enormous kitchen.

"You said to be here at seven," Kaia hollered back, looking for a place to set the doggie crate. There wasn't a spare scrap of real estate unoccupied by gifts or brunch fixings or purses.

Her mother pointed at the clock. Seven-ten.

Kaia offered up an apologetic smile. "I almost died, remember."

Mom sank her hands on her hips. "That was two years ago. You need a new excuse."

"But you're really, really happy I didn't die."

Mom came across the immense kitchen to wrap her in a hard hug while Kaia was still holding on to the package. "I'm really, really happy you didn't die." She rested her chin on Kaia's shoulder. "Did you bring the hash brown casserole?"

Kaia cringed. *Oh crapple.* "I left it on the counter. I'm sorry. You want I should go back for it?"

"We've got more food than we can eat," Casey, the bride-to-be said. She was standing at the island folding breakfast sausages into triangles of crescent roll dough for pigs in a blanket, and looking gorgeous in a short blue cotton dress with Van Gogh sunflowers on it.

"I really don't mind," Kaia offered.

"No worries. Do not go back for it. The minister will be here at eight for the rehearsal and it will take us that long to get everyone up to the chapel." Casey piled a freshly wrapped sausage on a platter.

"Ridge is here," Kaia blurted.

Those three words brought the entire room silent.

"What?" Casey said.

"His plane just touched down."

"Bury the lead, will you?" Kaia's youngest sister, Aria, said. At five-seven, Aria was the tallest of the four Alzate sisters. She'd just graduated from Texas Tech and was back home for the summer.

Someone, Kaia wasn't sure whom, but she suspected it was Ridge's stepmother, Vivi, said, "Baa baa black sheep has finally returned."

"How does he look?" Tara, Kaia's next-to-the-oldest sister asked. "Still handsome as ever?" Tara was a nurse who worked at Cupid General Hospital in obstetrics.

"Where can I put this?" Kaia asked, wishing she hadn't brought up Ridge's name, and shot Casey a get-me-out-of-this look.

Before Casey could answer, a toothy toddler in blue jean shorts and cowboy boots tackled her around the knees. Kaia grunted at the exuberant impact and ruffled the kid's hair.

"KiKi!" squealed the toddler, who happened to be Casey's three-year-old nephew, Atticus, and the ring bearer at the wedding. He had a thing for Kaia, probably because she usually had an animal or two with her for him to play with.

"Kitty kitty?" he asked, cocking his little head to one side.

"No kitty," she told him. "Not today."

"I'll take that," said Lynne, Casey's older sister and Atticus's mother, and took the unwieldy wedding gift off her hands, leaving Kaia free to swing Atticus onto her hip, lift his shirt and blow a raspberry against his round little belly.

Atticus shrieked with joy and planted a wet kiss on the end of her nose.

Mom leaned over to pinch Atticus's cheek. "When are one of you girls going to cooperate and give me one of these?"

Simultaneously, all three of Kaia's sisters, Ember, Tara, and Aria, rolled their eyes.

"Hey," Kaia said. "Don't look at me. Ember and Tara are first in line."

"Go ahead." Tara groaned. "Throw us under the bus just because we were born before you."

"I might be the oldest," Ember said. She was the only sister who'd taken after Mom's Irish side of the family, and her flame-red hair matched her name. "But clearly you're more maternal. Go for it, Kaia."

"I would love to have one of these someday." Kaia tickled Atticus making him giggle like the Pillsbury Doughboy. "But first things first. Gotta finish up vet school, and oh yeah, find a husband."

"You don't need a husband to get one of those," Aria said. "All you need is a visit to a sperm—"

"The Song of the Soul Mate," Granny Blue Alzate interrupted, her voice wrapped with the earthy tones of her Comanche ancestry.

Granny Blue sat at the kitchen table chopping up mise en place for the omelet buffet. She was petite, eighty-three, and sharp as a hawk. Her dark eyes, deep-set into a wrinkled face, missed nothing and she did not put up with bullshit. But it was just as easy to earn her smile as her rebuke.

"Need a hand, Granny?" Kaia asked, passing Atticus to Lynne, who'd come back into the room. She bopped over to the kitchen sink, washed her hands, plunked down beside her grandmother, and started julienning red bell peppers.

"I have a question, Mrs. Alzate," Casey said.

"Please, you're part of the family now." She slid pieces of diced ham from a cutting board into a small bowl. "Call me Granny Blue."

"Granny Blue." Casey smiled an I've-got-the-world-on-a-string smile. "What *is* this Song of the Soul Mate stuff?"

Granny Blue shot Kaia a glance that said, how do you explain the inexplicable?

Kaia shrugged. She had no idea. She'd never experienced it. Didn't know if she believed in the legend.

"It's something that happens to the women in our family when they fall in love," Granny Blue explained.

Casey took the chair across the table from Granny Blue, leaned in. "Tell me more."

"Anyone want a Bloody Mary?" Aria interrupted from where she was standing beside the Vitamix.

"Me! Me!" Tara and Ember waved wildly. Kaia raised a hand as high as her shoulder.

"Not now." Mom frowned. "Those are for brunch. We don't want you girls half-in-the-bag for the rehearsal."

"Why not?" Aria said. "Being half-in-the-bag is what makes it fun."

"Father Dubanowski will be there." With a stern finger, Mom waggled for Aria to put the pitcher down.

"He's Episcopalian—he drinks."

"About this soul mate thing . . ." Casey leaned forward, propped her elbows on the table, and sank her chin into her upturned palms, getting closer to Granny Blue.

"If we're going to talk about that silly old myth, we definitely need alcohol. How about mimosas, Mom? Champagne versus vodka?" Aria made teeter-totter, weighing-it-out motions with her hand.

"No hooch." Mom shook her head.

"Bummer." Aria sank her butt against the kitchen counter, folded her arms over her chest. Looked defeated.

"Cheer up," Ember said, bumping Aria with her hip. "In a couple of hours you can have all the Bloody Marys and Mimosas you want."

"Within reason," Mom added.

"Are you guys purposely trying to stop Granny Blue from telling me about the legend?" Casey asked.

"Pay no attention to them. They're skeptics," Granny Blue said. "Scared of what they do not understand."

Kaia finished up the bell peppers, reached for the porcini mushrooms, and started chopping. She was on the fence about the family legend. She didn't believe it, but she wanted to.

"Well," Casey said. "I want to understand. Tell me."

Granny Blue stacked her palms on the table in front of her.

"It is simple. When the women from my bloodline kiss their soul mate, they hear a soft, but distinct humming at the base of their brains."

"That's just tinnitus," Vivi said. "Ringing in the ears. I hear it after I listen to loud music on my headphones."

Granny Blue stared at Vivi until she sheepishly glanced away. "It is *not* ringing in the ears."

"That's wacky. I mean, c'mon," Aria said. "How could kissing someone make your head hum?"

"Wish fulfillment?" Lynne asked, bouncing Atticus on her knee, playing giddy-up horsey. "Power of suggestion?"

"I do not know the answer to the mystery," Granny Blue said. "I only know that it is so."

"Too bad the rest of us don't have such a clear-cut signal," Vivi muttered, and everyone turned to look at her. "What? I'm not allowed to question my choices?"

No one was touching that with a ten-foot pole. The entire town had questioned Vivi's choice when she threw Ridge over for his father.

"Mom," Ember said. "Do you hear humming when you kiss Daddy?"

"I'm not from your granny's bloodline," Mom said, trying to look neutral. Kaia already knew Mom thought Granny Blue's head humming tale was bunk, but she respected her mother-in-law too much to say so.

"Is it a Native American thing?" Casey asked.

Granny shrugged, a casual gesture that said she didn't care if anyone believed her or not. "It is a *family* thing."

"But only for the women?" Casey asked.

"Only for the women."

"That hardly seems fair."

"Fair has nothing to do with life," Granny Blue said sagely. "It just is."

"So there's no way to know for sure if I'm Archer's soul mate."

Casey pouched out her bottom lip in disappointment. "No song for us."

"My granddaughters are lucky to have an undeniable way to know if they've found their true loves." Granny Blue leaned over and placed a wrinkled hand on the left side of Casey's chest. "But anyone can know for certain if they just get quiet, be still, and listen to their hearts."

Casey locked gazes with Granny Blue. "Archer *is* my soul mate."

"And so you know." Granny Blue smiled. Straightened. "You are smarter than all four of my granddaughters put together."

Tears formed in Casey's eyes. "I know."

"Did Casey just dis the shit out of us?" Aria asked.

"Language!" Mom scolded.

"Sorry." Aria did not look the least bit contrite.

"I didn't mean I was smarter than you," Casey apologized. "I meant I knew for sure that Archer is the one I'm meant to be with."

"That's good." Ember crunched a carrot. "Seeing as how you're about to marry him and all."

"Just like I knew about Armand," Mom murmured, and a dreamy smile came over her face.

"Ooh," Lynne said. "I've got a question. What if you were already happily married, and then you kissed someone else and heard the humming? What then?"

Casey whipped her head around to stare at her sister. "Why would you kiss someone else if you were happily married?"

"Not me," Lynne said. "But someone might. Just saying. Mistletoe at a drunken Christmas party or something."

Everyone looked at Vivi again.

"What?" Vivi glared. "Am I officially the town ho' bag? It was ten years ago, people. Let it go."

"Thank you for hosting the brunch, Vivi," Casey said. "It was very nice of you to offer. I know this can't be easy."

Vivi fluffed her hair, looked appeased. "You're welcome."

"Granny B," Aria said. "I've got a question. If it's true that our female DNA has a built-in soul mate detector, then why haven't any of us girls experienced it?"

"She makes a good point," Tara chimed in. "Between the four of us, we've kissed a lot of guys and none of us have ever heard the humming."

"That's because you have not found your soul mate," Granny Blue said.

"We're getting a little old," Ember said. Ember had even been married once, but no one ever brought up that ill-fated union. In fact, everyone pretended it had never happened. "You'd think one of us would have found our mate by now."

Granny Blue smiled slyly. "You can't hurry true love, as you found out the hard way."

Aria grabbed a banana from the fruit bowl, pretended it was a microphone, and started singing the Supremes' song.

Tara and Ember both grabbed bananas and joined Aria.

"Me too!" Kaia said.

Then all the women in the room were on their feet, bananas in hands, dancing around the room, singing a heartfelt rendition of "You Can't Hurry Love." Even Granny Blue and Atticus joined. The toddler was wriggling and jumping, throwing himself fully into the endeavor. The women surrounded the boy, everyone singing to him about being patient for love.

That's what they were doing when Ridge sauntered into the kitchen.

Everyone froze. And it was like that ominous moment just before a tornado hits when everything goes utterly quiet.

Chapter 5

ALL the women had been dancing and singing like doo-wop girls, but it was Kaia alone who nailed Ridge's attention.

For one thing, her voice rose above the others, sincere and adorably off-key, belting out the song like she was Adele. She was hopping around, banana to her lips, eyes bright, braids flying, breasts jiggling.

For another thing, she was fully, one hundred percent alive, and it stirred him. How did anyone come by such pure joie de vivre? For another thing, it was such an unexpected bonus, to witness how she'd flowered in womanliness.

And those eyes!

Dark and mysterious as the bottom of the ocean. Her eyes made him think of spelunking in Cupid caverns.

He appreciated her pert sense of rhythm, her delicate collarbone exposed by the cut of her T-shirt, the two piercings in each earlobe adorned with gold studs and twin dream catchers that swayed seductively when she moved her head. She wore a dozen multicolored leather strap bracelets on her right wrist and a heart-shaped necklace around her slender throat.

Kaia caught him watching her and everything came to a screeching halt. The joy drained from her face, quickly replaced by red-cheeked embarrassment.

Regret kicked him. He'd done that. Sapped the joy right out of her simply by walking into the room.

Kaia was the first one to toss her banana back in the fruit bowl. Immediately, everyone else followed her lead.

"Ridge," Vivi said breathlessly, pressing a hand to her chest, and it wasn't until that moment he even noticed his ex-girlfriend-turned-stepmother. "You're here."

"You always were sharp as a tack, Vivi," Ridge drawled.

Vivi hadn't changed much, still thin, and tanned, and artfully made up. Well, except for what was clearly a boob job. She wore a white, snug-fitting tank top with a plunging neckline, black short-shorts and gold flip-flops. Her hair was longer and fluffier, rocking the Texas big hair. She was a good-looking woman, but in his estimation she couldn't hold a candle to Kaia.

He bore Vivi no ill will. He'd always known she was all about the money, and he'd not ever considered marrying her.

Truth? In retrospect Duke had done him a favor. Vivi and his father deserved each other.

Vivi laughed nervously under his scrutiny. "Well, come on in. We're just waiting for the priest. Are you hungry? Thirsty? Where are your bags? I opened up your house. Had it cleaned and stocked it with supplies. It's unlocked and ready for you."

That was damn ballsy. Bringing up his house. Assuming he'd want to stay there.

He cast a covert glance at Kaia. Saw a worried expression at odds with her inviting smile. He yearned to dip his head to her ear and whisper. *Nothing to worry about, sweetheart. All is well.*

Vivi pressed a hand to her ample chest. "I hope you don't mind. I um . . . I had the master bedroom redone."

"Thanks for the effort, but I'm staying at Archer's place." Ridge kept his tone even, but his eyes sharp.

"Oh. Um . . . sure. . . . right. " Vivi hem-hawed. "I should have expected that since you're the best man. Of course you'll want to spend the night at his place."

He enjoyed watching her squirm. Petty? "Where *is* Archer?"

Vivi hovered, wringing her hands, looking uncertain, but trying not to show it.

"He and Armand went to pick up Father Dubanowski," Casey said, coming over to give him a hug. "It's so good to see you again. I had such fun in Banff."

Ridge tolerated the hug, stepped back as quickly as he could. He wasn't much of a hugger. "You look great."

"Thank you." Casey blushed and smiled. "I'm so thrilled you were able to make it. First thing Archer said after he asked me to marry him was, 'I can't get married without my best friend. We have to plan the wedding around Ridge's timetable.'"

"Archer is a lucky guy," Ridge said.

"No, I'm the lucky one. Not only am I getting the most wonderful man in the world, but I inherited this amazing family." She swept her hand at the women in the room. "No one could be luckier."

"The Alzates are pretty special," Ridge agreed.

The Alzate and the Lockhart siblings had grown up together on the Silver Feather. Back then, their father, Armand Alzate, had been the Silver Feather Ranch's foreman, and he'd lived with his wife and kids in the original Lockhart farmhouse built in the 1860s.

Bridgette Alzate had served as the ranch cook and housekeeper and she'd often played surrogate mother to Ridge and his brothers after Remington and Rhett's mother, Lucy, had died. Like Ridge, Archer was the oldest child of his family. The nine of them had been pretty close in those years—running wild on the ranch, riding horses, being young and carefree, getting up to all manner of mischief.

Thinking back on it now, it was the most idyllic time of his life. Thanks to the Alzates.

But things changed. Kids grew up. Went off to college. Dad married Vivi, and arthritis forced Armand Alzate to give up ranching and move into town, leaving Archer to take over as foreman.

"This is my sister, Lynne." Casey introduced a slightly older version of herself. Lynne had a toddler on her hip. "And this is her son, Atticus. Atty is our ring bearer."

The boy stared at Ridge owl-eyed, accusatory as if he could see right through him, knew all his secrets and every lie he'd ever told.

Kids made Ridge edgy. He hadn't been around them much. Had no idea what to say to them. Especially kids this age. They were just so damned vulnerable, but clueless as to just how vulnerable they really were.

Not knowing what else to do, he offered up an uneasy smile to the kid and the boy's mother, and quickly moved on to greet Kaia's sisters, mother, and granny.

Now women were another story. Women, Ridge knew how to handle. He charmed and grinned and flattered. Going through well-oiled motions.

Hi. How you doin'. Been too long. Prettier than ever. I've missed seeing you.

Smooth. Easy. Not particularly sincere.

Until at last he turned to Kaia, and everything he'd been thinking and feeling turned upside down.

"Hi!" she chirped, happy as a robin, and she disarmed the hell out of him by enveloping him in a fierce hug right in front of everyone.

His heart slammed into his chest, a train wreck of sensation—*bam, bam, bam*—twenty-boxcar pileup. Her scent wrapped around him, welcoming as home-baked bread. He froze, unsure of what to do. Alarmed because he was getting aroused right there in front of everyone.

Christ, he hadn't gotten a hard-on this easily since he was a randy teenager.

Quick. Think about something else.

Right. Drilling stats. Think about drilling stats. Except the word *drilling* put a wholly different picture in his mind than silver mining.

Fine. Forget drilling. Stock quotes. Yesterday's stock quotes. The current trend in silver stocks should put him in a downward mood. PAAS was down 0.31. SSRI down 0.16. TAHO down 0.23.

Finally, thankfully, Kaia released him and stepped back, and Ridge could finally breathe again.

"Hey," he said rather idiotically, as if ten years hadn't passed since the last time she'd hugged him in a parking lot at the University of Texas, his business diploma clutched in his hand. "Hey."

"Welcome home." She smiled and his world slid sideways.

Home.

There was that word again, a twitchy word that usually tied his stomach in knots. But now, standing here, looking down at Kaia's adorable grin, home didn't seem half-bad.

The front door opened, letting in the sound of voices. Seconds later, Father Dubanowski and the rest of the wedding party showed up. It had been a long time since Ridge had been around so many people in a nonwork capacity. He'd forgotten what things were like on the ranch, and with the Alzates. Everywhere they went, people congregated.

There were more greetings and backslapping and lively conversation as they sorted out transportation to the chapel.

Vivi volunteered to stay behind with the housekeeper and Granny Blue to get the brunch set up. Ridge ended up in Archer's Suburban with Archer, Casey, Lynne, Ned, and Atticus. Both sets of parents took the priest in the Alzate's Wagoneer. Ranger and Ember zoomed away on an ATV. Those two had been best friends their entire lives, and they tended to hang out together whenever possible.

Ridge watched Kaia walk off with her other two sisters and the two ranch hands, Zeke and Kip, who were serving as groomsmen, to the blue Tundra, and he felt a pluck of disappointment.

Kaia hopped into the driver's seat and waved as she pulled out. Was she waving at him or someone else in the Suburban?

The chapel was a fifteen-minute drive from the mansion down a dusty dirt road, but it was only a stone's throw from Ridge's house in the east quadrant. The house he hadn't stepped foot inside in over a decade.

When they pulled up, Majestic was tied to a hitching post outside the chapel, and Duke was standing on the front porch, arms akimbo, black Stetson pushed back on his head, larger than life. The Lord of the Land waiting for their arrival.

Everyone got out of the vehicles. There was more talking and hugging and backslapping. Ridge jammed his hands into his pockets, wishing they'd get the show on the road. He'd forgotten how small town folk took life at a leisurely pace.

He took out his phone—hey, why not do some business while

he waited—but he couldn't get any bars. He was in the boonest of the boondocks, and still no decent cell reception away from the mansion's Wi-Fi. Ah, the Trans-Pecos. He slipped his phone back into his pocket.

Kaia popped over to him. "You look antsy."

"Bored."

"Mom says boredom indicates a lack of inner resources."

"Meaning?"

"That fact that you're alive is reason enough not to get bored."

"Um, yeah, okay."

"You're not bored." She tapped her chin, eyed him up and down. "You're nervous."

He lowered his eyelids, sent her the most bored look he could conjure. "Do I look nervous to you?"

"It's okay to be nervous. You've been away a long time."

"Not long enough."

She grinned and wriggled like a puppy. "You were missed around here, you know. You cast a big shadow, Mr. Lockhart."

He snorted.

"Give us a smile." She prodded. "It's a glorious morning and you're home and your best friend is getting married to the love of his life. There is so much to be happy about and thankful for. I know *I'm* thankful you're home."

"Oh yeah?" He simultaneously raised one eyebrow and the opposite corner of his mouth in what Archer called his Pablo Picasso smile.

"You earned the number one spot on my gratitude list this morning. First thing I wrote down." She pantomimed taking notes. *"Ridge is coming home."*

"Gratitude list?"

"Yes, I make a gratitude list every morning while I have my cup of coffee. Perfect way to start the day. By remembering how lucky I am to be alive. I started the list after my accident. Keeps you from being bored with life. Try it some time."

"I'm sorry you had to go through that." He dropped the smile.

"I'm not." She upped the wattage on her grin and it did something to him. "It changed my life in so many beautiful ways. These days, I take nothing for granted. Now, whenever life puts an opportunity in my path, I always say yes."

"Even if it's a mistake?"

"There's no such thing as mistakes. Everything we do and experience is a chance to grow and learn. When you look at it that way, nothing can ever go wrong."

"Sorry"—he shook his head—"but that's a horse I just can't ride."

"I know," she said cheerily. "It doesn't matter. Things still happen for a reason whether you believe it or not."

"So the reason you almost died was because . . ."

"The Universe was teaching me to live in the moment and stop worrying so much about the future and regretting the past."

"Couldn't the universe have picked a kinder way?" He was mocking her, but she didn't take offense.

"Sometimes it takes getting T-boned by a milk truck to wake you up."

"Milk truck, huh?"

"Driver fell asleep at the wheel."

"Would the message have been different if it had been another kind of vehicle?"

She paused as if actually considering it. "Nope. Delivery method doesn't alter the content of the message."

"Um, okay. If you say so."

"Now you're getting it."

Kaia was a regular beam of sunshine. It rubbed him the wrong way. How on God's green earth did anyone get that cheerful? And stay that way? It wasn't healthy. Either that or he was just jealous. "Optimism. How annoying."

She laughed low and sweet, a soft wind-chime sound that ought to calm, but her naughty-arsonist grin lit a flash fire south of his belt. "Does someone need a hug?"

"Jeezus." He fished his sunglasses from his shirt pocket, slipped them on. "Do *not* hug me."

"You can't stop me." She trotted after him, arms wide. "I'm gonna hug you like I did when I was a kid. It used to drive you crazy, so I did it even more."

Ridge sidestepped her, but crashed into Casey's mom, Nancy. He apologized, and turned right into Kaia's hug.

"There . . . there . . . you antsy, uptight city feller." She poured on the Texas drawl. "Hug it right on out."

Oh hell's bells, pressed up against her body he was getting hard all over again. She was bound to notice. Quick! Stock quotes, stock quotes.

Fortunately, the priest picked that moment to clap his hands and announce, "Let's get things moving along, shall we?"

Kaia giggled and released him.

Ridge finally breathed.

"She's up to her old childhood tricks I see." Archer leaned in to Ridge. "Pushing your buttons."

"You out to keep her on a chain," Ridge mumbled, watching Kaia's butt bounce as she walked into the chapel ahead of them.

"She's irrepressible. No holding that one back." Archer slung his arm around Ridge's shoulder. "Man, it's good to have you home."

"Good to see you," Ridge mumbled. The jury was still out on whether it was good to be home or not.

KAIA STOOD AT the back of the church as the second bridesmaid, waiting her turn to follow Aria down the aisle, holding the banana-turned-microphone-turned-pretend-bouquet in her hand. All she could think about was the fact Ridge had gotten aroused when she'd hugged him in the mansion kitchen, and then again just now on the chapel porch.

Her face flushed from her cheeks to her scalp. *She* had turned him on.

That thrilled and scared her beyond words. The guy she'd had a crush on for years, her first crush to be exact, was hot for her.

Finally.

In her heart of hearts, she'd not ever believed he would ever reciprocate her feelings. He'd considered her nothing more than a bratty kid sister. But apparently, a decade apart had changed things.

Oh gosh, oh wow, what now? Be cool, fool. Right. Pay attention. Don't go spinning fantasies. It was a wedding rehearsal. Rehearse.

She took a deep breath, started down the aisle. Ridge was already standing at the altar in the best man spot next to Archer.

Ridge met her eyes across the chapel and smiled the tiniest bit. So slight she wasn't even sure he *had* smiled.

In an instant she was sixteen again, her knees going weak, her pulse rate kicking up, her stomach shaky and unsettled like the last time she'd seen him. College diploma in hand, his things crammed into a beat-up old pickup truck, denim jacket hugging his lean muscular shoulders, dark wild hair curling down his collar.

Today, his hair was close clipped in a CEO style, and a suit jacket had replaced the denim. But he still wore jeans and a cowboy hat and boots. How did a man age so well? Fountain of youth? Deal with the devil?

Knowing Ridge, it was probably the latter.

He'd always bucked convention, swam upstream, spurred gossip. That wild Lockhart boy born out of wedlock to a mother who abandoned him on his father's doorstep and then died in a car crash rumored to be suicide.

His past was a lot to overcome.

For most of her childhood, she'd lived just across the pasture from him, her family in the foreman's farmhouse where Archer now lived. Ridge and his brothers in the mansion.

Her family servants. His masters. Another divide between them.

Except Ridge was something of an outsider. Not fully fitting in either world.

As she grew older, and adolescent hormones took over, she'd grown acutely aware of Ridge's presence in that big house across that patch of desert ground.

Sometimes at night, she'd sneak up on the roof of the farmhouse with binoculars and watch for a glimpse of him through his bedroom window. Once in a while she got lucky and the curtains would be open and he'd strip his shirt off to do push-ups. She lived for those sightings.

Oh, the midnight fantasies she'd had!

The one day when he was a senior, she saw him sneak a girl in his room and her heart had been crushed when he kissed her. She'd stopped spying on him after that because she couldn't bear to watch him with someone else.

The music tempo changed, cuing her that it was her turn to walk down the aisle. She pulled herself from her memories, met Ridge's navy blue eyes.

He sent her a significant look.

A hungry look.

A *sexual* look.

Kaia was so wrapped up in that look she stumbled, almost tumbled. Righted herself. Someone inhaled sharply.

And Ridge sprang forward as if to save her.

She didn't need saving, but damn, in that moment, she wished she *had* tumbled so he could catch her in his big strong arms and hold her as if it meant something.

Chapter 6

AFTER rehearsal, the group moseyed out to the front porch again, chatting, laughing, and congratulating Archer and Casey on their impending wedding. A red-tailed hawk circled lazily overhead, gliding on the current.

Ridge stood off to one side, slipped on his sunglasses again, more for the incognito effect than to block the morning sun.

Behind the chapel was a brand-new barn that had never housed animals. Archer had told him it had been built solely to host wedding receptions. Three hundred yards to the right lay his house. He had to wonder why Duke had picked this spot to build the chapel and reception barn.

A dig at him?

Or had the location been Vivi's idea?

He hadn't laid eyes on the house in ten years, and he felt no sense of ownership. Couldn't even figure out what had possessed him to build on the plot of land his grandfather's trust forbid him to sell without his father's and brothers' permission? Probably some naive notion, that as the oldest, he would run the ranch one day.

Idiot.

The house was constructed of Texas limestone, with a wide stone porch and silver tin roof. Desert willows in the front yard landscaped with gravel, flagstone pavers and hearty, heat-loving plants—agave, aloe, bougainvillea. The porch swing had a fresh coat of paint. Someone had been looking after it.

Ridge set his jaw, fingered the straw Stetson in his hands. Archer and Casey were talking to her parents, Herb and Nancy. Kaia and her sisters were in a huddle discussing the upcoming bachelorette party that evening. His brother Ranger was offering Lynne and her husband, Ned, a private tour of the McDonald Observatory. Duke was deep in discussion with Kaia's parents about something he couldn't hear.

The toddler ring bearer was running around and between the vehicles, carrying a toy water gun, making blasting noises, shooting everything and everyone in sight. Including Majestic who was still hitched up to the post in front of the chapel, not far from where Ridge was standing. No one was paying any attention to the kid.

Ridge settled his hat on his head, eyed the boy.

"Pew-pew!" Atticus cried, zipping by and squirting Ridge's dusty boots.

Majestic flicked his ears, narrowed his eyes, nostrils flaring.

Uh-oh. Trouble.

The kid swung on the hitching post right underneath Majestic, back and forth, back and forth. With a chortle, the boy dropped to the ground and crawled underneath the horse.

Majestic cocked his back leg, the muscles in his haunches twitching, his nostrils flaring, eyes narrowing.

"Hey!" Ridge shouted, running for the boy. "Hey!"

The clueless adults turned to see what was going on.

"The kid! The kid!" His boots churned up a flurry of sand, but it felt as if his legs were slogging through molasses. One sharp kick from the ornery stallion could cave the kid's head in.

Damn Duke for bringing the stallion out here. He should have known better.

The adults stood openmouthed, clearly still not understanding the impending disaster. The boy stood directly behind Majestic, gazing at the big horse with his mouth open and his eyes wide, seemingly mesmerized by the stallion's flicking tail. Ridge knew exactly what that slow, deliberate tail flick meant.

Imminent doom!

Ridge dove to the earth, shoving the boy out of the way just as Majestic did what Ridge knew the stallion was going to do.

Kick.

Hard.

Majestic's hoof connected with the side of Ridge's temple and sent him flying flat on his back.

The boy howled at being knocked down.

The adults gasped and came running. Lynne scooped up her yowling son, hugged him close, burst into tears.

Ridge blinked at the sky. Saw stars at nine o'clock in the morning.

And moons.

And rainbows.

And unicorns.

And finally, after an elongated minute, Kaia's concerned face peering down at him.

WHEN KAIA CAME outside to see Ridge sprawled spread-eagle in the dirt, a red welt blooming at his temple, her heart catapulted into her throat and stuck there like cockleburs in Velcro. She'd been in the chapel talking to her mother about Dart, the new kitten she was fostering, but suspected she'd adopt, and she hadn't seen Majestic kick him.

His cowboy hat and sunglasses were flung several feet away, and a circle of people surrounded him.

Duke had untied Majestic and led him away from the group. Archer was crouched beside Ridge's head, Casey at his feet. Lynne stood next to Ned, clutching Atticus to her chest.

"Ridge saved Atty's life," Lynne kept babbling. "If it wasn't for him . . ." She shuddered, buried her face against the toddler's head.

Ned made soothing noises and rubbed his palm over his wife's shoulder.

Kaia paid no attention to any of them. She raced to her truck and got her medical bag. In two strides, she was beside Ridge, dropping to her knees and nudging Archer out of the way.

She might be a student, but she was in her final year of vet school and the closest thing to a doctor within fifteen miles. Never mind that her hands were shaking and her stomach quaking. Ridge needed her.

"Move back." She spread her arms and shooed the crowd. "Give him some air."

Everyone shifted, clearing out.

Okay. Good. She was in charge. Feeling more confident and in control, she took Ridge's hand, patted it firmly. "Ridge?"

His eyes were closed.

"Can you hear me?" She squeezed his hand.

He squeezed her hand in return. Strong, capable grip. Promising sign. "Yep."

"Can you look at me?"

He opened the eye that wasn't rapidly swelling, grinned roguishly. "Hey there, cutie."

The look in his eye, and his lopsided smile, shot an arrow straight through her heart. Good God, even laid out on the ground with a black eye, the man was a force of nature.

"How you doin'?" she croaked, sounding like a bullfrog with whooping cough.

"Great, now that you're here." The timbre of his voice was as deep and dark as his beard stubble.

Seriously, was he flirting with her? Her pulse cha-cha-chaed. Or was he just dingy from getting a kick upside the head?

The scent of his cologne drifted over her—a manly aroma of leather, bay rum, cardamom, and sunshine that set her nose twitching. Bits of dried grass clung to his thick whiskey brown hair, and the eye he had trained on her was bright and inquisitive and way too naughty, as if he knew exactly what she looked like naked.

And then there was that cocky grin, rising higher on the right side of his mouth than the left; a crooked, self-assured, never-mind-that-I-could-have-a-head-injury-come-play-with-me smile that un-raveled her on a dozen different levels.

"Hand me a flashlight from my bag," she said to Archer, and stuck out her hand.

Archer slapped the mini Maglite into her palm like a scrub nurse passing a surgical instrument to a surgeon.

"This might be uncomfortable," Kaia said to Ridge, "but can you hold your right eye open, so I can check to see if your pupils are equal and reactive?"

He opened his swollen eye, immediately squinted it closed when she shone the light in it. The pupils reacted equally. A positive sign that he didn't have a serious head injury.

"What's your name?" she asked.

"You know my name."

"But do *you* know your name?"

He gave her a look that said, *are you kidding me right now?* "Ridge Lockhart."

"What day is it?"

"Friday, June 3rd."

"Where are we?"

"Silver Feather Ranch."

"Which horse did you tangle with?"

"Majestic."

Ridge was oriented to time, place, and person, and he could tell her what happened, another encouraging sign.

"Did you lose consciousness?"

"It was a TKO," Ridge said.

She glanced over at Archer for translation and confirmation. "What did he say?"

"TKO stands for technical knockout. Means technically, he's out, but he didn't get *knocked* out."

"And that means . . . ?" she asked, adding a sting to her voice. Men and their sports analogies.

Archer chuckled. "He didn't lose consciousness. His head is too hard for that."

"What?" Ridge protested. "You don't trust my word?"

"Stubborn as you are about admitting when you need help?" She shrugged. "Not so much."

"I don't remember you being such a smart-ass." Ridge was smiling at her, but he was watching her closely.

Kaia bit down on her tongue. Wise not to show how easily he could push her buttons. "Can you sit up?"

"Sure." He popped up to a seated position. Instantly, he paled, the blood draining from his face, a palm going to his right temple. "Whoa."

She put a stabilizing hand to his shoulder, felt his muscles twitch beneath her touch. "Dizzy?"

"Briefly. It passed."

"Take a few deep breaths." She moved her hand, pressing it against his back. Felt the hard steady throb of his pulse. The man had the heart of a lion, big and strong and fierce.

Ridge scanned the crowd. "I'm fine, people. Break it up. Go about your business."

"You're getting a huge shiner," Casey said.

"Damn," he mumbled. "It's gonna ruin your wedding photos."

"No," Casey said. "The black eye will *make* them. We'll forever remember the day you saved my nephew's life."

Ridge's neck muscle stiffened. Kaia could tell the attention was making him uncomfortable.

"Everyone, I've got this." She made shooing motions. "Ridge is right. You all go on back to the big house. We'll be along as soon as he's steady."

"You need me to stay?" Archer asked.

"Naw," Ridge said before Kaia had a chance to ask her brother not to leave her alone with him. "Don't let me spoil your day."

"You didn't spoil the day," Lynne said. "You saved my son. You're a hero."

"No biggie." Ridge shrugged, looked embarrassed.

"You took a hoof for my kid," Ned said. "It *is* a big deal."

"I did what anyone else would have done," Ridge said.

"Except no one else did." Lynne hugged her son tightly and covered him in kisses. Atticus squirmed and giggled.

"We'll hold brunch on you two," Casey said, wrapping her arms around Archer's waist and drawing him toward the Suburban.

Slowly, everyone drifted away to their vehicles. A couple of minutes later, it was just she and Ridge.

"Are you okay?" Kaia asked more to fill the silence than anything else.

"Why? Do I look that bad?"

"You need to put ice on your temple, reduce the swelling."

"Good point."

Kaia rose to her feet, held out her hand to give him a boost up off the ground. The minute their fingers touched, a sharp snap of static electricity shot from him to her. Jarring. She sucked in her breath.

His good eye widened, telling her that he felt it too. The second he was on his feet, he dropped her hand. Fine with her. She didn't like that snap, crackle, and pop any more than he did.

"I heard Vivi say your house is open and stocked with supplies. Do you think she's got frozen vegetables in the freezer?"

"I have no idea."

"Maybe there's ice."

"May be."

"It's a fifteen-minute ride back to the mansion and a short walk to your house. How about we give it a shot? I'm afraid if we don't get some ice on it ASAP you won't be able to pry your eye open tomorrow. Archer doesn't need a best man with no depth perception. After we ice it, I'll drive you to the hospital."

He hardened his chin. "Not going to the hospital."

She sank her hands on her hips. "You could have a concussion."

"I've had concussions before. This isn't one."

"You don't know that for certain."

"I'm not leaving the ranch. Casey and Archer are expecting us for brunch."

"They'll understand."

He hardened his chin. "Not throwing a monkey wrench in their wedding plans."

"You already did. That shiner is gonna be epic if you don't get ice on it." She snapped her fingers. "Get a move on."

"When did you get so bossy?"

"Sometime over the last decade."

"It *has* been a long time, Kaia." He said her name in such a low, seductive way, it sent goose bumps dancing down her arm.

She bit her lip and tried not to smile. He could charm the skin right off a rattlesnake. "Ice pack. Now."

"I really like this side of you." He grinned. "Tough talking on the outside, but gooey on the inside."

"Who says I'm gooey on the inside?"

"You don't fool me, Braterminator. I know you too well."

"Then you know I hate to be called that." Lie. When she was a kid she loved that he called her the Braterminator. It made feel like a superhero.

"I could shorten it to 'brat' if that's easier for you to work with."

Kaia snorted. "Don't bother. You're not going to be around long enough for it to stick."

"True," he mused. "But if you let me call you brat, I might be tempted to stay a little longer."

"You are so full of hot air, Lockhart." Ignoring her pounding heart, she scooped his Stetson and sunglasses off the ground, shoved them into his hand. "Your house. Now."

She spun on her heels and headed for the house, trying not to let him see how much his teasing got under her skin. Considering how loudly he was chuckling, she had to assume he already knew.

Dang it.

Chapter 7

Kaia walked fast, but she couldn't outpace him. He had longer legs and a more powerful stride. Ignoring the pulse pounding through his right eye, Ridge sprinted to catch up with her.

Approached the steps he hadn't trod in ten years.

They reached the bottom porch step at the same time, but he sailed past to get the door for her.

The door knocker—a lion's head with an open mouth—banged loudly against the wood as he yanked the door open. Yep, he'd built the house without a doorbell. He'd avoided doorbells since he was three, and he hadn't been about to install one in his house.

His house.

Although he felt no pride in it, no real sense of ownership since Duke had tainted it.

He bowed low and swept his arm out, indicating she should go in ahead of him. "After you."

But in the bow, his head spun. Oops. Bad idea. He wouldn't tell her he was dizzy. She'd make a fuss and insist on the hospital. He'd be all right. He'd had worse. Shaken off worse.

Kaia snorted, stiffened her spine, and marched past him into the kitchen, medical bag in hand. He cocked his head, watching her hips sway, wishing both eyes were in good shape so he could fully appreciate the view.

Nice. Very nice. He could spend hours watching that swing.

She stalked over to the fridge, jerked open the freezer door, dug around, and found a package of frozen corn. She got a cup towel from a drawer, wrapped the corn in it, and tossed the package at him.

He caught it one-handed, cocked his head, grinned.

She dropped her gaze, hooked the tip of her boot around the rung of a kitchen chair, and scooted it out from the table. "Sit."

"I'm not a dog."

"Matter of opinion. Sit." She pointed.

"I'm guessing you don't have a boyfriend," he teased, putting the bag of towel-wrapped corn to his temple and easing into the chair. The cold ice instantly soothed his swollen flesh.

She folded her arms over her chest. "What makes you say that? I *could* have a boyfriend."

"Doubtful."

"Why's that."

"Most guys don't like being ordered around."

"News flash, neither do most women. Normally, I'm not this bossy," she amended. "But vet school and working at the shelter have taught me that when you've got a stubborn case, sometimes you have to get firm."

God, he was enjoying her. "You think I'm stubborn?"

"Lockhart, a pack mule in the Grand Canyon threatened with a three-hundred-pound tourist wanting a ride to the top in August heat isn't as stubborn as you."

"Colorful."

She leaned her butt against the kitchen counter, sized him up. "Your stubborn pride has kept you away for ten years. If Archer hadn't decided to get married, I wager you could have stayed away another decade without a second thought."

"And you're mad about that?"

"Hell yes."

"Why?"

"You were missed, dammit. Desperately."

"By whom?" He lowered his voice and his eyes. She'd missed him?

"By the entire community."

"Bull," he said, but felt a strange tug in the center of his chest. "I was the hellion of Cupid. I'm sure mothers and fathers, teachers and preachers fell to their knees and gave thanks when I drove away."

"God." She shook her head. "That chip on your shoulder is huge. I hoped ten years away would knock it off."

"Watch it, Braterminator." His lip twitched. "You're treading on thin ice."

"See? Still too stubborn to even have a conversation about it." She turned away from him, got two white pills from her medical kit, filled a glass with water, and carried it over to him.

"What's this?"

"Aspirin."

She was standing close enough that he caught a whiff of her shampoo. It was the refreshing scent of chilled watermelon and summer daisies. His mouth watered. If he'd been of a mind, he could hook one leg around her waist and pull her into his lap.

He considered it. Was tempted.

Quickly, she hopped back. "Don't you dare, Ridge Josiah Lockhart."

She remembered his middle name. Why that should thrill him, he had no idea, but it did. "Dare what?"

"You know." She waved a hand.

"So you *do* have a boyfriend?"

"If I was in a relationship it would be with a man, not a boy. But no, I do not have a boyfriend. I'm far too busy with school and work. Not that it's any of your business."

Something in the way she said it, the way she tensed her body told him there was more to the story. Had some man hurt her? Just the idea of someone hurting her had him clenching his fists and his blood boiling.

"I heard that," he murmured. "Not enough hours in a day."

"Does this mean you don't have a woman friend?"

"I do not." By design, he'd not ever had a romantic relationship that lasted longer than four months. Four months tended to be the time when women wanted to know where the relationship was going and that's when he bailed.

"Not even a friend with benefits?"

"Not currently." He laughed.

"What's funny?"

"I've missed the hell out of you, Kaia Alzate."

"You sound surprised."

"I am."

"You miss me? The Braterminator? The kid who vexed you and Archer to no end? Why would you miss that?"

"I know, right." He tried to wink, but couldn't pull it off with the swollen eye. "But vexing can be exciting."

"Or it can be . . . well . . . vexing."

The tone of her voice, low, lazy, like the slow easy swing of a hammock strung between two sheltering trees, triggered a visceral response in him. Tight chest. Shallow lungs. Queasy stomach.

His imagination was off, spinning visuals of how she looked early in the morning: sleepy-eyed, hair mussed, her mattress imprinted with the shape of her body, and the smell of fresh-brewed coffee stirring the morning air.

"Where are you living these days?" he asked, shifting gears to keep from getting aroused again. "Still staying with your family?"

"Why does it matter?"

"It doesn't. Just making conversation."

"I rent a house on Murkle Street until I go back to school in the fall. Behind the Dairy Queen."

"Older homes in that area and you're really close to those Butterfinger Blizzards."

"You remembered." Her smile could light up outer space.

"Hey, they were my favorite too."

"The house is on a two-acre lot and the rent is cheap and the landlord doesn't mind if I keep animals, and there is that proximity to the Blizzards."

"How many animals do you have?"

"Varies. I foster."

"Cats? Dogs? Birds? Rabbits?"

"Yes, yes, yes, yes, and goldfish, a couple of pigmy goats, Earl the donkey, and a potbelly pig named Lancelot. Although right now Lance is off providing stud service at a neighbor's farm."

"Lucky Lance."

"Men." She rolled her eyes, but did not look disgusted.

"I like the way nothing much changes around here. You're still elbow-deep in critters, Elly May."

"Take the aspirin," she said, "and I'll drive you to the hospital."

"Not going. I'm fine."

"You don't know that."

"Give me some credit, woman."

Her cheeks pinked and she glanced away again. He'd rattled her. Good. She looked cute in pink.

"Give *me* *s*ome credit, man," she sassed. "I do know a few things about medicine. Granted, it's on animals, but a lot of stuff translates."

"You're being overly cautious."

"And you're being underly cautious." Her scowl was a shovel, digging under his skin.

"It's just a black eye."

"You don't know that for sure."

"I've been in enough fights to gauge the damage." He doubled up his fist, posed like a boxer. "I'll live."

"It could be something serious."

"Would it bother you if it was something serious?"

"Yes, of course it would."

His pulse skipped a beat and his chest twisted tourniquet tight. "Why?"

"'Cause it would ruin Archer's day if you fell into a coma. He and Casey have waited a long time to find each other. Last thing he needs is you screwing it up."

"Tell it like it is." He exhaled. What had he expected her to say? That she cared about him and it would break her heart if anything bad happened to him? He'd been fishing, which was pathetic. "At least we're on the same page about Archer's wedding."

"Just different approaches. Yours is denial. It's common among stubborn men."

"And yours is being overly cautious."

Kaia threw her hands in the air. "Fine. Have it your way. No hospital. But if you pass out I'm not helping you."

"Sure you will. You can't help yourself. I saw the look in your eyes when you were hovering over me. You were worried."

She notched up her chin. "I'm still worried. I'm a compassionate person."

"You're . . ." He let the sentence dangle, and she shot him another sideways glance.

"What?" she whispered.

"All grown-up," he murmured.

"And you are stub—"

"Stubborn. Yes, we covered that. What else?"

"Late for brunch," she finished, leaving him feeling vaguely disappointed.

Keeping the ice bag of frozen corn to his temple, he downed the pain pills, chugged the water, and pushed back the chair. Lost his balance a little from getting up so suddenly, and stumbled against the table.

"Whoa!" Kaia leaped forward, reached for his elbow.

He put up a restraining hand, moved away to keep her from latching onto him. He hated being fussed over. "I've got this. I'm *fine*."

She clicked her tongue, shook her head.

He flashed her the brightest smile in his repertoire. Pure gold, the one that never failed to charm. But he couldn't quite pull off full stun because of the black eye.

She scoffed at his smile. Shot down again. "You look like a junkyard dog after a weekend bender."

"Feels a bit like that too."

"Still," she said with all the primness of an old maid accountant. "I'm very glad you came home."

"Are you?"

"Absolutely." She lifted up a perky, I've-got-sunshine-in-my-teeth smile. Enthusiastic. Classic Kaia.

He saw her in a montage of past moments, hugging animals, splashing in Balmorhea Springs, spinning on the tire swing in the front yard of the foreman's house. She smiled the same. A girl who existed eternally in the amusement park of her mind. He was glad that hadn't changed.

"It was brave of you," she said. "Coming back after so long."

"I have a butt load of faults, but when I commit to something, I'm loyal to the bone. My best friend gets married. I'm there."

Noticing him evaluating her, Kaia's gaze scooted to her hands and she tucked them in her lap. Small hands, delicate but work-roughened, nails clipped short, palms calloused, skin tanned. Several small scars dotted her knuckles, and twin silvered puncture marks puckered the outside of her left hand.

"Ferret bites," she explained. "Vicious little suckers if they feel trapped."

He laughed at her comical expression, but immediately regretted it because it sounded as if he was laughing at her pain. "They better not try that around me."

"You've got plenty of scars of your own. I remember when you got that one." She reached out and traced an index finger over the jagged scar staggering across his palm. He had a corresponding scar that ran the length of his inner thigh. "You cut it on the barbwire fence saving my silly hide from Clyde the bull."

"You terrified the crap out of me. Standing there in your red cape with a bucket of oats."

Kaia crinkled her nose. "I thought I could tame Clyde."

"Testosterone-fueled bulls pastured near heifers in heat are impossible to tame."

"So I discovered. But give me a break. What did I know? I was eight."

"And fearless as hell."

"Animals have never scared me. People on the other hand . . ." She peered into his eyes.

Ridge flexed his hand, felt the sting of the barbwire, as he recalled yanking apart the strands to toss Kaia to safety on the other side of the fence. And there he stood bleeding all over the corral,

Kaia's overturned bucket of feed spewed out on the ground, Clyde ducking his head, snorting and pawing the sandy earth.

Kaia had hollered, "Hey, hey!" and then yelled, "Run!" as Clyde charged.

Ridge had thrown himself over the fence like a pole-vaulter, dragging his jeans and his flesh across the long expanse of barb-wire, slicing his thigh wide-open. It had taken forty-six stitches to close the wound and the entire time the doctor was sewing him up, Duke bitched at how much it was costing him.

"In retrospect," he said, rubbing a palm down his thigh. "I might have come out better if I'd stayed in the ring with Clyde."

"I haven't thought about that day in years," Kaia said. "But it was a defining moment for me."

"Yeah?"

"I developed a healthy respect for nature."

"But you didn't lose your love of animals."

"I could never lose that. Animals are in my blood. I was born to care for them."

Her perky smile grew so bright Ridge was tempted to put on his sunglasses. Her smile overwhelmed sometimes. Too honest. Too true. Too compassionate. Too much of a reminder of what he was missing.

He cast around for something clever to say, light and deflective, but he had no grip on where this conversation was going. She was his best friend's little sister. He wasn't about to do what his male instincts were urging him to do.

Kiss her.

Kiss her hard. Kiss her long. Kiss her now. Kiss her as if they had a future. Kiss her as if they belonged.

"I hated that you got cut up over me," she said, tracing her finger over his scarred palm.

"You ran for help."

"Your father came and carried you back to the ranch. Blood was everywhere."

Ridge touched the scar on his hand. "When I got home from the hospital, you stuck a Barbie Band-Aid on me."

"I loved Barbie." Kaia sighed. "For me to share my Barbie Band-Aids with you was monumental . . . but I was feeling guilty."

"I was honored."

"Were you?"

"I proudly showed off Barbie at school."

"You didn't get teased?"

"I was the quarterback and the class president and captain of the debate team. People didn't tease me."

"Because they wanted to be you or be with you."

"Pretty much." He grinned, not the least bit embarrassed. "Barbie made people think I had a new girlfriend."

"You liked that?"

His I'm-the-best-at-everything-I-do shrug. "Fueled my reputation as a player."

Kaia snorted. "As if you needed any help with that. You kissed most every girl in Cupid high school."

Ridge lowered his lashes, pitched her a softball smile. "I never kissed you."

"Because I was your best friend's kid sister."

His head bobbed in agreement. "True."

"Besides, I didn't go to high school with you, old man. I was in seventh grade when you were a senior."

"You were off-limits in those days," he said. But not now. Six years wasn't such a big age difference between twenty-six and thirty-two.

She shifted, backed up, grabbed for her shoulders, hugged herself.

He wished he'd kept his mouth shut.

"We should go. They're holding brunch," she said in a quick-silver rush.

"Ah yeah, brunch." He didn't want to go to brunch at the mansion with a houseful of people who by and large made him uncomfortable.

But she was already in motion, headed for the door.

"Hang on."

She paused, peered at him, looked frustrated and antsy. "What?"

"I owe you."

"Wait until you get my bill." She laughed, an honest-from-the-belly laugh. A laugh that said she knew how to have fun, a laugh that curled up tight inside him, a laugh that made him nostalgic for all the times he'd hadn't heard it.

A laugh he was going to miss when he was gone.

Chapter 8

KAIA stepped onto the porch of Ridge's house, medical bag in hand and stared at the ATV parked in front of the chapel. All the other vehicles, including her truck, were gone.

After Majestic kicked Ridge, she'd been so focused on him that she hadn't paid much attention to how the rides back to the mansion had been divvied up. But of course, they'd needed her truck for transporting that many people.

And she wasn't about to let him drive with only one operational eye. Her resolve to avoid Ridge was already shot all to hell, but the thought of riding tandem with him left her quaking in her cowgirl boots.

Or, new thought, she could get one of her sisters to come and pick them up. Except cell reception this far from the main house was spotty at best, although occasionally texts could get through when calls couldn't.

Ah, life in the Trans-Pecos. It might as well be 1980.

The front door slammed behind her.

She could feel his eyes on her. But she wasn't going to look back. No siree. She trotted toward the ATV. Stopped.

She couldn't help herself. She looked back.

His head was cocked to the right and he had the makeshift ice pack pressed to his temple. Stetson and sunglasses were in place, giving him the appearance of a cowboy cop—authoritative, in control, self-assured. She felt a wallop of sexual heat blast into her.

Transfixed, Kaia gulped.

The left corner of his mouth tipped up, a lazy, seductive half smile. She wasn't going to encourage him by smiling back. Nope. Nope. Not gonna . . .

A smile kidnapped her face, took it freaking hostage, and held her for ransom in the heart of the hot, dusty desert.

Gak! Call the CDC. She needed an emergency Ridge vaccine. STAT!

Too late. His contagion had already spread. The man was pure sex on two legs. *T. R. O. U. B. L. E.* For so many reasons she couldn't begin to count them all, but primarily because she'd had a crush on him since she was a kid.

And he could break her like biscotti. *Snap. Snap.*

Shaking off the silly notion that she and Ridge could ever pair up, she pretended she wasn't the least bit unnerved to ride back with him on the ATV, and strapped her medical kit to the flat metal rack on the front of the four-wheeler with the attached bungee cord strap.

"I'll drive," she said firmly.

"I'm driving."

"You've got one eye swollen half-shut. I'm not arguing with you." She swung her leg over the seat, glanced back over her shoulder to see if he would follow.

He hesitated as if he was going to put up a fight. Bruised and battered, but full of cowboy swagger, tugging at her with masculine spunk.

And in a wholly feminine way she reacted.

Her body softened and her pulse quickened and her stomach fluttered. *Dear God, stop it.* She clamped her lips together to keep from grinning at him and starched her spine. "You coming?"

"No, but I'm breathing hard."

"Oh good grief," she muttered, but she could barely suppress a laugh that rose up in her when he flashed a devilish smile that sent desire and heat rolling through her body.

"I'm not giving in. You're injured. I'm in charge."

"When did you get so ornery?"

"I could ask you the same thing, except oops, you've always been ornery."

"Now that's a sweeping statement, considering you haven't seen me in ten years."

"Prove me wrong and get on without any further argument." She waved at a spot on the seat behind her.

He sauntered toward her, adjusting his Stetson lower on his forehead. "Bravo, you've learned to stand your ground, Brat."

She shrugged like it was nothing, but she was thrilled that he noticed. "You don't come within inches of dying without rearranging some things."

"Ornery suits you." He slid onto the back of the ATV behind her. "I like it."

Well, look at that, Mr. Alpha Cowboy CEO was going to do it. He was going to let her lead. Being the second-youngest of five kids, she was accustomed to being brushed aside and minimalized. But surprise, surprise, Ridge didn't steamroll her, and she appreciated it.

That is until he snaked a big, strong arm around her waist, and all the air evaporated from her lungs.

It took her a second to calm her raging hormones, fumble with the key dangling in the ignition, and start the ATV. She could feel his breath on the back of her neck and that was totally distracting.

She wanted to ask him to stop breathing.

Also, she wanted to tell him to stop smelling so good. Because he did. Smell good. He was getting all tangled up in her nose and her memories and confusing the hell out of her.

"Locked and loaded," he said, wrapping his tongue slowly around each word, making it sound bizarrely sexual. "Let's buzz."

"I'm driving here. We'll buzz when I'm ready."

He laughed like she was the most hilarious thing since *America's Funniest Home Videos*. "All right, honeybee. Buzz when *you're* ready."

Well, of course she was ready *now*. She didn't want to keep sitting here in the hot sun with his arm wrapped around her, going nowhere.

She popped the clutch, put the ATV in gear, and took off.

His arm was tucked right up underneath her breasts. Crossing boundaries. Invading her personal space. Too intimate by half.

It felt territorial.

It felt like foreplay.

Gak!

But she couldn't protest. He needed to hold on to her or risk falling off.

She drove. Going perhaps a bit faster than she should across the craggy terrain, anxious to get back to the house and off the ATV.

A dangerous part of her wanted to savor the feeling of being snugged up against his hard-muscled chest, his thighs strapped around hers. To revel in his warmth, the pressure of his legs, but she needed to focus on getting them from point A to point B as quickly and safely as she could.

Since her accident, she'd become an overly cautious driver. But not today. Not with this pulsing thrill shooting through her. Today, she felt headstrong and reckless and brave as hell.

The landscape whipped by at dizzying speed. *Slow down*. But he laughed in her ear as if he was enjoying the pace, and so, insanely, she sped up.

Idiot. What was she doing?

They flew across sand and sagebrush, thrust forward by paddle tires beating out a steady rhythm against the ground. Momentum rocked his body forward, pressing his hips against hers, each bump and rut pushing them closer together, each vibration a jolt of awareness.

As if in concert with the machine, the wind picked up, blowing warm air over their bodies, matching their ground speed with whirling energy.

A sense of inescapability, of baffling aptness, crashed through Kaia like thunder. This was what she'd been waiting for. A man worthy of changing her life for.

No, no. no. Not him. It could not be him.

A jackrabbit jumped out in front of the ATV. Startled, Kaia

swerved, plowed right over a tumbleweed kicking up a thick rooster tail of sand. She swallowed back the gulp of fear that leaped into her throat, eased off on the throttle, and inhaled a deep breath of dusty air.

"Good reflexes," Ridge whispered.

The vibration of his voice sent a quiver straight through her center. She felt dizzy, but it had nothing to do with the speed or the jackrabbit or hitting the tumbleweed and everything to do with the man at her back. His arm was latched tight against her belly and ribs, hard and firm, more holding her in place with his steady strength than hanging on.

His grasp reminded her how long it had been since a man had held her. Ages. Eons. She'd been too busy for a relationship. Too busy even for sex. Her life filled with school and animals and family, and then the wreck, where her biggest goal had been first, not dying, and then getting well, getting healthy, getting her life back.

Was that why she was so responsive to him? Because it had simply been years since she'd had sex?

Yes. That was it. She liked that idea. She'd go with that explanation.

She relaxed then. Loosened her grip on the handlebars. Lowered her shoulders. It was okay. She was just sex-deprived. That's all this was.

Whew. Now she knew the problem, she could deal with it. Not with Ridge of course. She wasn't going to have a wild weekend wedding fling with him. Not at her brother's wedding.

But this chemical reaction did call her attention to the fact she'd been neglecting her physical needs. It was something she would address once the ceremony was over and Ridge was safely in Canada where he could do her no harm.

"How was the ride back? Did you hang on to his hot bod for dear life?" Tara asked, mischief shining in her eyes as Kaia joined her sisters in the ranch house kitchen.

Thankfully, as soon as they arrived at the mansion, Ridge had offered to put the ATV in the barn and she couldn't hop off and sprint into the house fast enough.

"I drove." Kaia tossed her head. "He was the one doing the hanging."

"Ooh." Tara giggled and wriggled her fingers. "How was that?"

Kaia rolled her eyes. "It was a ride on an ATV."

"With his big strong hands on your body." Tara ticked her head back and forth like a human metronome.

"Ridge is so hot," Aria breathed, sticking her nose into the conversation. "Pure testosterone on two feet." She fanned herself vigorously. "He's such a badass."

"Just like his brothers." Ember sidled up, shot a look at Ranger, who was talking to Archer. "The Lockhart boys are yumminess personified."

"Are you lusting after Ranger?" Kaia asked Ember.

"Eww! Good grief no," Ember said. "He's my best friend in the whole world. Why would I mess that up? But that doesn't mean I can't appreciate how hot he is for someone else."

"I guess it's a good thing that neither Rhett or Remington can come to the wedding," Tara mused. "Can you imagine all four of them together in one place?"

"All the air conditioners in Cupid wouldn't be able to cool off that chapel." Aria panted.

"What are we whispering about?" Casey asked, popping over.

"The supreme hotness of the Lockhart men," Ember said.

Casey scoffed. "As if they can compare with Archer."

"We know you're madly in love with our brother, but Archer cannot compete against four Lockhart men." Tara clicked her tongue. "No one in Cupid can."

"I hate to disagree with you," Casey said. "But it's my wedding and my opinion is the only one that counts this weekend. Can we get this brunch started?"

Kaia let out a sigh and followed her sisters and Casey into the dining room, where the guests were lining up at the buffet of chafing dishes.

Her gaze was immediately drawn to Ridge, who was at the head of the line, his plate stacked high with food. He'd taken off the Ray-Bans, and she could see the bruise darkening at his temple, but the swelling seemed to be receding.

Kaia was the last one to get her food, and now there was only one seat left, and it had to be directly across from Ridge.

Damn her luck.

She sat down and, flanked by Lynne on her left, Casey on her right, she kept her eyes on her plate.

Or tried to.

"Could you pass the pepper?" Ridge asked.

Why did the confounded pepper have to be right in front of her? She glanced up and her gaze slammed into his sultry navy blue eyes and even sultrier smile. And why did he have to keep staring at her like she was some fascinating creature he'd hauled onto his boat during a fishing expedition? Especially when the entire table could see the way he was looking at her?

Kaia dropped her gaze to the pepper shaker, picked it up and thrust it at him.

In the handoff, his big, broad fingers touched hers.

Intentionally?

Her heart gave an excited little kick and it was all she could do not to react. Or look at him again.

All right.

She did look at him again, but only after he'd lowered his eyes to pepper his eggs, and she tried not to let him see she was looking. From her peripheral vision, she watched his Adam's apple slide while he drank orange juice. The sun slipping in through the big picture window splashed him in a luminous glow, accentuating that dark sexy stubble on his jaw.

And that mouth! Full and angular. A glistening drop of juice on his bottom lip, his tongue whisking it away.

Detonating tiny little bombs of desire inside her. *Boom. Boom. Boom.*

Good God, surviving this weekend was not going to be a slam-dunk.

Not a cakewalk.

Not duck soup.

Not even close.

RIDGE STUDIED KAIA across the table.

She smiled, easy and uncomplicated, her mouth promising lots of fun. Of course, she was the proverbial girl-next-door—sweet, guileless, honest. Contagious. Yep. She was infecting him with her cuteness.

And sass.

Nice as she might be, she also had a bright spark of wildness, sleek golden skin, and a fetching scent. Not to mention those mysterious eyes, dark and deep enough to drown a man and make him happy for his demise.

In that quick pulse of the moment, a powerful urge passed through him. An urge so strong it yanked the breath from his lungs and spun his head. The urge to stare into her eyes so long they ceased being two people and merged as one.

He couldn't deny it. Something was chaining them together, something more than history and familiarity. Something he never expected.

Sizzle. Sparks. Chemistry.

Freakadilly circus, it was overwhelming. And he had to sit here at the table, surrounded by their families, and pretend that absolutely nothing was going on.

"Oops," Casey said. "I forgot to put the honey butter spread that Granny Blue made for the biscuits on the table."

"I'll get it." Kaia hopped up from her seat before the bride-to-be had a chance to move, and darted for the kitchen.

Escaping?

Ridge waited a beat, and then pushed back his chair, picked up the bag of frozen corn he'd been using as an ice pack. He was encouraged to see everyone was caught up in conversation about the wedding and not paying him much attention.

"Think I'll refresh this," he murmured.

In the kitchen, he found Kaia with her head in the fridge, her lush little rump in the air as she bent over, opening containers, searching for the homemade honey butter. She was petite, small but sturdy. There was nothing fragile about her. Her jeans molded to her curves and . . .

She straightened, butter dish in hand, and turned to catch him ogling her. She arched a jaunty, you-are-so-busted eyebrow.

He chuckled.

"What?" she said.

"My corn has gone warm." He held up the limp bag of corn still wrapped in the cup towel.

"Sounds like a personal problem to me."

"Smart aleck."

They stood there a moment staring into each other's eyes again.

"I better get back out there," she whispered. "The Alzates do love their honey butter." She ducked her head, clutched the butter dish closer to her chest, and stepped to the right.

He moved at the same time she did, unintentionally blocking her way.

Simultaneously, they both corrected and scooted to the left. Blocking each other a second time.

"Um . . ." She grunted, dodged right.

But so did he, drawn as if by an invisible source to match her move for move.

She snorted. "You're doing it on purpose."

"Hand to God, I'm not."

Her upper lip twitched.

He placed his hands on her shoulders, felt an instant zap of electricity. It was all he could do not to jerk away in response to the heat. "You stay put," he said. "I'll go left."

"Having trouble finding the butter?" Casey called from the dining room.

"Got it!" Kaia said. "On my way."

But she didn't move.

Ridge shook his head, listening to his heart gallop, holding a package of warm, soggy corn. Good thing he was only in town for three days. If he was around this sexy nymph for any longer than that . . . well, there was only so much temptation a man could resist.

He leaned over Kaia, reached for the freezer door above her head. Caught a whiff of her fragrance that smelled so sweet and good that he almost buried his face in her hair, but instead wrenched open the freezer door and let the cold air blast him in the face.

Wake up!

Blindly, he grabbed at a bag of frozen peas, exchanging it for the corn, and stepped back, realizing belatedly he was keeping Kaia from going back to the dining room.

Her gaze was on his and she looked a little uncertain. "You okay?"

"Why do you ask?"

"You've got an odd expression on your face. Are you sure you didn't pass out when Majestic kicked you?"

Not the kick to the head that stunned him. It was she. "Don't worry about me. Better get back to the dining room. They're a tough crowd when they're honey butter deprived."

"Right. Thanks." She stepped forward, but crunched down on the toe of his boot. She jumped back and, in the process, her hip made contact with his crotch.

They sucked in tandem breaths, and every ounce of blood in his body drained straight to his dick.

"Sorry, sorry," she mumbled.

"Ridge," Archer called. "What in the hell are you doing in there with my little sister?"

"Nothing!" Kaia hollered, eyes widening with awareness and alarm.

Yeah, babe, me too. Me too.

"Oh snapdragons," she muttered, looking as dazed as he felt. "Stay in here until I get settled."

"Gotcha," he said, but she was already gone, leaving him reeling.

Stunned with the full knowledge that whatever was going on between them, he was in it up to his neck.

Chapter 9

Iт the end, it turned out to be the bachelor party from hell.

At seven that evening, Archer, Ridge, Ranger, Ned, Herb, Armand, Duke and Zeke and Kip loaded up in various vehicles and headed for Chantilly's Bar and Grill.

On the way to the venue, Ridge noticed little had changed. Cupid was a town trapped in time; a small-assed place where they rolled up the carpets as soon as it got dark, no sushi restaurants within three hundred miles, too many freaking eccentric artists running around sketching desertscapes.

One by one, he listed the town's shortcomings. Tried to convince himself that he did not miss it, even when his heart tugged as they passed landmarks and landscapes etched into his memory.

The water tower he and Archer had graffitied. The old Palace Theatre—now closed and boarded up—where he'd lost his virginity at sixteen with a college girl. The Grab N Go where he'd bought his first beer with a fake ID, only to get caught by a deputy who was good friends with Duke.

Nope. Not happening. He wasn't going to be seduced by nostalgia. He was glad he'd left. Happy. Thrilled. Lucky. Best thing that ever happened to him. Especially in the summer, when everything went so bone-dry a man couldn't even work up spit, and going outside without sunscreen put you in imminent danger of skin cancer.

Who could miss that?

As part of his best man duties, Ridge had gotten his secretary, Gilda, to reserve the party room and arrange for food and gag gifts. Archer had said specifically that he did not want strippers and Ridge honored his request.

He'd always thought strippers at bachelor parties were immature anyway. Come to think of it, bachelor parties were juvenile in general, but hey, it was tradition and Archer *was* getting married. He deserved a proper send-off.

The bar hadn't changed much in the past ten years. Same colorful Christmas lights were still strung from the rafters like a south-of-the-border cantina. Same oversized margarita glasses, same mosaic tile on the floor. There were new tables and chairs and a fresh coat of bright orange paint on the walls, but that was the extent of the facelift.

A perky, ponytailed hostess led them to the back room, and she was openly staring at Ridge.

Did he know her? He hoped not. He'd sown some wild oats in his day. Broken hearts. Not proud of it, but there it was.

It was another downside about returning home. Chickens roosting. History biting a guy in the ass . . .

The room had been decorated in typical trashy bachelor party fare—inflated love dolls, one of the walls set up for bra pong, sexy lingerie clothes-pinned to rope strung from the ceiling.

The dessert spread was equally bawdy. Cookies in the shapes of lush fannies, chocolate-covered frozen bananas on a stick, cupcakes that looked like breasts with nipples. Libations consisted of multicolored Jell-O shots molded in condoms, cans of Coke with mini bottles of Jack Daniel's attached for mixing, and black lager beer representing the death of Archer's freedom.

Party favors included shot glasses engraved with the bride's and groom's initials. Beer koozies emblazoned with BYE-BYE BACHELORHOOD. Emergency hangover kits that included breath mints, Alka-Seltzer, and mini-bar-sized bottles of vodka.

And the games—AstroTurf putting green, a roulette wheel, darts, and a poker table.

His secretary had outdone herself. Gilda deserved a bonus for pulling this off long-distance. If the party wasn't a success, it certainly wasn't her fault. Now it was up to him to make sure everyone had a good time and got home safely. No drinking for him. Besides, the last thing he wanted was to end up the best man with a black eye *and* a hangover.

At first, the conversation was stiff. Everyone feeling their way into the party. Guys unaccustomed to hanging out with each other stuffed in a small room filled with a sexuality-oriented theme. It took a few minutes, and a few shots of liquor, to get things lubed.

Ridge fed money into the old-fashioned jukebox, and got some tunes playing. Soulful ballads. Country classics. Hank Williams. Johnny Cash. George Jones. Merle Haggard.

With his pocketknife Duke split open the condom mold of a tequila-laced lime Jell-O, sucked it down, and followed that with a shot of red-hot cinnamon schnapps. His father looked fierce in his black Stetson, dinner-plate-sized silver belt buckle and freshly starched, sharply creased blue jeans.

After the two shots, Duke's ruddy complexion took on the look of a sandstorm sunset, clouded, dark, brooding.

Something was up with the old man, but this wasn't the time or place to pry. As far as Ridge knew, *he* could very well be that something. No point throwing gas on a blazing campfire. Monday. He only had to get through the weekend. Monday, he'd be gone.

Archer slung an arm around Ridge's shoulder. "Thanks for this. I know coming home was tough, and that you did it just for me."

"Couldn't let you get married without me. I know where all the bodies are buried," Ridge teased.

Archer chuckled. "We did tear up this town when we were young."

Ridge watched Duke pick up a putter and head to the AstroTurf green with Armand, his steps swaying rhythmically like a sailor who knew how to ride the swells.

"How's the eye?" Archer picked up a mug of black beer and took a sip.

"I'll live."

Archer shook his head. "It was reckless of Duke to take Majestic around a lot of people, especially a toddler."

"Yeah, well, you know." Ridge shrugged as if he didn't care, but it was camouflage. He'd always cared too much about what his father said and did. Spent his life doing the opposite. "Duke does what he wants. Doesn't think about anyone else. He hasn't changed a whit in ten years."

"That's not entirely true."

"No?"

"He's slowing down."

"He should." Ridge grunted, felt the sound root around in his chest. "He's chasing sixty."

"He has regrets."

Ridge raised an eyebrow, not believing that for a second. "He told you that?"

"C'mon, he's Duke. He's never going to come right out and say what he feels."

"So you could be way off base on the regret thing."

"Whether he admits it or not, your father is lonely. Remington and Rhett rarely come home, and you know Ranger. He lives and breathes the McDonald Observatory."

"Did someone say something about McDonald Observatory?" Ranger asked, sidling over with a Jack and Coke in his hand, eyes shiny with interest and liquor.

"See?" Archer grinned at Ridge. "None of you boys fell in the love with ranching the way Duke hoped."

"Four sons," Ridge muttered, feeling a crust of anger crackle up his spine. "And none of us good enough for him."

"I see your point," Archer said. "But Duke's got a hankering to have his family around him and lots of grandkids playing in the yard."

"Yeah, now that he's getting old, he's getting maudlin." Ridge snorted, the hotness of his breath burning the inside of his nose. "If he wanted a closer-knit family, he should have been a better father."

"Everyone has regrets," Archer said philosophically.

"I don't." Ridge clenched his teeth, heard them clack together.

"No?" Archer's tone was mild, but his eyes said he didn't believe a word Ridge was saying. "What about Kaia?"

Startled, Ridge drew back, eyed his buddy. "What about Kaia?"

"You don't regret not telling her you flew down to see her when she was in the hospital after her accident?"

"Why would I regret that?"

"I dunno." Archer lifted a shoulder, slanted his head. "You two were acting weird this morning when you came back from your house. Like something was going on between you. Maybe if you'd stuck around at the hospital until she came out of the coma you could have—"

"If I seemed weird in any way, it was because it was the first time setting foot in my house since . . ." He shrugged again. "Well, you know."

Archer studied him. "I thought maybe being in close quarters with Kaia threw you for a loop. You haven't seen her all grown-up. Peeking into her hospital room when she was in a coma doesn't count."

"Why would that throw me? She's your kid sister. There's nothing there." Okay, so he was lying. Self-preservation.

"My gorgeous kid sister."

"All your sisters are gorgeous."

"Tell me about it." Archer held up both fists. "Can't begin to tell you how many scars I got on my knuckles protecting their honor."

"I know," Ridge said. "I was with you a time or two."

"So really?" Archer prodded like a determined tabloid journalist. "No regrets?"

"I'm regretting that we're not playing poker," Ranger said. "Who's up for poker?"

"You'll win," Archer predicted. "You always do."

"Can I help it if I've got a poker face?" Ranger kept his face stoic.

Ridge waved a hand at his younger brother. "Since you're the card shark, round everyone up, and we'll play."

Two minutes later, the nine men were sitting around the poker table, Ranger gleefully dealing cards for Texas Hold 'Em. Poker was the only thing that interested Ranger beyond astrobiology.

At first glance, the two topics seemed incongruous, but both disciplines required cunning and cool objectivity. Something Ranger possessed in spades.

After Ranger's mother, Sabrina, divorced Duke over Ridge coming to live with them, she'd taken off with another man who didn't want kids, so she'd left her son behind. That was before Duke had married Lucy, and he and Ranger were cared for by a string of underqualified nannies, who didn't notice Ranger had contracted scarlet fever.

It was only when Bridgette Alzate intervened that Ranger got the treatment he needed, but by then the fever had caused complications with his heart. Ranger spent a big chunk of his childhood on the sidelines, unable to do much else except read. But all that reading had given him a whip-sharp mind.

Lively bachelor party conversation flew around the poker table. Food eaten. Alcohol consumed. Ice broken. Things warmed up.

It felt odd.

Sitting in the dim room, filling with cigar smoke from Duke's stogie, looking around at the familiar faces that had changed more than he'd expected over the ten years. He was here and he was interacting, but he didn't fit. He didn't belong. He was the outsider who'd gone away. Brooks & Dunn played on the Wurlitzer, "Rock My World Little Country Girl." Ridge listened to the lyrics. Thought of Kaia. She was one little country girl who'd rocked his world. Felt his stomach draw up tight. Wondered how the bachelorette party was going. Wished he could see her.

"Nervous about tomorrow?" Ned asked Archer, and bit into a fanny-shaped cookie.

Archer grinned. "Nope. Looking forward to starting my life with Casey."

"Don't expect too much from the wedding night," Ned said. "It's not what it's cracked up to be. You'll both be exhausted."

"I know where you can get some Viagra. Keep you *up* all night." Zeke snickered. He was a tall, stringy guy with rounded shoulders and a pockmarked face. His hair was the color of Oklahoma clay, and he'd been married three times because he had a tendency to fall hard and fast for the wrong type of woman. No one took him seriously about anything except ranching.

"Hey, hey!" protested Herb, a squat, tax accountant with square-framed black glasses, a baldpate, and a trustworthy voice. "You're talking about my daughter!"

"Plug your ears, pardner," Zeke advised. "It *is* a bachelor party."

Archer glowered. "Herb's right. We're not discussing Casey."

"Duke," Kip said, sloshing beer when he raised his mug. Freckled-faced, big-eared, and bucktoothed, Kip looked like *MAD* magazine's Alfred E. Neuman. He was a former bull riding champion and wore the big belt buckle to prove it. "Give Archer some of your boner pills. He's too shy to ask for himself."

"Kip, shut up," Archer snapped.

Duke chomped on his cigar, switching it from one corner of his mouth to the other. "I don't need no damn Viagra. I keep Vivi plenty pleased all on my own."

"You expect us to believe that?" Ned asked. "When you're married to a gorgeous younger woman."

"How 'bout those Rangers?" Ridge said, steering the conversation to safer shores. "Think they'll make it to the pennant race?"

Archer jumped on the new direction, talking about the latest pitcher the Texas Rangers had recently acquired as bets were made and chips added to the ante. Conversation lagged as everyone concentrated on what was turning out to be a sprightly hand.

Ridge had a pair of Jacks, so he confidently stayed in past the flop even though he could play off none of the three flop cards.

Ned dealt the turn card and another round of bidding followed. No one folded.

The river card. Another Jack. Giving Ridge three of a kind. He grinned and upped the bet. It was Zeke's turn to call or raise.

"Hmm." Zeke studied his two cards as if they would magically change to a winning hand. He drummed his fingers on the table, scratched his jaw, and shifted in his seat.

"Make a move." Duke's voice was a cheese grater, rough and

irritating. "Before I take those cards away and smack you with them."

Ridge tensed. Ah, just like old times. Tensions high. Duke growling some threat or the other. But on the bright side, this time he was not the target.

"On my salary, I can't afford to lose," Zeke said.

"Then fold," Duke grunted.

"I've already got sixty bucks in the pot." Zeke shoved a hand through his hair.

"Fish or cut bait," Duke said.

"Fine." Zeke folded, tossing his cards on the table. "Fold, pardners."

Duke narrowed his eyes, looked across the table at Ridge. "You got a pair of Jacks?"

The hairs on the back of Ridge's neck lifted. How had the old man guessed?

"'Bout as likely as you do," he said mildly.

"You never could bluff for shit." Duke's eyes challenged him as he tossed more chips on the table. "All right. I raise you a hundred bucks."

Ridge shrugged. "And I raise you five hundred."

Archer threw his cards in the middle of the table. "Too rich for my blood."

"Me too." Ned tossed his in as well, followed by Armand, Herb, and Kip. Leaving only Ridge, Ranger, and Duke still playing.

"All in." Duke pushed his entire stack to the middle of the table between splayed hands.

"All in." Ridge held his father's hard-edged stare and tossed his remaining chips on top of his father's.

"Looks like all the Lockharts are all in." Ranger laughed, and added his chips to the pile.

"Whatcha got?" Duke demanded of Ridge.

"You first."

"I'm not bluffing." Duke clenched his jaw.

"Neither am I."

They stared each other down.

"You are both ridiculously stubborn," Ranger muttered. "Two of a kind."

"We are not!" Ridge and his father snapped in unison.

"All right, here's the plan," Ranger mediated. "We all turn them over on the count of three. One . . . two . . . three."

"Three Jacks." Ridge flipped his cards over.

"Ha!" Duke chortled. "Three Queens. I win." He reached for the pot.

"Not so fast." Ranger laid out his cards one by one. "I've got four twos. Read 'em and weep, fellas."

"Burn!" Kip guffawed.

"Sonofabitch!" Cursing, Duke flung his cards across the room.

"Don't mess with the master," Ranger clasped his hands over his head in victory. "When will you ever learn?"

"Congratulations," Ridge said, getting up to stretch, his eyes on his father.

Duke's face was flushed, and a blood vessel at his temple throbbed wildly. He went to the refreshment table for another Jell-O shooter.

Ridge followed him. "Don't you think you've had enough?"

"Butt out." Duke swallowed the contents of a condom Jell-O shooter filled with grape vodka. "This is a bachelor party."

"Yeah, so don't ruin it."

Duke laughed a dark laugh. "Oh that's rich. You telling me what to do. The prodigal son returns and expects to be met with open arms."

"I have no such expectations from you." Ridge struggled to keep his voice and anger low. Duke was drunk. This wasn't the time or place to mine a fight with his old man, even though the blowup had been brewing for years.

"Sure you do. You swagger in here with your fancy airplane and your patented drilling method expecting everyone to fall at your feet. Thinking you're better than us. Thinking you're better than *me*."

"Wait just a minute." Ridge put a palm. "You sleep with *my* girlfriend in *my* house, and I'm the shitheel?"

"You still holding on to that?" Duke glowered. "Vivi picked me over you. She wanted a real man. Deal with it."

Ridge bit down on his tongue to keep from saying all the dark ugly things he'd kept tamped down for a decade. Vile things that seethed and twisted. Grisly things that wanted to explode all over his father and burn him with hot foul spew.

"Party's over for you, old man. I'm taking you home."

"The hell you say." Duke's eyes burned like lava, his words slurred, his knees wobbly. That last Jell-O shot sent him over the edge into full-on hammered. He raised his fists. "Put up your dukes. The time has come to have this out. Man-to-man."

"I'm not swatting a gnat with a bazooka."

"You calling me a gnat?" Duke pummeled the air like he was boxing a speed bag.

"You're acting like one. Annoying as hell."

"Coward." Duke took a swing at him.

Ridge ducked. "I'm not hitting a drunk old man."

"I'll show you old man." Duke threw a left jab.

Ridge, who hadn't had a drop of alcohol, easily sidestepped it. "And you wonder why I haven't been home in ten years."

The rest of the men had gathered to watch, ringing them as if they were at a boxing match. No one intervened.

"I'm not fighting you," Ridge reiterated.

"Pussy." Duke came at him with a barrage of punches.

Ridge waltzed out of reach. "Don't make me do this."

"C'mon, c'mon." Duke motioned him closer. "I can take you."

"Not even on your best days."

Duke jutted out his chin. "I dare you."

Ridge had been holding back on punching him for twenty years. His fingers twitched and he had to knot his hands to quell his anger.

"Chicken. That's what I thought." Duke swayed on his feet, hiccuped, reached for a mug of black beer.

But Ridge was quicker and moved the mug away. He grabbed his father's arm. "Party's over for you, old man. Let's go."

Duke jerked back. "I'm not ready to go."

"Time we all called it a night." Archer faked a yawn, stretched. "Big day tomorrow, and Ranger cleaned us out."

"Aww." Zeke groaned. "It's not even ten o'clock."

Armand and Herb were already heading for the door. They motioned for Ned to join them, and the three sidled out the exit.

Ridge stuck out his palm, insisted, "Give me your keys."

"I'm the father, not you."

"And you're drunk. Give me the keys or I'll take them off of you."

"Try it."

"Dad." Ranger stepped forward. "If you don't go quietly with Ridge, *I'm* gonna punch you."

"Oh sure, gang up on a defenseless old man."

Ranger snorted and sank his hands on his hips. "You're about as defenseless as a rattlesnake."

"Never have children," Duke told Archer. "They'll stab you in the back."

"Only if you steal their girlfriends." Ridge couldn't resist.

"Don't pretend she was the love of your life." Duke's eyes glistened through the alcohol sheen. His words slow and slurred.

"Doesn't matter. You seduced her when she was dating me. That disqualifies you from father of the year."

"Among other things," Ranger mumbled.

Duke laughed, deep but mirthless. "You know why Vivi picked me?"

"'Cause you're filthy rich?"

"No." Duke shook his head like a dog flinging off water. "Well, maybe a little. But she picked me because I'm not afraid to live. I know when to work and when to play and how to have a good time. All you care about is showing me up. Prove you're better than me."

That rankled, but Ridge refused to rise to the bait. Best move? End this as quickly and quietly as possible.

"You . . ." Duke pointed a finger at Ridge. "You hide behind work 'cause you think it will save you. It won't."

Truth? Work *had* saved him. Work kept him sane. Kept him out of trouble. Made him money. Helped him win. Dedication to hard work was what made him a good quarterback in high school and college. That push, the urge to constantly be more, get more, achieve more.

Everyone loved winners.

And here his father was telling him he'd lost Vivi for the very behavior that had attracted her to him in the first place?

Not damn likely.

The old coot was drunk and spouting nonsense. He wouldn't let him get under his skin, because that's exactly what Duke wanted. To scratch the thick hide he'd developed. Make him bleed.

"Nothing is gonna save you." Duke spat. "You're doomed like the rest of us."

Suddenly exhausted of it all, Ridge strong-armed Duke out the side exit.

"Hey, hey," Duke protested.

"I'll drive him home," Ranger said, joining Ridge, clutching Duke's other arm. Together they dragged their father toward his Ford King Ranch pickup. Archer, Zeke, and Kip following close behind.

Ranger held Duke by the shoulders, while Ridge dug the keys from his father's pocket, Duke cussing and fighting them every inch of the way.

Finally, Ridge got the keys free of Duke's jeans pocket.

His father raised his fist, swung wild, missed, spun, crashed into the side of truck, bounced off it, wheeled around and came after him again.

Ridge didn't want to fight his father, but if he didn't do something the old fart was going to end up hurting himself.

"Back off," Ridge growled.

"Don't you tell me what to do," Duke yelled like a pissed-off bull, lowered his head and charged.

Sighing, Ridge sidestepped his father's attempted gut attack, doubled up a fist and delivered a quick controlled jab to Duke's left cheek. And he went down like a sack of spuds.

Yep, bachelor party from hell.

"*Day*-am, Ridge." Zeke scratched the back of his neck. "Remind me never to piss you off."

Chapter 10

THE bachelorette pajama party at the Lockhart mansion was in full swing when Ridge and Ranger hauled a drunken Duke into the house.

Music blasted from the sound system. Scrapbooking supplies were spread out on the kitchen table. Empty bottles of wine and cartons of Ben & Jerry's were lined up on the counter. Nail polish, cuticle tools, cotton balls, and toe separators were laid out from the mani and pedicures they'd given each other earlier in the night.

From the minute Kaia saw Ridge's face, she knew the bachelor party had not gone well, and it was all she could do not to run to him.

Vivi rushed to take a grumbling, stumbling Duke from his sons and usher him to the master bedroom. Archer and Casey huddled in the corner sharing low whispers and stolen kisses. Tara, Ember, and Aria read the situation correctly, that the festivities were over, and began cleaning up. Ranger joined them.

Kaia met Ridge's turbulent, troubled eyes across the room. He turned away, headed for the front door. An emotion she couldn't name settled in the pit of her stomach, churned hard.

In hushed tones, Ranger revealed what had happened at Chantilly's between Ridge and Duke.

Kaia couldn't leave it alone. She had to go after Ridge, never mind that she was in a Minnie Mouse nightgown and leggings.

Without making an excuse, she slipped out the front door, closing it softly behind her. There was a light breeze in the air and she wrapped her arms around her, scanned the expanse of arid land.

The moon was a sliver of almond in the sky, and it took her eyes a minute to adjust to the darkness.

She didn't see Ridge at first, but he didn't have a vehicle of his own, and both Archer's SUV and Duke's Ford King Ranch pickup were parked in the yard. He couldn't have gone far.

"Ridge?" she called.

No answer.

In the distance she heard coyotes howl, and from the barn across the way, a horse nickered. Had he gone into the stables?

She started in that direction, but spied movement near Ridge's plane. She stopped, peered into the gloom. He stood in the shadows watching her.

"Hey," she whispered, drawing nearer to him.

"Hey." He was leaning his shoulders against the side of the plane, looking cagy and mysterious.

"Are you okay?"

He shrugged so slightly she wasn't sure he'd even done it. She moved closer until she could see the whites of his eyes in the dim lighting. "Do you want to talk about it?"

"No."

"Okay."

"So Minnie Mouse, huh?" He smiled like he had sexual fantasies about Minnie Mouse, but maybe that was just her imagination.

"It was either this or my Ruff Night sleep shirt with cartoon dogs on it. Minnie Mouse was newer."

"The Ruff Night suits you better."

Silence dropped like a curtain. She stood there, not saying anything, arms folded over her chest. Waiting to see if he'd fill the empty space.

He did not.

A minute passed. Two. Three.

Clearly, he was not going to start the conversation. She had three choices. Keep quiet. Leave. Or say something.

Kaia took a deep breath, plunged in. "You punched your father?"

"Yeah."

"Knowing Duke, I'm sure he had it coming, but—"

"I shouldn't have done it," he said his voice heavy with the weight of what he'd done, regret etching lines on his face. "But Duke was so drunk and worked up. He kept swinging at me and missing and knocking into things. I was scared he was going to hurt himself. A controlled punch seemed better than letting him flail wildly."

"This has been years in the making," she said softly, lacing her tone with extra kindness.

"That too," he admitted.

"Don't beat yourself up."

"Who says I am?"

"I know you," she said. "You put on this tough, I-don't-care act, but inside you feel things deeply. I've got two sympathetic ears. I'm a good listener. It's safe to unload."

He sized her up. "Go back to your party."

"It's winding down."

"I ruined the fun."

"You didn't ruin anything." She reached out, touched his arm.

Instantly, his muscles tensed beneath her fingers. Her knees quivered, and so did other, more feminine parts of her, parts of her that had been dormant for a long time, parts of her that ached to wake up and live again.

His eyes glittered. "You're playing with fire, Kaia."

The way he said her name drew a hot, slow shiver down her spine to lodge in her pelvis. What did he mean by that? Her heart thudded.

"Ridge," she whispered, curling her hand around his forearm.

"Please," he said in a clipped tone. "Just let me be."

"I know you're feeling badly about your dad, I—"

"That's not it." His voice was rough, husky.

Undaunted by the turbulence in his eyes, she held tight. "What is it then?"

"*You.*"

She dipped her head, studying him speculatively. "What about me?"

"*You're* what's driving me crazy."

She stared into his eyes. Run. Run like hell before it's too late. But she didn't run. Instead, an insane part of her stepped closer. "Oh yeah?"

"Oh yeah," he said thickly, his eyelids half-closed. "Whenever I'm around you all I can think about is kissing you."

"Wh . . . wh . . . wh . . . ?" she stammered, gulped, let go of his arm, stepped back.

He allowed his arm to drop heavily against his side, his gaze never leaving hers. "Does that scare you?"

Hell yes!

"Kaia."

"Yes?"

He crooked a finger, grinned. "C'mere."

She shook her head, but her feet, oh damn those feet, flew to him. She breathed. "Ridge."

"You're the only one who came to see if I was okay," he said.

"It's not that they don't care. People just don't know how to take you."

"But you do," he said.

"I have an advantage."

"What's that?"

"The power of the Braterminator. If I hadn't followed you and Archer around for half my life I wouldn't understand you the way I do."

"How do you know? Maybe I've changed."

"You haven't."

"You sound pretty confident."

"I am." She fell into his eyes, like Alice in Wonderland falling down the rabbit hole.

It was true. She understood him more than he knew. Understood that he viewed the world as a contest that he could win if he just worked hard enough and gathered all the trappings of success—a house, a plane, expensive sunglasses. He was eager and responsible and goal-oriented, persistent, organized, and passionate about his work.

On the flip side he could be a hard taskmaster, as much to himself as anyone else. He put work ahead of people. He was climbing, climbing, climbing, grasping for the ultimate brass ring that only he could define.

But Kaia knew something he did not. Once he reached that brass ring it would turn to dust in his hand. No achievement, no high-flying goal could ever sate the hole in him. Until he understood that, he would always be on the treadmill, working harder and harder for the elusive self-worth that would forever be out of his reach.

It broke her heart.

She understood because she too had been a workaholic, until the accident and what had happened afterward. It had changed her irrevocably and shifted her misaligned priorities.

Yes, she still wanted to get her doctorate in veterinarian medicine. It was her top goal. But what had changed was her motivation. Before the accident, she'd wanted to be a vet not just because she loved animals, but because the career was how she saw herself earning respectability.

Now?

Her only motive was to lead a better life. Becoming a vet would help her do that, but in the meantime, she could support herself doing what she loved most, taking care of animals, whether she had her degree or not.

That was the bottom line. Loving wherever she happened to be on the path. Not wistful for the past or dreaming of the future, but accepting, loving, and embracing the present moment.

And right now she was standing in the dark in front of an airplane with the man she'd had a crush on since she was a kid, and he was looking at her like she was something special.

As if he wanted her as much as she wanted him.

"I shouldn't have come back. I'm ruining Archer and Casey's

wedding. First this." He gestured at his black eye. "And tonight, getting in a fight with my dad. Everyone would have been better off if I'd stayed away."

"Not true," Kaia said. "We're all glad you're home."

"Not Duke."

"Yes he is. He's just too ornery to admit it. Look at it this way. He picked a fight with you. He must be feeling *something* if he bothered to pick a fight."

"You're such an optimist." Ridge chuckled, but it was a hollow, unhappy sound.

"You came home. It was a big step. Pat yourself on the back for that. No matter what bumps you hit in the road, you made the effort. You showed up. That's good enough."

"Doesn't feel good enough."

"Feelings change and shift. They're not permanent."

"Ride 'em out, huh?" He gave her a half smile. That smile, combined with the black eye, made him look totally roguish.

"Something along those lines."

He was so close she could feel his radiating body heat. Sweat beaded between her breasts, trickled down her cleavage, turning her bare skin damp and salty. Her heart dashed at an alarming pace.

Yep, she was blistering, sweltering, stewing.

And he? Cucumbers weren't as cool as this guy. He didn't appear the slightest bit ruffled or disturbed. In fact, that cocky grin widened, as if he were fully in control. Which he was, because her legs were bobbing and her lungs couldn't seem to pull in enough of the clear night air.

He lowered his head, but never took his gaze from hers and his mouth softened and widened and he moistened his lips and she thought, *God, he's gonna do it, he's gonna kiss me.*

Her heart was slamming madly against her ribs, knock, knock, knocking. She could have run. She could have ducked. She could have hollered "Stop!"

But Kaia did none of those things.

Instead, she went up on her tiptoes, leaned in and moistened her lips too. Her entire body throbbed like an exposed nerve, burning, tingling, achy, and sore with need. She *needed* him. Desperately.

"Ridge," she whispered his name again. "Ridge."

He dipped his head lower still, and panic flooded her bloodstream. He was going to do it. He was going to kiss her. Yes he was. A kiss she'd been dreaming of for more than a dozen years.

He sank his big hands on her shoulders. They were heavy, strong, anchoring her to the earth.

Her legs were rubber bands. She had no idea how they were even holding her up. And the rest of her? She was swimming in heat. Red zone. She knew that. Temperatures rising. Trouble, trouble, trouble. The dam was going to break. Danger!

Impossible to explain how scared she was, and still, she did not run.

He wrapped an arm around her waist.

She sucked in an audible breath, debated her sanity.

His Adam's apple bobbed, and for the first time, he looked affected by what was going on between them. Their gazes were chained together and if a bomb were to detonate right beside them, Kaia doubted they would even notice.

A cloud slid across the sky, drawing a curtain over the slender moon, splashing everything in blackness.

"Kaia." He groaned.

"Yes?"

"Shh."

His mouth found hers easily in the dark, and he let out a low laugh as if completely delighted by what he found.

Her breath grew short as sizzling hot tingles swept from his lips to hers. It was an immediate and insistent chemical reaction. Urgent signals of yearning shot up and down her nerve endings. Vibrating sensation blasted over her cheeks and nose, a face mask of lightning. Brilliant pulses of indigo light throbbed before her eyes, multiplying rapidly until her entire body was engulfed with the hard, insistent thunder of sexual energy.

Her ears buzzed, rang, sang—a clear, high-pitched, joyous

sound, heavenly and honeyed. The sound of the universe whirling through space.

She could not believe what was happening. Tingles. Swirls. Hums. So much humming! Like a million bees swarming her brain, nourishing her with a steadfast drone.

Him, they buzzed. *Him. Him. Him.*

The electricity blazing through her was wild and raw. An urgent primal yearning that both consumed and disoriented her. She wanted to pull back and at the same time rush headlong into the feeling.

He deepened the kiss and in that deepening, the humming grew louder and louder and louder still.

Kaia was knocked agog.

Amazed.

Terrified.

Confused.

All these years, through all the times she'd been kissed, Kaia had not ever experienced anything like this. It left her with a million questions, primary among them:

What was happening to her?

His tongue skimmed along hers and it was the single most shocking, unsettling, fascinating, elating, and incredible kiss she'd ever received.

It occurred to her that she might actually be losing her mind.

And then she remembered.

The stories Granny Blue had told her. Stories she'd thought were nothing more than Granny's fanciful, Native American fairy tales. No different than tales from the Brothers Grimm or Disney princesses.

Legend. Lore. Myth.

Based on the fable that when your one true love, your lifelong soul mate kisses you for the first time, you will hear a sweet, ethereal, incomparable song in your head; a sound as solid and sure and unmistakable as any musical note.

She heard it now with such substance and clarity, she was ready to declare with *MythBusters* glee: Myth Confirm! There was such a thing as the Song of the Soul Mate. It did exist.

At least right now. Here. In her head.

How could this be? What odd quirk of science or fate had turned her into a human receiver, picking up airwaves thick with this love song?

Him. Him. Him.

Every cell in her body vibrated to the humming energy.

Did Ridge hear it too? She closed her eyes, tried to remember the specific details of Granny Blue's tale, but Ridge's mouth was too warm, the urges pushing through her too insistent for her to concentrate on anything but the man claiming her as his own.

"Do you hear that?" she whispered.

"Hear what?" he murmured, his eyes heavily lidded, his tone sultry. He dragged his mouth over her jawline, nibbling as he went.

"Never mind," she said, and melted against his hard, masculine chest. The hay-sweet air teasing her nostrils, and another scent . . . the smell of bay rum, male skin, and some exotic, sun-warmed spice like cardamom.

Running his hand up the back of her neck, spearing the spill of her hair between his fingers, he tilted her head back, urged her mouth open wider. She sighed into the soft heat and tang of him, dissolving into the intimate flavor.

He plumbed deeper, coaxing a shiver from her, a savory shock of awareness. The humming in her head escalated, setting her on a steady course to oblivion.

She didn't care. She wanted this. Wanted him. If truth be told, she'd wanted him for years. But she could not have ever imagined it being like this.

His hand moved up her spine, came to rest at her neck where her sleep shirt dipped in the back, touching her bare spine and sending another startling shiver skipping through her. She made an involuntary sound of pleasure. It squeaked from her lungs on a gentle sigh.

He wore jeans and a Western shirt and a belt buckle that was pressing into her navel. His shirtsleeves were rolled up to the elbows revealing tanned arms dusted with black hair. His wrists were muscular, his palm square, fingers broad. The jeans fit him snug, molding around powerful thighs. His lips seared hers, melting her legs straight into the earth.

She couldn't have moved if someone had hollered, "Flash fire!"

Making a low, desperate noise, Ridge swept his tongue into her mouth, exploring at first, then plundering. Taking her fully, completely.

Kaia had never in her life been kissed like this. Never mind the humming. Although it was as if a chorus of angels were singing "Hallelujah" over a bullhorn. This kiss was an entity unto itself.

Maybe it was because she'd imagined it for so many years, waited so long for it. Maybe it was because Granny Blue's legend was true, and this was how she knew she'd found her soul mate. Or maybe it was just because Ridge Lockhart was the hottest thing on two legs and he seemed to feel the same way about her.

Whatever the cause, she was in heaven.

It felt so perfect. So right.

He tasted like her fondest memories—marshmallows roasted over a campfire, homemade peach ice cream eaten on the front porch swing, chilled watermelon slices on a hot August day.

He tasted both familiar and foreign, like déjà vu in an exotic land you knew you'd never before visited.

He tasted like all the times she'd wanted to take a walk on the wild side but had been too afraid to step from her comfort zone.

Or maybe it was all of the above.

He tasted, quite frankly, of bravery and freedom. He'd been the one to walk away from Cupid. Fly the coop. Make a huge splash in the big world beyond the arid borders of the Trans-Pecos.

She felt proud and jealous and sad, an odd triad that had her clinging even tighter to him, wanting to suck as much emotion from this moment as she could. Wanting to infuse herself with his life force.

Their first kiss would never come again. She closed her eyes and allowed every cell in her body to strum with the sweet hum of their music. To steep in the bubbling bliss.

Everything about him stunned her. His strength. His scent. His taste. His sound.

Sudden light illuminated them. Bright and startling. For one crazy second she thought maybe they were being transported straight up to heaven.

Flood lamp.

Someone had turned on the flood lamp and they were standing directly below it. The front door of the mansion opened behind them. Voices spilled out. Party was over. People heading home.

Her instinct was to pull away, afraid of getting caught kissing him. Afraid her family would see and make a thing of it.

But instead of letting her go, Ridge took her by the hand and led her to the other side of the plane, where they fell into darkness again.

As he drew her into his arms for another kiss, she giggled. "Should we stop?"

"You're right," he said, leaning his head back so he could peer into her eyes. "We shouldn't be doing this."

"If we keep this up, we're going to get caught."

"I know." But instead of stopping, he threaded his fingers through her hair, held her face while he seized her mouth once more.

Setting off that beautiful tumult of humming again. *The One.* The song sang. He's The One!

Resistance pushed through her veins. She tried to think of a dozen rational explanations for the humming, why Ridge couldn't be The One. But her ears flooded with the sound, and her mouth filled with the taste of him, and it was all so overwhelming she could barely remember what her own name was, much less all the reasons why this couldn't be happening.

Bottom line? It *was* happening. Logical or not.

Ridge made a guttural sound, low and deep at the back of his throat. In the distance, she could hear party guests calling out good-nights, car doors slamming, engines starting.

Background noise. The real action was here, on the shadow side of the plane.

He plundered her. A pirate taking over a listing ship.

Glory!

She welcomed it. Hungered for more. Wanted to go on kissing him until the end of time and beyond. She opened her mouth wider, tilted her head back farther, urging him on. She flicked her tongue, doing creative things that occurred to her spontaneously. Things she'd not tried before.

He groaned, tugged his mouth from hers, breathing heavily. "Woman," he croaked. "You're a hazard."

Doubt zipped through her. She put a hand to her mouth. What had she done wrong? "Did I . . . um . . . did I mess up?"

A chuckle slipped from his lips and his eyes softened. "No way, sweetheart. The last thing you did was mess up. You've just got me cocked and ready and no way to relieve the tension."

"Oh," she said, dissolving into the murkiness of his dark eyes. "I thought I was doing a bad job of kissing."

"No, ma'am. Quite the opposite." He glanced down and she followed his gaze, showing her how aroused he was.

Her cheeks flushed. "I didn't mean to . . ."

"You are freaking adorable, you know that, Kaia Alzate? You make me forget all about my troubles."

"What troubles are those?"

He gestured toward the mansion. "Family drama. But let's not talk about that."

This time when he kissed her, he was incredibly gentle. Taking it soft and slow. Tender raindrop kisses that sent ripples of sensation surfing over her body.

"We really have to stop this now," he said.

She moaned and leaned against his shoulder. "I know."

"We have to get up early tomorrow. All this wedding stuff."

"I know, I know." The humming was ebbing, receding, soft echoes inside her head.

"If it was another time, another place, things would not be ending here."

His words gave her heart wings. Oh how she wished it was another time and another place.

"You gotta go home now," he said. "And I have to go to Archer's place. Otherwise, I can't be held accountable for my actions."

"One more kiss?" she pleaded, and ran a hand over his chest. She wanted to stir the humming. Make sure it was still there. That it was real.

He swore under his breath. "Kaia, don't."

"Please . . ."

"Home, woman." He took her by the shoulders and turned her so she was facing away from him. "Go home before I forget all my scruples."

"Kaia?" Ember's voice called out into the night. "Where are you?"

She glanced over her shoulder at him.

"Your cue to go." His face was unreadable. "Good night, Kaia." Then he pivoted and walked off into the night.

Chapter 11

HER phone went off before dawn, playing barnyard noises, jerking Kaia awake. A cow mooed. Loudly. Followed by a braying donkey.

"Gotta change that ringtone," she mumbled, fumbling on her nightstand for the cell.

Judging how dark it was outside her window and how groggy she felt, Kaia doubted she'd slept more than a couple of hours. She hadn't fallen asleep until well after three o'clock, obsessed with the humming she'd heard when Ridge kissed her.

She blinked at the phone—five twenty-five a.m. Archer's name on the caller ID.

"S'up?" she answered, stifling a yawn.

"Are you hungover?" her brother asked.

"Are you?"

"Were you sleeping?"

"Kinda."

"Is Ridge with you?"

"Why would you even ask that? Why on earth would you assume Ridge was with me?"

"I dunno. He likes you."

"A lot of people like me. That doesn't mean they're in my bed."

"He never turned up at my house last night."

"Ridge is missing?"

"I'm getting married today. I need my best man. Ridge better not pull a disappearing act."

"Well, he's not in my pocket."

"Last night was a disaster. What if he left town for good? Do you *think* he left town for good?" Archer asked on an extended exhale.

"Is his plane still there?"

"Yes."

"Settle down, Groomszilla. If the plane is there, Ridge is around," she said logically. Normally Archer wasn't one to freak out easily, but this *was* his wedding day. "Don't panic. Ridge won't let you down. He *will* turn up. Did you check his house?"

"Yes. He's not there either, and none of the beds have been slept in. Where else could he be?"

"Did you try calling him?"

"*Duh*. He's not answering. I left a bazillion voice mails."

"Phone reception at the ranch can be spotty."

"He should have at least gotten my texts."

"Maybe he doesn't have his phone."

"Why wouldn't he take his phone? His phone is like oxygen to him."

"Speaking of oxygen, try taking a deep breath, big brother."

"This day has to be perfect, Ky. Casey deserves perfect."

"Calm down. I have an idea where he is," she said. "I'll check it out. In the meantime, chill. Drink some coffee. Or better yet, go back to bed and try to get a couple more hours of sleep. Your wedding isn't until four o'clock. Plenty of time."

"Find him!"

"I'll do my best."

Kaia threw off the covers, upending Dart—the kitty she was fostering—who dropped gracefully to the floor for a morning stretch. Got dressed in jeans and a T-shirt, fed all the animals, let the dogs into the fenced backyard, and put out fresh kitty litter.

She made coffee, filled two thermoses to go, and stuck a couple of power bars in her purse. "Later, dude," she told Dart with a quick scratch under his chin and headed out the door.

She climbed into the Tundra and took off. The first flush of dawn pinking the crepuscular sky. She combed her fingers through her hair, trying to tame the thick mass.

At this sleepy hour on a Saturday morning, it took her less than five minutes to get across town to the Brooklane Baptist Church.

She pulled up to the cemetery. The gates were closed. She parked on the side of the road, stuck the power bars in her back pocket, and got out, balancing the thermoses in each hand.

She slipped the thermoses through the wrought-iron rungs, then climbed the locked gate, dropped down on the paved road in the cemetery, retrieved the thermoses, and headed south.

Long before she reached the tombstone, she spied him, in the muted dawn. He was dressed in the same black clothes he'd worn the night before, kneeling at the grave, his Stetson in hand, looking bleak as a raven in the rain.

She stopped. Her heart tumbled to the soles of her boots, and she almost went back to the truck, reluctant to disturb him.

He raised his head, and his navy blue eyes landed on her.

She painted on a bright smile as if they weren't in a cemetery and he hadn't spent the night at his mother's grave.

He got to his feet. He looked flattened. She wanted to run to him, to hug him and never let go. To tell him that everything was going to be all right. But of course, she did not.

"Mornin'," she chirped. Raised the thermoses. "Look, coffee."

"One for me?"

She nodded, came closer. Handed him the thermos that held heat better than the one she kept for herself, and a power bar.

He took a long sip, grinned like she'd given him gold bullion. "You remembered. Extra cream. No sugar."

"How could I forget? Same as me."

A hooded oriole sang a sharp, nasally "wheet, wheet" morning song, welcoming the rising sun. From a crack in the cement between tombstones, a small striped, whiptail lizard strolled out.

"I see you've had company." Kaia nodded at the lizard.

"He's not much of a conversationalist."

"Best pet for you since you've never been a big talker."

He smiled at that, a pat smile more automatic than authentic. "Archer send you?"

"You didn't come home. He worried."

"How did you know where to find me?"

She shrugged. "Last we talked, you were feeling guilty about punching your dad. Put two and two. Figured you'd come to the place that reminded you of why he deserved punching."

He scratched his head, settled his hat in place. His right eye was less swollen this morning, but it was a striking purple color.

"You're too insightful for my own good."

"How did you get here?"

"Walked."

"In cowboy boots?"

One shoulder went up like a half-mast flag. "I might have some blisters."

"It's fifteen miles from the ranch. It must have taken hours."

The other shoulder joined the first at his ears. "A baker gave me a ride on his way to open the doughnut shop."

"Archer is freaking out. I'm just going to text him and tell him I'm bringing you back." She pulled out her phone, sent her brother the text, trying not to notice how extremely hot Ridge looked in black jeans, black T-shirt stretched over his biceps, black boots, and black hat.

The man in black.

"Ready?" she asked, unnerved to find she was breathless. This was Ridge. She'd known him all her life.

But after last night, after those confounded kisses, after that sweet serenade of humming, she was a bundle of throbbing nerve endings.

"Ready." He put his palm against the small of her back. Bold. Intimate. Perfect.

His hand was big and rough and she could feel the pressure against her T-shirt. Ludicrously, now his touch felt both comforting and petrifying. As if he was righting her on a slippery rug.

That he'd just pulled out from under her.

Her entire body tensed.

He dropped his hand. Loosely, casually, as if it had meant nothing. It hadn't meant anything, right? She was reading way too much into a simple touch.

At the small of her back.

Perilously close to her butt.

Every spurt of blood passing through her veins bathed her in a fresh batch of heat and simmered like stew on a burner. Unnerved, she stepped away from him.

Ridge took another sip of coffee, studied her over the thermos as he peeled open the power bar. The murky look in his eyes had her convinced he was feeling the shift between them, as well.

"Um . . ." She cleared her throat. "Um, let's get out of here."

She rushed to the truck, not even checking to see if he was following. But somehow he ended up opening the passenger side door at the same time she opened the driver's side.

As they drove through town, not knowing what else to say, she told him the local gossip, what things had changed over the past ten years, who'd gotten married, who was divorced, who'd had babies, who'd passed away.

That loosened him up and he started talking about Calgary, and he told her how different it was from their hometown. Real mountains, not the foothills Texans called mountains. Green. Cool. Wet. Soothing.

But he conceded there were things he missed about home. Balmorhea State Park and the cool artisan springs. Stargazing because nowhere else on earth had a night sky like the Trans-Pecos. The quirkiness of desert folk. Weird little desert trails and random salt lakes that sprang from nowhere. The incredible shift of colors and light at sunrise and sunset.

"I've never really been anywhere except to A&M," she said. "I have nothing to compare home to."

"It's a big wide world out there." He was watching the road ahead, his chin high, his angular lips parted slightly. "You gotta get out more."

"Maybe someday I'll get a chance to explore. I've never even ridden in a plane before."

"Would you like to go up in the Evektor?" he offered.

"Wow, that would be awesome." She clapped her hands briefly before putting them back on the wheel. "But I doubt we'll have the opportunity before you have to go back to Calgary."

"We could go up this morning." He checked his watch. "Before the hubbub of the wedding hits. It's not even seven yet."

That thrilled her. "Really? Do we have time?"

"We should be able to squeeze in thirty minutes."

"That would be . . . so . . . so amazing."

He smiled. "I love the way your face lights up when you're excited. It makes me feel happy."

She grinned at him, happy that she'd made him happy. Especially after the troublesome night he'd had.

Fifteen minutes later, they were back at the ranch. They placated Archer, assuring him they would return by eight a.m. Ridge gassed the plane with fuel from a tank used by the crop dusters and did a preflight check.

When he was finished, he turned to Kaia and grinned like a man accustomed to having the world on a string. "Ready to soar?"

"Oh yes." A thrill chased up Kaia's spine, and she squinted against the morning sun, wished for sunglasses. As if reading her mind, Ridge settled his sunglasses on her face.

"Hey, you're the pilot," she protested. "You need these worse than I do."

"I have another pair in the plane," he said.

"Always prepared, huh?"

"Never know what might come up." He nodded. "It's always good to stay ahead of the competition."

"Who are we competing against?"

"In this case? The wedding."

The sky had taken on an opalescent orange glow as the sun banked off a column of dense white clouds, shooting bands of light poking through in spots like magical fingers.

He held out a hand to help her up the steps. Once they were belted in, he turned to her and said with a wicked grin, "I'm glad I'm your first."

For a startling second, she thought he meant her first love, but realized he was talking about the plane trip. "Me too."

He started the engine and her stomach fluttered. Her first time in a plane.

Giddily, she curled her fingers into her palms. She cast a glance at Ridge as he fiddled with the controls. She'd pulled her hair back into a ponytail and the tip of it rubbed across her shoulders as she turned.

His face was alight, his eyes bright, lips drawn into a smile, body relaxed. He was happy in the cockpit. The happiest she'd seen him since he'd returned.

"Excited?" he asked, engines churning loudly.

"Beyond." She grinned helplessly, part of her scared to death, the other part yearning to fly.

"Me too," he confessed as he taxied down the narrow airstrip.

And then they were off. Rising up in the air, the buildings below growing smaller below them.

It was very smooth, the climb. It was just the two of them enclosed in a whole new world together. Or at least it was new to her.

She assumed he'd taken many women up in his plane. She had no illusion that she was special on that score. He was rich and good-looking. He owned his own plane, his own business, his own house—hell, two houses—one here and one in Calgary.

Honestly, his wealth intimidated her. She didn't own anything besides a yard full of animals and a passel of student debt. She rented her home, and she was still paying on the eight-year-old Tundra she'd bought used after her old Chevy was totaled in the accident.

The engine hummed sharp and smart and it reminded her of another humming. The ground looked so faraway, her Tundra little more than a blue dot parked beside the landing strip.

It made her sad. Seeing everything fall away. Kaia pressed a hand to her stomach, felt a slosh of loneliness.

"Don't look down," he said. "Eyes on the sky."

She raised her head, looked out the windshield. "What do you call the windshield on a plane?"

"Windshield." He laughed. "Although some people say windscreen."

Sky stretched all around them. Wide-open. Inviting. "How long have you been flying?"

"Five years."

"Is there anything you don't know how to do?"

"Relax," he said.

"Huh?" she said, forcing herself to unclench her fist. Flying was thrilling, but she was uptight. How had he known?

"According to my critics," he explained, "I don't know how to relax."

"Oh."

"What they don't get is that working is *how* I relax."

It was peaceful, until they flew through a patch of clouds and the plane bobbled wildly without warning. Kaia gasped and grasped the leather seat with both hands.

"What's happening! What's happening!"

"Just a little turbulence. Nothing to worry about," he said, watching her cling to the seat as if it could save her life.

Her cheeks reddened, and she pressed a palm to her heart. "Oh whew. I didn't mean to flip out. Sorry."

"Fear of flying?"

"No. Dread fear of crashing."

"I've gotcha, Kaia," he said, his voice full of strength and certainty. "I'm in charge here. I'll keep you safe. *Always*."

Somehow, she believed it. She gave a smile and teasingly said, "My hero." Except it came out sounding more reverential than jokey.

The plane leveled out and she peered through the side window again, gazing at the white wedding chapel, reception barn, and Ridge's house below.

It was so peaceful up here. She could see why he loved this. No cell phones. No texting. No multitasking. No interruptions. Just the sky.

"I'm going higher," he said.

"Thanks for the heads-up."

"Here we go," he said, working the controls. By seamless increments he brought them higher into the clouds until they were engulfed by low-lying mist.

Kaia giggled, giddy with it.

"Ah." He exhaled deeply, as if he'd entered a mythical realm.

Suddenly, she realized he was casting a spell, strange fairy-tale magic as mesmerizing as the humming she'd heard when he'd kissed her—rare, priceless treasures.

On an impulse, she matched her breathing with his, aligning their patterns. She pretended he was the thrust of the plane and she the ephemeral clouds.

"Kaia," he whispered, and she wasn't sure if he'd actually said something or she imagined it.

She opened her eyes, glanced over.

He was staring at her.

"Where did you go?" he asked.

Nowhere. Everywhere.

"I'm right here," she said. "Right here with you."

"We better get back."

"I know," she said, her heart reluctant. "Archer is already strung like a guitar string over this wedding. We don't want to add to his stress."

The clouds separated and they left them behind, streamers of a delightful dream. A glimpse of what could be. A single tear collected in the corner of her eye, and she quickly daubed it away.

"Thank you," he said.

"For what?"

"Coming after me this morning. Knowing where to find me. Hanging out with me in the clouds."

"My pleasure," she said, because it was.

He circled the plane, and angled toward the landing strip. Up here things were quiet, simple.

She exhaled slowly. She liked being in the sky. He'd opened a door and showed her endless possibilities.

And that was the scary thing about him, wasn't it. Showing her things far beyond her reach. Opening a window into a high-flying world she had no idea how to navigate.

Chapter 12

THE white, steepled chapel bulged at the seams. People spilled out of the pews, and some even stood along the back wall. Ceiling fans rotated furiously to stir the air, but the congregation was too large, the summer day too hot, the air conditioning unit too small to compete with the desert heat.

Sweat collected along Ridge's collar, beaded at the nape of his neck, as he waited at the front of the altar beside Archer with Casey's ring on his pinky finger.

The minister droned on.

The afternoon sun filled the stained-glass window with beautiful splashes of orange, gold, and purple, casting everything in a misty, fuzzy glow of joy. Late-arriving wedding presents were being stored in the chapel's overhead loft and soft rays of light caught the foil wrapping, adding shiny glitz to the homey affair.

Ridge's gaze drifted over to where Kaia stood in the row of attendants behind Casey. The aqua bridesmaid dress fit her like a glove, and her hair was pulled back in a loose upswept hairstyle that showcased her cheekbones. Briefly, she met his eyes, offered up a slight smile, and then quickly shifted her gaze back to the bride and groom.

Thankfully, the service was brief and beautifully simple. The couple's vows were suffused with humble reverence and had Ridge battling a sappy sentimentality seeping into the pit of his stomach.

But if there was ever a time for tender emotions it was at the wedding of his oldest childhood friend, and so Ridge tolerated the mushy stirrings and avoided looking at Kaia.

They'd shared a world-rocking kiss. But so what? It didn't have to go anywhere. *Shouldn't* go anywhere. He was leaving Cupid on Monday. He'd even considered leaving tomorrow what with the bad blood churning between him and his father.

He swung his gaze to the first row of the pew on the groom's side, where Duke, sporting a shiner that matched his own, sat beside Vivi. A sting of guilt burned through him. He regretted having to throw that punch. Wished there could have been another way.

"Do you have the ring?" the priest asked, snapping Ridge back to the ceremony.

Because no one was going to trust three-year-old Atticus with Casey's wedding band, the boy had brought two fake rings down the aisle on a satin pillow. Leaving Kaia in charge of the groom's ring and Ridge in charge of Casey's band. To have it handy, he'd stuck it on his pinky.

"Yes," Ridge said. He tugged at his little finger, trying to slip off the ring. But it wouldn't budge.

Father Dubanowski's laser gaze zeroed in on Ridge.

"Gimme a sec," Ridge said as sweat popped out on his forehead.

The priest shifted his stare to Duke and his black eye. A stern expression crossed his beefy face as if to say, *Lockharts. Brawling. Drinking. Hardheaded. Pains in the ass.*

Yeah, okay, maybe it *was* the Lockhart way.

A hush came over the room. Only the sound of the whirling blades from the ceiling fan overhead punctuated the silence. Father Dubanowski cleared his throat. Loudly.

Ridge yanked on the ring. It would not budge. His fingers must have swollen in the heat and it wasn't coming off. He threw Archer a panicked look.

"Get the fake ring off the pillow," Archer mumbled from the corner of his mouth but kept his eyes and smile focused on his bride.

Feeling like forty kinds of fool, Ridge cast around for the pillow. Where had Atticus left it? His throat tightened and he searched the altar, didn't see it. It was official. He was the worst best man in the history of weddings . . .

And then there was Kaia, unpinning the fake ring from the pillow where it sat on the ground in front of the podium. Quickly, she straightened, handed it to Ridge, and stepped back into place as Ridge passed the ring to Archer so he could put it on Casey's fingers.

A ripple of humor passed through the crowd.

Ridge didn't have the stones to look Casey in the face. He kept working on the ring while the priest continued with the ceremony, twisting the band back and forth. But it felt like it was getting tighter instead of looser. Why hadn't he just put the damn thing in his pocket like a normal person?

Archer kissed Casey and the audience applauded. The couple turned and headed out of the church, leaving the groomsmen to hook up with bridesmaids and proceed in their wake.

As Zeke took Kaia's arm and escorted her up the aisle, the muscle at his right eye ticked.

"Don't feel badly about the ring thing," said Lynne, Casey's matron of honor, when he took her arm. "If there wasn't a glitch or two in a wedding, there would be no juicy stories to tell."

"I gotta get this ring off."

"Soap should do the trick," Lynne assured him.

He hoped she was right.

Once the wedding party was on the front porch, the photographer motioned them over to the side so the congregation could get out behind them.

Ridge let go of Lynne's arm as she joined her husband, Ned, who'd been escorting Tara.

Ridge sidestepped to get out of the way and crashed into Kaia.

"Hold on, cowboy." She laughed and put up a restraining hand. "I know I'm small, but don't plow over me."

The feel of her hand on his elbow unwound him. He glanced down, found himself falling into the vortex of her dark eyes. He couldn't speak. Couldn't move. Could only stare at her as if she held the meaning of life. Wedding guests flowed around them, smiling and chatting. Simultaneously, as if they'd planned it out, they both pressed their backs up against the outside wall of the church to give people room to move past.

"Thanks for saving my bacon with the ring," he said.

"You're welcome." She smiled so brightly it hurt his eyes.

"You look . . ." He gulped. "Stunning."

She pressed her lips together and glanced away. Was he saying too much in front of people? Probably. But he couldn't seem to help himself.

"Congratulations," Kaia reached out to hug Casey, who was waiting beside Archer as he slipped Father Dubanowski a white envelope. "It's official. You're an Alzate now. I'm so happy to call you sister."

"Thank you, thank you! I still can't believe I have my own real life fairy tale." Casey sighed dreamily.

"I've been meaning to tell you how beautiful the bridesmaids' dresses are," Kaia went on, and Ridge couldn't help feeling she was grasping for conversation with Casey to avoid talking to him. "I'll be able to wear this one many times. You have such great fashion sense."

Casey's face brightened at Kaia's compliment. "It took me ages to find the right ones. Not just the style and the fit, but a color that flattered everyone's complexions. Thankfully, except for Ember, you Alzate girls have that amazing dark hair and olive-toned skin."

"Your hard work was worth it," Kaia said. "The wedding was the perfect balance of country and sophistication. It's like something from a bridal magazine."

"I had lots of help." Casey gave a humble smile. "You've all been saints putting up with my bridezilla moods."

"Not even for a second were you a bridezilla. When Archer said you'd agreed to be his wife, I felt like our family had won the lottery."

"Oh, Kaia." Casey enveloped her in a jasmine-scented hug. "You make me feel so special."

Ridge swallowed. Yeah. Kaia had that effect on everyone. You couldn't be around her for very long without feeling her warmth and goodwill. She sucked you right in with her guileless charm. That's where he kept getting tripped up. Falling for her sweet, sunny disposition.

"And you, mister . . ." Casey turned to Ridge. "I want that ring before Archer and I leave on our honeymoon tomorrow."

"I blew it."

Casey waved a hand. "You were fine. It added a little humor to the ceremony. But I'm putting Kaia in charge of making sure you get that ring off."

"You're not leaving for your honeymoon after the reception?" Kaia asked.

"No, we've decided that instead of driving to El Paso tonight and staying at an airport hotel, we can hang out at the reception longer, sleep in our own beds, and drive to El Paso in the morning. Our flight isn't until noon."

"That means I need to find somewhere else to stay," Ridge said.

Casey nodded to Ridge's house across the way. "Vivi already had one of the hands move your suitcase over. Although I understand you probably have mixed feeling about that."

Mixed hell. His feelings were unequivocal. The last thing he wanted was to sleep in that house. He would have appreciated some advance notice and the option to decide his own lodging, but he didn't say anything. He could avoid *that* master bedroom. Sleep on the couch or floor. In the grand scheme of things, what did it matter where he slept? He'd be gone soon.

"Wedding party!" the photographer called, shooing people into the best lighting. "Over here!"

Once the wedding party was assembled and the photographer got a good look at everyone, he did a double take, mumbled under his breath, "What's with all the black eyes? How am I supposed to create art with so many black eyes?"

"Why, didn't anyone tell you?" Kaia asked. "This is a bushwhacker wedding."

The whole group laughed, and in that priceless moment, Ridge absolutely adored her.

THE RECEPTION BARN had been constructed along with the chapel to service weddings, and animals had never occupied it. Hay bales were situated around the cement floors for authenticity. Six long wooden picnic tables, placed vertically, lined the middle of the room. A seventh, horizontal table was set up at the front for the wedding party. White linen tablecloths were topped with peach-and-aqua runners. Flickering white candles in mason jars, surrounded by garlands made of rope and baby's breath served as centerpieces.

Kaia searched the barn for Ridge, spied him standing off to the side of the wedding party table, looking drop-dead handsome in his Texas tuxedo. He held a longneck beer bottle loosely between two fingers, his other hand clasped behind his back. It was as if he were in a protective bubble of his own making, separate from everyone else, impervious to the festivities, his face as stony as his name.

She started toward him, but then an out-of-town guest, a beautiful woman that Kaia hadn't met, came up and started a conversation with Ridge. Jealousy smacked Kaia in the stomach and she stopped her in her tracks.

Vivi stood inside the doorway passing out toy cap guns, to use to salute the bride and groom when they left the reception in lieu of throwing rice, and drinking a chocolate martini. From the shiny look in her eyes, it wasn't her first.

"Cap gun?" Vivi asked, extending the toy six-shooter tied with aqua-and-peach ribbon streamers that matched the wedding colors.

"Sure." Kaia reached for the cap gun, but Vivi held on to it. Startled, Kaia stared at her. "What is it?"

"He's going to break your heart, you know."

Kaia frowned. "Excuse me?"

"Don't play coy. I saw you kissing him last night."

Kaia didn't bother denying it. She let go of the cap gun and stepped back. She was not going to get into a tug-of-war over a toy cap gun.

"I'm not still hung up on him, if that's what you're thinking." Vivi hiccuped.

"I wasn't thinking that." She totally was.

"I'm worried about you."

Um-hum. Sure. "Thank you for your concern."

"FYI, Ridge is incapable of love," Vivi said. "His mother broke his heart and he's never recovered. I blame her for abandoning him the way she did. He just can't trust women."

Kaia bit down on her tongue to keep from saying, *Maybe you screwing his dad has something to do with his mistrust of women.* This wasn't the time or the place, and besides, it wasn't her battle. She and Ridge were not a couple. They were not dating. He had kissed her. That's all it was. The kiss meant nothing.

Except, she'd heard the Song of the Soul Mate.

C'mon. She had to stop this. Other than the fact that the humming had started the moment his lips touched hers and had stopped when he finished kissing her, she had no proof it was anything more than tinnitus.

"Consider this a friendly warning," Vivi said. "I want the best for you."

I call bullshit she wanted to say. Instead, Kaia forced a smile, mumbled, "Thanks," even though it was idiotic to thank Vivi for trying to stir up trouble, and she turned away.

"Wait," Vivi said.

Kaia rolled her eyes, sucked in a deep breath, and turned back around. "What is it?"

"You forgot your gun."

For a second, she hesitated, not wanting to look like a fool if Vivi held on to the cap gun again. Finally, she put out her hand.

Vivi settled the toy into her palm. "Be careful."

Kaia wasn't sure if she meant with her heart or the cap gun. "Will do."

"I'm here if you ever need to talk."

Yeah, right. Kaia had three sisters, a cool granny, and an understanding mom. She couldn't imagine any circumstance where she would turn to Vivi for advice.

Someone else came up for a cap gun, and Kaia made good her escape, heading for the wedding party table and Ridge. When his eyes found hers, his face lit up. Her heart flip-flopped. Vivi was right about one thing. The man *was* a heartbreaker.

They were the first ones from the wedding party at the table. "Where is everyone else?" she asked.

"Playing in the photo booth. The wedding planner went after them."

"There's a photo booth? I didn't know there was going to be a photo booth. I love photo booths."

"Yep." His eyebrows went up on his forehead in amusement. "There's a photo booth."

"Wanna go in it after dinner?"

"Together?"

"Um, yes. What fun is a photo booth by yourself?"

"Maybe we could get Casey and Archer to go with us."

"I'm sure Casey and Archer have other things on their mind than getting in the photo booth with us."

"Ranger and Ember?" he said.

"Why, Ridge Lockhart." She cocked her head, and sailed him a grin. "Are you afraid to be alone in a small space with me?"

"Hell yes." He laughed.

"Because of last night?" she whispered.

His eyes turned somber. "Last night shouldn't have happened."

"But it did."

"We could pretend it didn't."

She stared him squarely in the eyes. "Could we?"

"I can if you can."

"I can't."

"Me either," he admitted.

Wow. They stared at each other, still suffering the aftershocks.

"Are you nervous?" she asked.

"About?"

"The best man speech."

"No. I give speeches to large groups all the time."

"Look at you, Big Wheel." Her heart skipped at the idea of him in full command of a stage. Truth was she couldn't imagine him not being in full command of anything. Well, he did have his fumbles now and again. He wasn't completely a superhero. She nodded at his left hand. "You're still wearing Casey's wedding ring."

"I tried soap. Didn't work."

"Panicking yet?"

"I don't panic."

"Ever?"

"It's rare," he said coolly.

"I dunno. It felt like you were a little panicky at the altar."

"Nope." He pressed his lips together, suppressing a grin.

"You wouldn't admit it if you were panicky."

"Now you're catching on."

"Want me to help you get that ring off?"

"Would you?" Relief lightened his eyes.

"Can't have Casey mad at you, can we?" She held out her hand. "Come on."

"Where are we going?"

"My truck."

To her surprise, he didn't ask why, and sank his hand into hers. Trusting her? That was new. Ridge Lockhart didn't trust anyone. But his skin was on her skin, lighting her up like fireworks.

Kaia dropped his hand, explained, "We don't want to give people something to talk about."

"No," he agreed.

She went ahead of him, moving around the parked cars until she got to her Tundra. She unlocked it, found her purse, dug around inside for dental floss.

Silence settled over them. They could hear the festivities over at the barn, conversation, laughter, the band tuning up.

"What's the dental floss for?" he asked.

"Watch and learn." From her oversized purse, she also dug out a Swiss Army knife and a small emergency sewing kit.

"You don't have to help me," he said. "I could figure this out for myself."

"I know that." She looked at his sexy mouth and tried not to think about kissing him. "Finger."

"What?"

"Give it to me."

"You know you set that up perfectly, but I'm not going there."

"I didn't mean . . . oh gosh . . . I guess that *did* sound suggestive." Do not blush. She was not going to blush. Her cheeks burned. *Dammit.*

He eyed the knife, the sewing kit, and the dental floss. "What? Are you going to cut my finger off and sew it up with dental floss?"

"I'm not even answering that."

"So . . . what's the knife for?"

"Cutting the floss, the little metal cutty thing came off the roll."

"And why do we need dental floss in the first place?"

"Stop asking questions and trust me. Can you do that?"

Trust was not his long suit and they both knew it. Slowly, he extended his little finger. "Be gentle. My pinky is in your hands."

In the dome light, she cut the dental floss, and threaded it through a needle from the sewing kit. "Hold still," she said. "I don't want to poke you."

"Talking dirty again?"

"Hush." She was blushing once more, but hey, at least she had an olive complexion and the flush wasn't so easy to detect. She could feel the warmth of his breath on her skin. Remembered his kisses. Her head hummed just thinking about it.

"Is it hot in here, or is it just you?"

"Ridge!"

She could feel his stare burning into her as she slipped the needle underneath Casey's diamond wedding band. Then she wrapped the waxed string around his finger all the way up to the knuckle.

Winding it snuggly, but not so tight as to cut off his circulation. Beginning at the bottom of his fingers, she unwound the floss, the ring moving up the string along with the unwinding.

"Look at that." He sounded amazed. "It's working."

"Was there any doubt?"

"You know uncommon things."

"I do."

"Part of your Native American secrets?"

She laughed. "No. One of my physical therapists in rehab was nuts for dental floss. She showed me all kinds of ways to use it. Cutting your food. Starting a fire. Removing old photographs that got stuck together."

"File this under Things I Never Knew."

She finished unwinding the floss and Casey's ring dropped from his finger. "Voilà," she said. "You're a free man."

"With a whole new respect for dental floss." He laughed, but it was a shaky sound full of nervousness.

Truth be told, she was shaky nervous too.

Chapter 13

Back inside the barn, everyone else had taken seats.

This time, Kaia and Ridge were the last to arrive.

"You go ahead," she told him. "So people won't know we were together."

He ironed his lips together in a firm line, nodded like he was fine with it, but there was disappointment in the way he pivoted and loped away.

Oh dear.

She was still sorting out her feelings, and she didn't want her family and friends weighing in on the relationship. Mainly because it *wasn't* a relationship and she was afraid they'd blow things out of proportion.

Following the excellent meal of tenderloin medallions, risotto, and haricots verts, the speeches began. Waiters dressed as cowboys moved around the tables passing out glasses of champagne and sparkling cider.

As best man, Ridge was up first, and when he stood, Kaia's eyes were instantly drawn to him. And she wasn't the only woman ogling him.

He glanced down the table and caught her staring at him. The covert smile he sent her landed in her stomach like a firebomb, scorching her from the inside out. He dipped an index finger in his champagne glass, moistening it. Anchored the base of the glass on the table with his other hand, circled his wet finger around the rim, and produced a high-pitched keening.

Everyone turned to stare at him.

"Now that I have your attention." He raised the champagne glass, glanced out at the crowd. "For those of you who don't know me, I'm Ridge Lockhart. Archer and I have been friends for as long as I can remember. For those of you who do know me, well, I hope you don't hold our friendship against Archer."

That drew a collective laugh.

Ridge looked over at Archer, who sat to his left beside Casey. "We've had our share of adventures together, played sports, pulled pranks, chased girls, and suffered through our share of bratty little brothers and sisters tagging along after us."

With that, and it wasn't her imagination, Ridge gazed pointedly down the table toward her.

Kaia gulped, ducked her head, and stared at her peach cobbler.

"We vowed to be lifelong bachelors," Ridge went on, turning his attention back to Archer. "I kept up my end of the bargain, but then Casey came into his life and changed everything."

The crowd murmured a collective "aww." Kaia's heart went all mushy at the loving look her brother exchanged with his bride.

"Archer, I have a baffled respect for anyone who has the courage to ignore the high divorce rate and plunge headfirst into matrimony."

An awkward silence fell over the room. Archer shifted uncomfortably and Casey looked as if Ridge had gut-stabbed her. Kaia's mushy heart tripped into her stomach.

Gosh, Ridge sounded just like Hugh Grant's commitment phobic character in *Four Weddings and a Funeral*. Vivi was right. If she allowed it to happen, Ridge *would* break her heart.

So don't allow it to happen.

"But you guys aren't me. You clearly have what it takes to make it for the long haul," Ridge continued. "My hat is off to you. I know you'll have a long and happy marriage."

A tight smile stretched Archer's mouth and Casey wrapped her hands around her new husband's forearm and leaned into him.

Ridge raised his glass higher. "Let's all toast the happy couple and wish them well."

"To the happy couple!" the guests said in unison.

Numbly, Kaia parroted the phrase, downed half her champagne with one swallow. Reality check. Ridge was not the marrying kind. He'd just announced it. No matter what the Song of the Soul Mate might have hummed to her. He was not The One.

Never mind. It was okay. Forget the humming. She wasn't disappointed. Okay, maybe a little, but she'd get over it.

Ridge sat down, and Casey's dad started his speech. The rest of the speeches passed in a blur, and the next thing she knew the band was launching into the first song for the bride and groom to dance together. The Black Eyed Peas' "I Gotta Feeling."

During the liveliest part of the song, Casey started bouncing up and down and waving people out onto the dance floor with them. Archer had a happily dopey expression on his face as he gazed adoringly at his bride, moving his feet in an I-can't-dance-but-I'm-giving-it-hell shuffle.

When that song finished and the band broke into "Save a Horse Ride a Cowboy," the women cheered and the dance floor flooded with boot-scooting line dancers. Kaia shot a glance at Ridge, but Vivi was already claiming him, taking him by both hands and dragging him into the fray.

And boy, the man could dance!

Her jaw dropped.

Kaia sat watching and clapping, enjoying being a spectator, but then Duke came and without even asking, spun her out of her chair, not taking "no" for an answer.

"You're dancing with me, girly," he announced.

Not wanting to make a scene at her brother's wedding, she helplessly joined Ridge's father on the dance floor, but she couldn't shake the feeling she was a pawn in the middle of some grudge game between Vivi, Duke, and Ridge. And that was a triangle she wanted nothing of.

Duke's black eye was as vivid as Ridge's and he was sweating and pausing to mop his face with a handkerchief.

That song faded and the notes of the next tune started up.

"Angel Loved the Devil." A waltz. She was certainly not going to slow dance with Ridge's father.

She opened her mouth to tell Duke she needed water, but before she could get a word out, there was Ridge standing beside his father. They stared at each other with mirrored black eyes.

"I'm cutting in," Ridge stated, not asking permission. Damn those Lockhart men and their high-handed ways.

Duke hardened his chin. "I was here first."

Kaia sank her hands on her hips. "I'm not a pork chop. I'm not dancing with either one of you. Zeke . . ." She reached for the ranch hand who was passing by. "Dance with me."

Zeke grinned like an opossum and took her up on the offer. Leaving both Duke and Ridge looking put out. Good. Served 'em right.

But she couldn't help watching Ridge over Zeke's shoulder. And when he smiled, damn her hide, she smiled right back.

"YOU'RE GOING TO blow it with Kaia," Duke said to Ridge.

"I didn't ask your opinion."

"It's for the best that you do blow it. She's a good girl. Doesn't need the likes of you fouling her up."

"Screw you, *Dad*."

"Back at you."

"We're such a lovely family."

"When I saw you getting cozy with her I thought, now there's a Titanic romance. Gonna hit an iceberg and sink quick."

"Why would you say something like that?"

"Because I know you. The minute things get tough, you take off. I know you don't think you do it. I know you tell yourself tall tales about why you run away, but the bottom line? You don't show up for life. That's why you shouldn't get cozy with her. She deserves someone who'll stick around."

Ridge turned his jaw to marble, tightening his muscles until they quivered with repressed anger. "We're *not* getting cozy."

"You think I'm blind?"

"I think you have no right to weigh in on anyone else's romance."

"Touché," Duke said mildly, surprising Ridge with a mashed-potatoes voice. "She is gorgeous. You've got good taste."

"Back off."

"I'm married, you idiot," Duke scoffed.

"I don't trust you. You have a history of stealing my girlfriends."

"If Vivi was so easy to steal away, she wasn't yours in the first place." Duke snorted like a longhorn lost in a mesquite thicket. "There's one thing you fail to understand about me and Vivi, son."

Ridge prickled at the word *son*. "And that is?"

"I love her."

It was Ridge's turn to snort.

Duke thrust out his chest. "And she loves me."

"Whatever you need to tell yourself."

"It might not be the most functional relationship in the world," Duke admitted. "But it works for us. We've been married ten years, and still going strong."

"Angling for husband of the year?"

"Smart-ass."

"I inherited it from somewhere."

"Your mother's side."

Ridge narrowed his eyes. "As if you knew the first thing about my mother."

Duke stared at Ridge, his face pale beneath his tan, eyes red and exhausted. "You think I'm hard? Boy, you don't know the meaning of the word. Try having my old man for a father. Compared to that, you got lucky. You got cream puff."

"I know, I know. Gramps used to beat you with a bullwhip."

"I got the scars to prove it." Duke yanked his shirttail from his pants and lifted up the hem to reveal a crisscross of old scars striping his back. "I don't hold it against him though."

"No?"

"My father knew this was a harsh land and you had to be tough to make it in the Trans-Pecos."

"Well, thank you for not beating me with a bullwhip. I feel so blessed."

Duke closed his black eye, rubbed a palm over the cheek Ridge had punched. "You got your shot in."

"Excuse me," asked a sweet voice. "May I have this dance?"

Ridge looked over, and there was Kaia smiling at him and holding out her hand. How many times had she held out her hand to him since he'd been home? Open, accepting, welcoming.

"Sorry," Ridge told Duke. "I have a lady to dance with." He swung Kaia out onto the dance floor in time to "My Silver Lining."

Damn if she wasn't *his* silver lining. His throat tightened as he looked into her kind eyes. His chest squeezed and all he could do was hold on to her.

They moved as if they'd been dancing together their entire life. They fit. Hand in glove.

"You okay?" she asked.

"If you keep rescuing me, I'm going to have to turn in my man card."

Her smile was gentle as a light blanket on a cool desert night. "Everyone needs a helping hand now and again. Even the most independent men."

The phone in his pocket buzzed.

He was so busy staring into Kaia's eyes that he almost didn't register that his cell had vibrated, shouldn't have answered it, but upon the third buzz, he couldn't resist. He'd been waiting on news from his staff about the pending contract with a silver mining company in China. If this deal went through, he would be twenty times richer than his father.

And that felt good. Damn good.

"Just a sec," he said, waltzing her over to one side of the dance floor and reaching for his phone.

She glared. "Seriously?"

He held up one finger, motioning for her to give him a minute. Yep. It was from his lawyer. There were several missed calls. Apparently, Phil had tried to phone him, couldn't get through with the spotty cell reception, and ended up texting him a novella. Not a quick read.

A you-gotta-be-kidding-me-right-now expression crossed Kaia's face and she sank her hands on her hips. "Are you seriously phubbing me?"

"Phubbing?"

"Phone snubbing."

"I don't mean to be rude, but my employees and customers expect me to answer texts and emails right away."

"Even at night?"

"Yes."

"Even on the weekends?"

"Yes."

"Even when you're attending a wedding?"

"Yes."

"Bad habit."

"I know."

"You need to set boundaries."

"Boundaries?" he teased. "What are these things you speak of?"

She chuffed out a breath, shook her head ruefully. "I can see I'm not going to change you. Go ahead. Take care of business."

Then she turned and walked away.

Dammit! He switched off his phone and ran after her.

"WAIT, WAIT." RIDGE grabbed her elbow.

At his touch, Kaia's pulse quickened. If there was one thing her accident had taught her, it was how to set boundaries and stick to them. Phubbing was unacceptable behavior in her book. Yes, he was a busy and important man.

But this was a wedding and he'd been dancing with her. It wasn't prima donna behavior to expect his full attention in the moment.

"I'm sorry," he apologized.

Although she insisted on being treated with respect, she wasn't a hard-ass. Turning toward him, she dialed up an all-is-forgiven smile. "Apology accepted."

Relief filled his eyes, and he held out an inviting hand. "Come back and dance with me."

"Did you finish reading your texts?"

"No. That can wait."

"Because of me?"

"Because of you."

She took his hand and he wrapped his right arm around her waist, spun her back out onto the dance floor with the rest of the dancers bopping to a bouncy beat.

"When did you learn how to dance?" she asked.

"Took lessons," he said.

"To meet girls?"

"For business functions. Learned to play golf too."

"Should have guessed. With you, it's all about the job."

Not denying it, he shrugged, as if to say, *what else is there?* "You're cutting a pretty good rug yourself."

"Dancing was part of my rehab."

"I hate you went through that."

"That's life. Bad things happen sometimes."

"But you made lemonade."

"I'm not a whiner. Whining doesn't change things and dwelling on the negative just makes you miserable. No point."

"Casey might be the bride," he said, admiration combed through his voice, "but to me, you're the most beautiful woman in the room."

"That's out of context," she said, struggling not to be charmed.

"I've been thinking it all night."

"I'm sure Archer doesn't agree."

"We're not talking about Archer."

"What *are* we talking about?"

"How you are unequivocally, remarkably gorgeous, and *that* happens to be the least interesting thing about you."

She was flattered, but she didn't want him to know. "How many woman have you used *that* line on?"

"It's not a line." He paused for a long beat. "Not with you."

Her heart flipped. How she wanted to believe him. Instead, she changed the subject. "Is it weird?"

"Is what weird?"

"You and Vivi."

"Why should it be weird?"

"Um . . . I dunno. Maybe because she dumped you for your dad."

"Ten years ago."

"Vivi and your dad—"

"Let's not talk about them. We have such a short time together. Let's enjoy ourselves."

"You're right," she said, wrapping her arms around his neck and dancing closer. It was her only brother's wedding day. Be in the moment. Celebrate!

He tightened his arms around her, and she rested her head on his shoulders, let the music sweep her away. Enjoyed the magic. Savored the experience. Tried not to have any expectations beyond the sights, sound, smells, touch.

She inhaled him. He smelled so good.

His head was bowed, her chin tilted up. Looking into his eyes, her heart pounded. He held on to her hand, his grip both tender and firm. His other arm was resting at her waist, just above her hip.

Their bodies were close, not scandalously close for the crowd they were in, but still, Kaia was certain someone would say something about how close she was dancing with Ridge.

Let 'em talk. Tonight, she didn't give a damn.

They swayed to the music, gliding as if they'd been born to dance together. He interlaced his fingers with hers.

His bow tie was in the direct line of her vision. It looked so whimsical, that satiny black bow against his tanned skin.

The tip of her shoe caught on a crack in the cement floor. Her knee bobbled and she stumbled.

"Gotcha," he said, his arms going around her completely, hugging her tight.

"Why look." She laughed. "This time you saved me."

Her blood was churning and her brain was humming and she just knew she was going to do something very stupid tonight, but she didn't care.

His breath smelled of cinnamon mints, and heated her cheek. His intoxicating bay rum and cardamom scent filled every space in her head.

He was hope and adventure and pure sex on two legs. She raised her eyes to his as if he was the answer to every prayer she'd ever prayed.

The music stopped. The band taking a break. People drifted away. Heading for the bar or more wedding cake during the lull.

Kaia and Ridge stood welded to the dance floor, anchored by each other's gaze. He was staring at her as enrapt as she was.

It was heady. Knowing she'd tacked down his attention. He looked slightly breathless, as if he'd run to catch a bus, and his hair was tousled, and yet, he was handsomer than ever.

Transfixed, Kaia gulped.

What was happening to her? Why these feelings? Why now? Why Ridge?

She knew why Cinderella fled when the clock struck midnight. It wasn't just because her coach was turning into a pumpkin. There was much more to it than that. Old Cindy had been downright terrified by the promise of possibilities of what might happen if she did not run away.

Kaia's heart thundered and a panic bloomed in her chest. She had to leave him before she did something irreversible. "Thanks for the dance," she croaked. "It was . . . fun, but um . . . I gotta go."

"You're leaving?" Disappointment tinged his eyes.

"Um, yeah." She started backing up. "I gotta get up early."

"Tomorrow is Sunday."

So it was. "I have lots of animals to feed. It takes time." Okay, lame excuse—she acknowledged the lameness. She'd already paid a neighbor to take care of the critters while she was away.

He moved toward her.

"Bye," she chirped, waved a hand, spun around, and took off, her airway constricted and shots of bright white lights whirling before her eyes.

She pushed her way through the throng, and all she could see were strangers, even though she knew almost all of them. Faces blurred, dropped out of focus. Voices grew louder, amplified inside her head, filled with mindless, numbing chatter. She stumbled again, regained her balance, felt her heart chug.

Antsy to get away from Ridge, from her subterranean feelings, Kaia ran.

But she couldn't outrun herself.

She raced into the shadows, headed for where she'd left her Tundra parked outside the chapel. Stopped when she got there, saw numerous vehicles surrounding it. She wasn't getting out of here without making half a dozen people move their cars. That meant tracking them down.

Shoot.

She heard footsteps behind her, hoped it wasn't Ridge, and ducked deeper into the shadows around the side of the barn. Stood with her back and arms plastered against the wooden wall, trying to catch her breath and make sense of the emotions whirling around inside of her.

"Snap out of it," she scolded. "You're overreacting. Letting your imagination go wild."

She stood panting, and after a while, when she could finally draw in a deep breath, she slipped into the darkened chapel and climbed the steps to the overhead loft. She would hole up in here until people started leaving and she could get her truck out. She couldn't go back to the party.

Couldn't let anyone see just how much dancing with Ridge Lockhart had unraveled her.

Chapter 14

PUZZLED, Ridge waited a minute before following Kaia into the chapel. If she needed space, he would give it to her. On the other hand, if she was upset, he wanted to ease her troubled mind.

Thing is, he wasn't sure what he'd done to upset her. One minute they'd been dancing and having a good time; the next, she'd looked completely panic-stricken and couldn't get away from him fast enough.

Was it the fact he'd gotten an erection? He'd tried not to press right up against her when they'd been dancing, but the dance floor had been packed, necessitating close contact.

And how did a guy go about apologizing for that. *Sorry you're so hot I got a boner?* No, definitely do not say that.

It was a lot to take in. The fact that he wanted to bed his best friend's kid sister more than he'd ever wanted to bed anyone. It felt disloyal, taboo, and incredibly hot.

The chapel was dark save for the party lights shining in the windows. The band started up a rendition of "You Are the Best Thing."

Ridge pulled the door closed behind him and sauntered inside. Heard his boots scraping against the floor, inhaled the dry smell of wood and hymnals, felt the boards creak under his weight.

He walked the aisle, looking down each row to see if Kaia was skulking in a pew. She wasn't on the first floor, but he'd seen her come in here. She had to be in the loft.

Should he leave her be or go to her?

His brain told him to split, but his body, his bones, his blood, pushed him up the ladder to the loft.

His pulse quickened with each step and he realized it had been quite some time since he'd been this excited. She was not playing hide-and-seek. He'd scared her. He should go away and leave her in peace.

Smart thought. He would do that.

He didn't.

The loft platform was so close to the roof that he had to duck his head as he stepped off the ladder. He could see her sitting in the open window surrounded by wedding gifts, knees drawn to her chest, bridesmaid dress hugged around her legs, gazing out at the party below, the moon glow casting her in silhouette.

"Kaia?" he murmured. "Is it okay if I sit with you?"

"It's your family's chapel," she said. "I can't stop you."

He paused. "Do you want me to go?"

She didn't say anything for so long he was already backing down the ladder when she spoke. "I don't mind if you stay."

Not a rousing "yes, sit down, take a load off," but he would take what he could get.

He eased over, careful not to rise up and whack his head on the beams. He sat next to her, not touching her, stretched out his legs to dangle them out the wide-open hayloft-style window.

"Hey," he said, trying not to sound breathless. Why was he breathless? Had to be the heat. He wasn't used to it anymore.

"Hey, yourself."

"Will you get irritated with me if I ask how you're doing?"

Her mouth curled into a half smile. She sat looking sexy in a fancy dress and bare feet. He wondered if she had any idea the effect she had on him. "I'm not irritated."

He sat with her, saying nothing, a cocoon of darkness and silence surrounding them. It was as if they were on a completely different planet than the people at the party in the barn across the way. Just the two of them, snug and warm.

Intimate.

Crazy how intimate.

In a little more than thirty-six hours, Kaia Alzate had turned his world upside down. Kaia of the sexy laugh, sweet smile, and rocking hot bod.

"I made a mistake," he said.

"What mistake?"

"Waiting so long to come back home. I didn't realize . . ."

She inhaled audibly, her chest lifting, those gorgeous breasts rising high and pert. "What?"

"Never mind." How could he begin to tell her he regretted not being here to watch her grow into womanhood? Regretted all those moments they could have had together that they could never get back. Regretted he hadn't realized how much she truly meant to him until now.

"You're worried about your dad?" she guessed wrongly.

He took her comment as an excuse, because he was worried about Duke's health. No matter how big a jackass his father might be, Ridge cared about him. "He's drinking too much, and he needs to drop about thirty pounds. Archer told me he's got high blood pressure . . ."

Kaia squeezed his hand, offered up a reassuring smile. "You're here for him now. That's all that matters."

"Not for long."

"But you'll be back. You won't let another ten years pass before you come home."

"I'm headed for China after this," he said. "I'll be there for at least six months. Once the contract negotiations are over, I'll be staying in Beijing to train them in my drilling technique."

"Oh," she said, sounding disappointed. "I see."

"I have to go. We're about to sign a huge contract. That's what the phone messages were all about. I've been working my entire life for this. I even taught myself Mandarin."

"Really?" She giggled. "That's impressive. Say something in Mandarin for me."

"Nǐ hěn piào liang."

"What does it mean?"

It meant, *you are very beautiful*, but he wasn't going to tell her that. "It's just a greeting."

"Nǐ hěn piào liang," she parroted. "This is so cool. When did you find time to learn Mandarin?"

"Audio recordings when I commute."

"You don't waste a second, do you?"

"Not if I can help it."

"I'm happy for you." Her kind eyes cradled his. "It's everything you've ever wanted."

"Yes," he said, but he couldn't help thinking his victory felt empty.

How could that be? Making a success of his life was all he'd ever wanted. Making more money than Duke. Showing his father he didn't need a lick of his help to make it on his own.

He couldn't hold on to her gaze any longer. Looking at her stirred impossible feelings he didn't even know how to describe. Wasn't sure he even wanted to feel them. Feelings complicated things.

"It wasn't such a bad idea," he said.

Kaia frowned. "What wasn't?"

Ridge knocked on the low ceiling above their heads. "A wedding chapel for cowboy weddings. Gotta give Vivi props for that."

"It was a pretty wedding."

"I'm not keen on the idea that they built it so close to my house and parcel of land. But I'm pretty sure that was just Duke getting his dig in."

"Maybe your father figured that since you were never going to claim the house, why *not* build the chapel here?" she said, playing devil's advocate. "And it's not like you're home for good. Even if you manage to smooth things over and return to Cupid occasionally, as much as you work, I imagine it won't be that often. So the chapel isn't really going to be a problem."

"Probably not." He studied her, wondering how she felt about that.

She shifted, glanced away. "I'm thirsty. Are you thirsty?"

"I could go get us something from the bar."

"Or we could go make coffee at your house. I saw a brand-new coffeemaker when we were over there yesterday."

His body tightened in the most masculine way.

She was suggesting they go to his house. Was she sending him a signal? And she was suggesting coffee. As if she wanted to stay up late. Or was it just wishful thinking on his part?

He nodded. "Or we could do that."

She got up and eased past him, headed for the steps.

It was all Ridge could do not to ogle her ass. It was a losing battle considering it was a world-class ass and she filled out that dress so well. Okay, cards on the table, he didn't even try not to stare.

The way her rump moved stole the breath right out of his lungs. He took off after her. Caught up with her at the chapel porch. Took her arm, guided her around the parked vehicles and across the patch of ground between the chapel and his house. The lights were out, but the door was not locked.

He put a hand to the small of her back and guided her inside, switched on the lamps, but drew the curtains to block the lights from the outside. He didn't want anyone wandering over.

And locked the door behind them.

Kaia's eyes were wide when he turned back to her, but she didn't protest the locked door.

He led the way into the kitchen. "I'll put the coffee on."

"I can do it."

"I know that," he said. "But I'm gonna do it. Have a seat."

He searched in the pantry, trying to figure out where Vivi put the coffee when she'd stocked his house. Finally found it in the refrigerator. He loaded up the coffeemaker with a dark roast.

He bustled around making the coffee, poured them into identical mugs, brought it to the kitchen table. Sat beside her.

They did not speak. He could hear the steady ticking of the clock on the wall, marking off the seconds. Tried to think of something neutral to say as she stared into her coffee cup.

Ridge cleared his throat. "When do you graduate from vet school?"

"Next summer, if all goes according to plan."

"What could hamstring it?"

"Money." She shrugged, a casual gesture but he sensed something more behind it. "But if it takes longer, it takes longer. There's no rush."

Ridge sipped his coffee. She blew across the top of hers to cool it. He thought about offering her money. But she was so proud and independent he didn't want to offend her.

"You want to make this an Irish coffee?" he asked. "I saw some Baileys in the fridge."

She lowered her lashes, dished up a sly grin. "Are you trying to get me liquored up?"

"I'm trying to get *me* liquored up."

"Why?"

"Do you have any idea how much you throw me off balance?"

"Not any more than you throw me."

Their eyes met.

"I should go." Kaia jumped up suddenly, accidentally kicked the leg of the table, and sent hot coffee sloshing from the mug. It splashed her lap. "Ooh, ooh, hot, hot!"

He set down his cup, leaped up, took hold of her arm and propelled her toward the bathroom. "Get out of those clothes before you get burned. Strip. Get in the shower. Rinse off. Now! I'll see if I can find something for you to wear."

"Okay."

He closed the door after her. Heard her rustling around. His pulse pounded. "You okay?"

"I'm fine. Getting in the shower now. Find me some clothes."

"On it," he said, even though he had no idea what, if any, clothes were in the house.

He went to the master bedroom and was surprised to see the queen-sized bed he'd caught Vivi and his father having sex in a decade ago had been replaced with a new king-sized bed.

More props for Vivi. He was certain she was behind the bed change. Remorse? Her attempt at seeking his forgiveness? She need not have worried. He'd forgiven her years ago. It was his father he couldn't quite forgive.

He stepped to the closet, found a brand-new white terry cloth bathrobe. It would be huge on Kaia, but it was something to cover up with.

Ridge rapped on the bathroom door, but the shower was running, so he didn't know if she'd heard him or not. He tried the knob.

It was unlocked.

He opened the door, intended on resting the robe over the towel rack, but he caught sight of her naked body through the clear glass shower door.

Mesmerized, he couldn't move.

Her eyes were closed and she had her face stuck under the spray of water. His jaw dropped. The fantasies he'd been having about her paled in comparison to the sizzling woman standing there. Instantly, he got hard.

Leave!

He left the robe and scooped up her coffee-stained bridesmaid dress from the floor and ran out of there. He paused in the hallway to take a few deep breaths before heading into the laundry room, but then realized the dress should be dry-cleaned.

What now?

He paced, thinking of her clad only in a robe. Stop it. No expectations. She'd come here for coffee, not sex. But he couldn't help wishing and hoping that she had ulterior motives.

To what end? A onetime sexy romp?

Kaia deserved better than that. She deserved happily-ever-after, and he was not the guy who could provide that. He was going to China for six months, and in the fall she'd be headed back to College Station to finish her schooling.

Bad timing all the way around.

Ah hell, how had he gotten himself into this situation? Ridge ran his palm up the back of his neck.

Better question, how was he going to get himself out?

Chapter 15

Ridge was waiting for Kaia in the living room when she got out of the bathroom, her skin damp from the shower.

The sight of him slid into view before she had fully braced herself for it.

He was leaning back in the expansive leather chair, holding a tumbler filled with an inch of Baileys Irish Cream over ice. He sat in a relaxed posture, but his eyes were sharp, focused, a blue-jeaned executive in his Texas tuxedo. Sharp as a honed blade in a suede sheath.

She opened her mouth to say just that, but then stopped, put the tip of her tongue to the apex of her upper lip. He might take it the wrong way and that bothered her. Why?

Unless . . .

Kaia shook off the thought and tightened the belt on the oversized terry cloth bathrobe. Felt completely naked underneath the heat of his frank perusal.

"Have a seat." He waved at the matching chair next to him.

Not really knowing why, other than he'd issued an edict, she sat.

He stabbed his fingers through his hair. Showing his nervousness for the first time. Ah, the iron man did have a chink in his armor.

The air between them was thick with tension a chain saw couldn't whittle.

He lifted his head. Slammed his gaze into her like a head-on collision.

Kaia realized she was trembling. Hoping he hadn't noticed, she said, "You didn't put my dress in the washer, did you?"

"No. I was going to wash it, but realized it was dry-clean only."

"Oh whew. That dress cost me two weeks' salary." It dawned on her then that she had nothing else to wear home. It had to be either the coffee-stained dress or the bathrobe. Clearly, she'd go with the coffee-stained dress.

"I poured you a drink." He nodded at a second tumbler of Baileys sitting on the small circular table situated between the two leather chairs. "Figured you could use it."

"I'm not much of a drinker."

He raised an eyebrow. "No?"

She crossed her arms over her chest, feeling exposed. "I don't like the way alcohol makes me feel."

"How's that?"

"Different. Unlike myself."

"Isn't that the purpose of drinking?"

"But I like being who I am," she said.

He snorted, as if he was jealous of that or didn't believe her, and took another swallow of the Baileys.

This wasn't smart. She shouldn't have come here. She had no idea what he wanted from her.

Or what she wanted from him. It was all muddled. Her childhood crush mixed with this overpowering, but momentary lust.

And the Song of the Soul Mate. Don't forget that.

"Screw it," Ridge said, set down his drink, reached across the space between them, and yanked her into his arms.

Kaia gasped, startled and thrilled at the same time. Her head swam. She loved being in Ridge Lockhart's take-charge embrace.

His mouth hovered above hers, full and lush and beautiful. He smelled of Baileys, coffee, and the cinnamon mints served at the wedding—strong, bracing, and spicy sweet.

The moment his lips touched hers, that crazy swell of humming buzzed along the back of her brain again, louder and more insistent than it had been the night before.

It was a steady throb. A relentless river of vibration. A sweet rhythmic whir that simultaneously lulled her and shocked her into alertness.

Him. Him. Him.

Kaia couldn't quite remember how they got from the living room to his bedroom. Kissing was involved, and a slow two-step to the tune of the humming in her head. She floated on a current, every murmur, every caress, every sigh, colored with dreamy magic.

"I'll take that Baileys now," she said, once they were in his bedroom.

"Do you want to feel like someone else?"

She already did, a strange new woman eager to explore a provocative land. "Liquid courage," she clarified.

He stared at her a long moment, his eyes dark and unreadable. "We don't have to do this."

It wasn't a question of want, but rather, pulsing, unrelenting need. She needed to be sated. She needed to be with *this* man. Hungered for him and him alone. Craved him.

"Yes," she croaked. "I'm sure."

"Be right back." He vanished and quickly returned with the tumbler of Baileys.

Their fingers brushed in the handoff. Kaia inhaled a sharp, urgent breath.

"Yeah," he whispered. "Me too."

The glass trembled in her hand. She held on tightly, hoping he wouldn't notice. Once she'd regained a modicum of control, she brought the drink to her lips, took a bracing sip. Winced at the cloyingly sweet, creamy taste.

She set the glass down on a dresser, felt the warm liquid slide through her bloodstream, closed her eyes, and slowed her breathing.

"Kaia?"

Gradually, she fluttered her eyes open, shifted her gaze to meet his, and the world stopped spinning. Either that, or it sped up so fast it felt like it had frozen still.

The humming in her head spread, blooming, growing until it filled her entire skull with ethereal song.

This was insanity.

She knew that. It was simply ringing in her ears. Except the noise wasn't coming from her ears. It emanated from the base of her brain. A primal, eternal sound, heavenly as harp music.

Having sex with Ridge would be a game changer. He would mark her indelibly. She knew it as surely as she knew her own name.

There was danger here. She could fall in love with him. He could break her heart. Mostly likely *would* break her heart. He could break her in a way from which she might not ever recover.

And yet, she wanted him. Uncontrollably. The need was relentless, pushing at her with gusto and force.

He opened his arms and she threw herself into them. She could no more resist him than the ocean's tide could resist the pull of the moon.

So she just surrendered. Let the tide come in. Allowed the waves of emotion, need, and longing slap her into swiftly moving currents.

He pulled her against his chest and his mouth claimed hers again, and sweet joyous relief surged through her.

She felt a click, a solid settling in. As if they fit like puzzle pieces. It felt so right in his arms, and wrong for her to be anywhere else *but* here.

Desperately, she reached up to cradle his cheek with her palm. He made a guttural noise low in his throat and deepened their kiss.

She thirsted for him, for his touch, for his taste, for his sound. She was the lock and he was the key and together the entire world was open to them.

The strangest, inexplicable sensation came over her, a feeling that without him she would forever surf adrift on the ocean. A rudderless boat lost at sea.

"Kaia," he whispered into her mouth. "My sweet, sweet Kaia."

She tugged his head down, encouraging him to take the kiss as far as it would go. Frantically, she helped him get naked, stripping off his jacket, pawing at the buttons on his shirt.

It felt both odd and comfortable to be standing before him, working at his clothes with hot, fumbling fingers. As if they were lovers.

Could she use the word *lover* for a onetime hookup? Probably not. Lovers suggested a long-term relationship, and that's all this was, a onetime thing. Soothe the ache. Scratch the itch. Douse the fire.

The front of his white cotton shirt parted, giving her a glimpse of his tanned skin, toned muscles, and a sprinkling of dark chest hair.

She twirled a finger in the soft springy tuft; his golden muscles tensed beneath her touch. She heard his harsh intake of breath, and the thrum of her pounding pulse.

His warm skin turned silky beneath her palms as she slid them up his chest, hooked her thumbs into the seams of his shirt at the armpits, and stripped the shirt from his broad shoulders. Let it drift to the floor.

And there she had it, an unobstructed view of his gloriously ripped torso. Heat radiated off him in waves, blistering into her, burning her up.

Hot desire hummed at the base of her brain. Swelled. Grew. Vibrated down her spine and throughout her entire body until she was nothing but a single quivering string of sexual energy.

"Unbelievable." She exhaled a puff of pent-up air.

"You're what's unbelievable," he said in a dusky voice full of hidden meaning and dark mystery.

She sighed. It was a shaky sound, uncertain and nervous.

He ducked his head, peered down at her. Smiled a devastating smile that sent her heart skip hopping. Checkerboard heart.

Jump. Jump. Jump. Jump. *Queen me.*

Ridge laughed as if he knew exactly what she was thinking, and his navy blue eyes churned, mystic and dark as the night sky.

"Your laugh sounds rusty," she said, wanting the emphasis off her. "Like you don't use it enough."

"I don't," he admitted. "I'm serious about my business, and I work eighty hours a week. Not much time for laughter."

She wanted to tell him how sad that was, but she hated to derail what was happening between them. Especially when he was looking at her as if he couldn't wait to eat her up.

Yum.

He cradled her jaw in his palm, tilted her face up, and feathered a line of blazing kisses from her earlobe to her chin.

Kaia moaned softly at the sweet tingles spreading throughout her body. She parted her lips, leaned into his hard, delicious chest.

More. She wanted more. Needed so much more from him.

Reaching up, she wrapped her arms around his neck, entwined her fingers, tugged his head lower, and planted her mouth against his. A groan of pleasure escaped him, and she could taste the sweet flavor of Baileys on both their tongues.

With each sip from her lips, he tantalized her with a sequence of leisurely kisses, escalating pressure and heat. This was different from the hot, urgent kiss they'd shared beside his plane. That had been frantic, spur-of-the-moment, fueled by the fire of secrecy and situation.

But these kisses? These here? They were an invitation—a tantalizing temptation, a slow seduction, an unhurried waltz. These kisses suggested dazzling possibilities of cool sheets on a sultry night and infinite, wide-open bliss.

At once, they pressed closer into each other, the material of her terry cloth robe rubbing against his bare chest. Her breast growing warm and heavy, her nipples hardening.

He eased the robe down, planting kisses from her neck to her shoulder as he went, first one side and then the other. A crop of kisses, planting seeds of lust she knew he would be harvesting soon.

She shivered.

"Cold?"

"Hot."

"Like a fever shiver?"

"Like a fever shiver," she echoed.

"Good." His smile was wolfish in the dim light, and then he kissed the hollow of her throat.

His cell phone rang.

"Do you need to get that?" she whispered.

"No," he said, finding the cell in his pants pocket and switching it off without even checking the caller ID.

"Are you sure?"

"Absolutely. Right now, you're the only thing that matters."

"I don't mind if you need to take the call."

"I mind." He kissed her again.

She drowned in the sweetness of his heat, the haunting humming in her head, the heartrending beauty of here and now.

"What do you want?" he whispered, brushing his fingers against her temples and peering deeply into her eyes.

"I want you." She snuggled against his chest.

He kissed her forehead, his lips warm on her skin. "No. What do you really, really want?" He placed a hand over her heart. "Deep down inside."

"Sex!"

"Don't be glib."

"Why not? You're glib. In fact, you're the master of glib."

"But *you're* not. Tell me, Kaia. What do you want?"

"You," she said. "I want you to take me to bed and do all kinds of naughty things to me. Make no mistake, Ridge Lockhart. I'm not some fragile thing. I like a good time as much as the next woman. This is about sex. Let's just have a good time. I don't want anything more from you than that."

"As you wish," he said, took her hand, and led her toward the bed.

Chapter 16

KAIA didn't want anything more than sex.

He should have been relieved. If any other woman had said that, he *would* be relieved. Instead he felt . . .

Ridge searched his brain, looking for the word that described what he was feeling. He was such a master at sweeping emotions under the rug he often had trouble identifying them when they cropped up. He was fairly familiar with anger, but with subtler emotions, tender emotions? Well, he was inept.

Then he saw an impish smile tug the corners of her full mouth. Overwhelmed, he caught sight of their images in the bureau mirror on the other side of the bed.

Finally identified what he was feeling.

Disappointment.

He was disappointed with her for *not* wanting more, and with himself for not protesting when she said she only wanted sex. Because *he* wanted more than sex, had known it, and denied it, from the second he'd seen her again.

That split-second clash with his mirror doppelgänger opened his eyes, his mind, and his heart and triggered a sudden, staggering question.

Who was he?

A man who skimmed along the surface of life, collecting, achieving, constantly chasing success, but finding it was never enough? Or he could be the man who searched for something deeper, more meaningful?

Was he the guy who forever bailed out when relationships got complicated? Or could he be the man who dug in and found a way to make things work when he finally found the woman he wanted?

Was he going to let fear of intimacy define his life? Or could he take a chance, go out on a limb, and commit to something that scared the hell out of him?

A terrifying thought swirled through his head.

What if he'd avoided love for so long that he couldn't undo the pattern? What if his path was carved in stone, and he could not veer from it even if he wanted to? What if he laid his heart on the line and Kaia ultimately rejected him?

What if he was incapable of love?

What then?

Before he could fully explore the stunning new realization, she was nibbling on his chin, driving all thoughts and fears from his mind. All except one.

Kaia.

He had to have her.

No woman had ever derailed him like this. He was crazy with need for her, blind and deaf with it.

He'd even turned off his cell phone for her. And he hardly ever turned off his cell phone for any reason.

She sank against his chest. He could feel the steady beat of her heart pounding into him.

The robe hung halfway down her shoulders, still held in place by the tie at her waist. His fingers reached for the sash, and he slowly unknotted it.

A soft sigh spilled from her lips as the sash slipped to the floor, a sweet sound that stirred the air and his arousal. One flick of his finger sent the robe falling, pooling around her feet, and exposing smooth creamy flesh.

Leaving her wearing nothing but a pair of skimpy white lace panties and the gold heart-shaped necklace at her throat.

Pure.

She looked so pure. Pristine. Perfect.

He stepped back to admire her in the light. Felt his pulse quicken. Damn, she was beautiful. How had he gotten so lucky?

Her eyes smiled, gentle and accepting and filled with kindness.

Ridge rested his hands on her hips, felt her body heat seep through his palms. Holding her steady, he slowly sank to his knees, tasting her with hot, damp, open-mouth kisses. Gliding from her pert nipples, to her taut belly, on down.

God, she was magnificent, with her curvaceous hips, firm thighs, shapely calves, and coltish ankles.

And scarred hip.

He drew in a deep breath at the sight of the long, purplish scar, a bifurcating scar that ran from her right hip bone down to the top of her right thigh.

His heart ached for her. Felt the squeeze of her pain deep within his soul. Life was so damn unfair. Such a wonderful person like Kaia should never have to know this level of misery. More than anything in the world, he wished he could erase the suffering she'd gone through. Make it disappear.

Tenderly, he pressed his lips to her scar.

"Don't," she whispered, shifting away from him.

He raised his head. Looked up into her face, saw fear, uncertainty, and hesitation in her eyes. "Does it still hurt?"

She shook her head. "Don't you dare feel sorry for me. I don't want or need your pity."

"I don't feel sorry for you."

"Don't you?" Her tone turned accusatory.

"No," he said, mildly surprised by her reaction. Where was this coming from? "Why would you even think that?"

She closed her eyes, swallowed visibly.

"I . . ." Eyes still squeezed shut, and breathing shallowly, she licked her lips.

"Yes?" he whispered.

She shook her head.

Okay, clearly she wasn't ready to talk about what was bothering her. She didn't owe him an explanation. He wouldn't push her. Letting the topic drop, he went back to kissing her and found his way to where he'd been before, this time avoiding her scar.

His lips hovered at the waistband of her panties, the last thin barrier of her modesty. He was on his knees now, pressing his face against her, smelling her, the fresh, glorious scent of his woman.

His.

He was playing with fire and he knew it. Didn't care.

Ridge pressed a kiss against the light fabric, heard her sharp intake of breath, felt her thread her fingers through his hair, gently twist. Her body trembled against him.

"Ridge," she whispered. "I want . . . please . . . let's—"

"Gotcha." He grunted, knowing exactly what she meant. If they didn't get to the bed soon, they were both going to explode.

He wrapped an arm around her waist and stood up, swinging her up into his arms as he went. He carried her to the bed, laid her out on the mattress, stared down at her.

She sat up, reaching for his waistband, tugged him closer, fumbled with his belt buckle. He chuckled as she ripped and yanked, undoing the snap of his pants, tugging down the zipper.

"Hang on," he said, stripping off his pants and hopping around to pull them over his shoes.

Kaia laughed, the sound choked with joy and frustration. "Hurry, hurry."

He kicked off the shoes, wrestled out of his pants, landed on the mattress beside her.

Snatching his face between her palms, she laughed again and buried him in a greedy spree of kisses.

He tipped her onto her back, straddled her, and gazed down at her, awestruck by the fact she was in his bed.

"Protection?" she asked.

"Right here." He leaned over, grabbed his pants, found his wallet, and pulled out a roll of condoms.

"A whole roll?"

"I believe in being prepared."

Her giggle bounced around the room. "I like that about you. Now get that underwear off, mister."

"Yes, ma'am," he said in a cowboy drawl and accommodated her, stripping off his boxer briefs and tossing them over his shoulder.

Starlight drifted through the raised shade of the long window on the left side of the bed. Her breasts rose on each inhale, the nipples pink and peaked, shining in stardust glow. The lower part of her body lay cloaked in shadow, her hands cradled against her low abdomen, covering the scrap of panty.

Her eyes grew solemn as she watched him watching her. Her breath was so slow and shallow it seemed she was scarcely breathing at all. The blend of light and shadow cast a spell, weaving wispy magic around them.

He dipped his head, getting closer, peering into her face. Her full lips puckered, waiting for his kiss, and her dark chocolate eyes glistened.

Tenderly, he sewed kisses over her mouth.

Soft, light, teasing. He touched his tongue to her upper lip, and she parted her teeth, willingly, eagerly, letting him in.

Eyes wide-open, staring into her. Visibly, Kaia gulped and shuttered her eyes close, allowing her lashes to drift down.

Was she overcome by the intensity of their contact? Or was she trying to hide her feeling?

He pulled his mouth from hers, gently traced his index finger in a small circle against her temple. "What's going on inside that head of yours?"

The ghost of a smile tucked her lips up. "Shh. I'm savoring the moment since it won't come again."

Her comment startled him, but she was right, this was definitely a onetime thing. He lived in Calgary now, and she was wrapped around her family like roots. Long-distance romances failed.

Especially since he worked eighty hours a week, fifty-two weeks a year. Lockhart Enterprises was his focus.

Everything else took second place.

For how long? whispered a quiet voice at the back of his head. *For how long?*

He shoved that voice down the laundry chute of his mind. He'd been an overachiever all his life. It's who he was. He couldn't change that. When he had nothing to do, he grew listless and dissatisfied. He needed to be valuable, to distinguish himself, to be admired for his accomplishments.

That's what drove him. What would always drive him.

Without his company, his job, he had no identity. He'd be a failure. And more than anything in this world, Ridge feared failing.

Yeah? Try not to fail at giving Kaia a good time.

Exactly, head in the game.

He took one of her nipples into his mouth, suckled it.

Kai shuddered beneath him, a hiss in her breath. "Is this really happening?" she murmured sounding dazed. "I'm in bed with big brother's best friend?"

"You're here, sweetheart. Yes, you're here with me." He shifted, moved to stake her lips again, irresistibly drawn to capture her full bottom lip between his teeth, pull her into him.

She moaned heedlessly, arched her back, and pressed into him. "Oh yes. More."

"Whatever you need."

He drew her bottom lip deeper into his mouth, flicked his tongue along it with sweeping strokes, stoking her engines, revving her up.

She ran her tongue over his upper lip, exploring him the same way he explored her—fervently, all-in, holding nothing back.

Ridge chuckled at her enthusiasm. But of course, that was Kaia. She did everything at full tilt. What a woman!

Her palms cupped the back of his head and she coaxed him deeper into the kiss. Her lips held the promise of exciting things to come.

More.

He had to have more—more of her taste, her smell, the daring thrust and parry of their tongues dueling together. More of the nimble slide and glide of heat and moisture.

Each kiss, each moan, each touch sent escalating fever burning brighter, hotter, bolder. His body urged him to rush, to push, to gush toward the pinnacle, but he would not.

This moment was special.

Kaia was special. He was determined to take his time. He wanted . . . no he *needed* . . . to travel every inch of her, explore her, fully experiencing her delightful dips and curves.

He would memorize every dip and curve, every angle and plane. To find what made her hiss or giggle or sigh. When he should push, when he should back off.

But all that required strength of character and a depth of self-control he wasn't sure he possessed.

"What is it?" Kaia asked. "What's wrong?"

It was only then he realized he'd stopped kissing her and had shifted off to one side.

She sat up, looking confused and disappointed, ran a hand through her mussed hair. Her shoulders tensed and she bit down on her bottom lip, that lush bottom lip that had just been tucked between his teeth. "Have I done something to upset you?"

"No," he said fiercely. "Never."

"Then why did you stop?"

"Taking my time."

"Making me lose my mind." She feigned peevishness, screwing up her face in a pout that managed to look wholly seductive.

"You're not the only one losing your mind." He growled.

"So let's go crazy together." She reached for him.

He moved back. "We have to slow this down or you're not going to get a thing out of it."

"Don't have much faith in me, huh?"

"Don't have much faith in myself."

"You underestimate us both."

"No, you overestimate my self-control. Especially when you look and smell and taste so good."

She lowered her head to hide a shy smile, and even in the dim light he could tell she was blushing.

Throbbing need hit him harder than ever. Bent him over like a willow tree in a windstorm. Whirled him around. Dusted him up. Sending him to a place he'd never been before and where he wasn't quite certain what to do, even as every cell in his body vibrated with energy and vitality.

He was kidding himself. He could no more slow this down than he could hop a speeding freight train. Either way he went, he was going to get obliterated.

They were both sitting up now. Tailor style. Face-to-face on top of the covers. They locked eyes. Their lips lightly parted.

Tension stretched taut.

Kaia reached out and placed her palm on his chest, fingers spread. A beautiful starfish of a hand, the back of her knuckles pressed securely into his skin.

Slowly, she sent her fingers crawling down his torso, tickling and teasing him with each deliberate stroke. Delight lit her eyes, her fire within blazing hot and ready.

She might be eager, and willing, but when her hand reached his waist, she pulled back and cast him a sidelong glance, canting her head, evaluating, trying to gauge his reaction.

He wondered how experienced she was. Archer had told him Kaia had not ever had a serious boyfriend, that she'd been too dedicated to her studies and her goal of becoming a veterinarian. That, he understood.

But was she . . . could she be . . . He certainly did not want to take her virginity. If she'd waited this long to surrender her innocence, she needed to give herself to the right person. The man who would be her forever mate.

"Kaia," he said, surprised to hear his voice crack. "Is this . . . am I . . ." He swallowed hard. "Your first?"

She laughed then, a sound full of amusement. "You think I'm a virgin?"

Chagrined, he backtracked. "Archer told me you'd never had a serious boyfriend."

"Archer doesn't know everything, but I'm twenty-six. What? Did you think I was waiting around, pining over you?"

"No," he said. "Of course not. It's just that you seemed a little . . ." Oh crap, he was mangling this.

"Green?" she supplied.

"Inexperienced."

"Granted, I'm not the most worldly woman in the world," she said. "Which is part of what's got me hesitating. You're used to sleek, sophisticated, city women. You've dated a lot. You know your way around the bedroom. Me? I'm a farm girl with no pretentions of being anything more than I am."

"That's what I lo . . . er . . . like about you," he said, catching himself before he said the word *love*. Why did that word burn hot in his throat?

"I'm afraid I won't be enough for you. I'm pretty simple when it comes to sex. I'm not much into toys or outlandish bedroom outfits or fetishes or . . . oh who am I kidding. I've never tried any of those things. Maybe I would be into them." She shrugged. "Who knows?"

"We don't need any of those things," he said. "*I* don't need any of those things. Hell woman, those white cotton panties of yours have me twisted inside out. I don't think I could handle you with whips and chains and a black bustier."

"I *do* know how to crack a bullwhip," she offered. "If it's a bedroom skill you prefer."

"The only thing I prefer is you. Just as you are."

"Really?" Her smile was so authentic, so genuine, so full of relief, it melted his heart to a hot puddle in the square center of his chest.

"Sooo . . ." She blew out her breath through puffed cheeks. "Where do we go from here?"

"Where do you want to go?'

She reached over for the roll of condoms he'd dropped on the nightstand. Ripped one open with a quick, tearing motion, cleared her throat and positioned herself on her knees in front of him.

Her fingers were hot as they manipulated the latex over his erection. She met his gaze, her eyes brilliantly dark and inviting.

Groaning, Ridge wrapped his arms around her, flipped her over onto her back beneath him.

They stared into each other. He moistened his lips. She licked hers.

"I'm so ready for you," she whispered.

He peeled off her panties, touched her, testing. She was moist and swollen, her delicate tissues engorged with desire.

She parted her legs, letting her knees drop to each side, welcoming him in.

Clouds outside the window shifted and an opalescent slice of moonlight draped fresh light over her succulent figure, showing him exactly what she was offering.

Heaven.

He saw clearly her pert, round breasts, nipples ripe and hard with need. Ridge gave those lovely peaks his full attention, each sweep of the tongue, each brush of his fingers spinning her further and further into orbit.

Who was he kidding? He was spinning too. Buzzing. Humming. Whirling with need.

His lips caressed her velvety flesh, smooth and supple and salty. Skimming down her body to the place that made her quiver and shiver and mewl his name.

The dark triangle of hair at the apex of her thighs was a lovely place to lay his head and breathe in the scent of her. She smelled like a mermaid, briny and sunbaked.

"Do you mind that I don't shave down there?" Kaia asked. "I know a lot of women do. Probably most of the women you've been with do, but I . . . well, I'm a natural kind of girl."

"I know that," he said. "And I don't mind. Not in the least. In fact, it's womanly."

"I could wax, if you prefer. I'd do it. For you."

"No. Be yourself. Don't twist yourself up trying to be right for any guy. A man should appreciate you for who you are or take a hike."

"Well." Her breath hitched. "Well."

"Stop worrying about what I like and don't like," he said. "Just relax."

"Easy for you to say. You've probably done this a thousand times."

Ridge sat up again, knocked gently on the top of her head. "What do you take me for? A man whore?"

"C'mon. You're gorgeous. I know women fall at your feet. Are you trying to tell me you don't hook up constantly?"

"I *don't* hook up constantly. I'm too busy."

"But you're a guy. A very virile guy . . ."

"Who doesn't get out as much as you might think."

"Oh no?" She rose up on her elbows, leaned over to claim one of his earlobes between her wicked little teeth.

Tenderly, he pressed her back down on the bed and used his mouth to enter her sweet moist threshold, touching the center of her femininity with his tongue.

Her body tensed, tight as a bowstring drawn taut. A soft moan of sheer pleasure slipped over her teeth as she bit into her bottom lip.

He gave her more of what she was sighing for. Circling and swirling, paying attention to places that gave her goose bumps.

When she was ready, fully wet and open and begging for him, he slid into her soft, yielding, womanly body, and thought insanely, *home.*

He'd finally come home. It was crazy, and he knew it, but he couldn't stop thinking it. *Home. Home. Home.*

She squeezed him, hot and slick and tight.

He struggled for control and a scrap of skill. He was good at this. Or thought he was. But with Kaia, he felt brand-new, a fumbling teenager who didn't know where to start.

Desire drove him. Need seized him. Gnawed and clawed and

scratched. Instinct pushed him hard and fast. Mate. Claim her as his. Shatter her defenses. Dismantle her until she lay quivering and spent in his arms.

But he wasn't a beast, despite his Neanderthal urges. She deserved the best he could offer, and a rough quickie wasn't going to cut it. Not with Kaia. Not with the woman who felt like home. He held his breath, fought to slow down, lessened his movements.

"How are you doing?" His voice sounded deep, alien, raw, and rough. It shocked. The primal quality, the way need had him growling.

"Fine. Fine. More than fine . . ." She laughed shakily. "I'm rapturous."

"Already?"

"I *am* hoping for more." Her cheeks darkened prettily and her expression turned shy, vulnerable. She lowered her eyelids, sent him a soft smile. That look, so sweet and special, seemed designed for him and him alone.

With a mewling noise, she twined her arms and legs around, pulling him deeper into her, sinking her fingernails into his back, urging him on.

"Please," she whispered. "Don't stop. I want *all* of you."

That's all he needed to hear. He gave her everything he had, sinking into her with powerful thrusts. She let out a cry of speechless glee. A sound that stoked his blood and set his cells singing.

He cradled her as he drove into her, his arms around her waist, hands cupping her fanny. She moved with his rhythm as if they were made for each other. As if they'd been doing this for years. As if they'd do it for the rest of their lives.

They gathered speed, rocketing together at an impressive rate, riding, gliding, sliding down the splendid spiral of escalating joy.

Pleasure.

All he wanted was to give her the maximum amount of pleasure. Wanted to leave her wrung out and shaking and thrilled to the core. Wanted to leave her aching and longing to come back for more.

They twirled and spun, caught up in a tornado of their own making, their own whirlwind world. It howled through him, a wild wind—blasting, blistering, blustering, buffering.

He could not speak, could not blink, could not think, save for one inevitable instinctual command. Make this woman his. Brand her. Bind her. Ruin her for any other man but him.

Belong.

He wanted to belong to her. Wanted her to belong to him. Not in a grasping, controlling, possessive way, but in the perfect way two puzzle pieces fit together. Meant to be.

Meant for each other and no one else.

They'd crossed a threshold and no matter what happened from here on out, there was no going back. No undoing what they'd just done.

The thought hit him just as he flipped into the apex of sensation shooting through his body, tearing and ripping at him, pulling him into a million little pieces. Was she shattering with him?

Shambles. He was in glorious shambles.

But he wasn't going to allow himself to completely let go until he was sure she'd achieved her ultimate release. She was his main concern. Her pleasure was his pleasure.

He stared down into her face, their bodies locked around each other. "Look at me, Kaia."

Her eyelids fluttered open.

They peered into each other. Felt the heft and weight of being together like this. One. Joined. Fused. Inescapable.

She moored him, even as she spurred him to the pinnacle, sharing and surrendering and submitting completely. Her delicious scent mingled with his, the smell of the passion, hot and musky and sublime.

He could feel the vibrations rising up her and he captured her mouth with his. Her back arched against him as he dove as deeply into her as he could dive. He drank in the taste of her, inhaled the flavor of her ecstasy—sweet, divine, perfect.

And a second after she cracked, he followed, tumbling after her, his release explosive, shaking him to the core until he was nothing but rubble.

Never in his life had he experienced sheer annihilation of his ego self. He didn't know where he ended and she began. It was total union.

No separation. No boundaries. They were complete. A circle. Whole. Unbroken.

Kaia.

What had she done to him?

He was marked. She'd marked him, scarred him gloriously. She'd given him herself, a precious gift that took his breath and left him trembling.

In his thirty-two years on the planet, he'd been with a lot of women, but none of them had ever left him feeling like this.

No words could describe it. No image could capture the purity of what they'd shared.

"Whew." She expelled a breath of air, and the sound was music to his ears; her chest rose and fell in short ragged gasps.

He was still panting too.

"That was . . . you were . . ." Her cheeks pinked. "Well . . . no words. I have no words."

"Same here." He was speechless and breathless too.

He wrapped his arms around her and tugged her to his chest, rolled over until she was lying on top of him, peering into his eyes. She curled into him, feminine and feline. Their arms and legs entangled. Bound. They were bound together.

God, he loved the feel of her against him. Soft skin. Warm body. He couldn't get enough of holding her.

They lay together for a long time. Holding each other close. Murmuring sweet nothings.

If he'd thought that having sex with her would sate the cravings that had been building since the moment he'd seen her hopping out of that pickup truck, he was dead wrong. Truth be told, he wanted her now more than ever and already could feel his body rousing again, eager for another round of lovemaking.

It had been a very long time since he'd been this unstoppable. He thought those teenage years of a quick postcoital bounce back were long gone. But he hadn't bargained on Kaia Alzate.

His need for her roared like a forest fire, fueled by their lovemaking instead of banked by it. He should have been sated. He was not.

Weird. Wacky. Inexplicable. But there it was.

They were bonded now, in a way he could not express or explain. It was instinctual, primal. They were woven together, not just by their past, but by the potential of a future. A future he'd never before considered.

Chapter 17

"WELL," Kaia said, paused and said, "Well" again, unable to put into words all the thoughts, emotions, and sensations flooding her body and her brain. The sweet humming was receding now, but it still reverberated in her head, lingering like a tuning fork struck hard.

"Deep subject," he teased, and toyed with her hair, a possessive, intimate gesture, reserved for lovers who belonged to each other.

Lovers.

They were lovers.

But not for long. He'd be flying home to Calgary on Monday. No point in doing this again, no matter how badly she might want to. He had his life and she had hers.

She unpeeled herself from the mattress and sat up, dragging the top sheet with her to cover her breasts, unable to meet his eyes. But she could feel the heat of his gaze on her skin.

"Kaia?"

Finally, she looked at him. He was on his side, propped up on one elbow, the sheet draped over his hips, his bare chest on full display.

His eyes were murky, mysterious. His jawline darkened with whiskers. An urge to run her fingers over that scratchy stubble carpeting his angular jaw captured her, and she simply could not resist.

Leaning over, she traced his chin, marveling that she was here with him. Grateful, oh-so-grateful, that they'd had this one wickedly delicious night.

His arms went around her neck and he tugged her gently toward him for a soft kiss. Her lips were sore, a good kind of sore, the best kind of sore.

"Give me a few minutes to recover and we can do this again," he said.

She laughed. "That's a big boast."

"Don't sell yourself short. You inspire me to great heights." He nibbled her earlobe. His warm breath sending shivers over her skin dampened by his tongue.

"I'd love to take you up on that offer," she said, gazing into his eyes. "But if my truck stays parked in front of the chapel after everyone else has gone, it's going to look suspicious."

"You don't want anyone knowing about us?" He kissed her forehead.

"No."

"Why not?"

"You've forgotten how claustrophobic small towns are. I'll never hear the end of it."

"Would that be so bad?" he asked with a wicked laugh. "People gossiping about us?"

"Yes," she said. "Yes it would. I'm the one who has to live here, and live down the reputation you'll stamp me with. I'd be just another silly girl sideswiped by Ridge Lockhart."

"Do you really believe that about me?"

"Doesn't matter what I believe. It's all about perception."

Ridge captured her chin between his fingers, forced her to look him squarely in the eyes. "This was special. *You're* special."

Yeah? Maybe. But so what? He was off to China and she had to finish her degree. "It *was* great sex."

What about the humming? Huh? What about that? Song of the Soul Mate stuff. It meant something. But she wasn't about to tell him about that. Keep it light. It was the only way for her to survive.

"There's more where that came from." He wriggled his eyebrows like Groucho Marx.

"Listen," she said, imagining she was a sophisticated city woman accustomed to casual affairs. "I really do have to go. The Cupid grapevine aside, I have animals that need my attention."

"Ten more minutes," he finagled, snuggling her against his chest.

Her bones were rubber. How easy it would be to sink into him and let nature have her way.

His intoxicating bay rum and hot male scent enveloped her, and all she wanted was to bottle the fragrance and put it in her pocket so she could pull it out and take a big whiff of him whenever she wanted to remember this night.

"Did you know you have a heart-shaped freckle on the back of your neck?" he asked, tracking his finger over her nape. "It's cute."

Kaia plastered a hand to her neck. She did not know she had a heart-shaped freckle there. "Probably just dirt."

"Let me see." He lifted up her hair, licked the flat of his thumb, rubbed it against her skin where she supposed the spot was. A sweet shiver ran through her body. "No, no. Not dirt. It's a freckle."

He pressed his lips to her neck and the shiver turned into an all-out tremor. How easy it would be to surrender into this, into him. It took every ounce of willpower she possessed to sidle away. "I had a wonderful time tonight. Thank you."

"But . . ."

"I really don't see this going anywhere, Ridge. You've got a life in Canada. I've got a life here . . ."

"Can I at least have your cell number?"

"No."

"Why not?"

She shook her head. "It's for the best. You'll be out of the country. I'll be finishing school. We're both too busy for a long-distance relationship."

He paused, and for a moment she thought she saw disappointment on his face, but he quickly covered it up with a jovial mask. "You're right," he agreed. "Wishful thinking."

Silence fell over the room. Each of them lost in their own thoughts. Things were awkward now. Strained.

Suddenly, she wanted to be anywhere but here. She needed to get off by herself, think things through. She slid from the bed, using her pillow as a shield as she searched for her underwear.

"Don't get up," she said.

"I hope you don't mean that literally," he said impishly. "Because I already am. Up, that is."

Kaia darted a quick glance at him, and sure enough the covers were tented below his waist. She felt her cheeks flush, ducked her head.

"Down, boy," she quipped, spotted her panties, and slipped them on.

"Kind of hard to do when you just gave me such a clear shot of your beautiful butt."

"You're incorrigible," she said, alarmed by the surge of hope that bloomed in her chest.

"And you love that about me." He gifted her with a saucy smile and sultry, half-closed eyelids. "If you change your mind, you know where to find me."

"At least until Monday," she said. Reminding herself more than him that their short-lived romance had an expiration date.

He threw back the covers, got up, giving her a full frontal view of his total male gloriousness. "At least let me walk you to your truck."

"I'm a big girl," she said. "I know this ranch like the back of my hand. There's nothing to fear out there in the dark. I can see myself out."

Yep. Nothing to fear in the dark, because everything that scared her to the bone was right here in this room.

HE WASN'T GOING to romanticize it. They'd had sex. Very hot, very great sex, yes. But it *was* just sex.

Hell, Kaia had made that abundantly clear.

And yet, there was a small part of him that held out hope for more, a secret part that melted at Kaia's endearing smile and dared to think, *what if?*

She was a lot of fun, and it had been a long time since he'd allowed himself to fully play. There was another feeling inside him, a deeper, darker feeling that he did not want to label. She made him *want* things. Things he never thought he wanted—like a wife, and a family of his own.

Whoa-ho, he went there.

He wasn't the kind of guy who did well with family commitments. He'd had no role models for how to make a marriage work. No clue how it was done. People said love was enough. That love would get you through anything.

But Ridge wasn't stupid. He knew that wasn't true. He'd loved his mother more than anything, but she'd had no qualms about checking out on him. Hell, if he couldn't keep his mother interested enough to stick around how could he expect anyone else to?

Love was a gamble. Apparently some people got lucky at the game, found someone they truly cared about, made a life together, stuck it out through thick and thin. Kaia's parents were like that.

But not Ridge. Not his family. On either his father's or his mother's side. Not a single Lockhart male in the past six generations had been able to make marriage stick.

Sure, many of the Lockhart ancestors had been widowed during the settling of the West, but there had been just as many divorces, or just as many wives taking off, disappearing without warning. What made him believe he could make love work when none of his ancestors had before him?

Besides, his home was in Calgary. Hers was in Cupid. No way was he moving back to the town that held nothing but painful memories and his father. The Trans-Pecos wasn't big enough for the two of them.

A longer relationship between them did not make sense on any level. Tonight was the apex. He'd had fun. It was the best sex he'd ever had in his life, but it *had* been just sex. No wedding bells. No heavenly angels singing. No with-this-ring-I-do-thee-wed happy ending.

But he couldn't help chasing after her.

He paused just long enough to jam himself into his jeans and boots, but he didn't even bother with a shirt, just went running after her.

The party was still going on in the barn, although a lot of cars had already left, giving her room to get out. She was unlocking the door of the Tundra, looking sexy and mussed in the coffee-stained bridesmaid dress.

"Kaia," he called softly.

She stopped, raised her head. "What is it?"

He caught up to her, feeling a little breathless. "Before you go," he said, "I've got to know."

She paused, shifted her weight from foot to foot on the high heels she'd worn to the wedding. "What is it?"

"Why did you get mad when I kissed your scar?"

Her hand went to her right hip, as her mouth turned down. "It doesn't matter."

"Then what does it hurt to tell me?" He stepped closer. Saw the vein at her throat pulsing hard. It was all he could do not to pull her into his arms and whisper, *shh, shh, shh, everything will be okay*, until the pulsing slowed.

Kaia cast a nervous glance over her shoulder at the barn, where music was still spilling out. "If I tell you will you go away?"

He nodded, when all he wanted to do was throw her over his shoulder like a caveman and haul her back to his bed.

She leaned her back against the door of the truck, her keys clutched in her palm, closed her eyes, cleared her throat, opened her eyes again, let out a steadying breath. "It's hard for me to talk about."

He couldn't resist coming closer, but she held up a stop-sign palm, warning him off.

"Please don't," she said, the crack in her voice letting him know that while she longed to touch him again, she couldn't stand it if she did.

Respecting her wishes, he took a step back, even though everything inside him wanted to rush to her and draw her close.

"Listen," he said. "Forget I asked."

"No. It's okay. Maybe it's time I talked about it. But not out here where everyone can see."

He glanced over his shoulder at his house.

"The chapel. It's safer," she said, but didn't explain what she meant by that.

Nodding, he went into the darkened chapel ahead of her and took a seat in the last pew. A minute passed, he turned to watch the door, wondering if she'd decided to take off and leave him in the lurch. But he didn't hear the Tundra start.

Finally, she appeared, her curvy figure silhouetted in the doorway, clutching her high heels in one hand. On silent bare feet she made her way to him, settled in beside him. Close, but not close enough for him to touch her without leaning in. Her shoulders inched up to her ears.

"Who was the guy who destroyed your self-confidence?" he growled.

"Am I that transparent?" Her voice was weary, sagging with a heavy emotional weight.

He shook his head, smiled softly, held her gaze. "No," he said. "It's just that you're normally so happy that I knew something more had to be behind your edginess when I kissed your scar."

"I didn't mean to be edgy—"

"Hey, I'm not judging you for it. You're entitled to your anger. But it did make me curious. You don't owe me an explanation, Kaia. None at all—I just thought maybe talking about it would help."

She laughed.

"What?"

"Ironic."

"What is?"

She swatted him playfully on the shoulder. "You. The strong, silent type here encouraging me to spill my guts, when your cards are smack up against your chest."

"Ah," he said. "I get it. You want tit for tat. Okay, you tell me your ugly secret and I'll tell you mine."

She crinkled her nose. "Maybe we shouldn't do this."

"Why not?"

"Swapping stories leads to getting to know you better and getting to know you better leads to liking you more and liking you more leads to . . ." She trailed off. "Do you see where I'm headed?"

"Back into my bed?" he asked hopefully.

"You are such a *guy*," she said, and swatted his shoulder again, but her voice held a teasing note.

"So who was he? The guy who took your joy."

"Don't worry about him. I got my joy back."

"Okay," he said, disappointed she wasn't able to tell him her story, but fully understanding her reluctance to splash in water under an old bridge.

"It's not that I don't want to tell you. I . . . I don't know how to start," she confessed.

"Leave it lie. You're right. Maybe we shouldn't talk about it."

In the silence they heard distant voices, laughter, and a car door slam. Through pursed lips, Kaia hauled in a deep breath and slowly released it. Ridge reached over to take her hand and she did not pull away. He smiled into the darkness.

He gave her space. Letting her get to it in her own time.

"After my accident, I met a guy at the rehab hospital. He was there visiting his father and we had a lot in common. Both came from a family of five kids. Both loved animals. He was charming and I was vulnerable, feeling insecure after my accident . . ." She bit her bottom lip.

He stayed quiet, holding space for her to continue in her own time and way.

"After I got out of the hospital, I still needed a lot of therapy. He was so attentive. He wanted to start dating, but I wasn't in any shape for that. He told me he was happy to just be friends, and I took him at his word." She traced the coffee stain on her dress with her finger.

It was all he could do not to pull her into his lap and kiss her until she forgot everything but the feel of his lips on hers.

"He insisted on driving me to my appointments, and in the beginning it was so nice. He called me several times a day to make sure I was doing okay. I'm not going to lie, I was flattered by his attention and blind to what was behind it. But I wasn't sexually attracted to him and had no desire to take things to that level."

He squeezed her hand. Letting her know she was safe with him. It was the most he could offer her right now.

"Then things started to change. He moved into my apartment complex so he could be near me. If I didn't answer the phone immediately when he called, or I drove myself somewhere, he'd yell at me. Tell me I was still too sick to be going out without him. Honestly, I was flattered that he cared so much." She shook her head. "I was *so* stupid."

"No," he said sharply. "Not stupid at all."

"By the time I realized how possessive he was, and how dependent he'd made me on him, my self-esteem was in the toilet."

Ridge clenched his fist, his teeth, and his anger.

"The more I tried to stretch my wings, the more controlling he became. Then he got verbally abusive—"

"Did he ever hit you?" Ridge growled, anger a black thing in the pit of his stomach.

"No." She shook her head. "Not while I was still friendly with him. When I couldn't take any more of his yelling and cursing at me and I told him I didn't need that kind of negativity in my life, he begged my forgiveness. Said he was just concerned about me, begged me to give him a second chance."

"And because you're a forgiving soul who believes the best about people, you did," he guessed.

"Foolishly, yes." She cringed, hitched in a deep breath, and finally got out the rest of the story on a long rush of air. "But of course, he didn't stop. I was too ashamed to tell my family what was happening. Finally, I couldn't take it anymore and I moved out of the apartment complex while he was out of town. But then he started stalking me. Endless phone calls. Showing up at my school and at my job."

His entire body flushed hot then cold. He didn't want to hear anymore, but he knew she needed to tell it.

Her voice grew softer. "One night as I was leaving evening classes, he cornered me in the parking lot. He told me he loved me. I told him it was over between us. We argued. He attacked me."

"No!" Ridge said hotly, hoarsely, her words hitting him solid as a blow.

Her nod was barely there, as if she had no energy for it. "He choked me. Said if he couldn't have me, he'd make sure no one else ever did. I thought I was going to die."

It killed him to think of her suffering like that. Ridge knotted his hands into crabapple fists.

"It was terrifying. If another student hadn't happened by when he did . . ." She trailed off again, brought a hand to her neck.

Thank God for that other student!

Ridge's fists were squeezed so tightly the veins on his knuckles bulged. If the man who'd hurt Kaia had been there, Ridge would have beaten him to a pulp.

"He dropped me and ran off. The other student took me to the police station and I got a restraining order against him. The cops went to arrest him, but he'd disappeared. Even so, I was too afraid to stay in College Station by myself. That's the real reason I took a break from vet school. Not because of the accident. But because of him. I needed to come home."

Ridge grunted. Anger pulsed through him with every beat of his heart. Not knowing what to say that wouldn't scare her or make things worse, he said nothing.

"With the help of my family and a counselor, I worked through the emotional baggage. I've put it behind me, and honestly, I hardly think about him anymore. But once in a while, like when you kissed the scar, the fear bubbles to the surface."

Simultaneously, they both blew out pent-up breaths. Ridge ached to draw her into his arms, to promise her no man would ever hurt her again, but her tense body language warned him off.

"Did the police ever catch him?"

"Yes," she said, her voice growing even heavier than before.

Relief loosened his muscles. Thank God the stalker had been apprehended. "Did he go to prison?"

"No." Her answer was matter-of-fact, to the point, but her shoulders drooped, and she crossed her arms over her chest. Pulling herself in, making her body small.

There was more to the story and it was hard for her to tell.

Ridge's gut clamped down. Had the justice system failed? Was the son-of-a-bitch still out there? Still threatening women? Still searching for Kaia?

"What happened?" Ridge heard outrage boil in his voice. Felt it like an electrical jolt. "Why isn't he rotting in a prison cell?"

She shook her head. Moistened her lips. Paused for a long time. Finally spoke. "He killed himself."

"Good. Saved me from having to track him down and do it for him," Ridge said fiercely, a kneejerk reaction.

But then he immediately felt a punch of guilt. As horrified as he was that Kaia had been through such an ordeal, the troubled man had committed suicide. Obviously, he'd been in great emotional pain and hadn't gotten the help he needed. Society had failed him.

She laughed, a strange, mirthless sound of relief, followed by a troubled noise of shame as she dropped her face into her hands. He touched her shoulder, felt her muscles bunch. He lowered his hand. Unsure if he was helping or making things worse.

Raising her head, she bravely met his eyes. "It was sad." Pity rearranged her face. "He was mentally ill. I'm glad I don't have to worry about him anymore, but what a tragic way for a life to end. I . . ." Her voice cracked. "He was nice to me at first. I had no idea he was so unhinged. I wish . . ."

Remorse.

He could see it on her. She was a good person. And a man had died. No matter how deranged he might have been, no matter how much he might have hurt her, the depth of Kaia's compassion triggered regret.

And Ridge loved her all the more for her kind-heartedness. The way she was able to step outside her own experiences and walk a mile in someone else's shoes.

"The police found him . . ." She had to pause again. He could tell how much the story was taking out of her. "Hanging from a tree in the park where we'd once picnicked, a suicide note in his car."

"Jesus, Kaia." Ridge pulled his palm down his face, a tumult of feelings knocking him every which way—anger for what had happened, sorrow for what she'd suffered, fear that there were plenty more trouble people out there, and distress that he hadn't been there for her when she'd needed him most. But how could he have known?

"I survived."

Yes, she had. Brave woman. "I'm sorry as hell you had to go through that."

"I just wish he could have gotten the help he needed." There were tears in her eyes. "I wish I'd seen the signs before things got as bad as they did."

"You're a much better person than I am," he said. "I can't grieve for him. Not after what he did to you."

She raised her head, met his gaze. "He was a boy once. He had a father who loved him. He had family and friends who suffered as much as I did. I can't forget that. And I can't help thinking I could have done more to help him."

"His mental health wasn't your responsibility."

"Whose responsibility was it?" she asked, searching his face as if she genuinely wanted an answer.

"Not yours."

"That's easy enough to say, but it doesn't stop me from feeling like I should have done something. But then again, another part of me is relieved I don't have to constantly look over my shoulder, waiting for him to pop up. I'm not proud of those feelings, but there they are."

"Aww." He shook his head. "You poor kid."

"No! Don't you dare feel sorry for me!" she barked, and shook a finger in his face. "Don't you dare!"

Whoa! Her quick about-face brought him up short. He held up a palm, lifted apologetic eyes.

"*He* used to say that to me all the time. I'm not a poor *anything*. I'm lucky and blessed and loved. Yes, I've had struggles and challenges, but it's made me stronger, not weaker."

Ridge slapped a hand over his mouth. Dammit! No wonder she'd reacted the way she had when he'd kissed her scar.

"The last thing I want is anyone's pity."

"I get that," he said.

She squeezed his hand.

He squeezed back.

"I was stupid," she whispered. "So trusting. I grew up in a place where most people have your best interest at heart. I'd never brushed up against someone like him before."

Tears tracked down her cheeks. It struck him like a blow—her shame. She blamed herself for the way that crazy bastard had treated her.

"But I forgave him because I needed to do it for me. I realize now he had mental issues and I wasn't adept at reading the signs."

"Kaia," he said gently. "Look at me."

Reluctantly, she raised her head, but skimmed over his eyes, fixing instead on his brow.

He reached out, cupped her chin in his palm.

She tensed but didn't draw away.

"Kaia"—he repeated her name, drilling down, and tapping in—"look at me."

Finally, she met his eyes and he felt the jolt of their connection. It was strong. Unmistakable. The instant they peered into each other, the magnetic pull yanked their gazes together, until he was unsure if he *could* look away, should he want to.

"You're being too hard on yourself."

"No." She hitched in a breath. "I'm not being hard enough."

He rubbed the flat of his thumb against her knuckles. Felt her shiver. "Beating yourself up for someone else's bad behavior solves nothing."

Her laugh was a bark, short and bitter. "I was such a poor judge of character. That *was* my fault."

"You are a trusting soul, and you shouldn't have to apologize for being who you are."

"Who I am landed me in a world of hurt."

"Sweetheart, please. Ease up on yourself."

She cocked her head and studied him for a long breath. "You could take your own advice and get a couple hundred miles farther on down the road of life."

"What does that mean?"

"You're pretty hard on yourself, Ridge Lockhart. You're not responsible for either your mother's or your father's behavior."

"Touché," he agreed. "But right now, we're talking about you. You are a strong, competent, capable woman with a huge heart, but you can't save the entire world. And you have to take care of yourself before you can take care of anyone else."

"I'm starting to figure that out."

"You have family and friends. You don't have to carry this burden on your own. We're here just waiting to help you. All you have to do is ask." He touched her jaw, tilted her chin up. "Are you hearing me?"

She squirmed away from him. "Your turn."

"What?"

"You promised me, remember? My dark secret for yours."

He had made that promise. Wished he hadn't. Cast his mind around for another story he could substitute for it.

Luck was with him. The light in the chapel came on and Ember and Ranger walked in looking for Ember's lost purse.

And Ridge was off the hook.

Chapter 18

Early on Sunday morning after her night with Ridge, Kaia went to see Granny Blue.

The front porch was typical of the small adobe houses in Cupid, covered with a red tile roof awning, and just wide enough to accommodate a rocking chair. The cane-bottomed rocking chair in question was weathered and creaky. It rested atop the jute rug Granny had woven herself.

A short square table squatted beside the rocker. Atop the table rested the rainbow yarn of a newly started knitting project; a white candle burned halfway, a deck of Tarot cards worn thin from use, and a tin of cherry-scented pipe tobacco.

Granny Blue didn't smoke, but Pawpaw had, and she kept the tobacco to sniff when she got lonesome for his smell.

Through the open front door, the sounds of Benny Goodman's "Moonglow" scooted out.

Kaia stepped onto the porch and immediately set off a chorus of barking, yipping, and whining as Granny Blue's exuberant pack galloped out to greet her.

Laughing, she plunked down on the wooden planks and allowed herself to be covered in hounds, five dogs in all.

Mixed breed rescues. Smoke, Sage, Aggie, Tim, and Molly. She petted and cooed to each one in turn as the rest surrounded her, sniffing her hair, wriggling their bodies, wagging tails, hopping on her back.

Grandfather Alzate, who had a natural affinity for animals, was the one who'd taught her to love and cherish all God's creatures.

One of her favorite memories was the day when she and her

grandfather found a litter of motherless infant kittens living in a drainpipe. The local vet had decreed they would not likely survive and warned Kaia not to get attached to them. Even her parents hadn't been optimistic about the kittens' chances, and they warned her not to name the babies.

But Pawpaw had other plans. He vowed those kittens would live, and he helped her pick out the names. Mittens for the gray tabby with white feet. Dusk for the full gray one. Fluff for the smallest one with an excess of fur.

He showed her how to hold them delicately, how to make a soft warm bed for them, how to feed their tiny mouths milk from an eyedropper. He taught her a Native American healing song to sing to them and told her fiercely, *Never be afraid to love with all your heart, Kaia, girl. Death can steal us away at any time. So love now. Love hard. And never apologize for it.*

From that moment on, Kaia had gone all in. Loving each and every animal that crossed her path with a fervency that sometimes troubled her parents. And with each pet that died, she grieved, but the animal's passing never stopped her from loving anew.

But while she loved all creatures, great and small, dogs were secretly her favorite. She loved dogs for their sheer enthusiasm and die-hard loyalty.

"Hello, hello." She greeted each exuberant dog in turn. "I love you too."

In unison, they licked her face.

"Guess what?" she confided in them. "The most amazing thing has happened. You're not gonna believe."

"That must be Kaia squeaking the boards on my front porch." Granny's voice drifted through the open door. "The dogs go mad for you."

"That's because I have treats." She giggled and took five small squares of dried liver from the front pocket of her shirt and doled them out.

The dogs quivered with delight.

Granny Blue appeared in the doorway. "Ah, water has rolled

in," she said, in that cryptic way of hers, referring to the fact Kaia was born in Pisces, a water sign. "And here I was so thirsty."

The dogs turned and raced into the house, Kaia following.

Benny Goodman cut off in midswing as Granny lifted the arm on the record player, and switched it off. Sighed nostalgically. "Nothing like vinyl."

"Morning, Granny."

She pulled Kaia into her arms for a fierce hug. Hugging Granny wasn't easy. Kaia had to bend so low her chin almost touched the top of Granny's head and cradle her thin shoulders carefully so as not to hurt her frail bones.

If a good stiff wind kicked up, it would blow tiny Granny Blue halfway across the desert.

Her grandmother wore a faded brown calico housedress, and well-worn, leather-soled moccasins. The open room that served as living room, kitchen, and dining room was lit only by sunlight shining in under the partially raised shades. The Saltillo floor tiles had been designed in the pattern of a medicine wheel. Kaia knew the medicine wheel four directional quadrants by heart—physical, emotional, spiritual, and mental. She didn't know how much of the old lore she believed, but she trusted Granny Blue's wisdom.

The room was minimally furnished—a rustic couch handmade from piñon wood and topped with goose down cushions covered in colorful Native American designs, a round antique end table, another rocking chair, and a square table circa 1980, painted University of Texas burnt orange that served as a stand for an old tube TV. In the corner of the room was a kiva-style fireplace.

The cedar dining room set was older then Kaia's mother, and Granny Blue waved a hand at one of the sturdy chairs. "Sit," she directed, just as the teakettle on the stove whistled.

All five dogs sat at once, eyes trained on Granny Blue.

"You already had the kettle on?" Kaia plunked down at the table, used the toe of her boot to scratch the back of the nearest dog. The other four gathered around her foot, waiting their turns.

Granny Blue smiled an ambiguous smile. "The cactus rose bloomed this morning."

"You knew I was coming?"

"I knew someone was coming. You must pay closer attention to the world around you, Ky. Signs are everywhere if you will but look and listen." Granny plodded to the stove, lifted the kettle's handle with a knitted potholder, and poured water into two teacups already sitting on the sideboard.

Granny Blue carried the cups to the table, went to the cupboard for a tin filled with various flavors of teas and a sleeve of Fig Newtons. She sat down across from Kaia, eyed her a moment, and then plucked a tea bag from the tin and passed it to her.

Kaia made a face. "Echinacea?"

"You need to keep your strength up," Granny Blue mused.

"What makes you say that?"

Granny Blue shrugged, a common response she gave to questions that had no solid answer. "A feeling."

"Could I have peppermint instead?"

"Are you having digestive issues?"

"No, I just like it, and it goes better with Fig Newtons."

Granny Blue shook her head, but slid the tea tin toward her.

"Thanks." Kaia claimed the peppermint tea, and they both dunked tea bags into the water steaming from their cups.

They sipped in silence, munching on Fig Newtons, and then Granny Blue said, "What is your news?"

"Who says I have news?"

"You don't visit on Sunday mornings. Something is different."

Kaia poked the tip of her tongue against the inside of her cheek, trying to think of the best way to broach the topic. "I . . . um . . ." She cleared her throat, took a sip of tea.

Studying her intently, Granny Blue leaned forward, but said nothing. Warm wind stirred through the open window, blowing wisps of silver hair that had strayed from her braid against her noble cheekbones and craggy jaw.

"I . . . well . . ." Kaia moistened her lips, pressed a palm to the back of her head, couldn't quite meet Granny's fierce dark-eyed gaze. "I've got questions. Lots of questions."

"What is puzzling you, Ky?"

"Before I say anything, please tell me again the story of what happened when you met grandfather."

"You've heard the story dozens of times."

"I need to hear it again."

Granny Blue's face and voice melted into downy softness. In that moment, Kaia saw exactly what she must have looked like as a young woman.

"Ah," she said. "I see. Tell me what you've been hearing."

Kaia chuffed out the breath of air she'd been holding. "A beautiful, soft humming noise buzzing right at the base my brain, and I need an explanation for it."

Granny Blue lowered her eyelashes. "You know the explanation."

"I don't. Not for sure. It could just be ringing in my ears. Tinnitus. I should go to the doctor."

"It's not tinnitus."

"Maybe. It could be. I pray it is."

Granny Blue's eyes opened wide and she looked slightly alarmed. "Oh, my dear sweet child. Who kissed you?"

"Please," Kaia begged. "Tell me how to stop it."

"If it is the Song of the Soul Mate"—Granny shook her head, her expression both joyous and rueful—"it is unstoppable."

Kaia gulped, squeezed her fingernails into her palms. She'd been terrified Granny was going to say that. "Hopefully it's *not* the soul mate thingy."

"But my child," she whispered "why would you wish away our cherished family blessing?"

"Or curse," Kaia said. "Depending on how you look at it."

Granny Blue clucked her tongue. "Right now, you sound as stubborn as Ember. Normally, you are as easy flowing as the water sign you were born under. Who has you so scared?"

Ridge Lockhart, that's who! But she wasn't saying that out loud. Not yet.

Not while she was busy logging all the reasons they were incompatible. He was rich. She came from modest means. He was her older brother's best friend. He used to call her Braterminator and tug on her pigtails. She was still going to school and didn't need the distraction. He was off to China for six months. She was—

"I resisted too." Granny Blue laid her wrinkled, sun-spotted hand atop Kaia's. "It's only natural. Finding your soul mate can be quite scary at first."

"Honestly, I did not think it was real. I thought it was just a story you told us, like Cinderella. I never believed I would actually hear . . ." Kaia fanned her palms beside her ears. "*This*."

"I cautioned you," Granny Blue said. "But you had to have proof, and now you do."

Her soft words held such unyielding faith, Kaia's gut squeezed, sloshed with peppermint tea and cookies. She was glad she'd chosen peppermint now, hoping it would soothe her jittery stomach.

"What happened between you and grandfather? Was it love at first sight?"

"Oh no! The first time I saw him I thought he was the cockiest rooster in the barnyard. Although . . ." She took a sip of her tea and grinned. "He was the most handsome man I'd ever seen."

"So you had no idea when you met him that he was your true love?"

Her grandmother's smile turned wistful. "Not at all. It wasn't until he kissed me under the starry night sky and I heard the Song of the Soul Mate that I knew he was the one."

Just to have something to do with her hands, Kaia ate another cookie.

"I miss that man, his kisses and that humming, every single minute of my life."

She heard the heartbreak in Granny Blue's voice, felt the depth of her grandmother's sorrow all the way through her bones. "Aww, Granny." She squeezed her grandmother's hand.

"Don't feel sorry for me." Granny Blue smiled past the single tear streaking down her cheek. "I'm blessed beyond measure. And now you"—she reached out to stroke Kaia's chin—"whether you believe it or not, have heard the Song of the Soul Mate. It is a great gift."

"But who's to say it's not just some genetic malfunction in the brains of the women in our family and it has nothing to do with love at all?" Kaia fretted, alarmed at her tightening chest muscles.

"But you didn't hear the hum until after this man kissed you, correct?"

Kaia nodded. She couldn't deny it, no matter how much she might want to. Ridge had kissed her, and then she'd heard the humming. Every single time.

"You have doubts, it's understandable. But like it or not, once you've heard the Song of the Soul Mate, he is inevitably yours."

"But what if he is with someone else?" Kaia said. "What if he's married?"

"Is he?"

"No."

"Did you know that your grandfather was engaged to be married when I met him?"

"What?" Kaia pressed a hand to her mouth, slightly scandalized. "You stole grandfather away from his fiancée?"

The dry desert breeze made her skin feel hot. Fig Newton crumbs sprinkled the tablecloth in front of her. In her rapt attention to Granny Blue's story, she'd finished off the entire sleeve of cookies. With the flat of her hand, she swept the crumbs into a straight line, and then brushed them off the table into her saucer.

The dogs sat up, watching her, curious as to what she harbored in the saucer. The ceiling fan overhead rotated in lazy circles.

Her pulse pounded, and her head hummed. Just the thought of Ridge's kisses set it humming. She felt weak, dazed.

Granny Blue's eyes were pinned on her. She smiled a faint, far-away smile, remembering something she did not share.

"What would have happened if he'd married the other woman?" Kaia asked.

"He didn't."

"But what if he had?"

"Then we both would have been miserable for the rest of our lives." Her bittersweet gaze came back to Kaia. "When he stole that kiss from me, he broke his vow to his intended. His tribe took it as a sign he had a fickle character." She paused. "They did not understand the Song of the Soul Mate. It was not a gift his people possessed. That's why we moved to the Trans-Pecos. For a start fresh."

"It must have been hard. Leaving your home and your family for a man you barely knew. Did you ever have moments of regret?"

"Never." Granny Blue breathed out a fierce breath, the thin line of her nostrils flaring. "How could I regret finding the other half of my soul?"

"Wow."

"Although," Granny said, touching an index finger to her chin, "your grandfather and I regret that we caused the other woman pain. But when you hear the Song of the Soul Mate"—she shook her head—"everything changes and there is nothing you can do to stop it."

"It sounds awful. Out of control."

"It is awful only if you resist," Granny Blue said with ironclad conviction. "If you embrace what is . . . well, it is like a fairy tale. Happily-ever-after."

"Until one of you dies," Kaia whispered.

Granny's eyes burned bright. "No," she said. "Not even then. The Song of the Soul Mate sings throughout all lifetimes."

Kaia crinkled her nose. Granny had some eccentric beliefs that clashed with her own, and she wanted to deny the fanciful lore. But she was open-minded enough to admit something mysterious was going on.

"So tell me about your first kiss with Grandfather."

"The minute his lips were on mine it was as if the earth shifted off its axis, and I thought I heard a choir of angels singing. I realized it was the Song of the Soul Mate my mother had told me about, the same way I told you and your sisters."

"How sweet!"

"But then your grandfather told me he was engaged and he never meant to kiss me but that he was so taken with my beauty he was unable to resist. He was completely tormented by that kiss, but so was I."

Kaia ran a palm over her mouth. "I can imagine."

"I was too young to be falling in love, far too young to hear the Song of the Soul Mate. I hadn't even finished high school, and the man I loved was already promised to another."

"What did you do?"

"We tried to forget each other—of course, it was the only honorable thing to do—but we were miserable apart! My heart felt as if it had been ripped from my chest. I couldn't stop thinking about him and when I thought about him I heard the humming. It would not stop. How I prayed for it to stop! I did not want a reminder of everything I was giving up."

"But then Pawpaw broke up with the other woman and came for you."

She smiled slyly. "He did. But that's enough about my story. You are the one who is hearing the soul mate song for the first time. Tell me about it."

Kaia shrugged, reluctant to let the cat from the bag. Once she spoke his name, she'd never be able to take it back.

"Who is this man that has set your head singing?" Granny asked.

Kaia ran a trembling hand over her mouth, met Granny's hard-edged stare. Took a deep breath and bravely said, "Ridge Lockhart."

A beat of silence passed between them. Then two. Three . . .

"Oh no," Granny Blue whispered.

"Oh yes. Now do you see why I am so worried?"

Chapter 19

I<small>T</small> was ten a.m. when she got home from Granny Blue's, and Kaia had no more than walked through her front door when her cell phone rang.

The minute she saw Ridge's name on her caller ID, she started grinning, answered it with, "How did you get my cell number?"

"Ember," he said.

"Don't ever have sisters. They'll throw you under the bus every time."

"Thanks for the tip." He chuckled, and the deep-throated sound had her curling her toes inside her boots.

"What do you want?" she asked, hopefully wary that he wanted to see her again.

"You want to go do something?" he asked.

Bounce went her heart. "Like what?"

"Hang out."

"Are you asking me on a date?"

"We don't have to slap a label on it."

"Hanging out is what kids do. If you want to date me, just ask."

Ridge snorted, and she could almost see him shaking his head and smiling, the way he did when she'd both irritated and delighted him.

"All right then. Would you like to go to . . ." He paused as if he was trying to think of a good place to take her.

"In case you've forgotten, there are a limited number of date options in this town. Dinner and a movie, bowling, line dancing at Chantilly's, going out to watch for the Marfa Lights, and/or hitting the new ice-cream parlor on the road into town. Otherwise, for date stuff, it's a three-hour drive to El Paso."

"You forget," he said. "I own my own plane."

"Braggart."

"Up for a flight to El Paso?"

"Nope."

"You're turning me down?"

"I'd planned on giving blood this afternoon at the hospital, and I'm usually a little light-headed for the rest of the day after I donate."

"Could you donate another day?"

"It's for Natalie Vega's baby girl, Amelia. She's got Von Willebrand's disease and occasionally needs a transfusion."

"Who's Natalie Vega?"

"Oh yeah, I forgot you haven't been keeping up with us for the past ten years. I'm talking about Natalie McCleary, who owns the Cupid's Rest B&B. I think she was a couple of years ahead of you in high school. Anyway, she got married a few years ago to Dade Vega, a former Navy SEAL. He now works for Border Patrol."

"Man, I hate to hear that her kid is sick. Will she be okay?"

"Prognosis is really good if she gets medical treatment when she needs it," Kaia said. "Kids with Von Willebrands can live a normal life. But Natalie and Dade have both been through so much heartache. It doesn't seem fair that their baby daughter has a chronic illness. Luckily, Natalie and Dade have a strong marriage, and their three-year-old, Nathan, is healthy as a horse. Folks in town do what they can to help them out. For me, since I'm so busy and saving up to finish school, it's donating blood."

"I see." The timbre of his voice shifted, deepened.

"What?" Kaia rubbed a palm across her face wondering if she'd said something wrong.

"You."

"What about me?"

He clicked his tongue like he was guiding a horse. "You are one amazing woman."

"Me?" She scoffed. "I'm no better or worse than anyone else. Just a hometown girl doing right by my friends."

"Who cares so much about other people that they regularly donate blood? Be honest—how many people do that?"

"You've been gone too long," Kaia said. "Big city living has made you forget what it's like to live in a tight-knit community."

"You might be right," he agreed.

Silence lapsed between them as she cast around for something to say.

"Could you wait until tomorrow to donate blood if I invited you to spend the day with me at Balmorhea State Park?" he asked, referencing her most favorite spot in the Trans-Pecos. "What do you say?"

"Is this officially a date?" she squeaked.

"It's a date," he confirmed.

She grinned as if he could see her, but the smile quickly faded as reality set in. Having casual wedding sex with him was one thing; a sojourn to the place where they'd shared some of her fondest childhood memories was another.

Saying yes would be like diving headfirst into a body of water without first checking the depth.

"I'll pick you up in thirty minutes," he said.

"You don't even know where I live."

"Ember sold you out all the way," he said, and hung up.

She made a mental note to give Ember a good talking-to about passing out her personal information, and switched off her phone.

Her heart was skipping so fast she got a little dizzy and had to sit on the couch. Dart and her foster dogs, a Jack Russell named Buddy and a sweet-natured golden retriever named Bess, immediately jumped on her, knocking her down. Smelling Granny Blue's dogs on her, Buddy and Bess sniffed her up and down.

"Yes," she confirmed. "I've been cheating on you with Granny Blue's brood."

Dart, however, didn't seem to mind that Kaia had been cavorting with other beasts and staked out a claim in the middle of her chest, settling down to knead her skin with his paws.

"Going straight for the boobs, huh?" Kaia teased. "Whether cat or human, you men are all alike."

Dart looked her straight in the eyes and meowed as if to say, "Don't you know it, sister."

It fully hit her. Ridge was on the way! He'd be here in thirty minutes for their date—a real date with her favorite person in her favorite place.

Crapple, she was a mess.

At the speed of light, she let the dogs into the fenced backyard and dashed through the house, shedding her comfy animal-friendly clothes as she went. Her high-octane energy sent Dart hiding under the bed.

She hopped into the shower, taking her toothbrush and toothpaste with her. Two birds. One stone. Multitasking was a good thing. Thank God, the pedicure she'd gotten for Archer's wedding still looked good, but she hadn't washed her hair since Friday evening and it was currently pulled into a ponytail.

Who cared? She was going swimming.

Yes, but it was a swimming *date.*

Five minutes she was in and out of the shower, body scrubbed, teeth brushed, legs shaved. She did the frou-frou stuff. Deodorant. Cologne. Pull down the ponytail and fluffed her hair. Yes, later it would be wet and plastered to her head, but she wanted to make an impression.

She dressed quickly. Red bikini, topped with a denim skirt and pink tank top, slid her feet into sturdy pink hiking sandals. Slapped on a bit of waterproof mascara, blush, and lipstick—called appropriately enough—Cactus Blossom Red.

The front doorbell rang just as she finished putting on the lipstick. Good enough. Breathing a sigh of relief, she bounced into the living room.

Opened the door.

There stood Ridge, wearing knee-length swim trunks, a blue T-shirt that enhanced his navy eyes, and a pair of slip-on boat shoes. He held a wicker picnic basket that smelled of fried chicken, and a bouquet of blue forget-me-nots.

No way. Her favorite food and her favorite flowers? Where had he gotten fried chicken in Cupid this early in the day? And who'd sold him flowers that loved water in a desert town on a Sunday morning?

But he had a plane and plenty of money. He could get most anything he wanted with a snap of his fingers. She found that both sexy and oddly worrisome.

"Hey," he said, leaning one shoulder against the doorjamb, still looking like a total rascal with that blackened eye.

"Hey."

She gulped. "How did you get here?"

"Borrowed Archer's SUV. They took Casey's car to the airport in El Paso. He left me the keys."

"I see." Kaia didn't miss the appreciative look in his eye as his gaze roamed over her.

She wasn't the only one who'd just taken a shower. His hair was slightly damp, and she caught the scent of soap and the spicy tang of his bay rum cologne.

Her nose twitched. He smelled better than the fried chicken, and it took every last bit of fortitude she possessed not to move closer to him.

"Thank you for the flowers," she said a bit formally. "Forget-me-nots are my favorite."

"I remember," he murmured. "They reminded me of you. Bright. Fun. True blue."

She took a moment to bask in the warmth of his words. He'd remembered. If he was buttering her up in hopes of getting her into bed again, it was working. Big-time.

"Let me just put these in water." She took the flowers from him, tried not to react when their hands brushed and goose bumps spread up her arm.

He followed her into the kitchen. "You look good."

Something about the way he said it, so nonchalant and friendly, caused her to turn her head and peer at him over her shoulder.

"What is it?" he asked. His tone was innocent, but the expression in his eyes was deliciously wicked. "Did I say something wrong?"

"Right then you sounded like your old self. No hint of that Canadian accent you've picked up."

"Eh?" he said in a nasally tease, purposely trying to sound Canadian.

"You can take the boy out of Texas"—she grinned—"but you can't take Texas out of the boy."

"I suppose not," he said, and grinned wide enough to show off the dimple dug into his right cheek. That dimple loosened her knees and sent a rush of heat flooding straight into her pelvis. "But you *do* look gorgeous."

What was going on? He kept saying the most incredible things to her. As if he wanted a relationship. As if they had a future.

"Sweet talker," she scoffed.

He lowered his head, lowered his eyelids, and sent her a scintillating look. "I'm dead serious."

"I don't believe you for a second." She said it in a teasing voice, but her pulse was bouncing crazily through her veins. She put the flowers into a water-filled vase and tucked a strand of hair behind her ear.

"Ready," she said, her voice coming out a little frayed.

"I like your hair like that," he said. "Loose and wild. Suits your inner goddess."

There he was with the sweet-talking again. She ducked her head to cover her pleasure, mumbled "thanks," and flipped her hair over her shoulder, showing off.

"I'm just itching to get my fingers tangled up in it again." And with that rabble-rousing comment, he took her arm and guided her toward the door.

On the way out, she snagged her straw cowgirl hat from the coatrack, settled it on her head for protection from the sun and Ridge's hot-edged gaze.

THEY ARRIVED IN Balmorhea around noon, a perfect time for a picnic. They ate fried chicken underneath a canvas awning and drank sweet tea from thermoses, eating in companionable silence. When they finished, they kicked back on the blanket they'd found in Archer's SUV, waiting for their food to settle before going swimming in the clear, deep, artesian springs.

There were pictures in the family album of her first time at the springs. She was young, no older than two, wearing a pink bathing suit with big orange flowers and adorable little kid sunglasses. She splashed in the springs, a huge smile on her face like she'd found a stash of the most delicious candy on earth.

And later, other pictures, pictures that included her siblings' friends. Ridge was there.

In one photograph, her favorite, they were playing chicken fight in the water and she was on Ridge's shoulders as they battled against Archer and Tara. She was six at the time to Ridge's twelve, and she'd followed him around like he was a superhero. He'd been pretty good-natured about it, tolerating her childish adoration as part and parcel of hanging out with Archer.

The clear cool water was such a contrast to the dusty hot dry desert. It was her favorite place to visit, and every weekend she'd beg her parents to drive the sixty miles to Balmorhea from Cupid. But they'd been raising five children on a shoestring budget. Such luxuries were few and far between.

She often dreamed of the springs, woke to the feel of water on her skin, the slow churn of waves as she swam through it, the mineral taste pleasing to her tongue, the clear depths that beckoned her to dive deep, the fish and plant life that lurked beneath the surface a world away from her ordinary reality.

And now, here she was, in Balmorhea with Ridge Lockhart as an adult. On a date. Something she'd never imagined would happen.

"So tell me," Ridge said idly, cradling the back of his head in his palms as he leaned back against the wide base of the metal support beams that held up the awning. "What does Kaia Alzate do when she's not working, tending animals, or going to school?"

"Hmm," she said, kicking off her sandals and digging her toes into the soft blanket. She rolled onto her back and stretched her arms over her head. "I just enjoy being alive."

"No special hobbies or interests?"

"After what I went through? I'm interested in everything."

"Movies? Music? Sports?"

"Yes." She turned on her side to look at him. He was still sitting up, looking down at her, a mysterious smile playing across his lips.

He laughed and stretched out beside her.

"What about you?" she asked. "What do you do when you're not working?"

"I'm always working."

"You're not working now."

"No." His smile was electric. "Not right now."

"Let's put it another way. What do you miss most because you're always working?"

"Swimming."

The conversation lapsed into silence, but it was easy, companionable. After a while, Kaia said, "I know it was you."

"What was me?"

"The one who paid the deductible gap on my hospital bill."

"Archer rat me out?"

"No. I figured it out."

"How?"

"You're the only one I knew who had the money and cared about me enough to bother."

"I showed up at the hospital," he said. "But you were in a coma."

"Why didn't you tell me?" She studied his profile, felt a twist of pure love for this man.

He shrugged. "It wasn't about me."

"I appreciate it more than you can ever know."

"Know what I appreciate?" he asked, reaching over and lightly running his finger over the shoulder strap of her bikini top peeking from the sleeve of her tank top.

"What's that?"

"Your astounding body."

She tried not to let his compliment go to her head, failed. "Now I know the real reason you invited me on a swim date. Not because you know how much I love the springs. You just wanted to see me in a bikini."

"Guilty as charged," he admitted with a wicked gleam in his eyes, and stripped off his T-shirt. "I'm going in."

"It hasn't been an hour since we ate."

"Complete myth," he said.

She was so busy staring at his magnificent chest that it didn't even register what he was saying. She sat up and watched him saunter toward the water, the sun dappling his bare back as it filtered through the leaves of the oak trees planted along the path to the springs.

The man was a god, ripped and leanly muscled. His swim trunks hung low on his hips. She bit down on her bottom lip. Have mercy! He was the finest thing she had ever seen and he was here with her. And according to his kisses, he was The One, even if he didn't know it yet. It was all too much to absorb.

But damn if she wasn't going to try.

"Wait for me," she said breathlessly, snatching up the towels he'd brought with them and running after him.

Chapter 20

A FEW other people were also in the springs, but they were in the shallows. He'd picked the deep end for privacy. Ridge floated on his back in the water, watching Kaia approach.

She resembled the women in one of those ads photographed near waterfalls and clear running streams. Strolling toward him in that short denim skirt and chicly shredded pink tank top showing peekaboo bare skin and her red bikini beneath, straw cowboy hat, and a pair of pink hiking sandals.

She could rock a man to sleep with her hips. Her hair was a straight, dark, mesmerizing curtain that swayed when she moved. Her elbows swinging in easy pumps against her side, two beach towels dangling from her fingers.

Sweat trickled down his brow.

He was not going to survive. He rolled over in the water so she couldn't see how aroused he was getting.

"I love to watch you walk," he said lazily, stupidly throwing gasoline on the fire. "You move with such confidence."

Love.

He'd said the word "love." Shit, why had he said that word? His throat tightened and his chest swelled and his blood heated. He felt light-headed and lighthearted.

"Hey," she said, dropping causally to the ground at the edge of the springs. "Look in the mirror. You are the most self-confident person I know. You didn't let your rough childhood dissuade you. You pulled yourself up by your bootstraps and now you're on the verge of becoming a billionaire."

"Who told you that?" he asked.

"Everyone knows it. You and your drilling technique are the talk of the town. Whether you realize it or not, Ridge Lockhart, people in these parts are proud of you."

"People in these parts gossip too much."

"True," she said, not the least bit offended, sliding off her sandals, setting them aside, and dipping her toes, painted a pearly peach color, into the water. "But that just goes to show how much they care."

"Do you always put a positive spin on things?"

"For the most part." She gave a soft shrug, and slipped out of her tank top. Revealing that red bikini he'd been salivating to see all morning. God, she was gorgeous; her burnished skin glowed. He'd missed so much in the ten years he'd been away, so much about her.

"You know," she said, dragging one big toe back and forth across the top of the water as if she was stroking a beloved pet. "You never did keep up your end of the bargain."

He was so busy staring at her that he drew a blank. "Huh? What bargain?"

"Last night," she reminded him. "You promised to tell me your shameful secret if I told you mine. Then Ember and Ranger interrupted us."

"You have nothing to be ashamed of," he said, swimming over to her, remembering what she'd told him last night. It hurt him to think she blamed herself for what had happened. "You did nothing wrong."

"I still felt ashamed. That's why I kept it a secret."

Except from him. She'd told him everything. It made him feel special to know something about her that no one else knew. Not even her family.

He shouldn't let it go to his head. She most likely told him because she needed to tell *someone* and she knew he wouldn't be around. That was probably the reason she *had* told him. He won by default.

"Your turn," she prodded. "Do not leave me hanging, Lockhart."

"Take off your skirt and come into the water and I'll tell you," he invited.

She laughed. "You sound like the Big Bad Wolf."

Teasingly, he wriggled his eyebrows, sent her a leering grin. "I'll huff and I'll puff and I'll blow your . . ."

He let the suggestion hang in the air.

She laughed, shucked off her denim skirt, flung her cowgirl hat to the ground, and dove into the water. She surfaced beside him, her hair drenched, her face full of joy, looking at him as if he was the most incredible thing she'd ever seen.

Freakadilly circus. Coming here with her had been a major mistake. They were in the deep. No safe harbor. No touching bottom.

"Here I am," she said. "Now you have to tell me your story."

He dog-paddled. Trying to keep his head above water. She rolled over onto her back, floated beside him like a porpoise, happy and so full of life she blinded him with possibilities. She loved the water, belonged here. She could do this all day, whereas he was floundering. Trying to find footing that was not there.

"You've built it up too much," he said. "It's not going to live up to the hype."

"Stop trying to get out of it. You owe me."

Indeed he did. Because of her, he'd stopped checking his phone every five minutes. Because of her, the weekend he'd been dreading had turned enjoyable. Because of her, he'd started to remember all the things he missed about Cupid. Because of her—

"Sometime while we're still young would be good," she said, doing the backstroke in circles around him.

"You love every second in the water and you know it."

"Yes." She sighed. "The curse of being a water creature born in the desert."

He could take her away from the desert. Wanted to open his mouth and say they could move to Baja and spend their days sipping margaritas on the beach.

If he licensed his drilling technique to a big silver mining company, he could retire with enough money to last a lifetime with millions left over, and nothing to do but make love to Kaia for the next fifty years or so.

"Ridge," she said, and her voice was so full of concern he snapped his head around to stare at her. "You're struggling."

"What?"

"That's the third time you've sucked in water."

Huh? Was it?

"Let's head for the shallows."

Shallow water. Yes. Perfect. Good idea.

He followed her as she swam effortlessly the length of the springs toward the other visitors. She found a spot where they could be off by themselves and sit on the bottom of the springs with their shoulders above water.

They settled in.

She waited, watching him, not speaking.

"Like I said." He inhaled. "My story is not going to live up to the buildup. It's certainly not going to live up to yours."

She crossed her arms, leveled him a get-on-with-it look.

He shook his head, amused by her tenacity. "All right," he said, and started the tale he'd not ever shared with anyone, not even Archer.

"AFTER I LEFT Cupid," Ridge said, "after my father and Vivi . . . well you know . . . I was a train wreck. I spent an entire week in a drunken stupor, but then I shook it off and went in search of my mother's people. I was seeking some kind of connection, for the place where I belonged."

He scratched his chin. The raspy sound of his fingernails against beard stubble peppered the pause.

They'd been born in the same place, raised together, but there was a lot she did not know about him. He'd been gone a long time, and he'd never been one to dig deep into feelings. As if skimming along on the surface of life would keep him safe.

"You'd never tried to contact them before?" Kaia asked, keeping her gaze trained on his face, studying every nuance, every shift of expression, trying to ferret out what he was feeling.

He shook his head. "I'd done some research when I was a teen. Learned my grandmother's name and where she lived, but I wasn't brave enough to call or show up on her doorstep."

Kaia pushed her wet hair back from her forehead, tried to suppress the uneasy feeling crawling under her skin.

"My maternal grandmother was living in San Antonio in a rough section of town. I worked up the courage to ring the doorbell and when I told her who I was, she asked me what I wanted from her."

"Not exactly the reaction you were hoping for?"

Ridge snorted. "No openhearted embraces. No."

"Bitch," she said it succinctly, pulling no punches.

Ridge burst out laughing, but it was a brittle sound, dark and dry. "I learned she'd kicked my mother out of the house when she was fifteen, claiming my mother had come on to my grandmother's boyfriend," he explained.

"Lovely woman," Kaia said, lacing her voice with sarcasm. "I take that back. That word I said before? Go ahead and insert it here again."

"You're good for my ego, Kaia Alzate."

"Why, thank you." She beamed. "You're welcome." She stuck a toe out of the water, wiggled it at him. "Go on."

"I'd rather come over there and play piranhas like when we were kids."

"Piranhas!" she squealed, feeling eight years old again. "Don't get none on ya."

He gnashed his teeth like a hungry piranha and came for her, but she giggled and swam away. "Nope. Not until you finish the story."

"You're not letting me off the hook."

"No, so you might as well get to talking."

"Here goes." He spoke fast, his words tumbling over each other. "My mother called her when she was seventeen and pregnant with me, wanted to come home. Good old grandmother told her no and sent her money for an abortion. Apparently, she thought Mom had gotten rid of me. Because I came as a big surprise. She told me she wasn't giving me any money if that's what I was there for."

Kaia reached out a hand and gently touched his shoulder. "I'm so sorry."

His muscles tensed beneath her fingers, but he didn't shake her off. "Hey, I don't need pity any more than you do."

"I get your point," she said, keeping her hand on him. "It wasn't the family reunion you were hoping for. What did you do?"

"What was there to do? I left." His voice was quick, clipped. "And I got a job in a silver mine in New Mexico. I craved hard, back-breaking work to clean my head of all that crap. In the meantime, long-lost grandma did some sleuthing, discovered I was a Trans-Pecos Lockhart, and called me a few weeks later to put the bite on me for money."

"Oh no, she did*n't*," Kaia stretched out the last syllable and lowered her voice to show her disgust.

"Yep. She makes Duke look like a Prince Charming."

"Did you give her money?"

He looked chagrined. "She was going to get evicted."

"Ridge! You didn't owe that awful woman a thing. She didn't deserve a penny."

"I decided to take the high road."

"Or," Kaia pointed out, not unkindly, "you were trying to buy her love."

He barked an attempt at laughter that crashed and burned. "I'm not *that* pathetic."

"Everyone wants to be loved, and needs to belong somewhere. Nothing pathetic about that."

"Yeah, well, some of us need it more than others."

She wasn't sure what he meant by that. "What about your mother's father? Did you try to find him?"

"Another blue ribbon winner," Ridge muttered. "Under the

three strikes rule, dear old granddad is serving a life sentence in Huntsville for armed robbery. Under the circumstances, I decided to skip the family reunion. "

"Oh my." Her heart broke to pieces for him. She was so lucky to have such a supportive, loving extended family.

He spread his arms wide. "So there you have it, the rundown of my rotten DNA. Are you sorry you asked?"

"No. Not at all." She breathed. "But wow. Just wow."

"Wow?" He arched a dubious eyebrow.

"I always had a lot of respect for you before, but now, after learning all this?" Kaia looked at him with admiration and sadness. She didn't feel sorry for him. She knew how it felt when people pitied you, and the last thing Ridge engendered was anyone's pity. He was a self-made man, someone to admire and look up to. But she did hate that he'd had a crappy family. "You're something special, Ridge Lockhart. Do you know that?"

He shifted in the water, dropped his gaze. "Do we have any of that chicken left?"

"Look how far you've come." She feared her praise was making him uncomfortable, but he had to know how truly miraculous he was to have successfully pulled out of the toxic emotional environments he'd been planted in.

"Lots of people have it worse. I'm the son of a multimillionaire—granted, an illegitimate son—but Duke put a roof over my head, food in my belly, and paid for my education."

"And he slept with your girlfriend."

"Nobody's perfect," he grinned, making light.

She liked that about him. How he refused to play the victim.

"I've lived a good life," he said. "I've done what I had to do to take care of myself, and I have no regrets."

"But now, by working so hard you keep people from getting close. Some might argue that's running away from your problems, not taking care of yourself."

"Hey," he said. "I'm not the one who is hiding out from the world in Cupid."

That hurt her feelings, because he was right. She had been dragging her feet about returning to A&M, even though finishing her degree was the most important thing in her life. "Staying with the people who love you and have your best interest at heart is not hiding."

"No?"

"You stay busy as a way of keeping people at arm's length. You don't live life, Ridge, you attack it."

"There *was* chicken left," he said, getting out of the water and heading for the beach towels she'd left at the side of the springs. "I could have sworn I saw a leftover drumstick."

She followed him, watching him track watery footsteps over the cement. It was so arid in the desert, the footprints dried up almost as soon as he made them. "You're so preoccupied with one-upping your father and outdoing your DNA that you don't even know who you are outside the context of your history."

"I thought you were getting your degree in veterinarian medicine," he said tartly. "Not psychology."

"Ridge."

"What?" he asked, busily toweling water from his hair.

"Why *did* you come home?"

"Archer was getting married."

"You could have turned him down. Why didn't you just turn him down?"

He shot her a peeved expression. "Christ, Kaia, stop badgering."

"I'm not badgering. I—"

He looked so fierce it drew her up short. *Was* she badgering?

"What do you want from me?" he growled.

What did she want from him?

Why, to be hers forever soul mate. That realization was a leaden weight in the pit of her stomach. He had no idea that she'd heard the humming when he kissed her, when they made love. No clue to her deepening feelings for him.

But how could she be with him when he was unable to get beyond his upbringing and make peace with his father? There was a whole lot of emotional baggage he needed to unpack before he would be ready for a serious relationship.

Kaia pulled back. She wished she could tell him all this without sounding like a complete loon.

He was staring at her in a way that made her feel as if she'd made a major misstep. What did *he* want from her?

"I want you to be happy," she whispered, expressing the deepest wish of her heart.

"I *am* happy," he insisted.

"You don't seem happy."

He pulled his mouth sideways. "What do I seem like?"

"Lost. Lonely."

"I have everything I've ever wanted." He jammed his fingers through his damp hair.

"And still," she whispered. "Not happy."

He didn't argue the point, just hauled in a taut, audible breath. "When this deal goes through with China, when the money comes in, I'll be the richest Lockhart in the history of the Trans-Pecos. Richer than my father."

"And then you'll be happy?"

He didn't answer.

Kaia met his eyes, held his gaze lovingly, steadily, and whispered, "That's what I thought."

Chapter 21

W<small>HY</small> did it feel like he was sitting in a police station, hands cuffed behind his back, a spotlight shoved in his face? Kaia's inquisition was innocent enough and yet it felt like she was testing him on some moral level.

And then you'll be happy?

Her words spoken so kindly, so softly, shimmered in the air like a heat mirage.

And then you'll be happy?

Good question.

He was thirty-two and he'd achieved everything he'd ever dreamed of. Showing up his father, besting him in his own industry, earning more money than he could spend, eating in the best restaurants, wearing the finest clothes, driving the fastest cars, flying his own plane, having the prettiest women on his arm.

Why did he feel so empty?

How was it she'd put it? *Lost. Lonely.*

None of it—not the money, not the possessions, not his position, not the women—had made him happy. It was supposed to make him happy. Why wasn't he happy?

That, friends and neighbors, was the million-dollar question.

Christmas on a cracker. Now that everything he'd ever dreamed of was within his grasp, he didn't want any of it. How had this happened?

"What do *you* want, Ridge?" Kaia asked. "Independent of this need to show up your father?"

"I'd like for my father not to be an asshole."

"I have no magic wand for that," Kaia said. "But you know in your heart of hearts, he loves you in his weird way."

"I suppose. At least he didn't disown me like my mother and my grandmother did. But he might as well have disowned me. The results were the same. I felt all alone in the world."

Kaia slanted her head. "I've got news for you, Ridge."

"Yeah?"

"You've disowned yourself."

What the hell was she talking about? He frowned, grunted.

"Your mother obviously had some mental issues and so did your grandmother. Their behavior wasn't about you. It was about them. Duke too. He was trying to make a new marriage to Ranger's mom work when you showed up. He was between a rock and a hard place."

"Still, he didn't have to be a total dick about it."

"No, but you're still beating yourself up for the way they behaved. As if you were the cause of the problems. You weren't. But you internalized it and now you can't let it go."

"Oh yeah?" He narrowed his eyes.

"You're terrified that if you stop doing, achieving, moving and shaking, you'll cease to exist. Wanna know the truth?"

"Because you have all the answers?" His tongue tasted poisonous.

"Not all the answers. No, but I can see what you can't because you're too close to it. The truth is when you stop all the doing, achieving, moving, and shaking, that's when you'll finally be found."

Anger bubbled up inside him. Who was she to tell him how to live his life? She knew nothing about him.

"You've lost touch with the real you, and no amount of grasping and striving will help you find the peace you're so obviously searching for. You can own the biggest house, drive the fastest car, eat in the most expensive restaurants but that will never make you happy. You're using external things to salve those childhood wounds that cannot be healed by tangible things."

"Wow," he said, icing up inside, feeling as if she'd turned against him. "Seems like you got me all figured out."

"You never got over losing your mother at a young age. She

made the choice to leave you, but you keep holding on to that grief with both hands. Blaming yourself. You still think that it's your fault. That if you'd been a better kid she would have loved you enough to stay."

"Is that so?" he asked through gritted teeth, as if he'd just chewed glass.

"You've got a hole in your heart that's never going to heal as long as you keep seeing money and status as the Holy Grail." She reached out and touched his arm.

He pulled back, hurt.

She flinched, retreated, leaned away from him.

They stared at each other for a long, hard bite of time.

"I'm only telling you this because I care about you," she said. "I also know that giving up on the belief that you have to keep chasing that brass ring feels like failure to you."

"That's because it *is* failure."

"Oh Ridge." She said it so sadly, as if he'd disappointed her in some monumental level.

He hardened his face, hardened the quicksand in his heart. "You're just like every other woman I've ever met. You want to change me. Mold me in a role of your own making."

Kaia's mouth dropped, and she raised a protective palm to her cheek as if he'd struck her.

Immediately, he felt like a shitheel. "That came out wrong."

"No," she said. "It's how you feel. But you're wrong. I don't want you to change to suit me. I want you to find out who you really are. I only want you to be happy. What do you truly want, Ridge? In your heart of hearts?"

He had no answer for her. None. Things had taken a dark turn, and this was supposed to be a fun afternoon.

"I want that drumstick." He laughed.

Beautiful woman that she was, she let him get away with it.

"Easy enough," she said, opening the picnic basket and producing the one remaining piece of fried chicken, and extending it to him wrapped with a paper napkin.

Except now that he had the drumstick, he didn't want that either. He shook his head. "Lost my appetite."

She looked crushed, and he realized belatedly that she thought she'd offended him somehow.

"Not your fault," he croaked, pushing the words past dry lips. "Not your fault at all. I didn't mean to take everything out on you."

"You didn't." She put the chicken back in the basket, raised her eyes to his. "How can I help?"

He didn't answer her unselfish question. Instead, he yanked her into his arms so forcefully that she gasped a surprised little "oh!" and then erupted into a smile as he pulled her closer and dipped his head.

She turned her eager mouth to greet his.

He kissed her. Fiercely claiming her. Ah! This was what he'd been hungering for. This was what he wanted. *This* was what made him happy.

Kaia and her amazing lips.

She slipped her lithe arms around him, hugging his neck tight, pulling his head down, and lapping at his mouth with heat, moisture, and rampant zeal.

They kissed for minutes, hours, days, eons.

He lost track of all time and space.

They floated in a bubble of joy. Just the two of them. Surfing each other's lips. Surrendering to the moment. To the water and the sun and the sand and the sensuous feel of skin touching skin.

He breathed her name. "Kaia. Kaia. Kaia."

A mantra. A prayer. A song of his soul. Such a beautiful, powerful name to describe a beautiful, powerful woman. *Kaia*.

"Thank you," she murmured, pulling her mouth from his, but still clinging to his neck. "Thank you so much."

"For what?" he asked, slightly confused.

He should be the one thanking her for caring enough to put the screws to him and force him to look at himself in a new way.

For shining a light in the dark places he didn't want to go and urging him to see what he'd been so reluctant to face.

To understand the lonely, shallow man he'd become. A man who pursued success at all costs without even having an endgame, a man who viewed prestige as the ultimate goal, even when it turned to dust in his hand. A man with no real home, no place where he truly belonged, no one to make success worth having in the first place.

Her smile was a life raft filled with hope and encouragement. A smile that said, *grab on, I'll save you.* Did he dare trust that smile?

He tucked her into the crook of his arm, squeezed her tight. He wasn't sure what to say. All he knew was that he was overjoyed to be with her. *Kaia.* A sweet ray of sunshine in his stormy world.

She stared into his eyes, a look of wonderment on her face, the same stunning wonderment coursing through his veins.

"Thank you," he said in a voice as rough as the desert terrain.

"For what?" she asked.

"For being you."

THEY GOT PAST their argument and spent the rest of the day hiking Balmorhea State Park. They skipped stones in the lake, watched birds, and had several "remember when" discussions about their childhood, but kept things on the lighter side.

Being with Ridge like this was as comfortable as a favorite pair of old jeans, but it was exciting too, as they carved out a new way of being with each other. The best of both, familiarity mixed with the thrill of the unknown, because there was so much to discover about each other.

Ten years and three thousand miles had created a lot of distance and differences. It encouraged her that they were working on ironing those differences out.

When she was in the hospital recovering from her accident, she'd dreamed of moments like this. It was how she'd survived. Envisioning herself in Balmorhea. In water. Using her imagination to transport her to a happier time and place.

But now she was here, living the dream, she got anxious.

"I've thought about moving away from Cupid," she said, studying his face, waiting for a reaction. "When I graduate vet school. I've always wanted to live near water."

He looked cool, unruffled, unconcerned. Damn him. "You always were a water baby."

"Corpus maybe, or when I'm feeling really brave, I envision leaving the state. I'm thinking Florida."

"It's nice there."

"You've been?"

"Many times. Go for the Gulf Coast side."

"I've heard that. But then I think of everything I'd be giving up. My family, my friends, my entire community, and then poof . . ." She snapped her fingers. "The water dreams disappear. No matter how much I long for water, my family means more."

"You should follow your heart," he said.

Follow her heart? If she followed her heart, she'd throw herself into his arms and beg him to love her in the way she loved him. But Kaia had too much dignity for that. If she couldn't have Ridge, water was the next best thing. Maybe she *would* move away. For a few years at least. Get the water out of her system.

"But honestly," he said, "I can't see you leaving your family. You're stuck to them like glue."

"I've lived in College Station."

"Knowing it was just temporary until you finish school. There's a difference between moving off to get your education and starting a new life all on your own. It will change you."

She wanted to ask him to elaborate, to tell her what it had been like for him to leave everything and everyone behind. But the look in his eyes warned her off. He lowered his lashes, turned his head away, letting her know he was done with revealing secrets for one day.

After they left the park, they stopped outside of Cupid for gas at a kitschy truck stop filled with tourists.

He held the door open for her as they went inside, and out of now where, a long-legged preteen girl, engrossed in her cell phone, pushed between the two of them on her way out the door.

Startled, Kaia stepped to one side and almost lost her balance, but Ridge was there, righting her with his steadying touch.

"Tessa," scolded the girl's mother, coming up behind them. "Get your head out of that phone or I'm taking it away. You almost knocked those folks down flat."

The girl, thumbs flying madly over the phone screen, never glanced up.

Ridge tipped his hat. "No worries, ma'am. I've been guilty of paying too much attention to my phone a time or two myself."

"Honestly," the mom said, putting a restraining arm on her daughter's shoulder to keep her from crashing into a metal cage of propane bottles. "We get such spotty cell reception here on the outskirts of town, the only time Tessa really has to text her friends is when we come to the store."

"We should blame the Davis Mountains," Ridge said. "And the scarcity of cell phone towers."

Kais couldn't tell if he was being sarcastic or not. He was smiling, but he kept his hand securely latched onto her elbow. Just in case the preteen made another clueless move?

Whatever his motives, she was enjoying the feel of his hand on hers. Her mind hopped ahead, wondering how this day was going to end. Would he ask if he could spend the night? Knowing Ridge, he wouldn't ask. Just take charge and sweep her into bed.

Her heart fluttered crazily. Did she want that?

"If anything, I'm to blame for being too lax with her," said the mom, giving Ridge an appreciative glance.

Hey, hey! Standing right here, lady, she wanted to shout. Jealousy kicked around her stomach, made a nice muddy mess. The woman kept eyeing him up one side and down the other.

Oblivious to her surroundings, Tessa's thumbs flowed like lightning.

"See what I have to deal with?" The mother gave a sexy little moan and fluttered her lashes. "It's not easy being a single parent."

It took everything in Kaia's power not to roll her eyes. Seriously? Did women come on to him like this every day of his life?

"Tessa," Ridge said sternly.

The sound of his deep masculine voice calling her name managed to shake the preteen from her social media–induced trance, and Tessa finally glanced up.

Ridge sent her a fatherly look and Kaia could have sworn the girl's mom literally swooned, clasping her palms to her chest, bracing her wobbly knees against the side of the building.

"Yes?" Tessa blinked.

"Could you do me a favor?"

"What's that?" The girl looked suspicious.

"At least put the phone away when you're crossing the street. I'd hate to see you become roadkill. Those buzzards up there"—he waved at half a dozen vultures circling the pasture across from the truck stop—"look pretty hungry to me."

Tessa eyed the buzzards, uneasily switched off her cell phone, and shifted it into her pocket.

"Thank you for being so understanding," the mom said, and shooed her daughter toward the parking lot.

"Hmm, sort of like the pot calling the kettle names," Kaia whispered to him. "Mr. King-of-Phubbing."

"Takes a phone addict to know one," he said glibly, not the least bit ashamed. "Besides, have you seen me look at my phone even once this entire day?"

"We were in the state park out of cell phone range," she pointed out.

"Darn. That's what I get for hanging out with a smart woman." Ridge winked and guided her into the truck stop. "But FYI, I turned it off before I ever pulled into your driveway."

His conspiratorial glance eased her possessiveness and left her feeling petty for getting jealous in the first place. He didn't belong to her. She had no claim on him. Yes, they'd had spectacular sex last night and shared a few secrets. But hot sex and whispered confidences did not a relationship make.

Which begged the question, where were they going?

And what were his plans for the rest of the evening? Was he envisioning spending the night with her? She had certainly been hoping he'd stay the night. But what if she'd misread things?

Argh! Kaia pressed a palm to her forehead. She had to get a hold of herself. Splash some water on her face. Do some deep breathing. Knock off the constant mind chatter.

"Here's your chance to check your cell phone," she muttered, gave him a quick wave, and headed off to the restroom, her mind a jumble of doubt and second-guessing, her heart beating far too fast.

When she came out of the restroom, she couldn't find him. Assuming he'd also gone to the restroom, she perused the aisles, and honest-to-Pete, she didn't mean to end up on the prophylactics aisle, but she rounded the corner and found herself staring at rows of condoms.

She was about to run away, but glanced up and spied Ridge in the next aisle over.

"Ssst," she hissed, seized by impulse.

He raised his head, grinned when he saw her. "Uh-huh?"

"Should we buy these?" she whispered, holding up the box of condoms just high enough so he could see them over the top of the shelf.

His grin spread from ear to ear. "Why, Kaia Alzate, is that an invitation?"

"If you want it to be."

"Hell yes." Quickly, he joined her on the condom aisles, plucked the box of Trojans, ribbed for her pleasure, from her, took her by the hand and dragged her to the checkout counter.

Leaving no more doubts in her mind about whether or not he wanted to spend his last night in town with her.

Chapter 22

HE drove back to her house as quickly as the legal speed limit allowed—and maybe even a little faster than that. His left hand on the steering wheel, his right hand holding tight to hers.

By the time they reached her house it was dusk. The moon was so slender, barely a slice of light, and the stars were already visible.

She fumbled for her keys, ready to haul him into her house and jump his bones, but he slipped his arm around her waist and held her in place on the front porch. Night sounds came to life around them—a song of camel crickets, a blackbird's call, a dog barking lazily from a yard down the street, wind rustling the desert chaparral.

They stood together on her porch underneath the stars. He was looking at her, but his eyes were unfocused, his mind seemed faraway. She put her arms around his neck, drew his head down, and he was back with her.

Kaia wanted to ask him where he'd gone, what he'd been thinking, but before she could get the words out, he kissed her long and hard as if he'd been thirsty for years and she was a tall glass of cool water.

They were cloaked in darkness, mouths fused, bodies pressed tight. It was a goodbye kind of kiss. He was leaving tomorrow. Going back to where he'd come from.

Her head was humming. That same beautiful, hopeful song.

She should tell him about the humming. Just put it out there. Own it. But if she did that, he might not spend the night with her and she wouldn't even have one last sweet goodbye.

"Ridge, I—"

"Please don't tell me you're not going to invite me in," he said, his voice scarred and rough. "I need you tonight, Kaia."

"I need you too."

"Good." He kissed her hard.

Dazzled by the humming in her head, she finally got the lock opened, and let them inside.

Dart greeted them, reeling around their legs, meowing for dinner.

"I'm sorry," Kaia apologized. "I have to feed the animals."

"I'll help."

By the time they fed the animals inside and out, it was after nine o'clock. They took one look into each other's eyes and the next thing Kaia knew they were shedding clothes on the way to her bedroom.

What a blessing to have one more night with him!

They started out fast, but the minute they sank into her mattress, things slowed. Both of them wanting this night to last forever.

Kaia put the box of Trojans they'd bought at the truck stop on the nightstand and issued a challenge. "Let's see how many of these we can get through before dawn."

"Game on." He grinned, his teeth flashing white in the dim glow from the night-light in the shape of a horse that was plugged into the socket next to the bed.

And so it began, their glorious last journey, the beginning of goodbye. Kaia concentrated on every movement, every whisper, every caress, every scent.

Making love to Ridge showed her the world was multifaceted. A beautiful, mystifying world connected by a series of portals and dimensions, colors, shapes, and patterns; a world that flowed and ebbed as constantly and subtly as breath.

Being with him, body-to-body, skin-to-skin, heart-to-beating-heart shifted and merged, until they became an ever-changing, overriding, symbiotic energy that defied belief, and yet felt absolutely logical.

She was shattered and profoundly confused, while at the same time filled with bliss, ecstasy, and an engulfing sense of peace. It was as if a great storm had passed. Troubled waters parted and the sun was shining again, casting the world in a brilliant mosaic of bright, healing light.

As if the overwhelming waves of her life, which before were so constant, complicated, and challenging were now a sweet, calm, lulling sea full of fluid beauty and teeming with life and hope.

In that sharp moment of their total release, she was reborn.

Like an infant awaking for the first time in a brand-new world, she absorbed the wonder around her, in awe of everything she tasted, viewed, touched, heard, smelled. A baby in the arms of universal truth. In his arms she was both vulnerable and yet extremely safe.

She knew without question that if she ever ran to him, tears in her eyes, he'd want to know who he should beat up without even asking why.

In their achingly perfect joining, she saw everything with fresh eyes—herself, her life, the entire world, Ridge.

Love.

She was in love.

And Ridge was the personification of it all. Her beloved. There was nothing she could do that would ever change that fact. Whether they ended up together in the long run or not, he would forever be her soul mate, her one and only.

Engulfed in this knowledge, powerless to alter her fate, Kaia surrendered one hundred percent.

She stopped fighting, struggling, resisting. She let go and let it happen. Allowed emotions, sensations, thoughts, fears, and doubt to roll through her and flow out of her.

In his embrace she found nourishment, sustenance, comfort. Being with him transported her to a whole realm of possibilities. And she was so deeply grateful for this experience. For the transformation.

For Ridge.

He had given her the greatest gift she had ever received. He gave her permission to be who she was. Without hesitation or restraint or judgment. He accepted her just as she was.

How did she begin to describe what was happening? To put it in words others might understand? But there were no words. This wasn't something people could understand unless they'd experienced it for themselves, and then they would have to invent their own language for their experiences.

This . . . *this* . . . well, whatever ever you wanted to call it . . . love, belonging, perfection. It was so intimate, so personal, so sacred, it was completely surreal. Her feelings were illogical, fanciful, dreamy, and yet absolutely nothing had ever felt so authentic.

Impossible to gauge how this experience would impact Ridge, their relationship, and the rest of her life.

But one thing was clear, her gut, her intuition, her instinct, and the stirring of her heart had set her on a new path from which there was no turning back. There was no way to retreat after something like this.

None.

Kaia was forever changed.

She had opened herself up to his life force. His energy filled her, and she was activated. Alive in a way she did not question but could not fully understand. How could she go on in the same old way?

The discovery that she'd been trapped in a life she didn't even know was a prison shocked her.

Subconsciously, she'd been longing for something, lacking something, even though she couldn't quite put her finger on what it was. She'd been following her dreams, going to school, working with animals, enjoying life with her family and friends, but in the back of her mind there had been this nagging feeling that she was incomplete.

She'd had no idea of this power within her. An all-encompassing, electric indigo power that making love to Ridge unleashed.

It was dizzying, overwhelming, disconcerting. Her head and her heart were in the clouds. Flying in sweet paradise.

Would the emotions disappear once she came back to earth and got grounded in reality? Would this heavenly glimpse of her true self disappear in the day-to-day grind? Could she hang on to it long after he was gone?

Because he was going. Tomorrow. Flying off to Calgary and then to China. Six months gone.

Alarmed, she opened her eyes to see Ridge staring down into her face, eyes wide-open. He looked as gobsmacked as she felt.

She inhaled sharply. And he did too. Breathing the same air. Holding the same breath.

She wanted to simultaneously shout her experience from the rooftops, and to keep quietly sacred this delicious happening that was blowing to pieces everything she'd ever believed to be true about sex and love and her role in the world.

The ache inside her was deep and sorrowful. Knowing she was losing him just as she was finding him. She blinked away tears pushing at the back of her eyelids.

What twin emotions! Flip side of the same coin. With great love came great pain. You could not have one without the other. If you loved, eventually you would be hurt.

But oh! It was so worth the cost.

Even if he never loved her back.

SOFT STARLIGHT OOZED through the parted curtains of Kaia's bedroom window, spilling a gentle glow across Ridge's bare back. He was lying on his side, uncovered, one leg drawn up, the other leg outstretched, sleeping like a flamingo.

She smiled. Such fun to discover the little things she never knew about him. Fun to watch him sleeping as she listened to the Song of the Soul Mate humming in her brain. A steady strum of *he's your one and only.*

Oh, she was so screwed!

A girl who believed love was the only thing that made you whole was falling for a man who believed that love was the very thing that broke you.

"Hey," he murmured, his eyes fluttering open. "How are you?"

A smile claimed her mouth. "Amazing. How about you?"

Hair sexily tousled, he sat up, stretched his arms overhead, yawned. "What time is it?"

"Just after midnight."

"I should go."

"Did you forget the challenge?" She nodded at the box of condoms on the nightstand.

He grinned. "I did not." He leaned over to kiss her forehead. "But I was planning on leaving at three a.m. to get to Calgary by the time my office opens at eight."

"I see." Disappointment was a rock in the bottom of her stomach.

"I should have told you my plans," he said, swinging his legs over the side of the bed.

"It's already so late. Maybe you should just stay and get a few more hours' sleep before you have to go back to the ranch."

"I'm used to running on just minimal sleep. I'll be fine."

That was not what she meant. She wanted more time with him, but she didn't want to cling.

He leaned down to kiss the top of her head. It was such a sweet gesture her heart stuttered.

Lucky. She was so lucky to have had him for this precious time. That's the only way she could spin it so that she didn't completely break apart. Lucky, lucky, lucky.

"Go back to sleep," he said, pulling on his swim trunks.

It seemed a million years since they'd been swimming in Balmorhea, and yet at the same time, the flicker of an eye.

"One last kiss?" she breathed.

His grin was fast and loose like a tropical sunrise. He sank to his knees on the mattress, drew her into his arms for a parting kiss.

Ah. Bliss.

Humming so heavenly she wished she could submerse herself in it, in him for the rest of her life.

RIDGE DIDN'T WANT to leave.

He peered at Kaia, who was gazing up at him as if he were the sun and the moon and the stars.

His chest clutched like a manual transmission stuck in second gear, rumbling and grinding on a steep downhill incline. It was all he could do not to crawl back into bed, pull her into his arms and make love to her all over again.

He was hooked. Addicted. Obsessed.

But the only way to break an addiction was cold turkey. He had to go. He had work to do, and he wasn't going to get in the way of her finishing her degree. Plus, he didn't belong in Cupid. Never had.

"Have a safe trip," she whispered, her eyes full of the same sadness and longing that tugged at him. It was a sensation he'd never before experienced. A sensation that scared him to the bottom of his soul.

He had an overwhelming impulse to tell her to wait for him. To give him some time to figure things out. But how could he ask her to put her life on hold for him when he'd be in China for six months? It wasn't fair to her.

Damn, if he wasn't about to ask just that when her dogs pushed the bedroom door open and barreled inside and piled onto the mattress and buried her in wet doggy kisses.

Kaia giggled, covered her face with her hands.

Ridge stood there watching her with the dogs, wearing nothing but his swim trunks, affection for her swelling his heart. She was so uncomplicated, so honest, so fresh and real. A million miles away from his ordinary, high-speed, high-stress world.

He could taint her so easily.

"They need to go to the bathroom," she said.

"I'll let them out," he offered, and moved to the door. The dogs bailed off the bed, following him.

He was at the back door, the dogs at his heels, when he heard her call out from the bedroom, "Watch out for Dart. He's still a bit feral and he'll bolt if he sees an opening."

But it was already too late. The back door was open and a blur of orange fur zoomed outside ahead of the hounds.

"Dammit!" Ridge cursed and took off after the kitten, barefooted, in the pitch dark.

"RIDGE?" KAIA PULLED on her robe and padded into the kitchen. When she spied the back door hanging open, she knew at once what had happened. Dart, the little escape artist, had made good his getaway.

She should have warned Ridge sooner about the kitten, but she'd been wrapped in a cocoon of early-morning-after-great-sex bliss, and her brain was fuzzily warped.

"Snap out of it," she scolded, shook her head, and peered out the door. The dogs were in the fenced backyard, wagging their tails, but she saw neither hide nor hair of Ridge or Dart.

Cinching the belt of her robe tighter, she stepped out onto the back porch. "Ridge?"

Not far away, a coyote howled. She shivered. Oh dear. Little Dart was snack-sized, and the desert was filled with dangerous creatures.

"Dart," she called, hearing the anxiety in her voice. "Here kitty, kitty."

From the alley behind the shed, came a crash, followed by a muffled curse and another crash.

"Ridge?" She paused to jam her feet into the flip-flops she kept at the back door, and then sprinted across the yard. Buddy and Bess barked and ran along with her, clearly thinking she was up for some kind of game.

Something yowled. Twice.

Dart? Or was it Ridge?

Heart slamming hard into her ribs, she rounded the shed, reached the chain-link fence separating her property from the alley. Stopped, breathless and perspiring.

There stood Ridge in the light of the flood lamp, a wriggling Dart clasped in his hands, his bare chest covered in scratches.

"Gotcha!" Ridge crowed.

Kaia was relieved that he'd found Dart, but concerned for Ridge. She took the kitten Ridge triumphantly handed to her, cuddled him to her chest, felt the frantic rhythm of Dart's tiny pulse.

"C'mon," she said, noticing blood oozing from his scratches. "Let's get you cleaned and doctored."

"This is nothing."

"Nevertheless," she said. "We can't have you flying off with infected wounds. Ever heard of cat scratch fever?"

He looked as if he were about to argue, but nodded and hobbled toward her.

"You're barefooted!"

"Yeah. I was determined not to let Dart get away. Stepped on bull nettle."

"Good grief."

Still clinging to a wriggling Dart, she and the dogs escorted Ridge back to the house. Once inside, she crated the kitten and directed Ridge to the bathroom. Closed the toilet lid, motioned for him to sit.

He plunked down. She rummaged in the medicine cabinet for antiseptic and antibiotic ointment.

"This is going to sting." She knelt in from of him, dabbed the bloody scratches with an antiseptic-doused cotton ball.

Ridge hissed in a clenched breath.

His body heat radiated into her as she tended to the dozen scratches crisscrossing his muscled torso. He'd gotten injured saving her cat.

Between the black eyes and the wounds on his chest and the red welts on his feet where he'd stepped on the bull nettles, he looked like he'd tangled with the wrong character. He'd not had an easy time of it the past few days. She couldn't blame him if he never came back to Cupid.

"Thank you," she whispered.

"Don't thank me," he said. "It was my fault the little critter got out in the first place."

"Not your fault. Dart is slippery. He's always looking for an opening. This is the fourth time he's run away since I took him in three weeks ago. I'm terrified he'll get out and I won't be able to find him. The desert is not a safe place for a kitten on his own."

"You've got your work cut out for you."

"How's that?"

"You know what they say." Ridge's eyes met hers.

"What?"

"Once a runner, always a runner. Don't get attached."

"He's still young," she said, feeling strangely defensive of Dart. "I have a feeling he's going to make a great cat someday, and greatness takes time."

Ridge's eyes darkened, and an odd, humorless smile flitted across his mouth. "Then again, some animals just can't be tamed. Take Majestic for instance."

"That might be true, but I have hope," she said, surprised by a sharp tightness creeping through her stomach.

"And that," Ridge said, "is both your strength and your downfall."

"Meaning?"

"Sometimes things *are* hopeless. And nothing can hurt you more than false hope."

Kaia settled back on her heels, slowly shook her head. "That is the saddest thing I've ever heard."

"Oftentimes the truth is sad."

The tension in her stomach spread up to her chest, crawled like a hand to squeeze tight her throat. Was this his way of warning her not to have hope in their relationship?

She opened her mouth, wanting to say something that could change his mind, but before she could pry the words out, he yanked her against his bare chest and kissed her hard.

Instantly, the humming filled her head again. No joke. Not her imagination. If she believed Granny's legend, for better or worse, Ridge Lockhart was her soul mate.

In the midst of their earthshaking kissing, the phone in the pocket of his swim trunks buzzed. He ignored it.

The phone buzzed again.

And again.

And again.

"Dammit," he swore, pulling his mouth from hers.

"You turned it back on," she said.

"In the truck stop," he explained. "When you told me it was okay to check my messages. Hang on. I'll switch it off again."

He took his phone from his back pocket, glanced down at the screen, winced. "Oh no."

"What is it?" she asked, peering over his arm to see the screen. Saw several texts from Vivi.

Felt a lump of hard jealousy in her throat.

Ridge's face darkened, and in a controlled monotone he said, "Duke's had a massive heart attack. They're careflighting him to El Paso for immediate open-heart surgery."

Chapter 23

RIDGE wished it were Kaia sitting in the cockpit beside him instead of Vivi. This was the first time he'd been alone with his ex-girlfriend since she'd become his stepmother, and it was uncomfortable as hell.

Vivi was a wreck. Her hair hung oily and stringy in her eyes, her makeup was smeared, her eyes wide and full of fear.

A pile of wadded-up tissues littered the floor of the plane at her feet. She kept clenching and unclenching her hands in her lap, and then alternately rubbing her palms back and forth over her bare thighs.

She wore Daisy Duke denim shorts, red cowgirl boots, and a white halter-top. When he'd asked her if she wanted to change clothes—she and Duke had been line dancing at Chantilly when he'd collapsed—she yelled at him there was no time.

He knew she was distraught so he let it go. But if this thing stretched out for several days, as it most likely would, she'd need something else to wear. He'd buy her some clothes when the stores opened tomorrow morning. She didn't seem capable of handling the task for herself.

And he felt . . .

Angry, hurt by what Vivi and Duke had done behind his back. And he was confused too. He thought he'd buried all that mess, but apparently, he'd just swept it under the rug. He hadn't forgiven their betrayal. Kaia was right. He'd spent ten years using work to run away from his feelings.

Kaia. He thought of her sweet face, her lush body, her kind heart. Regretted that he was not going to wake up beside her.

Selfish. He was being selfish. His father might not make it through the night and he was thinking about the hot morning sex he was missing.

C'mon, tell the truth. It wasn't the sex he was missing. It was Kaia.

He and Vivi flew through the night mostly in silence with no sounds save for her occasional sniffles and the hum of the airplane.

To keep his mind occupied, Ridge did what he always did in uncomfortable situations. He thought about work. Sending his mind to China, envisioning the contract negotiations going as planned even though in light of recent developments, he was going to have to call his second in command to trek to Beijing in his place to meet up with Phil and the legal team.

He winced. The company he was dealing with had specific ideas about how business should go, and sending an underling instead of the president of the company could be taken as a sign of disrespect. Navigating a foreign culture could be sketchy. But first things first. El Paso. Duke. Coronary bypass surgery. Then he could deal with business.

It was then that Vivi decided to break the quiet. "Well," she said halfway into the flight, "are we going to discuss the eight-hundred-pound elephant?"

"Gorilla," he said.

"What?"

"The phrase is 'an eight-hundred-pound gorilla.' Elephants weigh several tons."

"Oh." Vivi crinkled her nose, and said with complete sincerity, "Maybe they're talking about a baby elephant."

"You're mixing metaphors."

"Huh?" Vivi blinked.

"It's two different sayings," he explained kindly. "It's either the eight-hundred-pound gorilla, or the elephant in the room."

Her brow furrowed. "So which one do I mean?"

Ridge shrugged. "Elephant. Gorilla. Whatever animal you want to call it. We do not have to discuss the situation. In fact, let's not and say we did."

"That won't work."

He sighed.

"Don't sigh," she said. "You always used to do that when I tried to talk to you about serious things. Listen to me, please. I need to get this off my chest. We never got closure because you ran off."

"What did you expect me to do?"

"Stay, fight for me."

"Like it's my fault you tumbled into my bed with my father?"

"I didn't say it was your fault, but you were always working, and I was lonely."

"So instead of talking to me about it, you went for my dad?"

"I tried to talk to you about it. You were always too busy to listen."

"To support your spending habits."

"Oh don't put that in my lap. You enjoyed buying me things. You *liked* showing me off." She inhaled deeply. "When it suited you."

"Yes, okay. You're a gorgeous woman and I liked having you on my arm. And we both know we weren't in love, but that was no excuse for stabbing me in the back . . ." He ground his teeth. "With my *father*."

"Ridge." She snorted and stomped her foot against the floorboard. "Will you just give me a chance to explain?"

"All right," he said. If she needed to unburden herself to feel better, he'd suck it up and hear her out. Maybe she was right. Maybe it was past time to get over this uncomfortable discussion. Get closure. It wasn't like he had much of a choice but to listen if she started talking. They were trapped in a plane together.

"This has been eating on your father too," Vivi murmured. "In fact, I bet your homecoming triggered his heart attack."

Ah, so that was his fault too?

"I'm not blaming you for the heart attack." Vivi read his

mind, and frankly, her insight surprised him. Generally, in his experience, she was pretty much all about Vivi. "I'm just saying he's been on edge ever since he heard you were coming back for Archer's wedding. Drinking too much, eating foods that aren't good for him."

"How is any of that my fault?"

"If you'd ever bothered to call or come home, you'd know he wasn't well," Vivi said. "But you were too stubborn or too selfish to forgive him."

"It's a two-way street, Vivi. He was the one in the wrong. He should have been begging me to forgive him."

"You know he's not built that way."

"Neither am I."

"So here we are." She fell silent.

For a moment the only sounds were the plane's engine. "How come you offered to host the wedding?" he asked.

"Archer is our foreman. It seemed the right thing to do."

Our foreman. As if the Silver Feather belonged to her too.

It hit him then, a load of emotional bricks dropped onto his head. Legally, he supposed it did. If Duke died without a will, Vivi would inherit the ranch. Did his father have a will? Surely, Duke had a will.

Ridge had no clue—*zero, zilch, zip*—what he was going to do if the old man didn't pull through, hadn't left a will and he and his brothers were left to battle Vivi over the future of the ranch that had been in his family for six generations. It surprised him. This territorial feeling. The fact that he cared. He'd had nothing to do with the Silver Feather in over a decade, and yet now the thought of losing it twisted him inside out.

Why?

Vivi was busy shredding a tissue into tiny pieces of white fluff. "You might not believe this, but if anything happens I don't know what I'd do without him."

Ridge grunted. He did not believe her. But he hoped for Duke's sake she was telling the truth.

"How was Archer's wedding?" asked Kaia's boss, Dr. Cheri Gunther DVM, bright and early Monday morning as they meet in the scrub room to prepare for surgery. Dr. Cheri was in her early thirties, round of body and face. She possessed an easy-going temperament, a down-to-earth bedside manner, and a new husband who worked at McDonald Observatory with Ranger Lockhart.

"Sweet," Kaia said. "Romantic. Adorable. I'm glad it's over."

"That taxing?" Dr. Cheri chuckled, joining Kaia at the scrub sink, where she picked up a scrub brush and turned the water on with her elbow. "I barely remember my wedding. It was such a hubbub."

"It *was* a nonstop blur, so much going on and so many out-of-town guests. I've barely slept in three days." Kaia suppressed a yawn.

She didn't mention that Ridge was the main reason why she hadn't slept. He'd texted her when he arrived in El Paso, saying Duke's condition was touch and go, and they were taking him into surgery. She hadn't heard another word since. She thought about calling or texting, but didn't want to pester. No news was good news, right?

"Are you good to go?" the vet asked, the safety of the animals her top concern.

It was Kaia's top concern, as well. "I've rallied. Two cups of coffee and I've got my second wind."

"If you want to leave after we finish the surgery," Dr. Cheri said, "just let me know. I can get Brenda to fill in."

"Maybe." As a part-time employee, Kaia didn't accrue comp time or benefits. "I'll see how busy the office is when we get done. Right now, I'm happy to be here."

"You might change your mind when you see what we've got on the docket this morning. A mastiff just came in through emergency with a bellyache, and the X-rays show the poor thing has three tennis balls in his intestines."

Thirty minutes later, over the dog on the surgery table, the satellite radio tuned to Cheri's favored rock station. Sense Field was playing "Save Yourself."

"So," Dr. Cheri asked as she meticulously made the midline incision on the anesthetized mastiff. "How was *he*?"

"How was who?"

"Ridge Lockhart."

Kaia peeked at Cheri. The doctor was focused on her work, but Kaia didn't miss the telltale flush spreading up the top of her mask to her temples and forehead. "Dr. Cheri, are you blushing?"

"What? Me? No. It's hot in here." Cheri's voice sounded funny, as if she had something caught in her windpipe and was trying to talk around it.

"Want me to move the light back?" Kaia reached for the handle on the big surgical light directly over their heads that generated a lot of heat.

"No worries. I'll be all right. I need the light close to see."

"I could ask Finny to turn down the temperature," she said, referring to the office manager.

"No really. It's okay."

They were silent for a while as they worked, and then Cheri said, "We were in the same grade in high school."

"You and Ridge?"

"Yes."

"You had a crush on him."

"Oh, didn't everyone?"

Yes. It was a sharp reminder that her infatuation with Ridge was nothing special.

"We dated a few times, and I'm a happily married woman now, and I am crazy for my Mason. But there's just something about your first crush that never quite leaves you. Know what I mean?"

She did indeed. Ridge was her first crush. Her last, come to think of it.

"Retractor." Cheri put out her gloved hand.

Kaia slapped the retractor into the doctor's palm. One day, she would be the one asking for the retractor, but right now, that day seemed very far away.

"Is Ridge still single?" Dr. Cheri asked nonchalantly.

"He is."

"I wonder if he'll ever slow down long enough to let any woman catch him," she mused. "Is he still sexy as sin?"

"Sexier," Kaia admitted.

Cheri looked up and met Kaia's eyes over her mask. "You had a crush on him too?"

Kaia lifted one shoulder.

"Huh. Imagine that."

"Imagine what?"

"I always thought you two were like brother and sister."

"We were raised that way," Kaia said, fighting against a sudden tightness pressing against her chest.

"But you have unsisterly feelings for him?"

"You've got a bleeder there." Kaia pointed and reached for the suction.

Cheri swung into action, cauterizing the bleeding vessel, and thankfully shutting up about Ridge. At least until three slimy tennis balls later when they'd finished the surgery and were closing up the mastiff.

"How long is Ridge going to be in Cupid? I'd love to invite him to dinner. Mason grills a mean sirloin," Cheri asked, after the mastiff had been transferred to the recovery area and they were stripping off their scrub gowns and gloves.

"He was planning on leaving this morning," Kaia said vaguely, leaving it at that. It wasn't her place to tell the vet about Duke's heart attack. Soon enough the gossip would make the rounds, but she wouldn't be the start of it.

"So soon?" Dr. Cheri sounded disappointed.

"He's headed to China for six months, where his company is introducing the drilling technique he pioneered. According to Archer, it's going to revolutionize silver mining."

Dr. Cheri sighed dreamily. "Ridge was always an overachiever."

"So is Mason," Kaia said.

"Don't worry." Dr. Cheri laughed. "I'm not about to throw my husband over for a guy who is allergic to commitment. Ridge Lockhart might be hot as blazes, but he's certainly no one's idea of husband material."

DUKE HAD MADE it through a five-hour open-heart surgery, but he was in ICU on the ventilator and hadn't regained consciousness.

Right now, it was just Ridge, Ranger, and Vivi in the waiting area. Rhett was on a plane home from Montana, where he'd been on the PBR circuit, and Remington was catching the next transport flight from the Middle East.

Ranger had had the presence of mind to drop by the mansion and pack an overnight bag for Vivi, saving Ridge from having to go clothes shopping for her. On the downside, he now had no excuse to leave the hospital.

He was stuck.

Ridge had gotten on the smartphone and played catch-up calls, texts, and emails. Because of the thirteen-hour time difference, he would have to wait until the evening to let Beijing know he would not be arriving as planned, but his second in command was on the way in his place.

God, he hated waiting. Hated hospitals too. And this was just the start of it.

He paced the length of the waiting room until a visitor glared at him, and he finally sat down. He crossed his legs, flipped through a magazine, uncrossed them again, and stared at the clock that seemed to be broken.

At four p.m. the ICU opened for visiting hours.

"Two at a time," a stern-faced nurse chided.

"Ranger and I will go in first," Vivi said to Ridge. "And then you can go."

Ridge nodded, understanding why it was easier for her to go see Duke with his brother at her side instead of him.

Ten minutes later, Ranger and Vivi came back out and it was his turn. He walked into the small private room punctuated by the whooshing sound of the ventilator breathing for Duke.

Seeing his larger-than-life father crumpled up in that bed, eyes closed, tubes snaking into his body, shook him. This was serious business.

Duke could die. This could be it.

They had a complicated relationship, but when push came to shove, Ridge loved the old son of a bitch.

Emotion flooded his system. His throat felt raw, and his stomach roiled. And he wished like hell that Kaia and her optimistic hope were with him.

Here lies Duke Augustus Lockhart caged by a machine that breathed for him. Unconscious. Unable to speak. A victim of a life of excess, lying in the darkened room that smelled of antiseptic and disease.

Dying by inches.

Was his father full of regret? Did he wish he could live his life over, make different choices?

What about his own regrets? What would he do differently if he had the chance?

Ridge swallowed, realizing he'd made just as many mistakes as his father.

"Visitation is over," said the nurse from the doorway.

He nodded curtly, went back to the waiting room. Vivi was on the phone. Ranger read a book. He sat apart from them. Closed his eyes. A lifetime of loneliness swallowed him whole.

"Ridge?"

He opened his eyes, bolted to his feet. Blinked to see Kaia standing before him. Ember was with her, and she took a seat beside Ranger.

"You're here," he said, a crazy impossible burst of joy pressing into the center of his chest so hard that it hurt.

"Of course I'm here." She stared at him as if he were a damn fool. "Where else would be? I got here as soon as I could."

At any other time a question such as this would have struck him as rhetorical. Either he expected her to be there or he didn't, no answer needed. But under the squeeze of circumstances and her intent dark eyes, his reason stumbled.

If he were being honest, would he admit he hoped she would show up? Subconsciously, had he been watching for her every time the door to the waiting room opened?

The concept was so distant and indistinct that he couldn't lay claim to it. The harder he tried to decipher the reason she *was* here the more uncertain he became about whether her question needed an answer. He never would have suspected that something as innocent as her steadfast belief that he should expect her to show up would cause so much bewilderment.

"I don't know," he said, feeling keenly aware that the remark was inadequate. "You've got things to do. Work. Your pets—"

"There is *nothing* more important than being here to support you," she said so vehemently that her voice cracked. "Ember told me she was coming for Ranger, and the clinic was slow this afternoon, so I left work early and came with her. I simply had to be here for you. Aria's promised to look after my animals."

She took his hand and led him to another bank of chairs along the back wall, out of earshot from everyone else. "Sit."

He didn't resist. Just allowed her to guide him down.

Suddenly, a childhood memory flooded him. One he'd all but forgotten. He and Archer had been out riding horses, and tagalong Kaia had followed them on her pony. They'd tried to run her off, but she'd refused to go.

Finally, they'd decided to ignore her. They'd been monkeying around, egging each other on to try riskier and riskier horseback stunts. Archer stood up in the saddle, balancing like a surfer on a board. To outdo his buddy, Ridge had attempted a handstand from the saddle.

It hadn't ended well.

Startled, his horse scarpered. Ridge fell off and struck his head on a rock. His horse galloped away. Spooked, Archer's spirited horse took off with his buddy astride. Leaving Ridge on his back, staring up at a wide expanse of sky, bloodied, dazed, shocked.

And then there was Kaia, peering down at him.

Her eight-year-old face serious with concern, she'd helped him to sit up and told him to put his head between his knees and breathe slowly and deep like she was a medical expert. From her saddlebag, she'd taken a canteen, wet a bandana, and pressed the damp cloth to the back of his neck. She'd sat with him until Archer came back leading Ridge's horse behind him.

He remembered being amazed at how calm she'd been. Doing what needed to be done. He'd felt humbled and embarrassed to have a little kid taking care of him. So embarrassed he'd never thanked her.

She was here now, doing it again. Taking care of him in a similar way. He looked up to see her holding a foam cup of coffee.

"Drink this," she said.

"Thank you." He took the cup, took a drink.

"You're welcome."

"Not just for the coffee. For everything you've ever done for me. Including that time in the desert when Archer and I were goofing around and I fell off the horse and hit my head and you were there to patch me up."

She smiled, a slight smile of acknowledgment. "You yelled at me."

"I did?"

"You said to go away. That you didn't need a little kid's help."

"I don't remember that."

"I do."

"I was an ass."

"You were in shock."

"You were eight. How could you know that?"

"I didn't at the time. You did hurt my feelings, but I was so in awe of you. No way was I going to leave you alone, even if you did yell at me."

He reached over and took her hand. Squeezed it. "Forgive me."

An angel's smile couldn't have been as lovely. "Always."

God, how had he gotten so lucky to have her as a friend?

"Have you eaten?" she asked.

He shook his head. The last thing on his mind had been food.

"Come." She stuck out her hand to him.

He didn't take it, even though he wanted to. "Where to?"

"You need to get out of here for a while. Get some food in you."

He shot a glance at Ranger, who was deep in conversation with Ember. Vivi was watching a game show on the waiting room TV.

She kept holding out her palm. "I'm taking you to dinner, my treat. We'll be back in time for the eight o'clock visiting hours."

Charged at the idea of being alone with her again, he sank his hand into hers. Then she went and invited Ember, Ranger, and Vivi to come along too.

He pushed back his disappointment, because that was his Kaia. So kind and openhearted, she wasn't about to leave anyone out.

Chapter 24

GUILT nibbled Kaia as she and Ember drove back from El Paso late that night. It had been a mad dash trip to show their support for the Lockhart brothers, but they both had jobs and responsibilities to get back to. She'd only had a few hours with Ridge, precious little of that time with just the two of them. Although they had managed a short private conversation in the hallway at one point.

"Are you all right?" Ember asked.

"Why wouldn't I be?" Kaia asked, guiding her Tundra toward Cupid city limits.

"You've hardly said a word the entire trip."

"Nothing to say."

"You slept with him, didn't you?"

Kaia bit down on her tongue. Her sister's insight floored her.

"Ky?" Her sister's voice held concern. "Talk to me."

"How did you know? Did Granny Blue tell you?"

Ember rolled her eyes. "Please. If the way you guys had your hands all over each other on the dance floor didn't give it away, Ranger and I caught you canoodling in the chapel if you'll recall."

"We weren't canoodling, we were—" Oh hell, why deny it. "Yes. I slept with him."

Ember's voice softened. "You heard it when he kissed you, the Song of the Soul Mate?"

"I don't know," she whimpered, but nodded fiercely, tears pressing at the back of her eyelids. "No. Yes. Maybe."

"I'm getting mixed messages here," Ember said, reaching across the seat of the Tundra to touch Kaia's arm. "Is this a good thing or a bad thing?"

"I don't know," she wailed again.

"Can I help?"

"Talk me out of this."

"How?"

"Tell me it's not true. Tell me there's no such thing as soul mates. Tell me it's nothing but ringing in the ears. Tell me it's a silly myth, and the only reason I heard the humming was because I *wanted* to hear it."

"You love him," Ember said.

"That's not what I asked you to tell me."

"You love him," Ember repeated, this time empathically.

"What *is* love?" Kaia backpedaled, in way over her head.

"You've loved him for a long time."

"Childhood crush. Infatuation. That's not love."

"It's more than that, and you know it."

"What if this humming, a belief in a soul mate, is just some form of mental illness?" Kaia asked. "You have to admit, it is a little crazy."

Ember studied her. "What if it isn't? What if it's all true?"

What if?

Kaia's stomach quivered. What if she and Ridge were mated? Fated? Put together by some universal force before they'd ever come here? Hands trembling, Kaia pulled over to the side of the road, put the truck in Park.

"Could you drive home?" she asked her sister, overwhelmed by the notion that they belonged together on some cosmic level beyond her control. It was fanciful and silly, but she couldn't shake the bone-deep feeling it was true.

"Sure, yes, for certain. But I think you need a hug first." Ember undid her seat belt and reached across the seat to hug her.

She dropped her head on her oldest sister's shoulder. "I should never have let things get this far. I should never have gone to bed with him. I tried to tell myself it was casual, it didn't mean anything, just sex—"

Except the sex had been top-of-the-mountain spectacular. So earthshaking spectacular in fact that it was easy to forget all the little steps leading up to it. Tending Ridge's black eye after he rescued Atticus from getting kicked by Majestic, the meaningful looks he'd sent her from the altar at the wedding, how he'd gotten her to open up about her stalker, the fun they'd had at Balmorhea, how he had the capacity to forgive his father and Vivi after they'd done him so wrong.

Small signs of the kind of man he was. Wounded but trying his best to heal, just as she was. Struggling to find how they fit. Yearning to show how much they meant to each other through actions and deeds.

"Have you told him about the Song of the Soul Mate?" Ember asked. "Have you told him you love him?"

Slowly, Kaia shook her head. "I . . . I can't . . . I can't be the first one to say it."

"Why not?"

"What if he doesn't feel the same way about me?"

"The way he looks at you—"

"What if it's just lust on his part?" Kaia said. "What if I spill my guts and tell him I love him, and then he has to try and let me down easy."

"But what if he feels the same way and he hasn't told you because he doesn't feel like this is the right time with all that's going on with his dad and his business?"

What if he did?

"Wouldn't you rather know for certain one way or the other?" Ember said. "If he doesn't love you back, then you can grieve and move on. If he does, well, wow, happily ever after. Because there's nothing worse than not knowing where you stand. You're frozen and can't move forward."

Ember was right. She was mired in quicksand over her feelings for Ridge. But was this the right time to tell him how she felt with his father so sick? He and Duke had a lot to work through. Their relationship was in shambles, but his father could be dying. It was time for them to make peace, and she shouldn't get in the way of that.

What would it hurt to wait for a bit? Give him the space he so obviously needed right now? She'd lose nothing by waiting except that she'd have to stay trapped in limbo for a little while longer.

She'd waited twenty-six years to fall in love. What were a few more days?

THE NEXT TWO weeks were hectic. Immediately after Duke's quadruple bypass, he suffered some serious complications—a life-threatening infection, blood clots in his legs. But the old man was tough and he fought hard.

Ridge was proud of him for that. Duke might be a hard man to love, but he was strong and determined.

Vivi got a hotel nearby. Together, they all decided that Ranger, Remington, and Rhett would take turns at the hospital, while Ridge, along with Zeke, would keep an eye on the ranch. Truth to tell, Ridge was happy to leave the hospital for Silver Feather, but he kept close tabs on Duke's condition and flew back and forth to El Paso a couple of times to check in.

In the days following Duke's heart attack, he took it on himself to pay bills, update the computer software, and institute some cost-saving ways to conduct his father's business.

He was surprised by how much he enjoyed the tasks and how easy it was to slip into the rhythms of ranch life. He'd forgotten how much he loved working with cattle and being on the land.

The dormant cowboy in him stirred, charged to life. He took to riding Majestic around the perimeter of the ranch every morning with the excuse of checking fences, but in all honesty, he did it because when he was on the stallion's back, he felt young again. In touch with the side of himself he thought long lost.

He also juggled his own affairs. Every evening at nine p.m., Phil Rhonstein would phone him from Beijing and they'd conference call with the legal team, often until the wee hours of the morning. Wading through the natural misunderstandings and misgivings that arose from not being there in person, troubleshooting and putting out fires on both fronts.

It felt better than he thought it would. Being back in the saddle again. Working hard. Keeping his mind and body busy. Focusing on work instead of his father's failing health.

Or what was going on between him and Kaia.

What *was* going on between them?

She'd texted him a couple of times to check on Duke, but mostly, she'd kept her distance. She was polite and kind and offered to help any way she could, but when he asked her to dinner or just to hang out, she told him he needed to focus on his family.

He sent her some gifts, just to make her smile and to let her know he was thinking of her. Small things. Fun things he knew she'd enjoy. A key chain in the shape of a cat with her name engraved on it. Her favorite candy bar. A Betta fish hand-delivered by her sister Aria because Kaia adored anything aquatic.

She acknowledged each gift in a text or phone call with her usual joy, but finally told him that while she appreciated his generosity, his family deserved his full attention.

He couldn't help wondering if he'd made a misstep. He told himself that she was right, that things were too fractured and uncertain for them to carve out the time to have a heart-to-heart and figure out where they stood.

But that wasn't true. It was just an excuse not to see her just yet. Not until he'd figured out what to do about his growing feelings for her.

He wanted her. Badly. Wanted her in his bed again. Wanted her more than he'd ever wanted any woman.

On Saturday, two weeks after Archer's wedding and the day before he and Casey were due home from their honeymoon, Ridge was in Duke's office, making out payroll when the housekeeper appeared in the doorway and told him he had a visitor.

"Who is it?" he asked, not even looking up from the computer screen.

"One of those Alzate girls."

"Which one?" he asked, yanking his head around and shooting to his feet.

"The spunky one," the housekeeper said. "I put her in the den."

A big smile split across his face.

Kaia!

Finally, she'd come to see him.

THE HOUSEKEEPER HAD parked Kaia in Duke's den and given her a glass of cold lemonade, while she waited for Ridge.

Feeling awkward now and wishing she hadn't shown up unannounced, Kaia shifted on the couch. She'd kept telling herself to give him space, but after almost two weeks of not seeing him in person, she couldn't bear it a minute longer.

But she had half an hour before she had to be at the dog care clinic to raise funds for the local no-kill animal shelter. She'd been unable to stop herself from dropping by to check on him.

She wasn't even sure what she was going to say. The den was intimidating, filled with mounted animal heads on the wall, a cigar humidor on the desk, and a ginormous portrait of the grizzled patriarch of Silver Feather Ranch, Levi Lockhart hanging over the fireplace. Heavy eyebrows framed sharp dark eyes, and his grim mouth was set in a disapproving line.

Was his humorless demeanor due to the harsh reality of nineteenth-century life in the Trans-Pecos? Or had old Levi simply been an asshat?

No wonder Ridge was so ambitious. For his whole life, having that stern man looking down on you like you'd never measure up. It would intimidate anyone. She wondered why Vivi had not vanquished old Levi to the attic. Probably one place where Duke dug his feet in.

"You don't scare me," Kaia told the old cuss. "You might have buffaloed your family through six generations, but the only reason you weren't killed off was because you did a nice thing once. I suspect you were more bark than bite."

"Talking to yourself?" Ridge's smooth voice asked.

Kaia jumped up. Embarrassed to be caught chatting up his dead relative, her right eye gave a nervous tic. At the sight of him, her defenses fell away.

He looked worn-out. Eyes red-rimmed, hair mussed, shoulders tensed from burning the candle at both ends. Her plans changed on the spot, and it was all she could do not to throw herself into his arms and cover his face in health-giving kisses.

"Hey," she said breathlessly.

"Hey yourself, beautiful." He gave up a smile for her, but it was as tired as his eyes. "What's up?"

"You've been working too hard. You should get away from the house, the desk, and your phone, and out of your own head. I'm kidnapping you."

"Kidnapping me, huh?" His eyes twinkled as he came closer as if just getting nearer to her increased his energy. "You think you're tough enough for that?"

"Just because I'm small doesn't mean I can't be persuasive." She crooked a finger, gave him a smile she hoped was beguiling.

"Amen to that," he said.

"C'mon."

"Where we going?"

"Do you trust me?"

He narrowed his eyes. "Yeah, but I like to be prepared."

"Are you always this suspicious?"

"Not suspicious, just need to know where I stand."

"Do you ever let go and let things unfold naturally?"

"Not much."

"Control freak."

"Guilty as charged. Not ashamed of it."

"I need you," she said in a throaty voice, and held out her hand.

"Well, why didn't you lead with that?" His knowing grin detonated a joy bomb inside her. "Just let me get my hat and sunglasses."

He looked so happy she didn't have the heart to tell him they would be playing with dogs today instead of each other.

"THIS WASN'T QUITE what I had in mind when you said you needed me," Ridge groused good-naturedly as he gazed at his surroundings.

Dogs of all shapes and sizes were everywhere. In kennels, on leashes, running around the dog park behind the animal shelter where they were standing. The volunteers wore bright yellow T-shirts with the name of the shelter emblazoned across the back and were working in teams of two, manning the "canine care" stations.

"I know." Kaia gave him a saucy smile and thrust an extra-large T-shirt at him. "But I'll make it up to you later."

"Promises, promises," he teased.

"Grab a brush." She nodded at the pile of brushes on a folding table beside the numerous metal tubs filled with soapy water. "We've got a lot of dogs to bathe."

They were positioned at the last station.

Amidst the endless barking, they wrangled dog after dog, bathing, brushing, clipping. Ridge did the heavy lifting. As a vet tech, Kaia was in charge of the medical stuff—giving shots, checking vital signs, examining ears and eyes, paws and mouths.

The dogs squirmed and wriggled, licked and whined.

Ridge didn't mind working hard and, growing up on the ranch, he'd certainly taken care of his share of critters, but he couldn't recall the last time he'd been drafted for dog grooming. The noise was deafening and he smelled of wet dog, and yet he didn't mind one bit. He was spending the day with Kaia.

He tried not to think too much about what that meant. Or what was going to happen between them once Duke was home and he was off to China for six months.

The standard poodle he had in the bathtub picked that moment to shake like a cement mixer, dousing him from head to toe. Ridge wiped excess water from his eyes with both hands, sputtered.

The alert poodle saw his opportunity, leaped from the tub, and went running around the enclosure.

Kaia burst out laughing. "Give Dagger an inch and he'll take a mile."

"I'm soaked to the skin."

She grinned, obviously unconcerned that she was responsible for the soaking of the CEO of Lock Ridge Enterprises.

"Oh poor baby, I'm so sorry," she said, sounding gleefully unapologetic. She was enjoying this. "Luckily, you're in the desert. You'll be dry in seconds."

"What does a man have to do to get some sympathy around here?"

"There are paper towels over there." She waved vaguely in the direction of some oversized plastic containers. Her attention was on the sheltie she was brushing with a FURminator. "But corral Dagger first."

To heck with the paper towels. She was right. With the heat of the arid sun, he'd be dry in no time.

Dagger had made himself small and crawled under the metal shelving holding dog grooming supplies. Ridge got down on his hands and knees, lowered his head to the ground, peered underneath the shelving at the quivering poodle. "Here doggy, doggy."

"You'll never get him out of there that way," Kaia said without glancing over. She fished a chunk of freeze-dried liver from the pocket of her jean shorts. "Daggy." She whistled. "Treats."

The poodle crawled out from under the shelving so fast he scrambled right over Ridge's back and raced for Kaia.

"Bath." She pointed at the tub from which Dagger had escaped.

The dog lowered his head and slunk back to the tub, trailing soap bubbles behind him.

"I'll be damned." Ridge got to his feet. "Will you look at that?"

Kaia tossed Ridge the treat. "Give it to him after you get him back in the water."

"Yes, ma'am." He tucked the treat in his pocket. Dagger eyed him with new respect as Ridge bent to pick up the dog and put him back in the tub. If he wasn't soaked to the skin before, he certainly was after holding the wet dog close to his chest. He gave Dagger the treat and the dog crunched happily while Ridge picked up the bath brush again.

"Is this is your typical workday?" he asked.

"Well this is a special clinic, but yes. Although I also go out with Dr. Cheri in the field sometimes, or help her in surgery." She turned her head to beam at him. "Isn't it grand?"

"Thanks for kidnapping me," he said, kneeling beside the tub and concentrating on rinsing Dagger. "I didn't realize how much I needed a break."

"Anytime."

"Even if you did give me the scut work," he joked.

"In my world, it's the only thing you're cut out for," she teased back, queen of the castle in her environment. "The basics."

"Is that an insult, Alzate?"

"Nah," she said. "I just like seeing you on your knees."

"You know," he said, cupping his hand as if he were going to throw water on her. "You *are* within splashing distance."

"You wouldn't dare."

"Try me." He could only see her profile, the rest of her face was hidden as she bent to run the special FURminating tool over the sheltie's front bib, but he could tell she was suppressing a laugh.

"You should know better than to dare a Lockhart." He scooted up the cup he'd used to rinse Dagger, filled it with water, got to his feet, and came toward her.

"Ridge . . ." She giggled, backing away from the sheltie, her hands raised in surrender. "Don't do this."

"Or what?" he taunted, advancing, his grin matching hers.

"Don't, don't, don't . . ." She squealed as he pounced, ducking her head, hiding her face in the crook of her elbow.

He took hold of the back of her collar, pretending he was going to dump the contents down her blouse. She brought her shoulders up to her ears, arms dangling at her side, looking like the cutest little female Quasimodo this side of Notre Dame.

"Did you really think I was going to dump water down your collar?" he asked huskily.

"With you? I don't know what to think."

"I have a much better way of getting you wet," he murmured,

and pulled her up against his chest, every urge in his body yelling at him to kiss her.

"Ridge!" She sounded scandalized. "There are people around."

He did not let go.

She resisted slightly at first, her body stiffening, hands curling into fists, and he manacled her wrists and pulled her hands behind her, rubbed his soppy T-shirt over the front of her, getting her as wet as he was.

"Stop," she said, grinning helplessly.

He pressed his mouth to hers. "My water girl. You know you love it."

Kaia inhaled sharply.

He *knew* she loved getting wet. Water, her weakness, and he would use it against her any chance he got.

"The dogs," she mumbled. "We're neglecting the dogs."

He let her go then, stepped back, his heart pounding, blood pulsing, breath shallow and fast.

"Hold on to that thought," she whispered in his ear. "Later. At my place."

"Hmm, I like the sound of that—"

She splayed a palm against his chest. "We need to talk."

Her words sounded worrisome and left him thinking, *Oh shit, what did I do wrong?*

Chapter 25

Right there during the dog care clinic Kaia made the decision to tell Ridge about the Song of the Soul Mate.

It had not been her goal when she'd kidnapped him. She simply wanted to spend time with him. But now they were here, now that he had kissed her again, she knew she had to tell him.

The past two weeks had been agonizing as she'd struggled to sort out her feelings and keep him at arm's length. She couldn't do it any longer. She had to know where they stood. Had to know how he felt about her. Had to know if they were on the road to happily-ever-after.

Or if she was better off letting him go and grieving the loss of her dreams.

Hope, that jackrabbit of emotion, hopped into her chest and bounced around with big thumper feet.

Whatifwhatifwhatif?

What if he felt the same for her as she did for him? She thrilled at the idea that he could love her too. Her hopes were a candle flame on oxygen, flickering higher, brighter.

Um, yes . . . but what if he didn't feel the same?

Shh, shh. She wasn't going to think about that. For now, she needed all the hope and optimism she could muster in order to open up and tell him everything that was in her heart.

And her head.

Because her brain was still humming long after he let her go.

He sat beside her in the Tundra, his masculine presence filling the cab of her pickup truck.

She cast a sidelong glance, admiring his manly profile, appreciating the straight line of his nose, the set of his angular jaw, the cut of his cheekbone. Cataloged the precious face of her beloved. Her breath caught. She loved him so very much.

But what if he did not love her back? Not the way she needed to be loved. What then?

Doubt crept in. Maybe she should just keep mum about the humming in her head. Say nothing. Don't rock the boat. Spend the night with him. Enjoy the moment.

It was not enough.

With Ridge, it had to be all or nothing. Either he was in or he was out.

She had to know the truth.

Be brave.

She lifted her chin, stared straight ahead. Saw her neighborhood come into view.

Felt her stomach flip upside down, a jellyfish floating on sea foam.

Once the words were out of her mouth, there would be no do-overs. If he told her he did not love her, how would she live without him?

The thought was a spike through her chest, sharp and bleak. Her lungs ached. If he dismissed the Song of the Soul Mate, if he walked away, she *would* survive. She'd survived a bad car crash, survived being stalked by a crazy man, she could survive losing him.

But she would never, ever love another the way she loved Ridge Lockhart. He'd etched an indelible brand on her heart. *That,* she was going to have to live with for the rest of her life.

She bit her bottom lip, got tangled up in his masculine smell that now included the scent of dogs and shampoo. And when he reached across the seat to place a hand on her knee, she jumped.

"Did I startle you?"

"A bit, my mind was elsewhere." She peeked down at his hand, big and tanned and nicked with small scars. His nails clipped and buffed.

There it was again.

The dichotomy that was Ridge Lockhart. A seductive combination of polished and rugged. He was a man of the world. He'd been places, seen things, knew important people.

He was out of her league.

She couldn't compete.

"You okay?" he asked, his voice kind, concerned.

She turned her head, raised a shadow smile, lied, "Fine. I'm fine."

His smile was warm and tender and inviting. Nothing to be afraid of. She knew him. Had grown up with him as a child. Had spent hot days and long nights getting reacquainted with him as an adult.

He didn't move his hand, the heat of it sinking through her skin, flooding her bloodstream. He gave her strength, infused her with energy and courage. Yes. She would do this and let the chips fall where they scattered.

"Do you honestly have any idea how gorgeous you are?" he asked.

The rumble in his timbre sent the rolling heat to every organ in her body. She tingled from head to toe, alive from his touch.

"Here we are!" She spoke too loudly, too perkily, killed the engine in her driveway. Hopped out. Almost raced up the steps to her front door without waiting for him.

He followed. Slowly. Loping.

Her heart was a bagpipe, expanding and collapsing, falling in on itself, wheezing with effort.

She got the door open, automatically put up a foot to block Dart. Frustrated, the orange tabby glared at the bottom of her boot. She'd left Buddy and Bess in the backyard so she didn't have to contend with them too.

"Back, back," she urged, gently pushing the kitten away.

Disgruntled, Dart stuck his nose and tail in the air and sauntered off to another part of the house.

Ridge came up behind her. "You didn't wait for me."

"I wanted to make sure Dart didn't get out." Okay, not totally true, but he bought it. She moved over the threshold. He followed.

"Well," she said, dropping her purse onto the floor and turning around to face him. How did she start? Ask him to sit and then just dive right in? Tell him, I love you and we're fated by the Song of the Soul Mate?

But that was a bit abrupt, wasn't it. Shouldn't she ease into the topic?

"Are you hungry?" she asked. "I could order a pizza. Or make grilled cheese sandwiches if the bread hasn't gone moldy."

"I'm hungry," he said, drawing her into his embrace. "But not for food."

His mouth found hers and she leaned into his kiss, even as she needed to tear herself away before he destroyed her reason. How easy it would be to let him sweep her away to the bedroom. To make love to him and forget all about her confession.

She forced herself to pull away. "We need to talk."

They stared at each other. Silence stretched between them so taut she could barely stand it. Finally, she dropped her gaze, plunked down on the sofa. Patted the cushion next to her.

"Please sit down," she said more formally than she'd intended. She was building it up, making a bigger deal of it than she should.

His brows knit in concern and he ran a palm along his jaw, but he sat beside her.

"What's on your mind?"

"How is your father?"

"Much better. He should be released from the hospital soon. But that's not what you wanted to talk to me about, is it?"

She shook her head.

They inhaled simultaneously.

"Kaia," he said, "what is it?"

"You'll be leaving then."

He nodded. "I have to go to China."

"For six months."

"That's the plan."

She emptied her lungs in one long exhale out through her mouth. *Tell him. Just say it and be done.*

"When will I . . ." She swallowed, entranced by his navy blue eyes drilling into her. "When will you be home again?"

"I don't know."

"I see, I see." She bobbed her head like a loony person. God, this was hard. He was going to think she was nutty as a pecan factory once she spilled the story.

His eyes scorched her face. "What did you want to discuss?"

She couldn't hold his gaze, stared down at her hands clasped in her lap. "You sure you don't want a pizza?"

"Whatever you have to tell me, it's going to be okay."

He said that now. Just wait until he heard about the humming.

She cleared her throat, straightened her shoulders, raised her chin, but kept her eyes downcast. Her chest was a vise, squeezing her heart, smashing her lungs. "Here's the deal . . ."

Here's the deal, I'm not sure I know how I'm going to survive six months without you . . .

Here's the deal, I've loved you since I was eight years old, if not before, and always will . . .

Here's the deal, according to Granny Blue and the humming in my head, you're my soul mate and we're destined to be together . . .

"Kaia," he prompted, placing emphasis on the last syllable of her name.

Just say it!

She wrung every ounce of courage she had in her body, and met his sultry navy eyes that were trained on her and her alone.

Lord help her, he was the most handsome man she'd ever come across. His thick hair was mussed from the morning of bathing dogs and he finger-raked it off his forehead.

"Here's the deal," she blurted, jumping in with both feet. All the way. No lead-up. No soft pedal. No preamble. Moment of truth. This was it. "I love you."

A heavy hush settled over the room. Neither of them breathed.

Ridge did not say a word. He didn't move. Or look away. His gaze frozen on hers. Had he heard her? Had she actually spoken? Was he so stunned he could not respond?

Oh dear, oh dear, oh dear.

Her heart stopped beating, or so it seemed. She tried to haul in a breath, but could not. Her lungs simply would not cooperate. She clenched and unclenched her fist, feeling goofy with shame. She wanted to bury her head under the sofa pillow, burrow deep into the upholstery, shrink herself down to the size of a dime, and get lost in cracks between the cushions.

She wanted, she wanted, she wanted . . . Oh God, he was still staring at her, unblinking. Silent. Stony. Ridged. A rock of a name. Ridge.

Her chest vapor locked. Her lips parted, panting, but she didn't have the strength to suck in air. Her head spun, dizzy as the day they'd pulled her from her crumpled car and settled her onto the ambulance gurney.

It was worse than she feared. She'd told him she loved him and he had not reacted. *Ohgodohgodohgod.* All this time. All the fantasies. It meant nothing. She'd bought into a myth, a fable, a silly lie.

The humming in her head was her imagination. Wish fulfillment. Desperation.

She closed her eyes. *Please God, kill me now.*

Nothing. No words from him. No movement. No touch. Nothing. She opened her eyes, found him sitting statue still.

In for a penny, in for a pound.

In a rush of words, the legend spilled from her mouth. Granny Blue's tale. The Song of the Soul Mate. The hum she heard whenever his lips touched her. The fact they were destined to be together.

She purged all of it. Held nothing back.

Her hands trembled. Hell, her entire body was trembling. Her heart was a bilge pump dramatically shoving blood through her veins. Hot and swift and hard. When she finished her story, he stayed stock-still.

Didn't react. Didn't speak. Didn't even breathe.

Stone. Marble. Granite.

"I know it's crazy," she said. "I know I sound like a crazy person.

It's irrational. It's nonsensical. I know that, I know that . . . but the thing is, it *happened*."

His eyes were twin flames of fire, burning into her. Unreadable and dark. Blistering her inside. Charring her to ash.

Shame cut through her, sliced her thin. If only she could take it all back. Pretend she'd never uttered a sound. In that moment, she died a thousand deaths.

The ringing of a cell phone jarred them both.

His eyes widened. Still, he did not say a word. Showed no emotion. He might as well have been a sea sponge for all she got out of him.

"You're ringing." Kaia nodded.

"I swear to God," he muttered, his voice low and buzzy as a rattlesnake's tail. He pulled the cell from his pocket. "I'm going to throw this damn thing away."

At the shift of topics, Kaia felt as disoriented as a first-time surfer clobbered by a big ocean wave, sputtering, coming up for air, grasping for her bearings. She gulped. Smiled.

"Promises, promises," she quipped, trying to keep things light, deeply grateful for the interruption.

He glanced at the screen, grimaced. "It's Vivi."

At his ex's name, jealousy rose up in her throat. She had nothing to feel possessive over. Yes, she loved him. But Ridge was not hers.

"The surgeon has been by to see Duke," he said. "They've released him."

"That's great news."

"Vivi wants me to fly him home."

"Of course."

He looked as if he were going to say something, but then pressed his lips together, bobbed his head. Got to his feet.

She was both relieved and disappointed. She remained seated, fearful that her legs weren't strong enough to support her weight. She'd laid her heart bare to him and he acted as if nothing had happened. She still had no idea how he felt or where they stood.

"Go on." She made shooing motions.

He hesitated, his gaze meeting hers again, but she took a page from his book, iced up her eyes. Detached. Disengaged. Disconnected.

"Get out of here." Her voice came out like gravel, spiky and rough. "Go now."

Before I fall to my knees and humiliate myself by begging you to stay.

KAIA LOVED HIM?

Ridge's heart was a whirligig in a sandstorm.

Blistered. Battered. Beat up.

He stood perched in the doorway, gazing back at her on the sofa, warring with his desire to stay and the hot fear telegraphing panicked messages through his nerve endings.

Her declaration left him shocked, stunned, blown away.

Not just because her story was far-fetched, unbelievable, loony flipping tunes . . . but because he ached to believe it was possible.

In truth, he felt it too. Love for her as big and bright as the sun. So bright that if he stared at her for too long he'd go blind.

And that's what scared him.

The intensity. The overwhelm. The loss of control. The terror that if he dared to let himself fully love her, and then he somehow lost her, it would be the end of him.

No one had ever told Ridge they loved him before.

Oh, he supposed his mother had, but he couldn't really remember. Duke wasn't prone to words of endearment, and none of Duke's wives had said it. Sabrina and Lucy had had kids of their own, and well, Vivi . . .

As for the women he'd dated, Ridge had always gotten out of the relationships if he got the slightest inkling that they were falling for him. But usually, he was careful to pick women who wanted to keep things casual.

Until now.

Until Kaia.

He opened his mouth to tell her he loved her too. But he'd never uttered the words out loud before, didn't know how to start.

It hit him then, and he knew why he couldn't wrap his tongue around, *I love you.* He was too damn broken for Kaia. She deserved so much better. She deserved someone who knew how to love with all his heart and soul. Someone who could and would put her ahead of everything else.

And Ridge just didn't know how to do that. Work was the only thing that had ever saved him. If he didn't have his work, he had no idea who or what he was.

"Go on," she said. "Your family needs you."

Still, he hesitated. Torn in two. Desperate for her, but committed to putting her needs before his own. If he told her he loved her, she would surrender herself to him one hundred percent—heart, mind, body, and soul.

It was a precious gift he had not earned.

She was so loving and generous and he could ruin her so easily.

"Later," he said. "I'll come back."

She nodded, but her face was pale, dark shadows under her eyes. "Later."

He met her gaze, sent her all the love he was feeling in that glance. "I will be back," he said firmly. "We'll talk this through."

"Okay." She smiled a gentle smile, soft and full of sadness. A smile that said she didn't believe him.

Not for a second.

Chapter 26

AFTER Ridge left, Kaia was devastated. She'd given him her heart on a platter and he had rejected it.

We'll talk this through.

Those four words gave her hope. But was it false hope? Was she stupid to keep holding on?

One thing was for sure. She would make herself crazy with second-guessing if she stayed here by herself. She had to get out of the house.

Aimlessly, she drove by Tara's place, trying to decide if she should confide in her most nurturing sister. She spied Aria's and Ember's cars parked in her driveway and pulled in.

Tara answered the door on her second knock.

"What's up?" she asked.

"We're planning a welcome home dinner for Archer and Casey for Monday night. C'mon in."

"How come I wasn't invited to the powwow?"

"We thought you had plans with Ridge." Tara ushered her into the living room, where her sisters were seated on the sofa, glasses of wine on the coffee table in front of them.

"Why would you think that?" Kaia said.

"Aria saw you with him at the dog clinic."

"You were there?" Kaia shot her youngest sister a look.

"I stopped by to see if you wanted to come hang out with us, but you and Ridge looked pretty cozy, so I backed off."

"Sounds like you two are working things out," Ember said, and patted the cushion beside her. "Come sit down and tell all."

"Nothing to tell," Kaia denied, but she sat beside her sister.

"Ridge was helping out at the dog clinic. That's all. After Duke's heart surgery and the complications of the last two weeks, he is finally getting out of the hospital fifteen days after he went in. Ridge left to go pick him up and fly him home."

"When I took a peek, Ridge was rubbing his chest all over yours," Aria snickered. "What was that about?"

Wisely, Kaia chose to ignore her.

"Want a glass of wine?" Tara asked, waggling the bottle of chardonnay that was almost empty.

Kaia raised a hand, wished she'd kept driving. Apparently she was in the hot seat over Ridge. Had Ember blabbed about the Song of the Soul Mate? "No thanks, I'm good."

"Don't be shy because it's almost empty. Aria brought two bottles."

"Oh?" Kaia shifted the attention to her youngest sister. "To what are we drinking?"

"I got a job," Aria said.

"Congratulations!"

"Thanks. I'm jazzed!"

Tara left the room and came back with the second bottle of wine, a corkscrew, and a glass for Kaia. Even though she didn't want the wine, she accepted the glass. She would be polite and toast her sister's new job, but then she'd be on her way.

"Doing what?" Kaia asked.

Aria grinned and tossed her head. "I'm working for Vivi."

"Huh? In what capacity?"

"As a wedding planner. At Archer's wedding, we got to talking. Archer and Casey had hired an outside wedding planner, and Vivi realized she was losing money by not including wedding planning along with the venue. But she can't do it alone, so she asked me if I'd be interested since I have a degree in public relations and, I quote, 'have a bubbly personality.'"

"Good luck," Kaia said.

Aria wrinkled her nose. "What does that mean?"

"It means good luck."

"You got a look on your face. It means something more."

"Pay no attention to my face," Kaia said. "I'm soured on Vivi because of the way she treated Ridge, that's all. I'm sure you'll love working for her. She's lucky to have you. Not only do you have a bubbly personality, but you're passionate about things that interest you. I can see you making a success of this."

"That means a lot." Aria grinned.

Sadie, a sassy Siamese that Kaia had coerced Tara into adopting last year, sauntered into the living room to see what was going on. Kaia's heart melted the way it always did whenever she was around animals.

Her sisters all ignored the cat because they knew if you went to Sadie and tried to pet her or pick her up when she wasn't ready, she would nip with her sharp little teeth. But if you waited and let her come to you, then you'd be rewarded with purrs and cuddles. Generally, Sadie's affections were random, unless Kaia was in the room.

"Watch how Kaia seduces Sadie," Aria whispered. "We're deep in conversation and without even being consciously aware of it Kaia started moving her fingers the minute Sadie appeared. Slow little scratching motions."

"Huh?" Kaia blinked.

"You're doing it now." Tara nodded. "You're scratching the leg of the couch."

"Yep," Ember confirmed. "Slowly, lightly, intriguing Sadie. Calling her to you without drawing attention. And here I thought you emitted some kind of magical, come-to-me allure."

"You think that's how she got Ridge wrapped around her little finger?" Aria teased.

Ha! As if. The reverse was true. He had her wrapped around his pinky.

Kaia stared down at her hand, felt the texture of the wood beneath her fingers. She should stop scratching. Deflect her sisters' attention. But then Sadie moseyed over to check out Kaia's fingers.

"Watch," Aria said. "She'll move to scratching the cushion."

"How long have you been observing her technique?" Tara leaned in, clearly fascinated.

"I can't do it now with you all staring at me." Kaia snorted.

"Go on." Ember waved a hand. "Show us your cat luring techniques."

"I didn't even know it was a technique," Kaia said. "It just comes naturally."

"Like Ember's red hair." Aria took a sip of wine.

Ember patted her curly locks. "Thanks to Mom's Irish DNA."

Sadie put her paws on Kaia's soft cushion, studied her scratching fingers with fascination. After a moment, she swished her tail and leaned in to sniff Kaia's fingers.

"Wait for it," Aria said. "Wait for it . . ."

Everyone watched Sadie.

The Siamese hopped delicately into Kaia's lap.

"Boom!" Aria pumped a fist. "And there you have it, the secret to Kaia's cat magic. The reason Sadie likes Kaia best is not just because she loves cats, but because she also understands them."

"Too bad those skills aren't transferable to men," Kaia lamented, rubbing Sadie behind the ears.

Sadie immediately started purring and the contented rumbling reminded Kaia of the romantic rumblings inside her own head when she kissed Ridge.

Kaia inched her fingers along Sadie's spine, thought of the way Ridge had stroked her in much the same way. Realized that in their relationship, he'd been the one holding the mesmerizing magic, and she'd been the one seduced.

Complicated feelings swirled inside her, and suddenly she wanted nothing more than to be home alone.

"I've got to head out," she said, transferring the Siamese to Tara's lap. "Let me know what you decide about Archer and Casey's welcome home dinner. Just tell me what to bring."

"Hey," Ember hollered as Kaia started across the living room. "You never did tell us what's going on between you and Ridge."

"Nothing," she said. "There's nothing to tell."

Then as quickly as she could, she headed for the door. How could she tell them something she did not understand herself?

SINCE THE EVEKTOR was a two-seater, it was just Ridge and Duke on the flight home. Ranger was driving Vivi back from El Paso. Remington and Rhett had already returned to their lives, once they knew Duke was out of the woods.

Ridge couldn't decide which was tenser, being alone in the plane with Vivi, or his father. The flight took an hour, but it felt ten times longer than the three-hour drive.

Duke's color was ashen, and he'd lost a good twenty pounds during the two weeks he'd been in the hospital. He kept wriggling around in the seat.

"Are you okay?" Ridge asked.

"Can't get comfortable." He grunted.

"You can let the seat back."

Duke fumbled with the seat, cursed. "Too many buttons. Stupid thing. Why did you have to buy such a fancy plane? Show-off."

Ridge took a deep breath and let it out slowly. His father was feeling frail and powerless. That made him grouchy. Ridge wasn't going to get sucked in.

Finally, Duke settled down, fell asleep, and snored all the way back to the Silver Feather. Ridge counted his lucky stars.

But then that left him alone with his thoughts. All he could think about was Kaia and that look on her face as he walked out the door.

And the story she'd told him. About the humming she heard in her head when he kissed her. Song of the Soul Mate she'd called it. The fable wasn't sane or rational, but he believed her. Believed she believed it anyway.

He wanted to believe it too.

What a terrific notion. That fate played a hand, and that the love of your life was predestined and all you had to do was find her.

Trick was, he *had* found her, but he wasn't worthy of her.

He'd trained himself not to feel *anything*. Feelings messed with your mind. Got you in trouble. He could be distant, self-contained, emotionless, and yes, he knew, hard to love. That's the way he'd always wanted it.

Until Kaia.

Now here she was, giving him a giant case of the feels.

When it came to Kaia, he was neither distant nor emotionless, let alone self-contained. All he wanted was to fuse with her, meld into her body, make her his forever and ever.

The very thought of being with her blazed a fire of burning desire through him so all-consuming that it left room for nothing else. He didn't care about work. He had more than enough money to last a lifetime. The desire to best his father had completely disappeared. All he felt for the old man was pity.

So go to her. Tell her that.

His pulse quickened at the prospect. But it had happened so fast. He felt crowded. Claustrophobic. *Terrified.*

It was nearly dark when they landed. Almost nine. Ridge came around the side of the Evektor to help his father out.

"I'm fine." Duke swatted at Ridge. "I can walk. I ain't no cripple."

"No, but you've been in bed for two weeks." Ridge took his arm anyway, dodged the next swat. "You're weak."

"Like you give a shit." Duke snorted. "You're only here because you feel guilty."

Ridge tamped down a sigh. Would it always be like this between them? "You got that wrong. I don't feel guilty about a damn thing. I'm here because I'm your son and you need help."

"Oh yeah? If you're such a great son, where have you been for the last ten years?"

"I'm as good a son as you are a father," he retorted.

"Hmph." Duke grunted, but stopped fighting to pull away.

"Yeah, that's right. Even Steven."

He got Duke into the house, but when he tried to direct him to the bedroom, Duke balked. "I wanna go to my office."

"It's nine o'clock at night."

"So what? I need to get back in the saddle."

Ridge knew when to pick his battles. This was not the time to buck the old man. "Okay," he said, and guided Duke into the office Ridge had been using, just as Phil Rhonstein phoned for their nightly conference.

He left Duke in the office and went outside to take the call.

"How are things today?" he asked, looking up at the wide expanse of stars, feeling the full impact of the night sky. The majesty of it still took his breath away. "We any closer to getting this sewed up?"

"Things are . . ." Phil hesitated.

"What?"

"Stalled."

Ridge jammed a hand through his hair. "What's the holdup?"

"Liu Yan," he said, referring to the Beijing silver mine owner, "is suspicious because you're not here. He thinks we're trying to pull something over on him. Now he's hired a new team of international lawyers to comb through the contract again. We're in wait mode."

His chest knotted up, and fangs of frustration sank into him. Honestly, he hated not being there, not being in control of the negotiations. Ridge huffed. "My dad's out of the hospital. He's doing better. Give me three days and I can be in Beijing."

"That's not necessary."

"Yes it is. I should have been there from the beginning. Billions are at stake."

"I know, I know," Phil said. "But we can work things out on this end. Stay put. Look after your father. You've got enough on your plate."

The last thing he wanted was to linger in Cupid when his Beijing deal was going to hell in a hand basket.

Well, except for Kaia. He would go see her before he left. Talk things through. Make things right so that when he came back from China in six months . . .

What? You're going to ask her to wait six months for you? How fair is that?

"There's nothing more important than family," Phil said.

Yeah, maybe for Phil, maybe for most people, but not for Ridge. In his entire life, the only people he'd been able to truly count on were the Alzates.

"Tell Liu Yan I'll be there on Tuesday," Ridge told Phil.

"What the fucking hell!" Duke's voice boomed from inside the house. "Where are you, you snot-nosed sonofabitch?"

"What was that?" Phil sounded alarmed.

"Family." Ridge sighed. "I'll call you later. Tell Liu Yan, Tuesday. I'll be there for sure."

"You really don't have—"

But Ridge was already hanging up.

Chapter 27

RIDGE pocketed his cell phone and reached for the handle of the sliding glass door, just as Duke yanked it open.

A vein throbbed at his father's temple, and his nostrils flared like a crazed bull charging a matador. Duke snarled. Lips curled back over his teeth. "What did you do?"

"What are you talking about?"

"Don't start that crap!"

Ridge shook his head. "Didn't learn a thing from the heart attack, huh? Take a deep breath, calm down."

"How can I calm down when the minute my back is turned you stage a coup!"

"A coup?"

"You go into my office, change things around . . ." He waved his arms wildly. "Get into my business accounts, move *my* money—"

"Oh, you mean how I modernized your banking, updated your software, and found a way to save the ranch seven hundred dollars a month? That's the 'coup' you're talking about?"

Duke ran right over that speed bump of information. "You had no right!"

"Vivi asked for my help. She's the one who gave me access to your accounts."

"You had no right! Coming in when I was down and out, throwing your swagger around. I know you're trying to show me up. You don't fool me for a minute."

In the back of his mind Ridge had been holding on to a thin rope of hope that Duke's illness would lead to some kind of reconciliation. Okay, maybe not a reconciliation, since they'd never been close in the first place, but at least an understanding so they could hold a conversation without constantly butting heads.

Dream the hell on.

His relationship with his father was what it was. Things were never going to change. All the wishing in the world wouldn't alter the facts.

"You're welcome," he said.

His father scowled. "What the hell for?"

"Staying behind, looking after the ranch for two weeks when I should have been in China taking care of my business."

"Nobody asked you." Duke hardened his chin, his voice going petulant as a five-year-old kid told he had to wear galoshes.

"Yeah, yeah they did. Vivi, Ranger, Remington, Rhett. They all asked me to stay. So I did."

"*I* didn't ask you."

"God no. Heaven forbid Duke Lockhart ever asked anyone for help."

"Goes to show you can count on me for something."

"Pigheaded? Yes. In that regard, you're as predictable as the sun comin' up in the east," Ridge drawled.

"I need a drink," Duke said. "Where'd you put the hooch you took out of my office?"

"Doctor said you need to lay off the liquor. Vivi's swept it from the house."

"Goddammitall." Duke sulked, his eyes turning dark and sullen.

"Look," Ridge said. "I'm sorry you're pissed off about the changes, but you're just going to have to adjust."

They exchanged a hard look. Duke's face razor-edged with anger.

"No whiskey at all?"

"Nope."

"When are you leaving?"

"As soon as Vivi and Ranger get here."

"For good?" Duke asked in a fisticuffs voice, but underneath the pugilism whispered a tremor of fear.

They were still standing in the doorway. Ridge outside. Duke in. Staring each other down.

"You should go to bed," Ridge said.

"And you should butt out."

"If you won't go to bed, at least sit down."

"Don't tell me what to do," Duke grunted, but backed up and sat down at the kitchen table.

"Want some water?" Ridge asked, coming into the house, pulling the sliding glass door closed behind him.

"I want some whiskey."

"Sorry, can't always get what you want."

"Throwin' that back in my face?"

"You told it to me when I was three and begging for my mama," Ridge said.

"She wasn't comin' back."

"I was *three*, you hard-ass." Ridge plunked down at the table across from him.

"I didn't tell her to leave you on my doorstep and run her car into a brick wall."

"You don't think you had a hand in it?"

"I couldn't marry her." Duke's voice softened. "I was already married to Sabrina."

"You might have figured out she was having a rough time hanging on and stepped in to help."

"I gave her money. What else was I supposed to do?"

Every bone in Ridge's body solidified into stone. A wrecking ball couldn't have knocked him down. He was that hard inside.

"She was pretty." Duke's voice softened, and Ridge could have sworn he heard traces of regret, but maybe that was wishful thinking. "And she smelled so good."

"Yes, she did."

"She'd be proud of you."

"I imagine she would."

They sat like boxers, eyeing each other from their corners after a tough round. Waiting for the bell to ring so they could flay each other again.

"So," Duke said. "You're flying away tonight."

"I am."

"Go on then." Duke flipped his hand. "No need to wait on Vivi and Ranger."

"I'm not leaving you alone."

"There's a housekeeper. She can look after me."

"It's not her job."

A moment passed. One tick of a clock. Then another. And another.

"Think you'll ever get married?" Duke asked.

Ridge shot him a quelling look. "Why are you asking?"

"Just filling the air."

"Can't say I'm marriage material."

"What about Kaia?"

"What about her?"

"You gonna throw her away same as Vivi?"

Zing. Bam. There it was. Sucker punch.

"I didn't throw Vivi away. You stole her from me."

"Bullshit. That's the sugar teat you use to soothe yourself with. Truth was, you were too busy trying to show me up to give a woman like Vivi the kind of attention she deserved. Stop blaming me for your failings."

"Oh, so that wasn't your bare ass I saw over *my* girlfriend, in *my* bed, in *my* house?"

"Okay, you got me there. I apologize for the circumstances," Duke said. "In hindsight it was crass. But I don't apologize for picking up the diamond you tossed aside as coal."

"Well all right then, that makes it okay." Ridge gripped the edges of the chair, his heart wedged firmly in his throat.

"You're doing it all over again," Duke accused.

"Doing what?" Ridge asked, his mouth so tight the words grated against teeth.

"Running away when you start to feel something."

"Excuse me?" Knees trembling, Ridge shot to his feet. "I've never run away from anything in my life."

Duke threw back his head and let out a donkey guffaw.

"What's so damn funny?" Ridge scowled, balled up his fists, and tucked them into his armpits.

"You!" Duke hooted, slapped both palms against his belly, and heehawed until tears rolled down his cheeks. "That is . . . whew wee . . ." He swiped at the tears. "That is . . . *priceless*."

"I don't have to listen to this." Ridge pulled his shoulder blades together, felt hot, ugly energy shoot up his spine like a bullet and lodge in the base of his skull.

"Oh, oh. What are you gonna do? Run away again?"

"I didn't run away. I left to make my fortune."

"And spent the next decade hiding out."

"I was not—" Ridge bit down on his tongue. The old man was trying to get his goat and he was allowing it to happen. "Fine. Think what you want. I know the truth."

"Do you?" Duke's laughter vanished. He planted his palms on the table, leaned in.

"I do."

"Whose truth? Yours or the rest of us?"

"And what *is* your truth, Duke?"

"Was I the best father in the land?" Duke shrugged. "No. But at least I own who I am, and I don't make excuses. You were the one who took off. If you'd stayed and had it out with me things would have been a lot different. I would have put you in charge of the ranch—"

"Is this your way of trying to make amends? If so, you pretty much suck at it."

"I'm saying you ran, so you have no right to come in here and mess with the way I do business. No right to change things to suit you without consulting me. No right to take over when I was down and out."

Ridge dug deep, grabbed hold of his steel self-control, and gripped it tight. "I was just trying to help."

"I don't need your help."

"You've made that clear enough," Ridge said. "I'm outta here."

"That's right. Scoot. Take off. Toodle-loo. Live up to my expectations. 'Cause leaving is what you do best."

AFTER KAIA LEFT her sisters, she'd gone to see Granny Blue. Only her grandmother could truly understand the emotions buffeting her, harsh as a west Texas sandstorm.

"Give Ridge time," Granny Blue said softly. "He's had a hard life. He's not used to being loved."

"He didn't say a word after I told him about the Song of the Soul Mate. He just stared at me as if I'd lost my mind."

"Most people are afraid to let go and trust their inner wisdom. You didn't want to trust it either."

"Until it happened to me." Kaia touched the base of her skull from where the humming emanated. Wished she could kiss Ridge and stir that sweet sound again.

"And you've had your whole life to hear about the legend. To prepare. He's new to this." Granny Blue had patted Kaia's cheek. "Give him time."

"How much time?"

"As long as he needs."

"Weeks? Months?" Kaia paused, gulped. "Years?"

"I can't answer that."

"What if he falls for someone else?"

"Have no fear, little one. The Song of the Soul Mate is never wrong. If you hear the hum when he kisses you, he is *yours*."

That all sounded well and good, but it did nothing to quell the fear in her belly. Granny Blue hadn't seen the stony look in his eyes when she'd told him about the humming.

"You must have patience. You must believe. You must trust. Understand me when I say this to you. You *cannot* lose him. He is yours. He has always been yours. He will always be yours. Nothing in heaven or earth can ever change that."

"All right." Kaia nodded, feeling marginally better. "I can't lose him no matter what?"

Granny Blue's eyes shone, her smile steady and filled with golden promise. "No matter what."

"But . . ." Kaia bit her bottom lip.

"What is it?"

"What happens if, no matter how much time I give him, no matter how long I wait . . ." She paused on a hiccup of emotions.

"Hope is your greatest strength, child. You've always been able to see past the thunderclouds when others could not. Hold on to that hope."

"But what happens if he is so broken, so afraid, he simply can't or won't accept our destiny?"

Granny's bright eyes shuttered and her smile evaporated. "I'll pray that does not happen."

A wisp of loneliness blew over Kaia so strong and mournful she felt it seep deep into her soul. "What if prayers just don't work? What if despite everything Ridge is incapable of loving me."

"Then . . ." Granny Blue's voice broke, brittle and mournful. "It will be the greatest tragedy of both your lives."

Chapter 28

IT was late when she returned from Granny Blue's. Almost ten o'clock.

Her mind worried over thoughts of Ridge, preoccupied, distracted. She forgot to bar the front door with her foot as she entered and the orphaned orange tabby kitten shot around her ankles into the night.

Sprinting for freedom.

"Dammit Dart!" she hollered, getting knocked down by Buddy and Bess as they chased after the kitten in an exuberant, we-wanna-play-too hullabaloo. "Get back here!"

Right. Like that was happening.

She grabbed hold of Buddy's and Bess's collars and wrangled them back into the house, shut the door, and went after Dart.

The half-moon was out, ghostly and white.

She walked around the house, calling "kitty, kitty, kitty," finally spied Dart scaling the only tall tree in the area. A big Texas walnut growing against the side of the house that someone had planted a long time before Kaia had been born.

Great. How was she going to get him down? She couldn't trust he'd come down on his own, and leave him be. Not at night. Not in the dark. Too many predators in the desert.

Remembering a trick she'd seen in the old movie *Roxanne,* where fireman C. D. Bales, played by Steve Martin sporting a fake Cyrano de Bergerac big nose, rescued a cat from a tree, Kaia went into the house for a can of tuna, came back outside, opened the pop-top lid, and set the can underneath the tree.

"Yum, yum. It's tuna. Dinnertime. Come and get it."

Dart crawled deeper into the leaves of the tree, eyed her suspiciously, but did not come down. Well so much for that trick. Steve Martin owed her a can of tuna.

"Dart, darling, come down, come down. Kitty, kitty, kitty."

Dart scooted higher into the tree. So much for her cat seducing abilities. If her sisters could see her now, they'd have a good laugh.

"If you're not going to come down, I'm going to have to come after you," she threatened.

Oh yeah? Oblivious to her threats, Dart never looked down, just kept climbing.

She blew out her breath so hard it ruffled the strands of hair that had floated loose from her braids. She went back into the house past Buddy and Bess, who jumped all over her like they hadn't seen her in ages.

"Yes, yes, good dogs." She paused to pet them.

She went to the pantry, retrieved the stepladder she kept there. It was just tall enough to boost her up to the first limb of the tree.

Back outside, under the glow of the porch lamp, she steadied the stepladder as best she could on the uneven ground. Thick, gnarled, tree roots poked up and she straddled the ladder between them. Climbed to the top rung. Slung one blue-jeaned leg over the lowest branch.

"Okay, we're cooking with kerosene now, baby."

Carefully, she moved to the next limb and the next. After several long minutes, she reached the thin, shaky limb where Dart was perched. Made the mistake of glancing down.

Crapple!

She had to be at least seven feet off the ground.

Don't think. Keep moving.

Dart, the little bugger, was being darn stubborn. Kaia scooted out as far as she dared on the limb, but the orange tabby edged out onto finger branches.

"I thought we had a deal. I take you in, give you all the love I have and in return, you don't act like a jerk when I try to save you from yourself."

"Mew."

"You know there are night animals that see you as a tasty treat. Coyotes, foxes, owls . . . If you don't want to be someone's midnight snack, I suggest you come to Mama."

"Mew."

"No? Is it me? Tell me, where did I go wrong?"

Dart's tail switched and he buried himself so deeply into the shadows she could barely see him.

"C'mere, sweetheart." Kaia fished a liver treat from her pocket, hoped he liked that better than tuna, and set it on a knothole in the branch between them. "There's more where that came from. Consider me your gravy train."

Dart hunched into a tiny ball, curled his tail around him tight, and stared narrow-eyed at her.

"What? When have I ever done you wrong? Name one time."

"Mew."

"Not buying it, huh?"

She heard the rumble of a truck engine, straightened up on the limb, and craned her neck to see who it was.

Archer's SUV.

With Ridge behind the wheel.

Her heart was a rocket, shooting to the moon. He'd come back!

From her vantage point hidden in the tree branches she could see him, but he couldn't see her.

Ridge got out of the pickup.

Kaia's stomach flipped and her chest squeezed tight and her pulse was a wild thing, writhing through arteries and veins.

What was he doing here? Why was he back so soon? Was everything okay with his father?

He sauntered up the sidewalk, headed for her house. He had no idea she was in the tree.

Kaia couldn't help taking advantage of the opportunity and ogled his backside. She leaned over the edge of the branch, watching his back pockets sway.

Nice, very nice.

He adjusted his Stetson, pushing it back on his head, as if he had something serious to tell her. He rang her doorbell.

She canted her head, appreciating how his tight-fitting Wranglers cupped his muscular butt.

Whew-wee! Perspiration broke out on her forehead and in um . . . other places.

She let go of the branch with one hand, used it to fan herself.

Dart picked that moment to dash down from his perch higher on the same limb and he came flying toward her, nimble as a squirrel. He ran straight at her, his kitten claws catching in her hair.

She shrieked.

So did Dart.

And the next thing she knew, Kaia was lying on her back on the ground, guppy-gasping for air.

"KAIA." RIDGE KNELT beside her. "Speak to me."

She would if she could, but she couldn't catch her breath.

He scooped her into his arms, held her close to his chest, and carried her into the house. She waved her hand, trying to get him to wait, to go look for Dart, but he wasn't paying attention.

"He . . . he . . . he . . ." She wheezed, partially from the air being knocked out of her lungs and partially because she was in his arms.

Gently, he settled her on the sofa, and looked down at her, concern knitting his face.

She nodded, still struggling to inhale with seized-up lungs.

"Shh," he said. "Wait until you get your breath back."

She nodded. Buddy and Bess came over to lick her face, thumping their tails and looking concerned.

"Dart," she finally got out.

"What?" He looked confused.

She swung her legs off the sofa, tried to get up, but dizziness swamped her. Whoa! She sank back against the cushions.

"Are you all right?" Ridge's voice was stuffed with concern and his hands were gentle on her body. "Are you hurt?"

"I'm fine, but . . . wait a minute. What are you doing here? I thought you went to pick up Duke in El Paso."

"I did. I'm back."

"So quickly? Why aren't you still with him?" she asked, hoping he'd tell her he couldn't stay away from her one second longer than necessary.

He shifted his gaze, glanced away from her. "We had it out. Big-time."

"Over what?"

"My mother. Vivi. Everything."

"That's good. Right? You finally cleared the air after all this time."

He shook his head. "Nothing changed."

"Oh Ridge, I'm sorry."

He shrugged like a snake shedding old skin, as if it were nothing, as if he wasn't lacerated inside. But Kaia knew the difference. She knew how desperately he craved his father's approval, even if he couldn't admit it, even to himself.

"I'm leaving," he said. "I came to tell you goodbye."

"Tonight?" She heard tension in her voice, felt it grip and crawl, squeezing her stomach, her lungs, her throat. Moving up to her head, throbbing at her temples. "You're leaving tonight?"

"I have to go," he said. "Immediate problems in China."

"I see."

"It's my livelihood, Kaia."

"I understand."

"People depend on me."

"I get it."

"It's—"

"You don't have to explain." She cut him off because she couldn't bear to hear anymore. He was leaving. She knew it was going to happen. But she'd convinced herself that they would have a few more days together. "I have problems of my own. Dart's missing. We've got to find Dart."

"The kitten?"

"Yes, the kitten. He got out of the house, ran up the tree. I tried to rescue him. He took off. He's out there. In the night. Alone."

"I'll go look for him." Ridge straightened.

"I'm coming too." She pushed off from the sofa, pushed through the dizziness. "There's a flashlight on the foyer table."

"You fell from a tree. Rest."

"I'm fine. Dart won't come to you. Remember the last time?"

He put a hand to his chest where Dart had scratched him. "Point taken."

"Let's go." She muscled past him, headed for the door.

"Stubborn," Ridge muttered, but he did not try to make her stay.

Ridge shone the flashlight in bushes and trees. They searched her entire two-acre lot, calling and calling and calling. Then moved to the back alley, peeking behind Dumpsters, looking over fences into the neighbors' yards.

No sign of Dart.

What if they didn't find him? What if he was gone for good? Anxiety was a corkscrew, punched into her chest, twisting and twisting. Tighter and tighter the later it got.

Finally, at midnight, the flashlight battery gave up the ghost, winked out. Plunging them in darkness in the middle of an open field a block away from her house.

"What do you want to do now?" Ridge asked. "If you want to get a fresh battery and search all night, I'm with you."

His words were a comfort. She appreciated the sentiment. But it was temporary. In his mind, he was already gone.

"You need to go," she said.

"I can stay until we find the kitten."

"We may never find him. He's hard to tame."

Kaia remembered what Ridge had said when Dart had taken off before. *Once a runner, always a runner.* She had not wanted to believe that. Had hoped her love would sway him to stay.

Hope.

Her greatest strength, according to Granny Blue. But was it also her greatest flaw? Hoping against hope Hoping when all hope was gone. Hoping a kitten would change his stripes. Hoping a man would too.

Foolishness. Utter foolishness. She could hope until she was blue in the face and it would not alter a thing. They were who they were.

Both Dart and Ridge.

She thought of an inane poster Aria had tacked on their shared bedroom wall when they were teenagers. *If you love something set it free. If it comes back it's yours. If not, it was never meant to be.*

"Are we giving up?" Ridge asked.

Heart scraping the ground, Kaia nodded. "It's over."

"Wait," he said, moonlight carving his face in silhouette, half light, half dark. "Are we talking about the cat?"

"No."

"Kaia." He reached for her, his voice dusky as the Milky Way overhead.

She stepped back, away from his hand, out of range. "You should go."

"We need to talk about what you said to me before I went to get Duke."

"There's nothing to say. You're leaving. You can't get along with your father. You'll never be comfortable in Cupid." *You can't tell me you love me.*

"Come with me."

Her heart skip-thumped, bump-bump, bump-bump. "To China?"

"Yes."

"I'm returning to A&M in September."

"You could come back then."

Hope. Hope. Hope. Her imagination flew to China with Ridge, pictured living there with him. How easy it would be. How exciting.

"No," she said, shocking herself by sounding so forceful.

"No?" He looked blindsided. Had he really expected her to say yes?

"It's better to cut bait now. Cleaner." She didn't know where the courage to say what needed to be said was coming from. The weak part of her wanted to sail into his arms and cover his face with kisses.

"But the humming you hear when we kiss . . . that legend. I thought . . ."

"The Song of the Soul Mate."

"I thought you believed in it."

"I do."

"So why are you breaking up with me?" He canted his head, gazed at her in hurt confusion.

"Sweetheart," she said as kindly and gently as possible, her heart breaking for him. He truly did not get it. "I can't break up with you. We were never together."

He chuffed out a breath, ran a palm up the back of his neck, looked utterly lost.

The breeze gusted. Kaia shivered in the darkness, crossed her arms over her chest. "You should go."

"If it wasn't a billion-dollar deal on the line—"

"It would be something else."

"What does that mean?" His voice turned flinty, flat.

"It's okay. I'm not judging you."

"What do you mean?"

She searched his face, trying to decipher what he was feeling. But he was so good at erecting barriers, hiding his emotions. His eyes were hooded, guarded. Cautious.

"You hide behind your work and achievements. It's your shield."

He blinked at her as if she were speaking a foreign language. "Huh?"

"You use success as a substitute for love and acceptance. It's understandable, considering where you came from. But the deal is, you don't even realize that's what you're doing. You think being a workaholic is a virtue, not an impediment to what you really want."

"And what do I want?" His sarcasm was a knife blade, cutting and cold.

"The same as anyone else." She offered him the kindest smile she could muster. "Love. Belonging. You just don't know how to open your heart and let it come to you."

"Got me all figured out, huh?" His eyes empty. Dead.

"You've got this one way of being in the world that has served you well so far. But now it's stopped working," she went on. She might as well tell him what she thought. She had nothing left to lose. He was already lost to her unless something shifted.

A grimace pulled his mouth down, but he said nothing.

"I love you, Ridge. I love you with all my heart and soul. That will never ever change." She paused. Giving him a chance to say he loved her too. Holding on to the seconds. Ten. Twenty. Thirty.

He did not speak.

All right. He wasn't ready.

She inhaled deeply. "But I can't put my life on hold for you, waiting for you to decide you love me back. And even if you could tell me you loved me, I can't be with you. Not until you get over this anger you have toward your father. Did he treat you badly? Hell yes. No doubt. No one will argue that point with you."

His eyes were a laser, searing her hot and long, but still he said nothing.

"But you *have* to forgive him if you want to move on with your life. You have to drop the baggage you've been carrying. The baggage you've used to push you hard and fast. You've built your entire identity on showing him up."

Ridge pressed his lips together so tightly they disappeared.

"News flash, you achieved your goal. You have bested him. You've made more money. You've made a bigger mark in the world. You've reached the pinnacle of success. You're on Mount Everest. There are no more peaks left to conquer."

He was breathing hard and fast, his chest puffing up like a fire-breathing dragon.

She lowered her voice to a whisper. "It's time to let all that go. It's time to find out who you are without Duke influencing your every move."

God, he was so stoic. Ridge. How apt his name.

Unbending. Inflexible. Stony.

"If you really want to be with me, you'll stay here." She moistened her lips. "You'll let your employees do their jobs in China. You'll forgive Duke and Vivi. You'll forgive yourself. And in the process, you'll find out who you really are. And once you find yourself, we can start to build something. If that is what you want. Until then . . ." She shrugged. It took everything she had inside of her not to show him how much this was killing her.

"You done?" he asked, tight-lipped and blank faced.

"Yes."

"You're wrong."

"If I'm wrong, then stay and prove it to me."

"I have to go."

"I know."

"I wish it could be different. I'm sorry."

"Me too," she said, her heart shattering into a bazillion little pieces. "But you've got nothing to apologize for. You are who you are. This is your way. What was it you said to me about Dart? Once a runner, always a runner?"

He cringed as if she'd hauled off and slapped him across the face as hard as she could. He flinched.

Then turned and walked away.

Leaving Kaia utterly broken.

Chapter 29

ONCE *a runner, always a runner.*

The words she'd thrown back in his face slammed into Ridge like high-octane pepper spray, burning his eyes, convulsing his throat, stunning his reason with the knowledge that she'd written him off.

Written them off.

At the ranch, the lights in the mansion were still on. Ranger and Vivi should have gotten back by now. He wished he could just jump in the Evektor and take off but he had to collect his things.

The doorbell glowed orange in the darkness. The same doorbell his mother had told him to push twenty-nine years ago.

He didn't push it this time. Simply walked right in. Went straight to Duke's office, grabbed his laptop, briefcase, and Stetson. Headed back to the front door.

Vivi came into the foyer from the living room. She wore elegant silk pajamas and looked as if she'd been waiting for him. "You're really leaving?"

"Yes."

"It's after midnight."

"There's a ticking clock. I'm needed in China." He settled the Stetson on his head, hoisted the strap of the briefcase onto his shoulder, and tucked the laptop underneath his arm.

"Excuse me." Vivi glared. "You're needed *here*. Your father just came home from the hospital after open-heart surgery."

"You and Ranger have got it covered. And I'll help pay for the home health nurse."

"Duke doesn't need your money." Vivi's eyes flashed anger. "He needs you. He could have died. You should spend time with him. Make amends."

"I have nothing to make amends for."

"No? How about the fact you can't forgive?"

"He's never asked for my forgiveness."

"You have to give him time."

"I don't have the time to give."

"I never thought of you as a selfish man until now," she said.

"So now I'm the dick?"

"Your father is a proud man, but he knows when he's wrong. He regrets the way he treated you. Truly he does. If you stay, we can fix this. We can be a real family."

He laughed harshly. "With you as the mom? No thanks. We can skip that little fantasy."

"You're being a jerk."

"Yeah well, I'm not the only one."

"I know your father is not an easy man to love," she said. "He's a hardheaded, opinionated, control freak, and he refuses to back down even when there's solid proof he's wrong. Come to think of it, he reminds me a lot of you."

Ridge shot her a cool stare. In the dim lighting she looked done in. Maybe she really did have feelings for the old man beyond the value of his wallet. Had he misjudged her all these years?

"You are more like him than you care to admit," she went on. "That's why the two of you haven't been able to make peace."

"If we're so much alike," Ridge said, "why did you pick him over me?" It wasn't that he'd ever wanted Vivi back, but it had been eating at him all these years. Why had she thrown him over for his father? Why had she stayed with Duke? He'd never expected them to have longevity.

"You mean besides the fact that I fell in love with him?" she asked.

"*Why* did you fall in love with him? What does he have that I don't?"

"Darling," Vivi said in a surprised drawl, as if he should have known her motives. "For one thing, you didn't love me, and we both know it. And, for another thing, at the end of a long day, your father knows how to put work aside, cut loose, and have *fun*. Can you blame a girl for wanting to kick up her heels a little?"

"I know how to have fun," he said, hearing the defensiveness in his voice.

"Maybe," she said. "But do you ever *do* it?"

Yes. Yes he did. With Kaia. He'd had more fun with her since . . . since . . .

Ridge ran a hand over his chin. He couldn't remember a time when he'd so much fun.

"You're so busy making money that you don't stop to consider *why* you're making it," Vivi went on. "Money is just a tool. It's not a reason to get up in the morning."

"I disagree," Ridge said.

"I know." Vivi sounded sorry for him. "And that's one of the reasons I'm with Duke."

"Don't hold back on my account. Let me have those punches."

Vivi let loose. "I was nothing to you but arm candy. A trophy. Something you could show off to your friends."

"I . . ." He opened his mouth to argue, but she was right.

"Hey, I'm not blaming you. I loved how you spent money on me. But the relationship had run its course. Served its purpose."

"You could have just told me that instead of bedding my old man."

"I'm deeply sorry for how I handled things," she said. "It still eats on me. You deserved better, and you deserve an apology from both of us. I know you probably won't get one from Duke, but I swear to you, from the bottom of his soul, your father regrets what he did."

"You're assuming he has a soul."

She touched his arm briefly, dropped her hand "I truly am sorry."

"Better late than never, I suppose," he said, softening toward her.

"Although, be fair, you never did give us a chance to apologize. You packed up your things without hearing us out and cut off all contact with your father and me. I understand why you did it. You were hurt and angry. I don't blame you. But by not giving us an opportunity to apologize, well, *we* didn't get a chance to heal either."

That startled him. He'd never considered that they were hurting too.

"Well hell, Vivi, thank you for that," he said because he didn't know what else to say, and damn, if he didn't feel a little bit better.

"When will you be back?" Vivi said, folding her arms over her chest.

"Don't you get it?" The briefcase was heavy against his shoulder, but he wasn't putting it down. He needed to get out of here. Now. "I'm not coming back."

"The work, right? It's always about the work."

"What else is there?" he asked, not to be sarcastic but because he truly had no idea.

Work was the one thing that had never failed him. Never let him down. Or disappointed him. He could not say the same for the people in his life.

"On their deathbed no one wishes they'd worked more," Vivi said.

"Someone might."

"*No* one does."

"I have to go."

"Wait right here," Vivi said.

"I gotta . . ." Ridge jerked a thumb over his shoulder, pointing in the direction of his plane, and he already had his hand on the doorknob. "Trail. Hitting it. Tell Duke goodbye for me."

"Stop!" she said so firmly and succinctly he did indeed stop.

"What is it?"

She reached over, plucked a white bud from the get-well rose bouquet sitting on the foyer table and thrust it under his nose. "Smell this."

"What for?"

"Because in all the years I've known you, you've never once

stopped to smell the roses, Ridge Lockhart." She shook the rose until a couple of petals peeled off and floated to the floor. "Smell it!"

"It's a figure of speech. You're not supposed to literally smell the roses."

"Yes, you are. Smell it."

He couldn't help but smell it. It was right under his damn nose. Soft. Floral. And totally irrelevant. He made a big deal of inhaling. "Okay, I sniffed it. Happy now? Can I go?"

"Take a deep breath."

"I don't have time." Ridge tapped his watch.

"Which is exactly why you should take the time."

"I'm outta here."

"You disappoint me."

Ridge gave a stiff-shoulder shrug. "Not the first time. I'm sure it won't be the last."

"Stay."

"Why?"

"You belong."

Ha! He didn't belong here. He'd never belonged here. Hell, truth be told, he didn't belong anywhere.

"You're hopeless. You know that?"

"Probably," he agreed, the smell of roses clogging up his sinuses.

"I give up. The only person who seems capable of getting through to you is Kaia Alzate, and you're pushing her away the hardest. She loves you, dammit. For once, just let someone love you."

"Vivi!" Duke called from the top of the stairs. "The boy wants to leave, let him go."

Ridge glanced up the wide double staircase at the end of the entryway. His father was leaning against the banister in his pajamas looking ashen beneath his outdoorsy tan. The bachelor party bruise at his eye was almost gone, but a shadow of color lingered. A quiver of regret seized him.

His father frowned, studying him hard as if trying to read his thoughts. His hair silvered, his forehead deeply etched with lines.

The man he'd once seen as a lion. The man who'd once controlled his life no longer held any power over him.

So much contention lay between them, so much stagnant water under the aging bridge.

"He's got to make his own mistakes," Duke said. "One day he'll see where he went wrong, but by then it will all be too late."

And as Ridge stood there feeling pity for the old man, he realized with shock, the old man was feeling sorry for *him*.

THE FOURTEEN-PLUS-HOUR FLIGHT to Beijing left Ridge wrung out and feeling like chopped liver hash on a stale cracker.

Or at least that's what he told himself.

His head throbbed and his shoulders ached and his butt was numb from so much time in the seat, never mind that he'd flown first-class. It was still too long to be stuffed into a winged metal tube at thirty thousand feet.

But the truth was, he'd been unable to think about anything but Kaia since he'd walked away from her in the dark.

Images flipped and fluttered through his mind, quick and vivid, a vision of Kaia in a teeny-weeny red bikini doing the breast-stroke in the springs at Balmorhea, an utterly disarming smile on her gorgeous face.

Kaia in his arms on the dance floor at Archer's wedding, her face turned up to him, head thrown back, long hair cascading over his elbow as he dipped her in an exaggerated back bend. Her laughter ringing in his ears.

Kaia in his bed, eyes wide and dark, pale light from the moon falling over her lithe body. The long scar at her hip, that jagged badge of courage, reminding him of how much she'd suffered and just how tough she was.

Kaia and her golden lips, telling him about the Song of the Soul Mate that had scared him so very much because he believed it too and believing it made him feel so out of control.

Kaia holding his gaze steady, assuring him that until he could let go of his emotional baggage and forgave the past she couldn't be with him. An assurance that knocked his heart sideways.

He loved her and that's all there was to it.

When he got to Liu Yan's headquarters, Phil Rhonstein met him with a toothy smile and a hearty handshake. "It's solved."

Jet-lagged, Ridge blinked. "What?"

"The contract. Liu Yan's signing off on it."

"How did that come about?"

Phil went into detail about the negotiations and ended with, "I told you we could handle it."

"Good work."

"No need for you to be here," Phil said. "You hired me for a reason."

Of course he needed to be here. This deal was the most important thing in his life. "I'm here for six months to train the miners."

"You've got a team that can do that for you."

"I'm here," he said. "I'm staying. Drop it."

"Sorry," Phil said. "I'd gotten the impression that maybe you'd gotten a social life while you were in Cupid. My mistake."

Before Ridge could think of a comeback, Liu Yan walked into the room and work took over. Just as it always had.

But this time, instead of feeling fulfilled by shoptalk, discussion of the Lock Ridge drilling method left Ridge strangely dissatisfied, and if it hadn't been the middle of the night in Cupid, he would have texted Kaia.

By the time the meeting was over, the impulse to text her had passed, and Ridge did what he always did when assaulted by complicated feelings. He threw himself into his work one hundred percent.

Work.

It was, after all, his one-and-only salvation.

Chapter 30

Dart didn't come home, and Ridge didn't call. Or text. Or email.

Not that day. Nor the next. Nor the day after that.

Kaia had to let go of them both.

At first, it made her stomach quiver, the idea that she didn't have to know the outcome or be in control in order to enjoy the unfolding of life in all its big messy glory.

Flow. She was water. Just let go and flow.

Once she got the hang of it, letting go started to feel natural. Inevitable. Freeing. She did not have to know what was going to happen tomorrow in order to enjoy today. Tomorrow was a mystery. The past nothing but a memory.

At times, though, she'd forget and slip back into the way she used to be. Worrying. Wishing. Hoping. Doing things to distract herself. Working all hours, eating when she wasn't hungry, listening for the humming in her head that had disappeared along with Ridge.

Let go.

Trust.

If she could do that, everything else would sort itself out. According to Granny Blue, they were destined. The only hitch was Ridge. It was all up to him.

A week had passed since Ridge left and she hadn't heard a word from him. Not a call. Not an email. Not a text.

The man who loved technology had chosen this moment to go for radio silence. And of course, she hadn't been bold enough to contact him. What would she say if she did? *I love you. Come home.*

It was what she wanted to say, but the ball was in his court. He was the one who had to come to her.

So when her thoughts grew worrisome, when her hopes were too much to bear, she would go see Granny Blue, who told her to simply breathe.

Pay close attention to how perfectly the air slipped in and out of her lungs. She would go outside and slip off her shoes and dig her feet into the warm sand, feel the grains shift between her toes and just be. She took long walks in the early morning as the sun was waking up, keeping her mind centered on the path and her walk.

She even stopped watching for Dart. Well, mostly. Her hope could still be seduced by the shift of shadows or the flutter of grass.

It was becoming automatic. The breathing, the walking, the being. It was easy, when you gave it a chance. Letting go. Why had she taken something so simple and made it so complex?

Awareness, Granny Blue had told her, was the key.

Life was really not that complicated when you took it moment by moment, stayed out of the past, and didn't invent a fictional future. Eventually, as she gained more and more control over her thoughts and feelings, she felt lighter, enlightened.

But enlightenment was a funny thing. If you thought you had it, you probably didn't.

Enlightenment wasn't some big neon sign glowing in the dark, bestowed by gods from on high. Rather, it was the eventual dawning that all the obstacles you'd been tripping over were of your own making, and only you had the power to dispatch them. Only you held the key to your own freedom by becoming aware of your mind chatter and how silly much of it was.

At least that's what Granny Blue kept telling her, and for the most part, that understanding helped her keep it together.

But then the dark clouds would drift over her. And the thoughts would close in. The ones she couldn't walk or breathe away. When the dark clouds came, she knew she had to get out of her own mind, so she submersed herself in animals. When her faith in people faltered, animals always cheered her up.

One sleepless night, she pocketed a flashlight and liver treats. Made a call to the police to let them know she'd be in the shelter after hours so they didn't send a patrol car and let herself into the kennels via the side exit door.

The sound of her key in the lock set the dogs to barking. Barking that filled her head with humming as surely as Ridge's kiss.

Stop thinking about him.

The second she stepped into the kennels and the dogs caught her scent, they immediately hushed and tails went wagging. She went from pen to pen, greeting each dog, rubbing heads and scratching behind ears. Cooing and talking to them like they understood what she was saying.

"Thinking time is over," she said to a mixed breed pit bull with an adorable spotted face, and tickled the dog's nose. "Yes it is. Oh yes it is."

The pitty sighed happily.

She sat down on the floor beside pitty's pen, the cement cool beneath her bottom. Bit her bottom lip to keep from crying. "Damn it, pitty, how do I stop loving him?"

The dog sympathized with a soft whimper.

"Nope. There's no hope for us."

The pitty rolled over onto her belly, pawed at Kaia's hand through the chain-link wire of her pen.

"I know. I should have seen it coming. Granny Blue's romantic legend aside, Ridge is Ridge. I can't change him. I don't *want* to change him. I love him just the way he is. Unfortunately . . ." Her bottom lip quivered and no amount of sinking her teeth into it could stop her sorrow. "He doesn't . . . or can't . . . love me the way I love him."

The pitty gave her a look.

"Well, yes, he did ask me to go to China with him. But I turned him down, and now he hasn't called or texted or emailed."

The dog barked.

"Ahh, so you think it's my fault? I should be the one to contact him?"

The pitty wagged her tail.

"Damn, dog," Kaia said, tears flowing down her cheeks. "How did you get so smart?"

The dog looked at her as if to say, "How did you get so dumb?"

TEN DAYS AFTER he arrived in Beijing, Ridge was dining on a lavish banquet in his honor at Liu Yan's palace, wishing he was instead at Kaia's little cottage sharing a delivery pizza.

He was at the pinnacle of his career, and it meant nothing.

He kept thinking about his last day in Cupid. What everyone had said to him. Duke. Vivi. Kaia.

Maybe they were right. Maybe he did use work as an excuse to bury his emotions. Maybe he had been running away.

It was a concept he kept butting up against.

From the time he was a kid, he'd always felt the only way to earn Duke's love and respect was to do something of value. Take care of his brothers. Play football. Be class president. Make money. Build a house. Win trophies. Invent a drilling method. Pilot an airplane. Learn Mandarin.

Where did it end? When would he be good enough? How much money did he have to have before he felt complete? How many skills did he need to master? How many awards did he have to achieve?

Why did he have to do things to feel worthy? Who would he be if he just stopped doing?

The idea was terrifying.

But it was also freeing.

What if he didn't have to constantly produce, produce, produce in order to be loved?

What if he was already loved, just for who he was?

Kaia had been trying to tell him that all along. He was loved. Ridge couldn't seem to wrap his head around it.

What if he didn't have to be the best of the best? What if second best was good enough? What if people accepted him just the way he was? And what if other peoples' opinions of him weren't so important?

What was holding him back from fully embracing that notion?

The answer came to him in Kaia's soft voice with such clarity that he sucked in his breath and bolted upright in his chair.

You don't believe you deserve love.

"Ridge?" Phil leaned over to whisper. "Are you all right?"

"Fine," he said, but his mind and body were on fire with the epiphany. Could the answer be that simple? Other people hadn't been rejecting him all along. He'd been rejecting himself.

His cell phone dinged, letting him know he had a text. Once. Twice.

But Kaia's lesson had sunk in. Mr. Yan was his host. He deserved Ridge's undivided attention. The phone dinged again, but he ignored it until he excused himself from the table. Slipped off to the restroom.

When he finally pulled the phone from his pocket and checked the text messages and saw they were from Kaia, his heart grew wings.

I lied, said the first text.

Intrigued, he scrolled to the next one.

I'll wait for you.

His chest tightened and his heart raced.

However long it takes.

He couldn't exhale. He staggered against the wall to keep from falling over.

I'll be here.

I miss you.

I love you.

And the last one.

I cherish the day when you can tell me you love me too.

Finally, finally, he could breathe again. And in that moment, Ridge absolutely knew exactly where he belonged.

THE MINUTE HE got out of his plane at the Silver Feather Ranch, Duke was there to greet him.

He'd called his father when he left Beijing, telling him he was coming home so they could have a long talk.

"Welcome home, son," Duke said, and stunned Ridge by giving him a hug.

"What's this all about?"

"Vivi threatened to leave me if I don't make things right with you this time," Duke said. "I can't lose her, so here I am, hugging you."

"Is she watching?"

"On the front porch."

"You'll do anything for her, won't you?"

"Pretty much."

"You're better for her than I ever was," Ridge said.

"I know that." Duke grinned and Ridge didn't take offense. Not at all.

They stared at each other, not in hostile tension as before, but in companionable silence.

Something monumental had shifted.

Not in Duke, but in him.

"I'm glad you came home," Duke said.

"Glad to be here." Ridge meant every word.

"After my heart attack, well, I've done some thinking and I want you to know I'm changing my will. I'm leaving the Silver Feather to you. Although I'm leaving the mansion to Vivi of course."

"What?" His jaw unhinged. A silver feather could have knocked him over. But this was Duke. Ridge had narrowed his eyes, hopeful but still guarded. "Are you just trying to stir up trouble between me and my brothers? Because I don't need your money or your ranch."

"I know that."

"Why then?"

"You're my son, what do you mean, why?"

"You have three other sons."

"You're the oldest."

"I'm the bastard."

"That doesn't matter. This isn't 1854."

"You always treated me like it was."

"I'm an asshole. Is that what you want me to say? There it is. I'm an asshole."

"Well, okay. We both already knew that."

"I admit it," Duke said. "I was furious when your mama got knocked up and put the screws to me for money. I took it out on you. I shouldn't have. That was wrong. Happy now?"

It wasn't quite an apology, but it was something. Baby steps.

"Besides," Duke went on, "you're the only one who loves the ranch like I do. Ranger's a good hand, but his head is in the stars. Remington's got a chip on his shoulder and a score to settle. And Rhett don't give a damn about anything he can't ride. You're the only one with soil in your blood . . ."

"Have you talked to them?"

"I haven't. They'll get their due. I'm not cutting them out. There's the silver mine and other real estate holdings. But the ranch is yours." Duke's voice faltered as if the conversation was taking way too much out of him. "I want you to have it . . . son."

"Thank you . . ." Ridge hesitated a moment, and then went ahead and grabbed the impulse seizing him. "*Dad*."

Duke looked stunned, pulled a palm down his face. "You called me Dad. You haven't called me that since you were—"

"Twelve years old, and we got into our first fistfight. I know."

"You don't have to wait until I die," Duke invited. "I'm not up to snuff and the doc says I have to take it easy. While Archer is an ace foreman, he's not family. You did a fine job with the business while I was in the hospital. I shouldn't have yelled at you. I just saw the changes you'd made. Good changes. Changes I should have made years ago and I felt inadequate and put-out-to-pasture and I took it out on you."

"Thank you for saying that." It was odd, hearing Duke admit he was wrong.

"You don't have to take it over now. I'm just saying the Silver Feather is your home. If you ever wanted to put down roots, you could."

"It's a generous offer."

"But you're not going to take it."

"I don't know."

"Are you heading back to China?"

"It all depends."

"On what?"

"How all this goes down."

"C'mon inside, boy. It's time we set things right."

Chapter 31

FOUR hours later, Ridge strode up the flagstone sidewalk at dark. No stars were out. The only sounds he heard were his footsteps against the pavers.

There were desert sounds too, of course, but his mind didn't fully register those. Inside that house was the woman he'd been waiting all his life for, and each scrape of his boots took him closer and closer, the sharp slap-slap marking off each step like a promise.

Two minutes.

One.

Thirty seconds.

A breath.

A heartbeat.

And then he was there. Her front porch boards creaked underneath his weight. The lights were out. Windows dark and shuttered. They stared at him like vacant eyes, dull and challenging. Filling him with an impending sense of dread.

All the hope that had gotten him this far vanished and doubt set in.

Did she still want him? What if she turned him down? Had he let it go too long? Had she fallen out of love with him? What would he say? How did he start to mend things?

He should go. Come back in the morning. Things would look brighter in daylight.

Why the hesitation?

Only a brief while ago he was running to get here. Breathless and anxious and excited and ready, oh so damned ready to have her in his arms again.

But doubt, that sneaky villain, crept in, whispered poisonous words. Telling him she was better off without him.

No. He was not going to let fear of intimacy chase him away again. Not now. Not when he'd come so far. He couldn't live one more minute without her in his life.

The woman inside that house was important. The most important thing in the world. Without Kaia, he had no world. She was his sun and his moon and his stars. She was the air he breathed. The water he drank. The soil beneath his feet. The burning fire in his heart.

One word from her lips would save his life. One sweet word.

Yes.

But what if she said no?

He stuffed his hands in his pockets, balled them into hard knots to keep them from trembling. His blood rushed through his veins and his heart throbbed. A hard, steady ka-pow, ka-pow.

It was quiet. Too quiet. No dogs raising the alarm.

Then he thought of something truly horrible. What if she had moved on? What if she'd cleared out the pets because she had overnight company? What if she had a man in there with her?

Ah damn. Ah shit. He'd not even thought about that.

Go! Just go. Leave. Call first.

But he did not. Ridge took that last step. Onto the welcome mat with a puppy's face on it. Raised his hand to the door. Rapped.

Quick.

Staccato.

Let me in. Let me in.

He waited. Held his breath.

Listened. Heard nothing.

Knocked again. Cocked his head, listened harder.

Was that the sound of socked feet padding toward the door? The porch light came on, bathing him in a halo of yellow.

Air leaked slowly from his lungs.

The door opened and there she stood in her oversized Minnie

Mouse sleep shirt. Even in the dim light, she looked beautiful, the fall of dark hair framing her dear face.

A face he'd seen in his dreams every night since he'd left. Her deep ebony eyes looked surprised, but lurking beneath the surprise, was that joy? Her gaze latched onto his and she flicked out her tongue to touch it to her full lush lips. Lips he'd desperately missed kissing. Moisture clung to her mouth, glistened with warmth and invitation.

As if he'd just seen her that very morning, Ridge said casually, "Hey."

For an eternal second she just stood there, not smiling, not talking, not moving, simply taking him in. Waking up to the moment, shrugging off sleep.

Then, with a voice as heavenly as harp music, she whispered on a sigh, "Ridge?"

He wasn't even aware he'd opened his arms wide until she rushed into them and flung her arms around his neck and buried her face against his shoulder. Her whispers turned to whimpers as she kept repeating, "Ridge, Ridge, Ridge."

Chest aching with emotion, he wrapped his arms around her waist, squeezing her against his chest. Held her. Just held and squeezed her as hard as he could without cutting off her breath.

She pushed against him, made hungry noises.

"Kaia."

In a frenzy, their mouths found each other, met, sealed, thrust, burned. He tasted her passion, her beauty, her kind sweet heart. His hand kneaded the soft skin at the nape of her neck, slipped down to her shoulders, and then to her back. Savoring each and every touch as if feeling her for the very first time.

She trembled in his arms. Her familiar scent encompassed him, wrapping him up in the cozy, homey aroma that was his Kaia.

He eased her back into the house. Automatically, he put out his foot to block the exit, but no orange ball of fur shot out. "Dart hasn't come home?"

Solemnly, she shook her head. "No."

Damn if he didn't feel a sting of regret that the kitten hadn't made it back.

"But you're here," she whispered, and wrapped her arms around his neck.

He closed the door behind him with the heel of his boot. Reached for the switch plate to simultaneously turn off the porch light and turn on the living room lamp.

The illumination was sudden and startling in the throes of their embrace, and it moved them apart for a moment to catch their breaths.

Lamplight chased the shadows away and highlighted her cheekbones, the jut of her chin, and the provocative thrust of her nipples beneath the white cotton sleep shirt.

She seemed leaner, as if she'd been skipping meals. He understood. He'd had no appetite without her either. He couldn't eat. Couldn't sleep. Couldn't do damn much of anything.

"Sweetheart, I've missed you so much," he murmured, and watched a brilliant smile bloom across her face.

There was much to say. So many words. He didn't know where to start.

She studied him closely, her eyes saying what her lips did not. *I missed you too, you big lug. Please tell me you've come home for good.*

Her expression softened and her mouth formed a gentle circle. She reached out her fingertips, trailed them over his face. Touched his cheek, his jaw, his lips. "Is it really you?"

"It's me."

"And you're really here? I'm not dreaming?"

"It's no dream." God, his legs were so shaky, it was a wonder he didn't topple over.

"Ridge . . ." Her voice caught, light and joyful. "Oh Ridge."

"I'm here, I'm here." He pulled her into his arms again. Pressed her against his chest, hand to her back, rested his face against the top of her head, smelled the honest clean scent of her hair, watermelon and daisies.

Smelled daisies and heat and Kaia's hot little body. Savoring this moment. Knowing he would never have another exactly like it. Basking in the glow. Loving every sigh, every caress, every taste, every glance, every scent.

Grateful. He was so grateful to be here. So grateful she'd texted. So grateful she'd given him a loving, welcoming reception.

Honestly, he didn't deserve it, but he was deeply appreciative that she was so willing to give him a second chance without a moment of hesitation.

"Are you . . ." She stopped, pulled back a bit so she could see his face but did not break the circle of his embrace. "How long will you be here?"

"This is it. I'm back for good. I've come home."

Tears blurred her eyes. "Oh Ridge, don't tease. If it's not true—"

"It's true. I'm selling the drilling company to Lui Yan and, get this, Duke just offered me the Silver Feather."

"What?" Her eyes widened.

He told her about his conversation with his father. About the old man's change of heart and attitude.

"I don't believe it."

"I didn't either at first, but he seems sincere."

"There will be challenges working for him."

"That's just it. I won't be working for him. He and Vivi would stay living in the mansion, but the ranch will be mine."

"What about your brothers?"

"Like you said, there will be challenges, but I'm up for them."

"This is what you really want? You're not just doing it for me?"

"This is what I really want," he said, his heart filled to overflowing.

What a blessing to love the very place that called to his soul, the place where he had belonged all along, but never knew it. The place he'd missed for ten long years.

She shook her head, her hair swirling in a dark arc around her shoulders. "I still can't believe it."

"It's true. I'm here and I'm home and I'm with you. There's nothing I want more."

Her bottom lip trembled as if she wasn't sure she could trust the changes in him. "Oh Ridge . . ."

As small as she was, it took no effort to pick her up off her feet, kiss her again, and carry her to the cushy sofa nestled in the bay window.

She quivered in his arms, her skin flushed, her eyes bright. She smiled when he laid her down, put her mouth against his and devoured him with desperation, letting him know she was as full of loneliness and longing as he was.

"I want you," she whispered.

"Not any more than I want you." He pulled back a moment to stare down at her, marveling at the blessed gift before him.

Looking at her clogged his throat and clutched his gut. She was everything he had not known he wanted. Everything his heart and soul needed. She was his. A sweet, feisty, gorgeous woman. Who loved him and was whimpering for him to take her, "now, now, now."

Touching her was so poignant, so filled with nuance and emotion. The fire he'd tried so hard to bank flickered, flared, flamed. No tamping down his desires. No going back. He never wanted to go back to the life he'd led before.

Through knowing her, he'd learned so much. She'd held a mirror to his face, showed him what he'd become, schooled him on what really mattered in life.

Family. Home. Love.

By teaching him how to slow down and observe the world around him, she led him from vain pride in his accomplishments to humble hope that he was enough just as he was.

It came as such a relief. The knowledge that there was nothing to get, nowhere to go, nothing to be but himself. A radical concept for a man who'd based his self-worth on the trappings of success.

She'd taken away his "to do" list and replaced it with experiences and memories that would last a lifetime. She'd created more space in his life, more room to feel and to express those feelings. Her love had trained him to tap into the rhythm of his body. And to listen, to listen to the song of his heart.

Through loving her, he'd learned how he used rationalizations to keep from delving deep into his emotions and his relationships. And in those lessons, he'd found the security and connections with others that had always seemed to be slipping through his fingers.

People were what made a life rich. People. Connections. Relationships. That's how you grew. Not through stubborn self-reliance and chronic hard work.

And the most lightning bolt lesson of all? He'd learned that he did not have to be responsible for everything and everyone. When he allowed others to share the burdens, mutual trust developed and he didn't have to go it alone.

This dear woman was his guiding star, and he loved her more than words could ever express. He'd gone from self-imposed prison to the most exquisite kind of freedom.

"Ridge," she called, and he realized he'd gotten lost in thought. "Are you all right?"

"Never been righter."

"Well, what are you waiting for?"

"I was thinking maybe we should wait just a little bit longer."

"What?" Alarm and disappointment sent her eyebrows shooting up on her forehead. "Why?"

"To do this right."

"Meaning?"

"Let's get married. It doesn't have to be a big showy deal. We can keep the wedding small. Just immediate family. Your call. Whatever you want."

She blinked at him, a rapt smile overtaking her face. "Wait. Let me absorb this. You're asking me to marry you?"

He slid off the sofa, went to one knee on the floor, took her hand. "I'm sorry I don't have a ring yet. I wanted you to pick out your own, but yes, Kaia Marie Alzate. I am asking you to marry me. Become my bride. Make my life. Take me as your husband from now until eternity."

"Oh, oh." She planted a palm to her mouth. "I wasn't expecting this. I thought we were finished. You didn't answer my texts and I just thought I'd ruined everything. And now here out of the blue, you show up on my doorstep asking me to marry you."

Nervously, he licked his lips. "Did you . . . find someone else?"

She cocked her head and looked at him so tenderly it bruised his heart. "Silly man. There will never be anyone else for me but you. You are my soul mate. My one and only. Whether we are together or apart, that will not ever change."

"Kaia, my beloved," he said as his eyes stung. "I am not worthy of you."

"Of course you are." She smiled and reached up to touch his cheek. "But we're better when we're together. Both of us."

"I don't deserve you."

"We deserve each other." She wrapped her arms around his neck, pulled him back down over her. "Now make love to me."

"You didn't answer my proposal."

"There's time for that later. Right now, I want you."

"That's my sexy kitten," he murmured, and gave up the fight as her mouth captured his and pulled him under.

He pushed his palm up underneath her sleep shirt, his hand drifting over the velvety expanse of her skin, felt tiny tremors trigger throughout her body wherever his fingers trailed.

She squirmed beneath him, pressing their bodies closer, moaning softly, egging him on.

"You are so damn beautiful." He exhaled heavily. "I've got something to confess."

"Oh no," she groaned. "Not more secrets."

"It's not a secret, just an admission."

"Okay." She pulled back to study his face. "Go on. I'm listening."

He stared into her eyes, mesmerized, and gulped.

Kaia laughed. "You're speechless. I didn't know that was a possibility."

"Are you kidding? I'm struck dumb every time I look at you."

"How long has this been going on?"

"I didn't want to admit it, even to myself, because I was afraid Archer would see the lust on my face and punch me out, but you've had this effect on me ever since you showed up at my college graduation."

Surprised, Kaia raised an eyebrow. "*Really?*"

"You wore this white lacy dress and the material was so thin I could see right through it, and you weren't wearing a slip."

"That's right." She smiled as if he were an apt pupil. "I purposely did not wear a slip, hoping you would notice. I had no idea you noticed. That evening you treated me the way you always did. As if I were nothing more than Archer's annoying kid sister. Just so you know, I was crushed."

"Unbeknownst to me, I've been carrying a torch for you ever since. I can be a bit thick sometimes."

"Clearly." Her grin forgave him for all sins.

He reached out to trace her chin with the pad of his thumb.

"You missed out on a big opportunity that night," she said.

"You were too young. Only sixteen. Which is why I kept my distance."

"I know that now, but I would have gone to bed with you in a heartbeat."

"Which is precisely why I left. You scared the living hell out of me."

"You broke my heart."

"I know. I'm sorry. Please forgive me."

"I'm not the girl I once was," she said. "I no longer worship at the altar of Ridge Lockhart."

"Good," he said. "I do not want to be put on a pedestal."

"I'm not even the woman I was when you sauntered back into Cupid with your golden boy smile."

"I've never been a golden boy. It's a myth."

"A myth you've milked."

He started to look a little panicky. "I'm trying to apologize here."

"So it seems. But I'm no longer a pushover."

"Why did you send me away that night Dart went missing?"

She paused, touched the tip of her tongue to her upper lip. "Remember that day at Balmorhea?"

"I'll never forget it."

"Do you recall what you said?"

"I said a lot of things. What specifically?"

"You said I was just like every other woman you'd ever met. That I wanted to change you. Mold you in a role of my own making."

"I didn't mean it. I was angry," he said. "That day stirred up a lot of old painful memories. You know my past, what I was like as a kid, how things were with Duke . . ." He stopped, cleared his throat. "I was always the outsider. The one who didn't belong. My whole life has been trying to prove myself worthy of the Lockhart name. It's all I ever thought about."

"I know that. And you were right."

"I was?"

"Not about me wanting to change you because I love you just the way you are, but because you believed I was trying to change you."

"I was running scared of my feelings."

"So was I. I was terrified you'd see that as me trying to control you, mold you. But I had to send you away so you could figure out for yourself who you were and who you wanted to be. You needed to figure you out. No input from me."

"So why did you text me?"

"Because." She bit her bottom lip. "I couldn't live one more minute without letting you know how much you meant to me. I love you, Ridge Lockhart. Always have, and always will. The Song of the Soul Mate just clinched what I already knew."

"My soul mate," he whispered, and nuzzled her neck.

"You're not scared of that?"

"Not in the least." He wrapped his arms around her, dragged her up against his solid chest.

"You could choose any woman you want."

His gaze tangled up in hers. "And I choose you."

"Why?"

"Fishing for compliments?" He laughed like she was the most amusing thing he'd ever seen.

"No. I'm serious. Why me?"

"Why? There are so many little things I love about you. Your adorable laugh or the happy face you make when you hug an animal. I love how you bite your lip when you're uncertain and the way you bounce when you walk like you're throwing yourself fully into life. I love learning a little more about you every day and I don't ever want to stop."

He took a deep breath. "But mostly, my darling, it's because when I'm with you, I'm a better man. You bring out the best version of me. Something no one else ever has. But you challenge me too. Push me out of my comfort zone. Give me what I need even if it hurts. Because there is no growth without growing pains."

"We've had a few of those."

"And I'm sure we'll have them again as we navigate our life together. Without turbulence we can't appreciate the clear skies."

"Pretty poetic for a businessman."

"Rancher," he corrected, and kissed her again. And for the first time in his life, Ridge Lockhart felt well and truly loved.

KAIA LISTENED TO the humming in her head, kneaded the beads of her necklace between her finger and thumb, and watched the sunrise brighten through her window. They'd made love all night long and the humming had not stopped.

There was, she noted, a lulling quality to the hum. It was not the annoying ring of tinnitus. But if she were to tell other people about the humming, they would assume it was something unpleasant that she needed to get rid of. They would not understand how the hum was now an integral part of who she was and clear-cut evidence of her true nature.

Love.

Granny Blue understood. But she was the only one.

She glanced over at the man in her bed, smiled wide. He was lying on his belly, arms flung out over his head, legs spread. He looked like a starfish, hogging the bed, her big man. She leaned over, pressed her lips to his bare back.

Immediately, he rolled over like a crocodile lying in wait for prey, grabbed her in his arms, flipped her onto her back and buried her in kisses. She giggled so hard that she couldn't catch her breath. "No . . . stop . . . wait. I . . . hafta . . . breathe."

He pulled back, but just barely. His big body trapping hers beneath him. His eyes were bright and alert. His dark hair was mussed and a cowlick standing up in back.

She inhaled sharply, overwhelmed by the miraculous beauty of him.

He didn't say anything, allowed her to breathe, and then he folded her gently against his hard-muscled chest and kissed her again.

And boy, what a kiss!

Deep, hot, sensual. His tongue slipped between her teeth, filled her mouth, hungry, searching. No preamble. No good morning. Straight to the point.

Here we go!

His body radiated heat and strength and divineness. The sheets smelled of him, all leather and cardamom and bay rum and Ridge.

That's when she registered he was clearly turned on.

She pressed against his erection, kissing him harder, happy, so very happy to be in his arms. She let her eyes flutter closed, reached her hands up to thread her fingers through his hair, tugging his head lower. All stray thoughts slipped away and the only awareness she had was of his hands, his mouth, his body, his masculine heat.

So much heat churning between them.

His palm swept underneath the sleep shirt she'd put on during the night when she'd gotten chilled, pushed it up over her belly.

Their mouths were glued. Lips seared. Tongues fused.

"Hang on." Panting, she wrenched her mouth from his. "We need to talk."

"Now, Kaia?" He gasped. "I want you so bad. Need you." He buried his face against her neck. Nibbled. Licked.

She shivered. Closed her eyes against the onslaught of glorious sensation. God, she needed him too!

Instinctively, she wrapped her legs around his waist, clung tightly to his neck. He fumbled blindly on the nightstand. Found what he was looking for.

Box of condoms.

Foil package.

He covered himself, kissed her again. And for the fourth time since he'd come home to her, they made love.

Afterward, they lay on top of the blanket, limbs entwined, breathing ragged and sated. Kaia slipped her palm into his, and he interlaced their fingers.

"Yes," she whispered.

"Yes what?" he asked, sounding sleep and sex-befuddled.

"Yes, you big lug, I'll marry you."

"Really?" He sat up in bed, glee in his eyes, looking happier than she'd ever seen him look. "Oh Kaia." His voice clotted. "You've made me the happiest man alive."

Kaia sat up beside him. "What was that?"

"What—?"

"Shh, shh." She waved a hand. Heard it then, plain as day.

The sound of a kitten mewling.

"Dart!" he said.

And they shot out of bed, dashed to the back door, opened it up to find Dart on the porch blinking up at them.

"You're back!" Kaia exclaimed, overjoyed. She scooped the cat to her chest, cradled him against her heart. "Will you look at this? Two prodigals returned at the same time."

Ridge hugged her against him as she hugged the cat, Buddy and Bess dancing around them.

"I guess you were wrong." She giggled. "Once a runner, not always a runner. I guess this means you're part of the family now."

"You talking to me or the cat?"

"Both." She grinned at him as Dart crawled up her arm to lick her face. "But I hope you don't mind having a few pets in your life."

"Sweetheart, I wouldn't have it any other way."

And when he took Dart from her, set the kitten on the ground, drew Kaia into his arms, and kissed her again, all she could hear was the happy humming of their soul mate hearts.

Epilogue

Like a blast from her past, Kaia dove into the water, lithe as a fish. No, she was not in Balmorhea.

She was swimming in the beautiful water feature Ridge had made for her at his house in the middle of the desert. A sweet oasis for his water nymph as he loved to call her. The pool was eight feet at its deepest spot, and shaded by a long wooden pergola. There was a curved slide and a diving board and a cascading waterfall.

Ridge had created a water-land paradise.

Tonight, they were having a blowout party to celebrate the ending of one chapter and the beginning of another. For the past year, as Kaia had finished her DVM, Ridge had been shuttling back and forth from Beijing to Calgary to Cupid and back again, winding up his business dealings as he turned the keys of Lockhart Enterprises over to Lui Yan.

The guests were due to arrive at six, but it was only four.

Ridge would be home soon. He'd called that morning to tell her he was on his way back from Calgary for the final time. The offices were now officially closed. The ink was dry on his deal with Duke. Ridge was now a rancher and proud owner of the Silver Feather Ranch.

At the moment, she was home alone, well except for Dart and Buddy and Bess, who were all napping in the air conditioning, and the place was quiet.

She got out of the water, wrapped Ridge's white terry cloth bathrobe around her. It was the same bathrobe she'd worn the first night they'd made love. The night he'd stirred her to untold heights. The night she knew she'd mated with the other half of her soul.

Dropping into the lawn chair, she sighed happily and pulled off her swim cap, shook out her hair. She stretched her legs out in front of her, admired her freshly painted toes. She'd gotten a pedicure in honor of Ridge's homecoming. His favorite color. Candy apple red.

She got up and went into the house, double-checking the provisions, making sure she had everything she needed for the party. Food. Drink. Music. She was ready. Since it was a pool party, she didn't even have to change. Just put on a cover-up over her swimsuit.

The sound of a plane buzzed overhead. Ridge was home!

She raced out the front door, put her palm to her forehead to shield her eyes from the sun as she watched his plane touch down. Fifteen minutes later, his ATV came into view, her handsome husband astride.

He pulled up to the house in a cloud of dust, a stunning smile on his face. "Do you have any idea just how gorgeous you look?"

She ran to him, giggling.

He held his arms open, and when she was close enough, he scooped her up and spun her in a circle, pressed his face to her hair. "God, how I've missed you."

"I've missed you too." She nuzzled his neck.

"How 'bout a kiss." He puckered up.

"Any time, any place." She kissed his lips that tasted of peppermint. The instant their mouths touched the humming in her head bloomed, swelled.

Ah. Song of the Soul Mate. Telling her the thrill of kissing her husband was meant to be. It would not fade.

They'd gotten married at the cowboy chapel just as Archer and Casey had. Where the girlhood dreams she'd doodled in her notebook all those years ago had come true and she became Kaia Lockhart.

Ember had been her maid of honor. Aria, Casey, and Tara her bridesmaids.

They used Atticus as ring bearer. He had experience. Luckily, the boy had learned not to walk behind horses, and no one got kicked this time. Archer served as Ridge's best man, of course. His brothers were groomsmen. Her mother cried. Granny Blue whispered, "The song is never wrong." Duke was on his best behavior. Kaia doubted it would always be smooth sailing with her father-in-law, but the man loved animals as much as she did.

"When are the guests supposed to be here?" Ridge murmured, his lips pressed against her throat. "Do we have time to get you out of that swimming suit and into my bed?"

She wrapped her arms around his neck and pulled his head down for another kiss, dreaming of the delights awaiting in their bedroom.

But the sound of the glass patio door sliding open interrupted them.

"Lookee here, they're at it again," Aria said, as her three sisters traipsed into the kitchen, carrying food and drink. "Sappy time."

"Don't be jealous," Ember said. "Your turn will come."

"Frequent kissing makes for the best marriages." Tara nodded.

"How would you know?" Aria asked. "You've never been married."

"Mom and Dad still kiss like that." Tara put a platter of her famous deviled eggs in the fridge.

"Bodes well for us." Ember settled a tray of crudités onto the kitchen counter.

"Touché." Aria swiped a celery stick.

Ember batted Aria away from the food. "Get out of that."

"So much for getting you out of that swimsuit," Ridge muttered.

"Later," Kaia whispered. "Anticipation is the most underrated form of foreplay."

"Oh," Tara said. "Are we interrupting Ridge's welcome home?"

"No, no," Kaia said, at the same time Ridge said, "Yes, yes."

"Should we go?" Aria pointed a thumb over her shoulder at the back door.

"I told you we shouldn't have shown up so early," Ember grumbled, and elbowed Aria.

"You're already here," Ridge said good-naturedly.

"The pool is amazing, by the way," Ember said, turning to peer out the door at the water.

"Why is that bottle of wine unopened?" Aria asked reaching for the merlot and a corkscrew. "It's almost five. Let's get this party started."

"None for me, thank you," Kaia said.

"Aww, c'mon," Tara said. "I know you're not much of a drinker, but just one glass. We're celebrating."

"I can't." Kaia smiled shyly and ducked her head.

"Omigod!" Ember squealed. "You're preggers?"

"Kaia?" The joy in Ridge's voice was unmistakable.

She turned to her husband, nodded. "I took three pregnancy tests while you were gone, just to make sure, but it looks like you're going to be a daddy."

His color paled and he swayed on his feet.

"Quick," Aria said. "Get him sitting before he passes out."

Tara was already on it, guiding Ridge down into a kitchen chair.

"This is so wonderful," Ember said. "You and Casey both expecting at the same time."

"A baby?" Ridge said. "You and me?"

"Well"—Kaia smiled—"I'm certainly not having a baby with anyone else."

"That is . . . I'm . . . you are . . ." Ridge couldn't seem to find the words. But that was okay. Kaia knew what was in his heart. Happiness radiated off him in waves.

"Spit it out, man." Aria danced around the room. "Tell her what you're feeling."

Ridge's eyes drilled into Kaia's. He patted his knee. "Come here."

Heart pounding, she went to him.

He pulled her into his lap. Smothered her with kisses. "I love you," he said with each kiss. "I love you, I love you, I love you."

The old familiar humming started the second his lips touched her, rising with each kiss, growing, surging until every cell in her body throbbed to the beat of their love.

Then he dipped his head and kissed her belly through her swim-suit, sending vibrations swirling through the very core of her.

"Dear, sweet Kaia," he breathed. "You've made me the happiest man on the face of the earth."

"You're not afraid?" she whispered.

"I'm freaking terrified." He laughed. "But I'm in this with you one hundred percent."

Tears pressed against the back of her eyes at the look of absolute joy on Ridge's face. He wasn't going to run and hide behind work.

The back door opened, and Kaia's parents came in with Archer, Casey, and Granny Blue.

"We're having a baby!" Aria announced.

"What?" Mom exclaimed. "Who?"

"Ridge and Kaia."

"When?"

"In about seven and a half months," Kaia confirmed.

Ridge pressed his forehead to hers, stared deeply into her eyes. "This kid is going to be the luckiest baby on the face of the earth."

As she sat in the shelter of her man's arms surrounded by her family, the seams of her heart swelled to bursting. And she knew with absolute certainty they were going to live happily-ever-after.

Here is a sneak peek at
New York Times bestselling author
Lori Wilde's

COWBOY, IT'S COLD OUTSIDE

Arriving Christmas 2017 only from Avon Books.

Chapter 1

BACKSTAGE at the one-hundred-forty-year-old Twilight Play-house, Paige MacGregor wriggled into her skimpy Santa Baby costume, finger-pinching red Lyrca leggings up around her waist, flashing her doughy-white belly to the full-length mirror, and quite possibly the ghost of John Wilkes Booth, and swore off Christmas cookies forever.

"Sorry, John," she apologized. "But if you don't want to see the sad evidence of my total lack of self-control, you shouldn't haunt theatres."

She was the first of the six Santa's helpers to arrive, and the quiet of the old limestone building offered momentary respite from the extravagant Dickensian hullabaloo ruling the town square.

At the narrow oval window overlooking the flat roof of Perk's Coffee Shop next door, Earl Pringle's pet crow, Poe, pecked at the pane, *tap, tap, tap,* and glowered with murderous intent, but then again Poe was a moody cuss.

He was tiny for a crow, barely larger than a grackle, but he cocked his shoulders and flared his wings as if trying to convince her he was indeed a ferocious raven.

She pretended to startle because she knew what it was like to be on the short side, and everyone needed an ego boost now and again, even small crows trying to prove worthy of poetic names.

Poe gave a "caw," satisfied that he'd scared her, and flew away to find new town folk to terrorize.

She moved to the window clouded with decades of dirt and grime, called, "Go forth and nevermore."

Hey, were those snowflakes?

Her obsessive-compulsive gene wished for Windex and a cleaning rag, but her curiosity gene overrode it. She undid the rusty latch, and with some effort, shoved open the window for a better look at the street below teaming with tourists. The smell of dark roast and yeasty pastries teased her nose, and her mouth watered.

No. No more sweet treats.

Behind the theatre and the town square, Lake Twilight stretched sapphire blue, a dazzling jewel in Hood County's crown. If she leaned out the window and craned her neck, she could just make out her Uncle Floyd's houseboat where she was crashing for the holidays and/or until she got her life straightened out.

Delicate white flakes coasted silently from the sky, sprinkling trees, roofs, cars, and heads of passersby. Her West Texas heart leaped joyously.

She'd grown up in the desert surrounded by oil and sand, far away from water and snow. And she was thrilled by the white stuff here in North Central Texas, even though she knew the ground was too warm for it to stick. For this one spectacular moment, Twilight looked like a shaken snow globe.

She took a deep breath, savored the sight for as long as she dared, then reluctantly, pulled back inside and shut the window.

With a dreamy sigh, she kicked off her Skechers, and plunked down onto the creaky rocking chair, the white paint distressed dingy and chipped by advanced age and a vast collection of butts.

Zipped herself into knee-length, black-vinyl, spiked-heel boots that were part of her sexy costume. Topped her chestnut, chin-length bob with a green elf hat and examined the results in the mirror.

Turned sideways, sucked in her gut.

"What do you think, John? Give it to me straight. I know I'm no Eartha Kitt, but put me in a couple of pairs of Spanx and I can pull off this hot elf thing. Right?"

She spun around to get a rearview, but her ankle turned in the stilletoe boots and she had to grab hold of the mirror to keep from toppling. "Okay, okay, Spanx *and* deportment lessons."

She took a second look, brushed her hair back from her face, and reapplied her lipstick. Good enough.

The other assistants would be here soon and they'd need the dressing room. Time to clear out.

Carefully, she minced her way down the stairs, went past the stage where the stagehands were setting up, and into the auditorium.

The Twilight Playhouse was one of the oldest existing theatres in the U.S. that still hosted performances, and it was the only building on the town square to have kept its primary function since the town was founded in 1875.

The theatre in fact predated the township, having been built the previous year, next door to what was then a saloon. Now, it was a fine dining restaurant nostalgically called 1874.

A few years back, when Emma and Sam Cheek took over as owners, the Playhouse had undergone a historically correct renovation, so while everything looked the way it had almost a century and a half ago, and the exterior was one hundred percent original, the auditorium was essentially brand new.

The theatre held three hundred people, and during the month of the December, every performance sold out. This year's Christmas play was *Elf* and on Saturdays and Sundays they held a two p.m. matinee.

Numerous green wreaths, with red velvet ribbon streamers connecting them, hung from the white limestone walls, festive and inviting. Stacks of programs sat on the apron of the stage, waiting for Santa's helpers to pass them out to theatregoers at the door.

From the slip of light filtering in through the open side doors, the Italian crystal of the colossal chandelier aggressively created rainbows, dappling the stage and orchestra pit in luminous prisms that twinkled and danced when the heating/air conditioning unit stirred the dangling glass.

Someone had suspended a wedding-bouquet sized clump of mistletoe from the chandelier's central branch, inviting the audience to indulge in stolen kisses. Aww, Christmas in Twilight.

Paige picked up an armful of programs, tucked them into her

elbow, and bobbled her way over the thick rose-patterned carpet to the theatre lobby. No one was at the main reception desk, but rummaging sounds came from the closet on the other side of the room.

"Emma?"

"Nope." Colorfully tattooed, multiply pierced, purple-dreadlocks Jana Gerard popped her head out from the closet.

"Oh."

"Sorry to disappoint. Emma hopped over to Caitlyn's flower shop to replace the blooms." Jana waved at the wilted poinsettia baskets on the long marble countertop.

From the closet, Jana dragged out a life-sized cardboard cutout of an acoustic guitar protected by a sheet of thin clear plastic that the Playhouse had used to decorate the lobby for last summer's performance of *Oklahoma*.

"What's that for?" Paige asked.

"Sesty's spearheading the Cowboy Christmas music fundraiser, and Emma said we could borrow the guitar." Sesty Langtree was a local event coordinator, and one of Jana's two bosses.

A few years back, Jana had moved to conservative Twilight from keep-things-weird Austin, and with her flamboyant appearance she stood out like a scarlet rose in a planter box of white lilies.

No one knew much about Jana and rumors dogged her heels, usually clad in leather spiked motorcycle boots. The speculating about her past ran the gamut from the absurd; she shot a man for cheating on her. To the sublime; she'd donated a kidney to a sick lover, friend, parent, sibling, child, but alas, they'd tragically died anyway.

While the truth of Jana's abandonment of the state capital for the close-knit lake town of Twilight was probably much more mundane, she did nothing to quell the gossip and at times actively flamed it with sly smiles and knowing glances.

Paige understood the temptation toward mysteriousness. Even though she had relatives in Twilight, and was not nearly as exotic as Jana, she too had been the topic of lively conversation when she'd taken up residence in Uncle Floyd's houseboat.

"Need any help?" Paige asked, as Jana hoisted the cardboard guitar onto her back.

Jana eyed her. "You've got your hands full, and I'm not real confident in your ability to walk a straight line in those heels."

"Me either," Paige admitted, but she set down the programs and moved to open the left side exit door. "Excuse me," she called to the crowd packing the sidewalk. "Woman coming through."

The throng shifted, cutting a narrow path for Jana to join the flow of foot traffic.

"Thanks." And Jana was off, swallowed up as the crowd closed ranks again. The only visible sign of her was the bobbing cardboard guitar surfing heads.

The other five assistants came bustling in through the door Jana had just exited from, red-cheeked and laughing. They greeted Paige merrily, and trundled off to the dressing room.

All the Santa's helpers had been told to get into costume early so the actors could have the dressing rooms. The helpers would work the lobby before the performance, greeting guests, passing out programs, selling refreshments from the bar.

The doors opened at one-thirty. It was now twelve fifty-five.

"You're gonna do great," she said, giving herself a first-day-on-the-job pep talk. "Don't trip and break your neck in the dang boots and you'll be fine."

She glanced around for something to do, spied the droopy poinsettias. A little water and time out from under the heating system and they would rebound. Taking the initiative, she whisked the five baskets away one-by-one to the closet, filled with posters, signs, and various stage props, that Jana had just vacated.

The side door of the Playhouse opened again, this time ushering in a red-cheeked Emma Cheek carrying a giant basket of white winter flowers. Emma was in her mid-thirties, barely five foot, two inches shorter than Paige. She possessed flame-red naturally curly hair, peaches and cream skin, and an easy smile.

Emma had once been a Broadway actress, and still occasionally starred in a movie, but mostly she kept busy running the Twilight

Playhouse, and riding herd on her veterinarian husband Sam, Sam's teenage son Charlie from another marriage, and their six-year-old daughter Lauren.

Emma stopped short and peered around the basket. "Where did the poinsettias go?"

"I moved them to the closet to make room for the new flowers."

"Why thank you, Paige. That was considerate."

"You're welcome."

Emma hefted the basket onto the marble counter, moving it this way and that, cocking her head to assess her handiwork, attempting to find the most strategic spot for all angles. "I would have taken care of the flowers sooner, but when I stopped by the clinic to drop off Sam's lunch, he had a whole different kind of meal in mind."

"Oh."

Emma wriggled her auburn eyebrows. "Word to the wise, a quickie on an exam table is *not* as sexy as it sounds."

"I . . . um . . . never thought . . . well . . . um, okay."

"Sorry, was that too much information?" Emma grinned as if she wasn't the least bit sorry. Her husband was one smoking hunk and she didn't mind letting everyone know they had a spicy sex life.

In all honesty, it wasn't Emma's frank talk that gave Paige pause, rather it was the realization that she'd not ever done anything as halfway intrepid as have a quickie on an exam table.

The bravest thing she'd ever done was to take up residence on a houseboat. And as far as sex went, well, she wasn't exactly a femme fatale. Never mind the Santa Baby costume she had on.

"Now if you want to talk sexy . . ." Emma winked.

No, no, Paige did not want to talk sexy with her employer.

"Room nine at the Merry Cherub has a seven foot jetted tub. Fun!" Emma paused, her face turning dreamy at a hot memory. "Or try midnight under the Sweetheart Tree in Sweetheart Park. And do bring a blanket."

"Um, doesn't that violate public nudity laws?"

Emma looked like a sly cat that had slurped up all the cream.

"Sometimes a girl has to let down her hair and take a walk on the wild side."

Wild side, huh? Yeah, well about that . . . not her strong suit. Paige was more the look-both-ways-ten-times-before-crossing-the-street type.

"But I shouldn't be standing here gabbing about sex. Got lots to do. Would you guard the doors and not let anyone unauthorized in until one-thirty? The town council has been my riding my butt about letting people in early." Emma rolled her eyes as commentary on the town council.

"It's five-after-one," Paige pointed out.

"Right, so keeping 'em out for twenty-five minutes shouldn't be hard. You'll only have to monitor the side door. All the rest are locked. You can unlock them all at one-thirty." Emma disappeared into the theatre in a float of red hair and the scent of violets.

Guard the door for twenty-five minutes?

Sure, she could do that. Paige marched over to monitor the side door at the same moment a guy pushed his way in, bringing a bracing breath of cool December air. She was just about to reroute him when their eyes met.

They both stilled.

Man. O. Man.

Snow dusted his thick ebony curls and broad shoulders clad in a faded denim jacket over a red plaid flannel shirt. He was average height, five ten or eleven, but he had a presence about him that made him seem much larger.

He was lean and narrow-hipped in a pair of well-worn Wranglers, and only the Patek Philippe watch at his left wrist and his handmade James Leddy cowboy boots said he was anything more than an ordinary cowboy.

But his smile!

Dazzling. White. Killer Diller.

Oh, that smile was the dangerous thing!

Sprung from full, angular lips that twitched irresistibly as he stared at her—into her—with laser beam focus.

It was a dynamite, TNT, nitroglycerin kind of a smile that detonated every nerve ending in Paige's body, firing off round after round of tingly, breathtaking explosions.

"Hi," he said and she forgot that she was supposed to say, *Doors don't open until one-thirty.*

Instead, her jaw dropped and her tongue welded to the roof of her mouth, and she made a guttural sound. "Um . . . um . . ."

His smile deepened, moved up to crinkle around his heart-stoppingly gorgeous gray eyes.

He came nearer, walking with a sauntering, old-west gunslinger gait, the door closing behind him, the sound of his boots reverberating across the polished marble floor.

And still she did not tell him to leave, mainly because she couldn't find her voice. It had gotten tangled up in his smile like a lasso around a bull's heels.

The way he moved, smooth and easy, slammed in her chest and snatched her breath from her lungs.

Couldn't talk. Couldn't breathe. Couldn't think.

She was a fish on a hook. Well and truly caught.

"I'm here for the performance," he said.

Wait outside, she should have said, but her tongue remained glued to the roof of her mouth, peanut butter stuck.

Her first day on the job and she couldn't complete one simple task. Tell this red-hot stranger to wait outside with everyone else until the doors officially opened.

But it was clear he was not a man accustomed to following the rules. What applied to regular folk didn't apply to Greek gods in cowboy clothing. Did it?

C'mon. Snap out of it.

"I'm sorry," she said, meaning to sound firm, but somehow her words came out alarmingly shaky. "But we've got a strict schedule to keep and we're not opening to the public until one-thirty."

"It's one-ten." He turned his wrists so she could see the face of his expensive watch. Show off.

"Rules are rules."

"Even in my case?" He gave her a look that said, *are you kidding me right now?* As if she should know who he was. As if he was somebody.

Cocky. He was amazing and he knew it.

His attitude rubbed her the wrong way. He wasn't different than any of the other people lining up waiting to be let in. Peeved and vowing not to be swayed by his lively eyes and knowing grin, she pointed to the sidewalk. "Out, mister."

"But—"

"No excuses."

"I'm—"

"Go." She snapped her fingers, gave him her fiercest scowl, even though her knees were shaky. He didn't have to know that.

Instead of leaving, he strolled closer. Paige's heart hopped onto a trampoline and flipped into her throat. Now what?

The stranger observed her with half-lidded eyes and intense interest, as if she were the most fascinating creature he'd ever seen. The hair at the nape of her neck tickled and her heart hiccupped. She wasn't accustomed to this kind of scrutiny from a gorgeous man.

"No one has to know you let me in twenty minutes early," he whispered.

He was fully in control. He knew it. She knew it. They both knew she was putty in the glare of his sexy stare.

Damn him.

"Leave," she said, and added unsteadily, "please."

"What do I have to do to get you to bend the rules?" he coaxed, dipping his head, lowering his lips. "Will a kiss do the trick?"

He was teasing, trying to get her goat. She could see it in his eyes, but the joke tumbled into the pit of her anxiety, pinged off her every nerve ending, chaotic as bouncing flippers in a pinball machine.

She supposed he was trying to scare her off, get her to back down. Standing here smelling his stunning scent, feeling the heat from his rock-solid body radiate into her, she wanted, more than anything on the face of the earth, to turn tail and run.

But she wouldn't.

Couldn't

For one thing, she'd promised Emma she'd guard the door. For another, if she took off running in the stilletoes she'd certainly fall and bust her ass.

Not. Going. To. Happen.

He must have seen something on her face, in her body language, because he stepped back, put his hand on the door. "Only eighteen more minutes now."

"And that's when you can come in." She pointed, surprised by how forceful and commanding her words shot out like a drill sergeant.

He grinned at that, devilishly, frankly amused, and latched onto her gaze with eyes the color of San Francisco fog. Not that Paige knew firsthand. She'd never been out of Texas. But she had dreams.

Big dreams.

Dreams she believed long out of her reach.

Those dusky eyes held the promise of landscapes she yearned for—windswept moors and craggy mountains, foamy ocean waves and red-rock deserts, stony castles and petal-strewn gardens.

He'd been around. Seen the world.

And his magnificent, experienced eyes left her winded and wondering and wanting.

Wanting so much more than she had a right to claim.

Dear Lord. She clicked the lock on that pitch of desire. Slammed it shut. Spun the tumbler. Steeled her gaze. Offered him nothing.

His eyes gentled, no longer filled with daring mischief, and nonchalantly shifted his attention to the door. Which she was grateful for because it meant he was going.

And when he turned, she had an unobstructed view of his butt cupped so enticingly in those faded Levi's. A cowboy's butt—firm, muscular, built for endurance, a masculine butt that dared her to touch.

She hauled in a short, shallow breath, and ignored her tingling fingers.

The sleeves of his denim jacket were pushed up enough to reveal tanned wrists roped with strong veins. Long, calloused fingers took hold of the knob. No adornment on his hands. No rings or tattoos. Plain. Durable. Bare.

Simple but not simplistic, he was a man of rugged style and surprising grace.

He opened the door. Going. Leaving.

Yay. So why did she want to throw herself onto the marble tile floor, throw her arms around his ankles, and beg him to stay?

"One more thing." He turned back to her, eyes twinkling, and stared at her a long moment without saying a word. But his mouth, oh his knowing mouth, quirked up at the corners as if to say, *I know you're as intrigued by me as I am by you.*

She gave him a polite, noncommital smile in return. He might be interested right now, but he wouldn't be if he knew the truth.

"What's this sweetheart legend I've been hearing about?" His voice was low, sexy, and cozy as a fleece blanket in front of a roaring fire on a cold winter evening. There was a lazy lilt. As if he'd spent time in the Deep South where words were stretched out slow and sultry.

But there was something steely as well. It was in the way his tongue hit the back of his teeth hard on the "t" sounds. Determined. Stubborn. A quality and tone that said when this man set his mind to a goal, come hell or high water, he would never, ever give up.

Paige shivered. Just a little. Barely.

But he noticed. His eyes darkened and narrowed, taking leisurely measure of her.

"Huh?" she said because she was so distracted by his potent sexuality she couldn't remember what he'd asked her.

"The wishing well, the old tree with lovers' names carved in it, the statue of a hugging couple in the park. What's that all about?"

"Uh," she said. "Rebekka Nash and Jon Grant, childhood sweethearts from Missouri. They separated by the Civil War. She was a Southern Belle and he turned Yankee solider. But they never stopped loving each other. Fifteen years later they met accidentally on the banks of the Brazos River at twilight, and they were reunited."

"Hence the name of the town?"

"Indeed."

"Ah." He laughed. A beautiful sound that sent her heart thumping. "There's nothing like a good romantic legend. Bet it stirs tourism."

"You got it."

His eyes drilled into hers. As if she meant something.

And then he left without another word. Opened the door. Walked out. Disappeared into the crowd. Gone forever?

Goodbye.

Good riddance.

Oh no, don't go.

Emma popped back into the lobby. Paige shifted her gaze from the door, where the cowboy and his world-class butt had just vanished, back to her employer. Emma wore a green-and-red elf costume that complimented her auburn curls and pixie smile. She was playing the role of Jovie that Zoey Deschanel embodied in the movie.

"How do I look?" Emma asked, patting her stocking cap and setting the big jingle bell on the end of the hat jangling.

"Like the star you are," Paige assured her. "You'll look all of eighteen in that outfit. You'll be the talk of the town."

Emma blushed, her gorgeous blue eyes glowing with delight, slow grin lighting up her face. "You made my day. I've been worrying I'm too old to play Jovie."

"No way. You're perfect." Paige returned the smile, felt cheery warmth settle in her stomach and heat her from the inside out. She loved making people happy.

It was her greatest strength, and according to her mother, her biggest flaw.

"You gotta be a little selfish sometimes," said her mother often—this from the woman who'd taken a powder on motherhood when Paige was ten and her brother, Parker, four. "Remember what they tell you on airplanes. Put *your* oxygen mask on first."

But if putting other peoples' needs before her own was Paige's worst sin, she would take it with her head held high. Because, c'mon, what was a little hypoxia if she could make the world a better place?